"You must forget yourself— completely forget. You are now a lusty lad,

"and you must learn to talk like one, and act like one, too." Tarleton roared with laughter.

"I see you intend to enjoy yourself at my expense," Elizabeth coolly observed. Her remark only brought forth fresh rounds of mirth.

"Aye, at your *costly* expense! Remember, there will be a matter of payment." He grinned at her wickedly.

"When we get to court!" she reminded him.

"Aye, we shall get to court." Tarleton regarded her gravely for a moment. "That I do promise you. And now, 'tis time I work your transformation. Lady Elizabeth, be gone! And in her place you shall be..." His roguish gaze danced over her. "Robin! For you remind me of that bright little bird. Aye! That has a pleasing ring to it! Robin—the jester's lad!"

Dear Reader,

When we ran our first March Madness promotion in 1992, we had no idea that we would get such a wonderful response. Our springtime showcase of brand-new authors has been so successful that we've continued to seek out talented new writers and introduce them into the field of historical romance. During our yearly search, my editors and I have the unique opportunity of reading hundreds of manuscripts from unpublished authors, and we'd like to take this time to thank all of you who have given us the chance to review your work.

This March, we are very pleased to be able to introduce you to author Tori Phillips with her Maggie Award-winning story, *Fool's Paradise*. This Elizabethan tale of a young noblewoman and the jester who becomes her protector is delightful, and we hope you enjoy it.

And be sure to keep an eye out for our other three titles. *The Pearl Stallion*, the story of an adventurous voyage by Rae Muir. *Warrior's Deception* by Diana Hall, a medieval tale about a marriage based on lies. And *Western Rose* by Lynna Banning, the story of a rancher and a schoolteacher who must work out their differences before they accept their love.

Four new talents, four great stories from Harlequin Historicals. Don't miss a single one!

Sincerely,

Tracy Farrell
Senior Editor

Please address questions and book requests to:
Harlequin Reader Service
U.S.: 3010 Walden Ave., P.O. Box 1325, Buffalo, NY 14269
Canadian: P.O. Box 609, Fort Erie, Ont. L2A 5X3

TORI PHILLIPS
Fool's Paradise

Harlequin Books

TORONTO • NEW YORK • LONDON
AMSTERDAM • PARIS • SYDNEY • HAMBURG
STOCKHOLM • ATHENS • TOKYO • MILAN
MADRID • WARSAW • BUDAPEST • AUCKLAND

ISBN 0-373-28907-3

FOOL'S PARADISE

Copyright © 1996 by Mary W. Schaller.

TORI PHILLIPS

After receiving her degree in theater arts from the University of San Diego, Tori worked at MGM Studios, acted in numerous summer stock musicals and appeared in Paramount Pictures' *The Great Gatsby*. Her plays, published by Dramatic Publishing Co., have been produced in the U.S. and Canada, and her poetry is included in several anthologies. She has directed over forty plays, including twenty-one Shakespeare productions. Currently, she is a first-person, Living History actress at the Folger Shakespeare Library in Washington, DC. She lives with her husband in Burke, VA.

To the young romantics in my life:
Tori & Rick
Elizabeth & Phil
and to my One and Only,
Marty
with thanks for all the roses and champagne
Godiva chocolate and May Day poetry
and especially moonlight waltzes in Venice!

Chapter One

∽∾∽∾∾

If you should lead her into a fool's paradise, it were a
very gross kind of behavior... for the gentlewoman is
young.

—*Romeo and Juliet*

On the Woodstock Road
Warwickshire, England
August 1586

"Thunder! Hold! Pray, do not abandon me now!" Even
as she spoke, Lady Elizabeth Hayward knew it was in vain.
The swift chestnut hunter galloped far down the woodland
road, racing back toward home.

Home to Esmond Manor? It was no longer her home,
now that Sir Robert La Faye had declared himself lord and
master. All he needed was the formal exchange of marriage
vows. That odious thought made Elizabeth more resolved
to face the unknown road ahead.

"I would rather die than marry that varlet," she muttered under her breath. Adjusting her dark blue travel cloak,
Elizabeth squared her shoulders for the long trek ahead of
her.

Repulsed by the preening nobleman she left behind her,
Elizabeth had slipped out of Esmond Manor at dawn with

only a saddle pouch containing food and a few personal
items. Her mind full of escaping her betrothed's brutish
manner, Elizabeth paid no attention to Thunder's habitual
skittishness until it was too late. One minute she was high in
the saddle and well on her way to Hampton Court and to her
godmother, Queen Elizabeth. The next, Thunder, balking
at a hare, pitched Elizabeth sideways onto the road.

"Thank the good Lord I have not broken any bones," she
consoled herself. "And, at least, I still have my money." Her
hand closed over the leather bag of golden angels and silver
shillings that hung from her girdle.

"There must be an inn or a farm nearby," Elizabeth told
herself as she picked her way along the verge, carefully
keeping her long blue velvet skirts out of the mud puddles.
"And the day promises to be fair."

She wondered how long it would take Thunder to return
to his stable. If he ran all the way, it would be no more than
an hour. "When he is found with all my things in his pack,
Sir Robert will know I have escaped my room and he will
come looking for me—that is, if he hasn't already discovered I've gone."

Elizabeth hoped that her faithful maid, Charlotte, did not
suffer from Sir Robert's anger. She touched her cheek,
where she could still feel the sting of his hand, though it had
been over a day since he struck her. The memory of that
pain and the twisted look on his face spurred Elizabeth
down the tree-shaded road, no matter what lay ahead.

"Sweet angels, please let there be no boars in this wood,"
she prayed, gripping a small pair of gold embroidery scissors that hung from a slender chain at her waist.

When Thunder had crested a hillock and Elizabeth first
sighted the wood, she judged its size to be small and not too
forbidding. Now that she found herself alone and on foot
in the middle of it, the thick foliage of the oaks and elms
appeared much more threatening. The friendly twitter of
unseen birds among the branches overhead did little to calm

her nerves. Elizabeth had never been abroad without an escort before. Nothing in her schooling at the Convent of Sacre Coeur in Reims had prepared her for such a desperate plight as this. Her ears strained to catch the slightest rustling in the thick undergrowth, which might announce the presence of a fox or a bear or...

"The keeper would a-hunting go..." The cheery song, heartily sung in a pleasing baritone, wafted on a breeze through the green wood.

Elizabeth stopped at the sound. Her heart thumping wildly in its cage, she gripped her scissors tighter. Never in her nineteen years had she been alone with a man other than her father or the manor's steward—not until the coming of Sir Robert La Faye. She shuddered as the leering face of that vile lord rose in her mind's eye. No man alive boded more ill for her than he! Elizabeth would take her chances with the unknown singer.

"...among the leaves so green-o!"

The songster sounded friendly to Elizabeth—and familiar. Only two nights ago she had heard that song sung before her father's festive table by a merry traveling player. Sir Thomas Hayward had hired a jester to entertain at the feast marking Elizabeth's betrothal to Sir Robert. Elizabeth bit her lip. Her wonderful, loving father, God rest his soul!

"Hey now! Ho, now! Derry, derry down! Among the leaves so green-o!" The singer punctuated his music with a great deal of splashing and gurgling noises.

The sounds came from a thicket to the left. Stepping cautiously into the tangled underbrush and parting the sapling branches of a hickory, Elizabeth saw the sparkle of a small river snaking in and out of the verdant surroundings. The singer's voice, now stronger, came from behind a large clump of holly bushes.

"To me hay down-down, to me ho down-down..." More splashing intermixed with joyful whoops accompanied the chorus.

Drawn by the song and the singer's apparent cheerful nature, Elizabeth crept up to the screening holly. Holding her voluminous skirts above the twigs and bracken, she clutched her tiny scissors.

A stick snapped underfoot. To Elizabeth, the resulting crack sounded like gunfire from a fowling piece.

The singer, on the other hand, did not appear to notice his secret audience. He repeated the chorus, though the direction of his voice changed slightly. Drawing her cloak more tightly about her, Elizabeth crouched down behind the holly clump and gently poked her fingers through its prickly, glossy leaves. In front of her, the river widened, forming a small pool. On the bank nearby lay a pair of brown woolen breeches and a beige homespun shirt. Their owner was nowhere to be seen, though she could still hear him humming the tune of his song. Elizabeth pulled back the branches a little farther in order to see what manner of man she had stumbled upon.

"Stand and show thyself!" a deep voice growled behind her.

Elizabeth stiffened, her heart nearly leapt from her mouth. Trembling more from fright than from the early-morning's chill, she slowly rose unsteadily to her feet. Hidden amid the folds of her cloak, Elizabeth's hand clutched her scissors. She would defend her honor to the end, if necessary.

Turning to face him, she gasped. The man pointed a long, wicked-looking dagger at her throat. The morning sun glinted off its sharp blade. Her assailant was hard muscled, dripping wet—and completely naked. Crystal rivulets coursed down his broad chest, angled at his slim hips and disappeared into his . . .

Elizabeth's eyes widened. She had never seen a man without his clothes before, and this particular specimen looked singularly well-made. The warmth of a deep blush swept over her. The churl grinned.

"Heaven protect and defend me!" Whirling, Elizabeth plunged blindly through the nettles and thorny bracken.

"Stop! Wait! Not that way!" her attacker called. But it was too late. In her haste, Elizabeth lost her footing on the slippery bank and fell headlong into the cold river.

Her heavy velvet overskirt quickly weighed her down. The fashionable bum roll around her waist greedily soaked up the water, pulling her beneath the surface. Panic gripping her soul, Elizabeth thrashed wildly to the surface. As she struggled to unclasp the hook of her woolen cloak, her pursuer grasped her around her waist, pulling her against his chest. She shook the water from her eyes and fought for breath. The strong arm around her tightened.

"Unhand me! How dare you!" Elizabeth flailed her arms helplessly as he half carried, half dragged her to the shore. "You will pay for this outrage! You do not know whom you have attacked!"

The varlet answered with a rich, almost musical laugh as he pushed her up onto the muddy bank.

"If I had let you go, you would have drowned," he remarked as he hoisted himself out of the river. "And I do, indeed, know full well who you are, Lady Elizabeth Hayward," he continued, shaking the water from his brown curly hair. Sitting down companionably beside her, he drew up one leg, hiding the most intriguing part of his anatomy from her gaze.

"How?" She drew back from him, trying to regain both her breath and her composure. She tried to avoid staring at his lithe body. "Who are you?"

"Do you not recognize Tarleton, the jester?" He pulled a sorrowful face. "I had the honor of entertaining at your noble father's home. I believe you were celebrating your betrothal." He laughed easily, the richness of that cheerful sound echoing in the woods around them. "Were you so entranced by your new love that poor Tarleton and his jests were all for naught?"

Tarleton? Aye, Elizabeth remembered the jester, dressed in a jacket of bright green and red motley, his little brass bells tinkling merrily with each caper and jig. The Queen's favorite player, he boasted, with no small show of modesty. Now he sat shamelessly naked beside her. A certain warmth seemed to radiate from him, enveloping her. Drawn to him, Elizabeth had the unconscionable desire to touch his strong, rough-haired leg so near her hand. Surprised, Elizabeth willed her heart to stop its unseemly fluttering.

"Truly I did not recognize you, Sir Jester, for you are without your cap and bells." She cast another quick, sideways glance at him through her lashes. "Indeed, you are without any clothing at all." She held her breath. *Now, he will either rob and murder me, or he will . . .*

Throwing back his head, Tarleton roared with laughter. "Well spoken, my lady! Permit me to make myself more presentable. And you should be thinking about getting out of your own wet attire." He stood up, towering over her.

"What?" Elizabeth's eyes widened at his bold words and even bolder stance. "Take off my clothes? Here, in the middle of nowhere?"

Tarleton disappeared behind a gnarled oak. "What I mean to say, fair lady," he continued from his leafy hiding place, "is if you sit on the cold ground much longer in those sodden clothes, you will no doubt catch a noisome cold, and you will be joining the sweet angels in heaven a good deal earlier than you planned."

"But I have nothing . . ." she began.

"Neither did our mother Eve have anything to wear in the garden of paradise." He reappeared, dressed in his shirt, breeches and a tan jerkin. He carried a pair of black stockings in his hand. "But I do have a spare shirt and breeches to which you are welcome."

Elizabeth gaped at him, startled by his scandalous suggestion. A teasing light twinkled in the depths of Tarleton's dark brown eyes. She was tempted to smile back at him—almost.

"I assure you, Lady Elizabeth, my clothes are clean. Your own good cook, Jane, washed them for me only a few days ago." He hunkered down beside his pack, rummaged through it, then tossed an oatmeal-colored shirt and black breeches to her. "I recommend that fine willow tree over there as your tiring room. I shall not peek—word of honor." His warm brown eyes grew serious as his gaze rested on her. "But, truly, my lady. You will catch your death if you stay seated thus. And I care not to have your sweet corpse on my hands."

Elizabeth swallowed hard as she glanced at his large, well-formed hands and wondered fleetingly what it would be like to be touched by them. She gave herself a little shake. How could she possibly think of him touching her? She barely knew him!

"Turn around," Elizabeth ordered sharply as she struggled to her feet. "And remember your promise—on your honor!" Snatching up his clothing, she flounced off to the willow.

"On my honor, my back is turned," he called after her as she slipped inside the willow's concealing green canopy. "Of course you know what the poet says about honor, don't you?"

"No, what?" she asked as she struggled to undo her lacing.

"'Some after honor hunt, but I after love.'"

"Oh! Don't you dare come any closer! I am armed," Elizabeth warned, using her scissors to cut through the tight, wet knots. "In truth, I will defend myself."

"Truly, my lady, you are a bundle of wonder!" There was a trace of laughter in his voice.

With a man of dubious nature and too-easy charm only a few yards away, Elizabeth dispensed with all ceremony in favor of speed. Wriggling out of the last clinging petticoat, she let it fall with the others in a soaking mass at her feet. *Ridiculous!* She kicked the useless things away. Whoever convinced ladies to wear all these layers of clothing ought to be hung by his own garters from a gibbet! Some Spanish fop, no doubt.

Tarleton's shirt hung down to her knees. As for the breeches, they were too wide in the waist and too long in the leg. On the other hand, they *were* warm, dry and surprisingly comfortable.

"Is my lady gowned in her—?" Tarleton began, but his easy banter exploded into laughter as Elizabeth stepped out of her leafy dressing room, clutching at her waist with one hand, while the other was completely lost in a sleeve.

Trying to maintain her shredded dignity in the face of his cheery reaction, Elizabeth cleared her throat and tilted up her chin proudly. "I thank you for the loan of your clothing, jester, but I will also thank you not to mock me. Tell me, if you can spare the breath, how do you keep these pantaloons up?"

"Usually, you tie them to your waistcoat. Alas, I have none that I can safely spare, but I do have something that will serve." Rummaging in his pack, Tarleton drew out a length of red satin ribbon.

"I was saving this as a gift for some special maiden," he remarked, handing it to her.

"Oh?" she retorted, one eyebrow raised. "And who would that be?" Pulling the ribbon through his fingers, she turned her back to him and threaded the makeshift belt through the eyelets. Elizabeth found herself extremely conscious of his virile appeal.

Tarleton chuckled. "I haven't met her yet. But never fear, my lady, I will someday. And I always like to be prepared."

"You sound very sure of yourself," Elizabeth said dryly as she stuffed the outsize shirt into the breeches.

Tarleton merely grinned in reply, then he went back to tending a small fire of dry sticks. Elizabeth admired his fluid movements and the easy grace of an acrobat. In profile, his face was pleasant and well-defined, his lips sensual with an infectious smile only a breath away. His flashing dark eyes promised pure mischief. Elizabeth snorted to herself. No doubt Tarleton would find his "special maiden" soon enough. In certain classes of society, some women might even call the jester handsome. As she tied the ends together, Elizabeth felt a certain smug satisfaction. At least, no one else was going to get Tarleton's prized red ribbon—not while she wore it tight around her waist. *What on earth am I thinking?* she thought, catching herself. *He's but a commoner, and I have enough troubles with a man as it is!*

"Come, warm your toes and dry your hair, my lady. Breakfast is served!"

"Breakfast?"

"Sweet apples, compliments of God's fair wind in an orchard, and the cheese..." He regarded the golden wedge ruefully. "Well, 'tis not moldy yet." As she sat down opposite him, he quickly averted his eyes.

"In truth, my lady, that shirt looks far better on you than it ever did on me, but I suggest that you tie up the band strings tightly before you display any more of your unmanly bosom."

Glancing down at her open neck, Elizabeth flushed. She snatched the collar shut and pulled the laces until they puckered.

Without looking at her directly, Tarleton offered her an apple slice on the tip of his knife. Plucking off the fruit, Elizabeth bit into it.

The apple's hidden sweetness burst generously in her mouth; its juice overflowed, escaping from a corner of her lips. Until this moment, Elizabeth had forgotten how really hungry she was. Tarleton's simple windfall was the most delicious thing she could recall ever eating.

"Another," Elizabeth commanded, her mouth still full. Nodding solemnly, he offered her a second slice, as well as a large wedge of cheese.

They ate in silence for a bit, then Tarleton spoke. "I did not expect to find myself playing host to so noble a lady in the greenwood."

Elizabeth shifted uncomfortably under his thoughtful gaze. She wasn't sure how much she wanted to tell him.

Tarleton continued, "I can't help but ask myself why such a fine lady is roaming about the forest, and falling into rivers? Is it because she is bored with life in a great manor house? Is she lost?" Pausing, he raised one eyebrow slowly. "Or, perhaps, she is running away?"

Elizabeth choked, then stared at the fire to avoid his compelling eyes.

"Ah," he murmured. "Methinks I have hit the nut and core of the matter. Lady Elizabeth, may I ask why are you running away from so great a fortune and so noble a betrothed lord?"

Elizabeth tried to ignore Tarleton's honeyed probing.

The jester spoke softly. "I believe there is some water in your eye, Lady Elizabeth. Use your sleeve, that's what the good Lord created them for." He drew closer to her side. "Tell me your story, sweet lady. I am a patient listener as well as a chattering monkey. You can trust Tarleton. Her Most Gracious Majesty often does. What happened since I left Esmond Manor?"

"All my happiness died," Elizabeth answered quietly, afraid to give freedom to the words that, until now, she had kept confined in her heart. "The morning after the feast, my father took suddenly ill, and . . . died."

"May God have mercy upon his soul." Tarleton's voice held an infinitely compassionate tone. "Sir Thomas Hayward was a good man, and a generous one, too. What happened?"

Elizabeth took a deep breath to steady her voice. "We don't know. Father was well when I greeted him early in the day, but toward the forenoon he doubled over in pain and turned a dreadful color. We put him to bed straightaway, and sent for a doctor. But, by the time he arrived in the afternoon, my father had . . . had died.''

Tarleton's eyes narrowed with suspicion. "Had your father eaten anything unusual? Did he complain of the taste of the food?''

"No-o." Elizabeth racked her brains to remember the details of that dreadful day. It had been a delightful breakfast. She and her father repeated to each other some of Tarleton's jests from the night before. Then Sir Robert joined them. "Wait! My father had a dish of mushrooms that the rest of us did not. My betrothed gathered some plump ones that morning, which he gave to my father.''

"An interesting gift." Tarleton compressed his lips into a tight line. "And what did the good Sir Robert do after your father died?''

Elizabeth shuddered as she recalled what followed. "He changed as suddenly as a weathercock in a high wind. Though Sir Robert was all smiles, I did not like him much. I told my father of my dislike after the betrothal feast. My father, who was kind and loving, said he would break off the match. But, before he could do so, he . . . he was gone.'' Elizabeth blinked rapidly several times in an effort to keep her tears at bay.

"Even as my father's body grew cold, Sir Robert suggested . . . nay, he *insisted* that we should be married at once. He said it would protect my interests.''

"And his," Tarleton muttered knowingly under his breath.

"I told him it was too hasty. How could I think of marriage when my father had just died?'' Elizabeth looked away, fighting back her grief. It must wait for a more private time.

Slipping his arm around her shoulder, Tarleton drew her closer to him. He smelled of wood smoke, leather and mint, a combination Elizabeth found oddly comforting.

"Surely Sir Robert meant kindly," Tarleton prompted.

"No!" Elizabeth gritted her teeth. "When I put him off, he grew violently angry. He was loathsome to look at, and he swore such oaths at me! Sir Robert called me a ninny, saying I did not know what was good for me. He said I was stubborn, and, when I told him he was acting as no gentleman should, he . . . he struck me across the face!"

Tarleton's grip tightened around her. "He deliberately hit you?" he whispered in a low, dangerous voice.

"Aye!" Elizabeth shivered. "Then he dragged me to my chamber and locked me in, saying I would neither eat nor drink until I agreed to be married immediately after my father's burial. If not, he threatened he would . . . force himself upon me!"

"Forgive my boldness, Lady Elizabeth, but methinks Sir Robert La Faye is in desperate need of a sound horsewhipping. How did you manage to escape?" Tarleton lightly stroked her hair. Elizabeth found his touch soothing. She laid her head against his shoulder.

"'Twas my maid, Charlotte. Last night, she brought me some food after Sir Robert had drunk himself into a stupor. She told me that he had taken over the hall as if he were already the master. After I ate, I made up a small packet of clothing, provisions and money, then I escaped on my father's favorite horse."

"Where are you going, my lady?" Tarleton questioned gently.

"To my godmother, the Queen. They say she is at Hampton Court."

Tarleton abruptly stopped playing with Elizabeth's fine, soft hair, and regarded her with surprise. "Her Grace is your godmother? But I've never seen you at court."

Elizabeth sighed. "I was too young. For the past six years, I've been away in France with my mother's family. I only recently returned . . . and found myself betrothed."

"And what do you seek of your godmother?" Tarleton asked casually, while his mind spun with the complications of the situation. God's nightshirt! This tiny lady was a prize, indeed! No wonder Sir Robert had been so anxious to wed her!

"I will beg Her Majesty to annul this loathsome betrothal. I would like to become one of her ladies."

"And you would be an ornament to her court, though not, I fear, in your present garb. In truth, you look a very poor lady but you make a very pretty lad."

Elizabeth felt his warm breath tickle her ear. She suddenly realized that she was clasped in his embrace, and, more shocking, that she clutched him tightly around his waist. Shivery tingles ran deliciously up and down her spine. Hastily drying her tears on her sleeve, she pulled away from his arms. Her blood pounded hotly in her ears.

"I meant no offense . . ." Tarleton began, seeing her confusion, but then he thought better of it and changed the subject. "How does it happen you are here and not halfway to Oxford by now?"

Elizabeth wrinkled her nose. "My horse shied at a hare. I am sure by now Sir Robert is out searching for me."

"He best not cross my path, Lady," Tarleton growled.

"As I walked along the road I heard you singing."

"Ah! So you were drawn by the sweetness of my voice and came spying upon me? And I thought you were a thief!" He chuckled at his mistake.

Elizabeth stared at him for a long moment, her mind weighing her few options. "Tarleton, can I trust you?" she finally asked.

"You are wearing my clothing. You have eaten most of my food. You have even threatened me with a weapon. Yet, you ask me if you can trust me?'' Cocking his head, he grinned impishly at her.

Though she did not mean to, Elizabeth found herself smiling back. How could any woman resist such a roguish smile? *Stop it! He's only a player, even if he is a handsome one.* Clearing her throat, she stood up. Best to deal with Tarleton in a more dignified manner, despite the fact she was barefoot in a forest. ''Will you escort me safely to Hampton Court?'' she asked. ''I can pay you well for your service.''

Reaching into her shirt, she withdrew the small money bag that she had hung around her neck. The coins inside clinked invitingly.

''Put that away, my lady!'' he said gruffly. ''Never show your money in public. Not even to me. I fear I am no saint.''

''Please help me, good jester. I have no one else,'' she beseeched.

Tarleton whistled through his teeth. ''I am a coward of the first degree,'' he admitted. ''I should be tied up and put into a darkened room to agree to such a mad idea, and yet...''

Elizabeth felt his gaze sweep over her. It made her quiver, as if she had just been washed with liquid fire. He looked as if he were planning to sell her to the highest bidder. *What if he is?* A cold fear replaced the other, more pleasant feeling. She knew Sir Robert would pay handsomely for her return.

Then the player slapped his thigh and laughed richly. ''What a most rare jest it will be! A jest of infinite value! Why, my Lady Elizabeth, this jest of ours will go down into legend. The university students will make up ballads of this jest! Provided, of course, that you agree.''

''Agree? Agree to what?'' she asked cautiously. Lord, how his eyes sparkled so devilishly!

''I will take you to the Queen. I was going that way myself. But you cannot travel with me as a lady. That would be unseemly. A fine lady and a gypsy player? Oh, no! Instead, you shall become my prentice! A most perfect counterfeit!" Tarleton jumped up and began to pace around the glowing embers. "I am near twenty-eight summers. 'Tis time I took on a young jackanapes to instruct in my honorable profession. Think of it! We shall stroll along the highways and byways as merrily as we please until we reach Hampton Court, whereupon you will magically reappear as Lady Elizabeth Hayward! What say you to that?"

Elizabeth wrinkled her nose. She wasn't too sure she liked this idea at all. It was one thing to wear his clothes until hers dried out, but to wear them until they reached the Queen? And strolling the highways?

"But why must I be disguised?" she protested. "I have money. We could go to the nearest inn where we can get horses and proper clothing. We can ride to Hampton in a matter of days. Why must I be a...a...?"

Tarleton grinned. "Apprentice jester! Apprentice to Tarleton, the Queen's most beloved royal fool! Why, half the lads in the country would jump at the chance I am offering you."

Elizabeth drew herself up. "In case you haven't noticed, I'm not a lad."

"Indeed, I *have* noticed, my lady." Tarleton grew serious again. "And so will every highwayman between here and Windsor, if we traveled as you suggest. But as two poor players? Who looks twice at servants? Remember, Sir Robert will be searching for a fair noble lady—not for a dirty prentice boy."

"Dirty?"

Yet Tarleton had a point. Elizabeth understood the need for disguise. Her mouth slowly curled upward into a grin. She would dearly love to outwit the boorish Sir Robert La Faye. How she would delight to make him a laughingstock when she arrived at court and told her tale! Dare she do it? She glanced at Tarleton and saw his dancing eyes, his tempting smile. She felt herself grow weak as his grin widened. She would have to watch herself with that smile. She must not appear ready to wholly fall in with Tarleton's madcap scheme. She didn't want him to think he was going to have the upper hand with her. After all, she was employing him, not the other way around.

"Very well, Tarleton. I agree but I am in need of shoes and stockings."

"God's teeth!" Tarleton cried delightedly. "I knew you were a game lass!" He slapped her playfully on her backside.

"Hold, knave!" Elizabeth backed away from him. Was he trying to impress her with that upper hand already? "You forget yourself!"

Tarleton shook his head. "Nay, prentice boy. You must forget yourself—completely forget. You are now a lusty lad, and you must learn to talk like one, and act like one, too." Tarleton roared with laughter.

"I see you intend to enjoy yourself at my expense," Elizabeth coolly observed. Her remark only brought forth fresh rounds of mirth.

"Aye, at your *costly* expense! Remember, there will be a matter of payment." He grinned at her wickedly.

"When we get to court!" she reminded him.

"Aye, we shall get to court." Tarleton regarded her gravely for a moment. "That I do promise you." Then he continued in a lighter vein. "And now, 'tis time I work your transformation. Lady Elizabeth, be gone! And in her place you shall be..." His roguish gaze danced over her. "Robin! For you remind me of that bright little bird. Aye! That has a pleasing ring to it! Robin, the jester's lad!"

Tarleton circled Elizabeth, his mind working quickly. He realized that what they were about to undertake was dangerous for them both. The roads were full of rogues and vagabonds who would make quick work of Lady Elizabeth should her true identity be discovered. Also, the law and the church took exceedingly dim views of women dressing in men's clothing. He smiled to himself. The challenge of the gamble appealed to his impish nature, and the risk raised the stakes to an interesting level.

"What must I do to be your apprentice?" Elizabeth tried to swallow her apprehensions when she saw a devilish gleam come into his eye. *Why do my insides melt when he looks at me like that?*

"First, we must hide your clothing," he said, going to the willow where she had left her wet things. "God's teeth! How do you ladies manage to move about in such attire?"

"We usually do not bathe in them," she reminded him with a smile.

Tarleton stuffed her finery, worth a scrivener's annual wage, deep into the rotted trunk of a fallen tree. "Some bird or squirrel will find himself a most sumptuous nest there this winter. We'll keep your cloak, for I think it will serve us well." Tarleton rolled the damp woolen garment into a tight bundle, tying it together with some cord produced from his wondrous pack. "Tonight, if we are blessed, we shall be by a warm fire and can dry it out properly."

"Oh, truly, Tarleton?" Elizabeth sighed, thinking of a fine inn, a hot bath, and a deep feather bed. Perhaps a good, brisk walk wouldn't be too bad, after all.

"That we shall see." Pursing his lips, he took out his dagger. "But there is one more thing I must do to turn you into a lad."

"Wh-what?" Elizabeth faltered, eyeing the sharp blade as he came toward her. "What mean you?"

"Fear not, sweet Robin," he reassured her. "'Tis but your hair. I must cut it. No lad I know has such tresses." He ran his hand gently through her disheveled locks. "I must fashion you into a gutter urchin."

"Cut it?" Elizabeth's lower lip trembled. "Gutter urchin?" This was more than she had bargained for. Her long golden hair was her pride. In fact, her maid had often teased her about her one vanity. "How short?"

"You are a boy now, remember?" Tarleton muttered gruffly. "So be a man and stop sniveling!"

Looking into his eyes, Elizabeth saw compassion there, though his words were rough to her ear. She nodded. Her disguise had to be perfect if it was going to work. "Do it quickly!" She gritted her teeth as she felt the cold steel against the back of her neck.

Elizabeth's hair was so soft to his touch that Tarleton was tempted to forget himself then and there. A man could lose himself among such silken tresses. Tarleton winced as he stepped back to survey his choppy handiwork. Shorn of her gleaming locks, which lay like spun gold on the ground around her, Elizabeth looked like a poor, orphaned waif.

Tarleton felt his throat tighten. "'Tis certain that I am not a barber, and praise the good Lord for that. When I can find a proper pair of shears, I promise to do a better piece of work." He was thankful she could not see the butchery he had made of her.

Elizabeth gingerly touched the short, stubby ends around her ears.

"I suppose it will grow back soon?" she asked hopefully.

"Aye, when you are safe at Hampton Court, and this adventure is but a strange dream." Tarleton cocked his head and tried to sound cheerful. "Besides, I understand the latest fashion is for short tight curls about the head."

"Even so?" she whispered, rubbing the back of her neck.

"Aye, or you may boil me in pickle brine!" Tarleton gathered up the strands. "Now to dispose of these."

He quietly pocketed one gleaming lock for himself, then, wrapping the rest tightly around a rock, he pushed the golden bundle deep into the muck at the edge of the river.

"Now, then, my boy, the sun is high, so let us be on our way." Stamping out the embers of their fire, Tarleton scattered the remains. "If you were a true apprentice, you would be carrying the pack."

"What say you?" Elizabeth's jaw dropped as she saw him heft it upon one shoulder. The bundle looked quite heavy.

"But since this is your first day, I shall let you off easy. Take the cloak instead." He tossed it to her.

Instead of catching it, Elizabeth ducked and the roll bounced off the oak behind her.

"How dare you!" she sputtered at his audacity.

"Pick it up, prentice, and dare me no further!" Tarleton grinned impishly as she snatched up the damp bundle. "You must learn to catch things, Robin, my lad. Things like balls, hoops, apples and coins—most especially silver coins. That, sweet lad, is our livelihood."

"Am I to walk in bare feet?" she asked, stumbling after him, as they made their way back to the forest road. Sticks, sharp stones and tree roots seemed to spring into the path of her tender flesh.

"Aye, for now. I have no spare shoes and yours were ruined, but we shall try to remedy that soon. In the meantime, 'twill do you no harm to go unshod. A lad of your age and station does not have soft, dainty feet."

"And what age and station am I?" she muttered, hopping a little.

"What age was Lady Elizabeth when last seen?" Tarleton looked down at his charge with amusement.

"I am nineteen, soon to be twenty at Michaelmastide. Ouch!" she ended, stubbing her toe on a large rock.

"Nay, Robin does not know when he was born, but he looks to be all of twelve summers, I'd say. Old enough to be on his own, but still unbearded and of treble voice."

"Twelve?" she murmured. It was too young to be out alone in the world.

Elizabeth remembered her own twelfth year. On her birthday, her father gave her a string of beautiful pearls that had once belonged to her mother, saying that Elizabeth was now old enough to take proper care of them. But she was still young enough to hide from her governess when there were lessons to be done. Elizabeth had never seen a street urchin, never given one a thought. When she was twelve, it seemed every day was filled with sunshine, a wealth of good things to eat, lively music, pretty clothes, warm hearths, lots of sociable hounds with cold wet noses, and shoes—most especially pretty shoes.

Tarleton's warm voice broke in among these pleasant memories, pulling her back to the harsh reality of her plight.

"Remember, prentice. You must act the part, as well as look it. Your safety will depend upon it."

Chapter Two

That first hour on the road south to Woodstock was the longest, most uncomfortable one that Elizabeth had ever experienced. The hard-packed dirt highway, full of ruts and strewn with stinking manure from all manner of livestock, presented new obstacles at every step. Her feet, accustomed to dainty satin slippers, were soon bruised and scratched. The damp roll of the bundled cloak soaked through Elizabeth's borrowed shirt; its cord bit painfully into her shoulder.

On the other hand, Tarleton, striding beside her, seemed perfectly at ease as he whistled all manner of sprightly tunes. Determined to prove to the cheerful jester that she could keep pace with him, she concentrated on putting one aching foot in front of the other. Just when she thought she would pitch forward into the dirt and never rise again, Tarleton clapped her companionably on the back.

"We'll take our ease here," he said, pointing to a grassy bank by the side of the road. "No use in wearing out our soles."

Elizabeth merely glared at this last witticism and wiped the perspiration out of her eyes with her sleeve. The grass felt cool and delicious between her throbbing toes. Collapsing in an exhausted heap against his pack, she idly watched the fluffy white clouds swirl lazily across the blue bowl of the sky above her. The caressing warmth of the noonday sun and the humming of a nearby bee made her feel drowsy. Her eyelids fluttered.

"Don't go to sleep now, Robin Redbreast. We have miles to cover before sundown." Tarleton stood over her, momentarily blocking out the sunlight. "I have a wineskin in the pack, if you care to move your head."

With a small sigh of regret, Elizabeth sat up. Didn't Tarleton ever feel tired, she wondered, watching him rummage through the canvas sack. Elizabeth gingerly massaged her burning feet.

"Ah! Here we are!" He waved a bulging wineskin in front of her face. "Finest vintage from your father's cellars."

"You stole our wine?" Elizabeth's eyes widened at his audacity.

"Nay, nay! Stealing is a sin. Jane, your sweet cook, gave it to me as a gift for—" Tarleton stopped suddenly, his face reddening a bit.

"For what?" Elizabeth snapped. Jane, she felt, was a little too free with the manor's provisions. "What did she buy from you?" Elizabeth prodded.

"She bought nothing of me. 'Twas a gift for an hour or two of pleasure," Tarleton replied, his eyes burning deeply into hers.

"Pleasure? You mean she...that is, you and she..." Elizabeth colored deep crimson at the thought of the manor's reed-thin cook caught within Tarleton's loving embrace. What sweet pleasures would a woman find there? What would it feel like to be held tightly against his chest? Elizabeth shook herself.

Tarleton, instead of looking properly shamefaced at his confession, laughed at her obvious discomfiture.

"Aye, my *boy!*" He arched his dark eyebrow meaningfully. "The pleasure of a woman's sweet love! There's nothing finer on God's good earth. Nay, do not blush so prettily. A growing lad needs to know these things." Lowering his voice, he added seriously, "You will hear talk like that—and far worse—on our travels, so best get used to it now."

"I can't help it," Elizabeth replied, wishing she could wipe away her pink cheeks. "I have always blushed easily. Indeed, when I was growing up, my family often teased me just to see me turn red."

Tarleton's eyes softened with understanding. Elizabeth was, after all, a gently bred lady. How could he expect to turn her into a lusty lad in only a few hours? Smiling at her, he continued lightly, "Be of good cheer, Robin! Have some wine. Sunshine in each drop." He held out the wineskin to her.

Trying not to notice the merry twinkle in his dark eyes, Elizabeth took the proffered bag and drank deeply. Tarleton was right, the sweetness of the vintage was a balm to her dry throat and raw nerves.

"Save a bit of that, my boy! 'Tis all we have for now." He drank from the bag, then corked it tightly. "Let us be gone." Taking Elizabeth by the hand, Tarleton pulled her to her feet. He held her fingers in his a moment longer than necessary, then he gently draped the rolled cape over her shoulder once more. "It is not wise to tarry in one place too long," he remarked, his voice husky.

A party of armed horsemen nearly ran them down in the midafternoon. They neither saw nor spoke to the jester and his scruffy apprentice by the side of the road as they left Tarleton and Elizabeth in the dust behind them.

"Did you mark their livery? Were they Sir Robert's men?" Elizabeth asked, glad to see the mounted figures recede from sight.

"Nay, the poxy knaves went by too fast." Tarleton smiled encouragingly at her. He did not tell Elizabeth that he recognized the lead rider. La Faye's henchman had tried to cheat Tarleton at cards in the kitchen of Esmond Manor. So, Sir Robert was indeed on the move! Tarleton ruffled Elizabeth's soft hair. "Foot it, my lad! We've some miles yet to go this day."

"Where are we going?" Elizabeth asked wearily. Only the occasional farmer's cottage dotted the distant fields. Visions of a hot bath danced maddeningly in her brain.

"To visit the Queen!" was her companion's jaunty reply.

"I mean tonight. You said we were going to stay in a nice place tonight." She stifled a yawn. She would not let Tarleton see how exhausted she was.

"Did I?" Tarleton cocked his head, then chuckled. "I do not recall that I said 'nice.' But at least 'twill be a roof over our heads."

"What *is* this place?" she asked warily. Something in the tone of his voice warned her that she wasn't going to like his choice of accommodations.

"An inn of the lowest sort, I fear, but this route is not traveled by the upper crust of society. And I thank you for reminding me of something." He stopped so suddenly in the middle of the road that Elizabeth almost ran headlong into him.

"What now?" she asked irritably, angry that Tarleton had deceived her with his earlier promise of a goodly inn.

"We shall be expected to sing for our supper."

Elizabeth's jaw dropped. "Sing in front of strangers? You are jesting!"

"No jests, I fear. 'Tis the hazard of my calling—and now yours, prentice. So, as we walk along, I shall teach you some fine tavern ballads. 'Twill lighten your heart—and help take your mind off your blisters." Guiltily Tarleton watched her tighten her jaw, as Elizabeth shifted her weight on her swollen feet. He vowed to do something about her lack of shoes at the first opportunity. He admired her courage. Not once had she mentioned her obvious pain. "Listen to the words carefully."

Clearing his throat, Tarleton broke into a rippling ditty. "She had a dark and rolling eye/And her hair hung down in ring-a-lets/She was a nice girl/A proper girl/But, one of the roving kind!"

The tune was merry enough, but the lyrics grew more and more bawdy with each successive verse, as the song extolled, with explicit detail, each and every one of the roving girl's myriad charms. Elizabeth's ears, as well as her cheeks, were burning by the end of the last chorus.

"You cannot possibly expect me to sing that!" she sputtered. "It's awful! It's...it's shameful! And not for a lady at all!"

"You are right, chuck," he agreed, daring to call her by a lighthearted term of affection. "'Tis not fit for a proper lady's ears, but we left the very proper Lady Elizabeth at the bottom of the river, remember? You, prentice, will stand high on a tabletop with your legs thrust boldly apart. You will throw back your head proudly, and you will sing that song at the top of your sweet lungs."

"Never!" declared Elizabeth, glowering at him. "I shall die first."

"No, you won't. Who knows?" he teased her. "You might even get to like it. And just think what a surprise 'twill be when you sing it for the ladies of the court!"

"I couldn't!" she gasped. Had the jester completely lost his wits?

"Oh, but you could!" He grinned, amused by her reaction to his suggestion. "In private, of course. Truly, those fine ladies at court will enjoy it just as much as the ruffians on the road do. The only difference is the setting. Now, my lad, sing!" He began the first verse again, making Elizabeth repeat each line after him.

Over and over that beautiful, high summer afternoon, the jester and his stumbling apprentice practiced "that awful song" until Elizabeth had it note perfect. Tarleton was pleasantly surprised to discover that his reluctant pupil was gifted with a clear, pure voice.

"Where did you learn to sing?" he asked as they rested later that afternoon, eating more of his windfall apples.

"In France. I was taught in a convent there."

"A convent?" Tarleton's eyes widened. "Sweet angels! Were you a nun?"

"No, only a student taught by them. My mother's family insisted upon it, and my father agreed. My mother was French, but she died when I was quite young."

"Are you a papist?" Tarleton eyed her sharply. Politics and religion were often the same thing in these turbulent times. Tarleton made it a practice to avoid both whenever possible.

"Only when I'm in France." She smiled. "Here I profess the new learning, but I pray privately in my own manner."

"Amen to that." Tarleton breathed a sigh of relief. At least, his employer would not be making any irrational or unhealthy moves, such as insisting upon attending a popish mass.

She arched her eyebrow at him. "I am sure that the good nuns who taught me to sing would not approve of your choice of hymn, Sir Jester. I'd be in penance for a month!"

"You have a beautiful voice, and you learn quickly." Tarleton complimented his apprentice. "As a reward, I will teach you another—"

"Oh, no! One is more than enough!"

Tarleton's lips twitched with amusement. "This one, I promise, will please you. 'Tis a love ballad, one that you could sing before your reverend mother without a blush. Listen!" He sang in a deep, rich tone. "'Under the greenwood tree/Who loves to lie with me/And turn his merry note/Unto the sweet bird's throat?' There, what thinkest thou?" he asked when he had finished.

"It's better than the last one," Elizabeth conceded.

"Then let us be merry, too long we have tarried!" Pulling Elizabeth to her feet again, Tarleton swung down the road, smiling to himself. Her hand felt even warmer and softer than before. "Sing, sweet Robin!" Tarleton cheerfully called to her over his shoulder.

The sun was low behind the haystacks in the fields, when the travelers came to the promised inn. Elizabeth's weary heart sank at the sight of it. The Blue Boar sat at the side of the highway like a squat, old, painted woman. Its cracked plaster walls had not felt the touch of a paintbrush for a decade, at least. Several shutters hung at rakish angles from the narrow, grimy windows. Its wooden sign creaked on rusty hinges above the battered door; the namesake boar more gray than blue in color. Determined to make the best of it, Elizabeth started toward the entrance. Tarleton yanked her aside.

"Around to the back, my boy. We are not paying customers. We've come to do business with the innkeeper." He pushed her into the cobbled stable yard, past stinking piles of kitchen refuse and manure.

Closing her eyes for a moment, Elizabeth reminded herself that she had indeed agreed to this charade. Squaring her shoulders, she tried to look as manly as possible. Roughly she pushed away a thin yellow cur who sniffed at her bare toes with interest.

Tarleton engaged the florid-faced innkeeper in deep conversation. After a bit of haggling, the man nodded, and pointed toward the stable. Tarleton swept him a courtly bow and strode off in that direction.

"Robin! Look lively, boy!" he called gruffly, snapping his fingers at Elizabeth. Bewildered, she followed him across the filthy cobblestones into the barn.

"Up we go!" Tarleton stood at the bottom of the loft ladder.

"Up there?" Elizabeth's heart dropped to her toes, and all her manly intentions fled. She drew in her breath to tell

Tarleton exactly what she thought of his proffered lodgings, but Tarleton moved faster than her indignation. Grabbing her roughly by the scruff of her neck, he practically threw her up the first two rungs.

"I said move, churl! Are your ears full of wax?" he yelled at her. "Damn your hide! I've a mind to give you a sound whipping, and no supper!"

Stunned by this sudden rough treatment, and shocked into silence by Tarleton's unexpected coarse language, Elizabeth blinked back her angry tears as she scurried up the ladder. On the top rung, a stray splinter drove itself deeply into her foot. Suppressing a cry of pain, she limped into the hay-filled loft.

Following close behind her, Tarleton surveyed the area with a practiced eye. Pulling her to a far corner where the sweet-smelling hay was piled the highest, he heaved the pack to the dusty floor with a contented sigh.

"Oh! Have done with me!" Elizabeth moaned as she threw herself into the straw, burying her head in her hands.

Dropping down beside her, Tarleton gathered the worn-out girl in his arms. Gently he rocked her back and forth.

"Don't..." She wanted to protest more, but her words were muffled in his jerkin. Instead, she relaxed into his cushioning embrace.

"Hush! Hush, sweetling!" he whispered softly in her ear. "Forgive me for all. Don't cry." He gently stroked her ragged hair, still silky despite its rough treatment. "There was a stable boy below, watching us. I acted as any master would have done to his apprentice," he explained. "A man's world is a rough one. Shush, fair one. We are safe. We have this fine, warm place for the night, and a supper, as well—if we sing prettily enough for it."

"We are to sleep here? In a barn?" Elizabeth's reserves of courage melted away. She was tired, sore, hungry and frightened in these strange, coarse surroundings.

"'Tis no Esmond Manor, I warrant you, but then again, there are far worse places we could be in. So be of good cheer!"

"You hurt me!" she whispered fiercely.

Tarleton winced at her accusation. "Not by choice. Please, sweetling, understand I do what I must for your own safety."

"Does that include laming me?" she snapped. The splinter felt as if it were on fire.

"Laming you? Nay, 'tis only a sweet stroll down a dry road on a sunny day. How is it that you are now lame?" he gently teased her.

"I have a splinter in my foot from the ladder."

Tarleton laid her down on the straw. "Which foot?" he asked, concern etched his voice.

"The right one, just under the largest toe. Ouch! That's it! Oh, please, don't touch it again!" She gritted her teeth as Tarleton ignored her protests.

"'Tis not a deep one, only large. I can pull it easily."

"Oh, no!" she moaned.

He held out the pack strap to her. "Bite on this, but don't cry out. We can't have that stable boy poking his head up here," he commanded sternly as he produced the wineskin.

Wincing from the pain, Elizabeth hesitated only a moment before putting the dirty cloth into her mouth. It tasted of earth and sweat; Elizabeth nearly gagged on it. Tarleton touched her cheek tenderly, brushing away a traitorous tear with his thumb. Then he smiled encouragingly at her, his gaze as soft as a caress. Something in his manner soothed her. Nodding, she bit down hard as Tarleton poured some wine on the wounded area. More tears burned in her eyes as he probed for the splinter. She gripped handfuls of the hay as the stabbing pain increased under his probing.

The jagged splinter was lodged deeper than he thought. Glancing at Elizabeth, Tarleton noted how white she looked, her eyes squeezed shut. His heart tightened.

"What manner of company are you keeping of late, sweet Robin?" he joked, trying to take her mind off the pain. "For I see that your sole has become very black."

His quip was rewarded by her fleeting smile.

"'Tis gone!" he announced triumphantly. Bright red drops of blood welled up in the spot where the splinter had been. Placing his lips over the injury, he sucked at the tiny wound.

A soft gasp escaped Elizabeth. Tarleton's lips were surprisingly gentle. As they caressed the burning skin of her foot, she felt a lurch of excitement within her. Her breath caught in her throat; her heartbeat hammered in her ears. His nearness was overwhelming.

"Oh!" she moaned again, softly this time, her pain forgotten.

Recognizing the sound for what it meant, Tarleton quickly released her foot. "I trust you are better now," he remarked in a tight, hoarse voice.

She was as intoxicating as new wine in autumn. He tried to shake off her heady effect. If Elizabeth had been any other maid moaning so passionately at his touch, Tarleton would have cheerfully pressed his advantage immediately. As it was, his loins throbbed hotly and grew tight. Elizabeth was a lady, he reminded himself—and the Queen's own goddaughter! He would be moonstruck to even consider the idea of a romp in the hay.

"Tarleton, I—" she began.

"What you need are shoes," he muttered gruffly. "Stay here, and rest." Leaping up, he built a low wall of straw in front of her. "Behold my lady's chamber," he whispered.

Not moving from where she lay, Elizabeth watched him through her thick lashes. His presence made her senses spin. For a long moment, she felt as if she were floating. As her heartbeat slowed, soft waves of fatigue enveloped her. The straw beneath her was fresh harvested and smelled sweetly of sun-filled summer days and flowering meadows. Basking in the warmth of Tarleton's low voice and the memory of the caress of his lips, Elizabeth drifted into a deep, dreamless sleep.

Tarleton smiled ruefully down at her; she looked like a kitten curled in the sun. She was so tiny, barely as tall as his shoulder. "How high is my love?/Just as high as my heart," sang the old refrain in his head.

"I will return soon," he whispered, watching her delicate eyelashes fan against her pale cheek. *Oh, my lady, what have I done to you? And what have I done to myself?*

Turning quickly, he left her.

Chapter Three

Elizabeth dreamed she was being shaken, as if a large dog held her in its mouth, whipping her back and forth like a rag doll. Dully opening her eyes, she was greeted by Tarleton's elfish grin. The corners of his brown eyes turned upward in the ghostly light of the new risen moon. In his hand, he held a pair of shoes. They were cracked, well-worn at the heels, and smelled strongly of their former owner.

Instantly Elizabeth was wide-awake. "Where did you get them?" she breathed excitedly.

"The tap boy. He's a lad about your size, and he was willing to part with them for a small financial consideration." Sitting back on his heels, Tarleton looked extremely pleased with himself. "I am sorry there was no time to get them embroidered with gold thread, but will they do? Are you well pleased?"

"Oh, aye! Very!" She dimpled with satisfaction.

"And to add to the merriment of the occasion..." Tarleton delved into his pack. "I have a fine pair of knitted stockings."

"Stockings! Why didn't you tell me before? Why do you make me walk barefoot all day?" Elizabeth's injured voice rose with each word.

"Hush!" he reminded her. "Without shoes you would have walked the stockings into shreds. Now you have both."

"Aye, they are wonderful!" She ran her fingers across them lovingly as if they were a pair of soft satin slippers.

"Your pardon, but didn't I hear you say thank you just now? I must have wax in mine own ears. I swore you mumbled something like that." Tarleton made a great show of banging the side of his head as if to clear it.

Elizabeth giggled, even though she realized she was being chided by one who was her social inferior. What did that matter now that she had shoes and stockings?

"Thank you, Tarleton. You do remind me of my manners. I must have left them back by the river." She laughed again happily. Unrolling the stockings, she began to pull them on.

"Hold! Those are my clean stockings. Wash your feet first."

"Wash? Where?"

"Here." Tarleton pointed to a nearby wooden bucket brimming with fresh water. "Give me your foot," he commanded in an odd but gentle voice. Obediently Elizabeth placed one in his hand. Tenderly dipping it into the water, he gently kneaded her bruises and blisters.

Sighing with pleasure, Elizabeth lay back in the straw. A small smile stole across her lips. The water dripped deliciously between her toes. The jester's knowing fingers massaged the soft pads on the balls of her feet, then stroked her ankle. Were it possible for Elizabeth to purr like a sleek cat, she would have.

Patting the one foot dry with a piece of huck toweling from his shaving kit, Tarleton took the other one, again working his gentle magic. He marveled how tiny her foot was, so like the rest of her. A small, nagging voice in his mind reminded him that what he was doing was wrong. He knew how easy it would be to seduce such a trusting young lady. He should have let Elizabeth wash her own feet, but he excused himself as being a weak-willed mortal in the presence of an angel. A most provocative angel who lay so se-

ductively in the hay, her eyes closed and her full lips parted
so enticingly. The barest hint of her white teeth shone; the
tip of her moist pink tongue caught between them. Holding
her foot, Tarleton's hands trembled as a hot surge of desire
rippled through him. Roughly he dried her toes.

"Methinks you are ready for civilized company now," he
muttered raggedly. "Put your shoes and socks on, prentice, and don't dawdle. There's work to be done."

Turning away from her, he pulled his bright-colored
jacket from the pack. The bells on its points tinkled softly
when he shook out the folds.

Elizabeth's eyes snapped open at the sudden change of his
tone. She was totally bewildered by his behavior—and her
own. She found his touch both disturbing and exciting.
*Tarleton must think I am a wanton to allow him to be so
familiar with my person,* she chided herself as she pulled on
the thick stockings.

As she wiggled her toes, her mood changed to joy. Never
again would she complain of the style or color of her slippers.

Dressed in his red and green motley, Tarleton beckoned
to her. "Follow me, and watch that ladder on the way down.
As much as it gave me pleasure to tend to your last splinter,
I doubt you wish for an encore."

Elizabeth sighed at the remembrance of his warm lips. *An
encore might not be so bad.*

At the top of the ladder, Tarleton whispered into her ear,
his warm breath tickling her cheek.

"Be warned. Play your part well. You are a dull-witted
prentice boy. Take no offence at what I say to you when we
are in the company of others. And if I should clap my hands
together while rebuking you, cry out as if you have been
slapped. 'Tis expected for masters to treat their lads in such
fashion." He swung himself down the ladder first. Elizabeth followed him gingerly.

"God's teeth, boy!" he bellowed at her from below. "The next time, I will throw you down the ladder headfirst. You would get to the bottom a good deal faster!"

Elizabeth thought she heard a snicker from somewhere in the darkness of the stable, and surmised it to be the eaves-dropping ostler. "Aye, good master," she answered, lowering her voice. "Pray be patient with me."

"Angels have patience, but you, I fear, are a long way from heaven!"

Grabbing her arm roughly, Tarleton pulled her after him across the yard. Though his voice was harsh, Elizabeth saw his grin flash in the moonlight.

He pushed her against the pump. "Water, churl! Ply the pump, and with a will!" Slapping one hand against the other, he whispered, "Cry out!"

Elizabeth responded with a weak, but passable cry of pain.

He grinned. "Good! Not a star performance, but 'twill suffice. Now, pump. Don't tell me you've never seen a pump before."

"Of course I have," she whispered back, grasping the worn handle firmly. "I've just never done it myself." As she pulled it up and down, Elizabeth dreamed of pitchers of warm, sweet rose water that Charlotte used to bring to her room. How she would love a bath right now! A hot, laven-der-scented bath before a cheerful fire! And with someone to scrub her back—someone with warm, gentle hands like.... Glancing guiltily at Tarleton, she banished her wanton thoughts.

Bending down under the gush of glittering water, Tarle-ton doused his head, shaking the drops out of his hair with a contented sigh.

"Your hair looks like a bird's nest, boy!" he observed, his deep voice echoing off the grimy plaster walls of the inn yard. After grabbing Elizabeth by the neck, he shoved her head under the tap just as he had done himself. Icy water streamed into her eyes and trickled down her shirt collar.

"Now, shake your head," he whispered, while she was still sputtering her surprise. "Let's smooth you up a bit." Elizabeth's tormentor smiled into her clean face. He lightly ran his fingers through the shorn golden stubble. There was a faint glint of humor in his eyes as he regarded his handiwork. "'Tis plain as the nose on your sweet face that I'm no lady's maid."

Swallowing hard, Elizabeth prayed her features did not betray her racing heart. "I wish I had my comb and brushes," she mumbled.

"Fine ladies have combs, but not guttersnipes and prentice boys," Tarleton replied in a strange husky voice.

Tarleton donned his coxcomb hat and tied the strings firmly under his chin. It was the cap that changed his appearance, Elizabeth realized. With his curly brown hair concealed, Tarleton the jester looked every inch a rogue and goblin, especially when he grinned so wickedly and wiggled his dark eyebrows. No wonder she failed to recognize him on their unusual meeting!

"Ready, boy?"

Looking with apprehension at the back door of the inn, Elizabeth shivered then nodded. Loud, boisterous male voices came from inside. Tarleton took both her hands in his strong, reassuring ones.

"Frightened?" he asked her gently.

She nodded again.

"Good," he continued lightly. "'Tis healthy to be frightened just before a performance. Don't worry, chuck. 'Tis a little like losing your virginity—the first time you're scared to death and don't enjoy it, but it gets better each time after that."

Elizabeth gasped at his frankness, but he allowed her no time to respond. Before she knew what was happening,

Tarleton pulled her through the door into the humid, smoky taproom.

"Room! Pray, masters all! Give me room to rhyme! We've come to show activity upon this pleasant time. Activity of youth..." Tarleton whirled and pranced, pointing to the quaking Elizabeth. "And activity of age..." He bowed deeply to the stinking assembly. "And such activity as ne'er been seen on this stage! I am Tarleton, jester to Her Most Gracious Majesty, and to her loving subjects!"

"Aye, Tarleton! Give us a jest!" cried a gravelly voice from the back of the dim room. "Tell the one about the pig, the sheep and the farmer's daughter!"

Without pausing a moment, Tarleton grinned devilishly, then launched into the most ribald story Elizabeth had ever heard. She kept well back in the shadows and reminded herself that she was a boy, who should not be blushing. Tarleton's crude story was greeted by a loud round of approving cheers and whistles. Immediately he told another tale, which was even more bawdy than the first.

What manner of man was this jester? Elizabeth wondered as she listened with bewilderment. When they were alone, Tarleton was polite and well-spoken with Elizabeth. Now he was someone else entirely—someone she didn't know at all.

Next in the repertoire was a tavern song concerning the life of a lustful boy, and how he hung on the gallows for it. Afterward Tarleton executed a short jig, pulling a giggling serving wench into his arms, much to the additional loud cheers of the patrons. Spinning around suddenly, Tarleton grabbed Elizabeth by the wrist, pulling her into the center of the room. She could feel her heart hammering against her breast.

"Good masters, your patience is my prayer. Gently to hear and kindly to judge this player! 'Tis my new prentice, Robin. Give us a song, lad, about the wench with the roll-

ing eye!'' With that introduction, he gripped her around the
waist, and plopped her on top of the nearest table.

Girding herself with resolve, Elizabeth wet her lips and
began. ''She had a dark and rolling eye/And her hair hung
down in ring-a-lets.''

Fixing her gaze on a spot just above the smoking fireplace, Elizabeth forced herself to forget the velvet-gowned
heiress of that morning. Now Lady Elizabeth Hayward of
Esmond Manor was a ragged jester's apprentice. What
would she be by the journey's end?

At the conclusion of the last verse, the patrons of the Blue
Boar clapped and banged their leather jack mugs heartily.

''Sing it again, sweet Robin!''

Elizabeth could scarcely believe her ears. Some loutish
churl on the side by the counter was ordering her to entertain him again—and he was calling her ''sweet'' in the bargain! She glanced over at Tarleton, but he acted as bad as
the rest, grinning and clapping at her.

''Sing again, Robin Redbreast!'' her erstwhile protector
commanded. He grinned impishly, challenging her to go
through with it.

Elizabeth ground her teeth. *All right, you shag-eared
jester! I'll show you just how good I can be for this ragtag
mob!* Taking a deep breath, Elizabeth threw the bawdy lyrics back into their pockmarked faces.

Her second rendition was received even better than the
first. At the end of the rousing last chorus, Tarleton swept
her off the table. Then he pushed her head down, forcing
her to bow to the unwashed rabble while he bantered to
them, something about ''Robin is a little slow and hasn't
learned his manners yet!''

Despite the sordid surroundings, the rough company and
the type of song she had just performed, Elizabeth surprised herself by grinning as she accepted the lusty applause for her debut. The rowdy noise was an intoxicating
wine to Elizabeth.

"What's the news, Tarleton?" an old woman's shrill voice asked.

While Tarleton recounted the comings and goings of the gentry in a witty and scandalous manner, Elizabeth retreated again to her shadowed spot in the corner, where she observed the scene more closely. She saw Tarleton's audience hang on his every word, especially his colorful description of a particularly gruesome execution, which had taken place in Coventry a month before. Elizabeth's stomach lurched at the gory details, and she was glad she had nothing in it to lose.

"And now, say I, let us drink a toast to my mistress!" Tarleton snatched a mug of ale out of the paw of the nearest man and held it aloft. "Here's a health unto Her Majesty, and confusion to her enemies!"

"And so say all of us!" the innkeeper quickly rejoined, looking anxiously around the room, in case there might be a Queen's man among the company.

"She's Great Harry's true daughter, fiery hair and all!" croaked an old man from the inglenook. "And so I say, here's to good Queen Bess!" There was a general cheer, and a great deal of slurping as the loyal citizens drank deeply to show their affection for their ruler.

Looking pleased with himself, Tarleton pulled Elizabeth out of her corner. "The evening grows apace, good friends, so my prentice has a sweet song to sing ye to your rest." He lifted her back onto the tabletop, and whispered, "The Greenwood Tree," to her.

Closing her eyes to blot out the uncouth surroundings, Elizabeth concentrated on her song of love and of warm summer days. The crowd in the taproom grew surprisingly hushed as her clear voice rose above them.

Tarleton felt his throat tighten as he listened. In his mind's eye, he saw Elizabeth sitting sweetly under a thick, green-leafed tree, her billowing satin skirts spread out on a carpet of tiny white-faced daisies, and her golden hair, long once

again, spilling down over her tight bodice. He saw himself
with his head pillowed in her soft lap; his eyes closed as he
listened to her sing this very song, just for him. He clenched
his jaw. *You are even a greater fool than you profess to be!*

Loud cheering and applause greeted Elizabeth's last note.
This time, she hopped lightly off the table and executed her
own graceful bow. Then she turned to Tarleton with a smile
that was half defiant and half pleased. Tarleton rewarded
her with a wide grin.

"Our play is done and that's all one!" Tarleton bowed
elaborately to the audience as if they were the finest lords
and ladies in the land. A smattering of silver coins rained
down on him.

"Look lively, Robin!" Tarleton stooped to retrieve them.
"'Tis your fortune at your feet!"

Obediently Elizabeth dropped to her knees and began
gathering up the money. The floorboards were sticky to the
touch; dirt and dried food filled the cracks between the
planks. Elizabeth wrinkled her nose. Feeling light-headed,
she passed her hand across her brow. Tarleton, noting her
pallor, was at her side, pulling her to her feet.

"Landlord! Food! Food for the inner man...and my
pale-faced boy!" he called, hauling Elizabeth through the
crowd to a small wooden booth in the back corner.

Elizabeth sank down with relief against the rough plank-
ing of the seat.

"There now, lad! What say you?" Doffing his cap and
rumpling his damp hair, Tarleton slid onto the bench opposite her. In the guttering candlelight, he looked like the
devil's own helper with a dark curl falling casually across his
forehead and his white teeth gleaming at her.

Now that their performance was over, Elizabeth suddenly felt limp. She was hungry and bone tired.

"How, now, chuck?" Tarleton reached across the pitted
table and lifted her chin so she was forced to look into his
dancing dark eyes. His thumb brushed against her lower lip,

sending a spark shooting through her veins. "You were a success! Look you!" He spilled out the money on the table. "'Tis a fair take, I warrant you. Much better than I expected. 'Twas your sweet voice that pleased them!"

A few halfpennies glinted among the farthings. Tarleton whistled softly when he came upon a groat. Elizabeth could only blink at him, then at the small pile of tarnished silver. She touched her shirt where the small money bag lay nestled between her breasts. As if he could read her mind, Tarleton leaned across the table.

"Look happy at your good fortune, Robin," he whispered. "'Tis a fine night's work for such players as you and I. This money will buy several meals for both of us."

Before Elizabeth could remind him that money was not a problem, the serving wench arrived with a tray of steaming bowls.

"Are you truly the famous Tarleton we have heard so many travelers praise?" she asked coyly, gazing at him with an open hunger.

Tarleton returned her smile. "Aye, on my honor, sweetheart. Am I not the Queen's own Tarleton, my lad?"

Elizabeth stared first at him, then at the girl. "Aye, so my master has often told me," she muttered gruffly, playing her new role. She did not like the way the serving girl was eyeing Tarleton.

"And are you not the luckiest boy in the realm to be apprenticed to the great Tarleton?" He smiled a challenge at Elizabeth, and wiggled his brows.

"Aye," Elizabeth responded in a stronger voice. Two could play this scene. "My master has told me that often enough, as well. Indeed, he drums it into my head hourly."

The wench and the jester laughed at her retort. Ignoring them both, Elizabeth regarded the watery soup placed before her. The black bread that accompanied it was hard as wood. Her empty stomach grumbled in protest.

"Be off with ye now," Tarleton told the wench, who had made no move to depart. "Let us dine in peace."

"Later, perhaps?" The maid leaned toward him so that her heavy breasts peeped boldly from the top of her smock.

"Perchance." He smiled, and followed up his half promise with a sound smack on her backside. She merely laughed and ambled away, casting several long looks at him over her shoulder.

Elizabeth pretended not to notice. To her annoyance, she found herself starting to blush.

"Eat up, my boy!" Tarleton turned his full attention to his trencher.

"How? This is impossible!" whispered Elizabeth fiercely.

"Not used to humble fare, I see," he whispered back, but his eyes were gentle. "Sop the bread into the broth. 'Twill soften it up even for your dainty teeth. Zounds," he swore, after tasting the dish. "She said it was chicken soup, but methinks the chicken did not pause too long in the pot."

Elizabeth's nose wrinkled with distaste.

"Eat it all, prentice," he cautioned her quietly. "And give thanks to God for it. There's many in the land tonight who would sell their mother's virtue for such a meal as this."

Elizabeth looked at him to see if this was yet another jest, but she could tell by the sudden soberness in his eyes that he had spoken the truth. She chewed the stale bread thoughtfully, and promised herself never to take finely milled manchet for granted again.

The wench returned with mugs of ale and a wedge of hard cheese.

"Surely there is something else I can do for so famous a player as yourself, sweet Tarleton?" she purred, arranging herself on his lap.

Elizabeth's eyes widened at her boldness, though Tarleton did not look the least annoyed. In fact, he seemed to enjoy the maid's attention.

"Well, now that you mention it, fair mistress, I have in mind a thing or two," Tarleton bantered, playing with the loose strings of the girl's smock.

"Aye, I have a thing or two that perhaps will stir your mind—and other, more manly parts, as well." She giggled, tugging her smock down even lower. "Do ye think of these things?" she cooed, pulling his head toward her ample charms.

Watching her, Elizabeth was fascinated and horrified at the same time. The more she saw of the brazen wench, the less Elizabeth liked her. The opposite seemed to be true of Tarleton.

"They are a right fine pair, I warrant you, sweetheart," Tarleton beamed, kissing first one fleshy mound, then the other. The girl giggled and arched her back. Now both her breasts were fully exposed, their dark nipples engorged and erect.

Tarleton slipped his arm around the girl's back, stroking and teasing her breasts with the other hand. The wench's low animal moans of pleasure sent icy shivers through Elizabeth. An angry feeling of possessiveness welled up inside her. Elizabeth longed to claw the girl out of Tarleton's arms.

"Surely there is some service I can do for you, sweet jester? Some small thing I can do to while away the night?" the girl murmured, kissing his ear. Over the wench's shoulder, Tarleton winked at Elizabeth.

The knave! Was Elizabeth supposed to enjoy watching this? She started to rise, but, in a flash, Tarleton's hard-muscled calves wrapped around her ankle, pinning her down. He arched his brow at his captive.

"I fear we are embarrassing my poor young prentice." He fondled the wench's breasts; all the time he held Elizabeth in his smoldering gaze. "The lad is young, and more than a little dull in his wits. This morning I had to free his head from a thornbush. As you can see, I had to cut away a good deal of his hair, and, alas, I am no barber."

Tarleton smiled winsomely at the panting girl. The wench glanced over at Elizabeth and giggled.

"So I see, sweet Tarleton. But I am sure you have other skills far better than the cutting of hair. In fact, I do believe I can feel one of those skills right now between your legs."

"Aye, mistress mine, but I perceive by the length of your sweet fingers—" here, he began to kiss and nibble at each finger in turn "—that you have a skill or two yourself. If you could render my prentice more presentable, you may find me—most rewarding. A snip or two here and there is all that's needed."

Elizabeth's own fingers curled tightly around her mug of ale and she considered throwing it at the churl. Gritting her teeth, she tried to remind herself that Tarleton's social life was none of her business.

Leaving off nibbling Tarleton's ear, the maid regarded Elizabeth professionally. Elizabeth felt herself grow warmer under the coarse wench's scrutiny.

"Aye, I can trim the boy's hair. And then...?" The maid traced the outline of Tarleton's smiling lips with a ragged, dirty fingernail.

Watching her caress Tarleton so familiarly made Elizabeth's skin crawl.

"Then you will find me . . . most grateful." Tarleton covered her mouth with his, kissing her loudly and deeply.

Baffled and angry, Elizabeth stared down at the crumbs on her platter and heartily wished both the wench and the smiling jester to hell.

Sighing contentedly, the girl adjusted her smock, then ambled away.

Elizabeth glowered at Tarleton, her green eyes blazing in fury. "If you think, for one minute, that I am going to let that...that horrid person touch me, you are moonstruck!" she hissed.

Tarleton chuckled, then lowered his voice. "You need a haircut, and she can do a proper piece of work on it. 'Tis part of her job to barber the inn's patrons. How I pay her is my business, just as it is now my business to see you safely to court!''

''And do you enjoy making a spectacle of yourself with that...?''

He regarded her evenly. ''The word you are looking for is *stew,* or *doxy. Slattern,* if you prefer that.''

Elizabeth's eyes shot green fire at him. ''Why are you doing this to me?'' she whispered fiercely.

''Because I must, for your sake, as well as mine. Look like a young lusty lad—and start thinking like one, too!'' Tarleton relaxed casually against the back of the booth as the girl returned, holding in her hand a pair of extremely sharp shears.

''Mind Robin's ears,'' Tarleton remarked lazily. ''He's hard enough of hearing as it is.''

The wench pushed Elizabeth's head down so that the candlelight could catch her gleaming crown and jagged neckline.

''By my troth, thou art a pretty chick!'' the girl crooned as she swiftly began to snip a little here and there. ''Such fine, soft hair! I've never seen the like. Ye will make a sweet youth when you have a beard coming. I should like to see more of ye then!'' She giggled wickedly.

Elizabeth held very still, wincing at each snip, feeling the cold of the steel against her neck. She dared not say a word, playing the part of the ''dull-witted prentice'' as Tarleton had called her. Inwardly she seethed with mounting rage.

''There! Look up, my pet! Say now, Tarleton. Art thou pleased with this small service?'' the maid asked archly.

Elizabeth blew the loose hair off her nose and glared at Tarleton.

Ignoring his furious apprentice, Tarleton beamed at the wench. ''The court barber could not do as well. You have a skillful hand!''

"I have more than that." The wench smiled invitingly, preparing to fling herself once more into Tarleton's lap.

"Sweet mistress, I would feel easier in my mind if you would put away that sharp implement afore you straddle me!"

Squealing with delight, the wench laid the shears down behind the booth. Only then did Tarleton release Elizabeth's foot, which was numb from his viselike pressure. Standing up, Tarleton stretched to his full height, then pulled the girl hard against him.

"'Tis true I am most marvelous sleepy, but I fear, I cannot spend it in your company, toothsome though you are. My spirit is willing, but my other parts..." Sighing deeply, he looked regretfully into her eyes. "They have given up on me this evening."

"You trickster!" The girl's face grew red, and her eyes narrowed like a prowling cat's.

Sliding quickly out of the booth, Elizabeth edged back toward the rear door. She wasn't sure what was going to happen next, but she knew she wanted to be as far away as possible from the fray that was brewing.

Tarleton smiled calmly. "Nay, nay, sweet minx! I promised you a fair payment for your fine services, and I am a man of my word." Still holding her close with one hand, Tarleton fumbled at his coin purse with the other. "See, sweetheart? As true a coin that was ever minted by Her Majesty's treasury, and 'tis all yours!" He glided a gleaming silver penny across the tops of her breasts, then dropped it down her bodice. "Now give me a kiss to remember ye by!"

The wench laughed delightedly, threw her arms around his neck and kissed him passionately. Tarleton returned her kiss with equal abandon. Sweeping her off her feet, he laid her down on the table. Drawing away from her slowly, he traced his fingers down her neck as the lust-soaked girl lay still amid the half-filled beer pots and dirty wooden soup bowls. The nearby patrons thumped their leather jacks of ale in appreciation and envy.

"I shall see thee again, sweetheart," Tarleton promised glibly as he reached around her, retrieving his cap. "Come, boy!" He snapped his fingers as he strode out the back door.

Elizabeth bolted after him, thankful to escape the smoky den and the serving girl's ire.

Chapter Four

"The wench made a fine piece of work of you," remarked Tarleton softly beside Elizabeth as they crossed the inn yard. He ran his fingers through her hair; the short strands whispered the loss of her golden tresses.

Angrily Elizabeth pulled away from his caressing fingers.

"Don't touch me! I am not your stew, nor your doxy!" she snapped, her green eyes flashing a withering look of disdain.

"Nay, I can see you are not that, prentice boy," he replied, spacing his words evenly. "You learn your lessons fast."

In silence they paid a visit to the inn's privy, though Elizabeth did not thank him when he guarded the door for her. Afterward, they climbed the ladder to the loft. From somewhere in the dark corner near the horses, she heard the loud snores of the ostler.

Tarleton shook out Elizabeth's dried traveling cloak. Spreading it on the straw, he placed the pack under his head and laid his dagger by his side. Elizabeth, meanwhile, turned her back to him, took off her shoes and stockings, then stared out at the moon, whose silver beams poured through the loft door. Behind her, she could hear Tarleton's rustling as he prepared himself for the night.

"Forget the wench, chuck, and let us be friends. Come to bed." His rich voice entreated her softly.

She stiffened and did not look at him. "Where do you intend to lie?" Until this moment, she had not given a thought to their sleeping arrangements.

"By your side," Tarleton answered easily.

Wheeling around, Elizabeth stared at him wordlessly. With the exception of his shoes and the jacket of motley, Tarleton lay fully dressed on one side of the cape, his arms folded comfortably under his head.

"I have a...a weapon, and I will defend myself, if necessary," Elizabeth warned him, feeling for her scissors case in the pocket of her breeches. The memory of him fondling the serving girl was all too fresh in her mind.

Tarleton chuckled. "Your virtue is safe with me," he continued in the same light tone. "You are paying me right well to preserve it. We will sleep this night, and every other night, as chaste as any bundling couple, I give you my word. Lie down and rest. We've a long day on the morrow."

Elizabeth considered his words, though she dared not look into his eyes. Truly, those devilish eyes could charm a badger from its den. "I must pray first," she said finally. "I always say a night prayer."

She knelt, folded her hands and bowed her head. The moonlight caught her cropped hair, turning the golden strands to a silver halo as she prayed amid the straw. *She looks like one of God's bright angels,* Tarleton thought. *Say a blessing for me, little one.*

With a small sigh Elizabeth ended her orisons, then she carefully lay down on the far side of the cape, keeping her back firmly turned toward her companion.

"Tarleton?" Elizabeth whispered in the dark. "Why does she do it?"

"Who?" He yawned loudly.

"The girl who cut my hair. Why does she give herself to men?"

Tarleton smiled in the darkness of the loft. He had wondered when Elizabeth was going to mention the girl. "For money, mostly. And perhaps for a bit of pleasure, as well."

"Pleasure?"

Tarleton was not surprised to feel her shudder. Elizabeth had never been in a place like the Blue Boar before. "Aye. We poor folk must take our pleasures when and where we find them. There is no promise that we will live out the morrow," he told her truthfully.

"And you? Did you want to...to lie with her?"

"What manner of questioning is this?" He chuckled softly.

Elizabeth cleared her throat. "You told me I must think like a boy, so I am asking a question that a boy would ask. Did you find her...pleasing?"

Tarleton glanced over at the huddled form a mere arm's length away. His lips curled into a grin. "She was pleasing enough in her own fashion, but not for me. I suspect she was diseased."

Elizabeth gasped. "With the plague?" she squeaked.

"With the pox." Tarleton stole another sideways glance, waiting for her reaction.

"Oh." There was a pause, while Elizabeth digested this unexpected bit of information. "Is that the *only* reason you didn't...stay with her?" Elizabeth's voice was muffled and a little bit hopeful.

Tarleton grinned even more broadly. "That, chuck, is a personal matter. Now go to sleep!" He rolled over, pointedly ending the discussion.

In the ensuing silence, Elizabeth became aware of a number of tiny rustling noises that made the hairs on the back of her neck stand on end. Was someone creeping up on them?

"Tarleton?" she whispered.

"What?" came the sleepy reply.

"I hear something!"

"Probably rats," Tarleton replied calmly.

"Rats!" Elizabeth moved closer to him. "Big ones?" She had heard horror stories of sleeping children being eaten alive by rats.

"Perhaps." He chuckled. "Perhaps they are only medium-sized ones."

"Rats!" She moved still closer to him, clutching the cloak.

"Perhaps only small rats," he teased gently, rolling over toward her.

"Rats!" She huddled against him.

"Perhaps they are only wee barn mice," he murmured, taking the quaking girl gently in his arms. "Mice who are more afraid of us than we are of them. Hush, sweetling. Sleep now." His lips brushed her hair.

"Rats...mice...and hard bread...and stones in the road..." Elizabeth's voice, heavy with fatigue, trailed off as she snuggled within the comforting warmth of his embrace.

"Under the greenwood tree/Who loves to lie with me?" Tarleton hummed softly, smoothing her hair across her brow. He felt her relax, the tensions of the day seeping out of her with each soft breath she drew. He could almost hear the beat of her heart as she nestled against him. Tentatively Tarleton laid his cheek against hers and allowed himself to dream of things that could never be.

"Wake up, sleepyhead!"

Elizabeth's limbs felt too heavy to move.

"Wake up, I say! The birds have sung their matins hymn, and we must put miles behind us today," he announced cheerfully.

Elizabeth opened her eyes slowly. Dawn's pearl gray light was just edging the bottom of the sky.

"Let me be!" she moaned, wrapping the cape tighter around her. "It's too early."

"Nay! I say we must be abroad." With a quick tug, he wrenched the covering off her.

Elizabeth sat up stiffly, rubbing the sleep from her eyes. The chill air prickled her skin with goose bumps.

"'Tis a cool morn," Tarleton observed, wishing he dared to comb the straw out of her hair with his fingers. Elizabeth looked enchanting with her face still soft from sleep. If she were not a lady he had sworn to protect... Tarleton roughly pushed the wayward thought from his mind. "'Tis best you wear the cloak," he told her gruffly. "If anyone asks how a ragtag lad such as yourself could afford so grand a cape, tell them 'tis mine. Put on your shoes, and let us be off."

"With no breakfast?" she asked wistfully. Grinning his puckish grin, Tarleton slapped his pack.

"I've breakfast enough for Great Harry himself should he be of a mind to pay us a visit from the underworld. Come now, look sharp."

Helping Elizabeth to her feet, Tarleton's hand lingered around her soft one. He longed to kiss her smooth, slender fingers. Instead, he roughly fastened her cloak around her shoulders, then led her to the top of the ladder. "Is your money still safe?" he whispered.

Touching the bag concealed under her shirt, Elizabeth nodded.

Placing his finger to his lips, Tarleton pointed below where the ostler still snored out of tune. He helped Elizabeth descend the ladder, catching her around the waist as she neared the bottom. He allowed himself the luxury of holding her close against his chest for a heartbeat, then he lightly placed her on her feet. A tiny smile turned up the corners of her lips as her wide green eyes held his. He wanted to crush her to him, to sweep her off her feet and carry her away to—where?

Pushing these dangerous thoughts to the back corner of his imagination, Tarleton silently beckoned Elizabeth to follow him. Together, they stole out of the inn yard in the chill, damp dawn. A stable terrier raised his head, but Tarleton crooned softly to him. The dog yawned and scratched lazily at a flea, ignoring the departing guests.

"What about breakfast?" Elizabeth suggested hopefully a few hours later, when the sun had burned off the morning's mist. "I'm starving."

"Starving? How can you say that when you had a huge supper last night?" Tarleton rolled his eyes, looking down at her with amusement.

Elizabeth snorted. " 'Twas a supper for Lent!"

" 'Twas a princely feast, and, if more princes ate such feasts, they would not grow so uncommonly fat!" Tarleton chuckled at his witty observation.

Elizabeth merely sighed and rubbed her shoulders. This was not how she had envisioned her escape to the Queen. In the space of one short day she had lost her horse, her clothes, her hair and most of her dignity. Then she remembered that her beloved Esmond Manor was in the thrall of the villainous Sir Robert La Faye. Truly, she was better off with Tarleton. Though he kept low company, there was a certain something about him—

"What's that you were mumbling? Speak up, Robin Redbreast!" Stopping in the middle of the road, he looked at her over his shoulder.

"I was merely wondering at the low company you keep, Sir Jester!" she retorted. Sinking down on the grassy verge, she rubbed her sore calves.

"Have you forgotten that I keep company with you?" He smiled his most impish grin.

Elizabeth pretended to ignore his beguiling charm. "Breakfast?" she prompted.

"I am your most humble and obedient servant."

Squatting down beside his pack, Tarleton drew out a folded cloth that held some of the cheese from the day before, and a half loaf of fine white bread. There was also the end of a hard sausage. To this he added three more apples, which he juggled deftly, eliciting a delighted giggle from Elizabeth. Last of all, he produced a small bottle of imported French wine.

"Where did you get all this?" she asked wonderingly as she sliced a large wedge of cheese. "And why didn't you tell me before that you had a most marvelous feast?"

"This food is what's left from your own kitchen. I was saving the wine for some suitable occasion." He gave a mock sigh.

Ignoring Tarleton's unrepentant free use of her father's stores, Elizabeth ate greedily.

"Methinks your manners went the way of your hair, Robin Redbreast," the player noted with wry amusement. "I pray they will return or the Queen will wonder what mischief I have done you."

Looking up at him, Elizabeth felt a swift flutter in her throat. His brown eyes spoke an eloquent language all their own—a language whose meaning she couldn't quite understand but which stirred her deeply.

Glancing away from him, she asked lightly, "Will it take long to reach Hampton Court?"

"Above a week," he estimated. When her face fell, Tarleton's lips tightened. He forced his voice to sound cheerful. "But we shall make each day a holiday, and the time will pass quickly. Just think what adventures you can tell the other ladies when you are safely at court! They shall be envious of your good fortune for you are traveling with me— Tarleton! The Queen's most favored—"

"Yes, yes, I have heard that tale before, good jester. Leave off another telling of it. You think most highly of yourself!" Elizabeth giggled.

"If I do not trumpet my own name, perhaps you will do it for me? A good apprentice should be proud of his master." Tarleton cocked his head at her.

"We shall see, Master Fool. We shall see."

Tarleton stood up and stretched. A tarnished silver pin, stuck in the weathered brim of his cap, gleamed dully in the sunlight.

"What's that?" Elizabeth asked, pointing to the trinket. She did not recall seeing it yesterday.

"What?" He glanced quickly down the road.

"That pin you wear. Is that another gift from some woman who was...grateful for your attentions?" Elizabeth bit her lip. Her voice sounded more shrewish than she had intended.

Touching it, Tarleton smiled.

"This? Nay, 'twas no love token. I paid good money for it at Canterbury some years back. 'Tis a pilgrim's badge."

Elizabeth gaped at him in surprise. The jester did not seem the religious type. "You went on a pilgrimage to pray at Canterbury?"

He laughed and winked at her. "Aye, chuck, to prey upon the pilgrims. I did right well by them, too. I bought this badge, in case of later need." He dropped his hat in her lap.

"I don't understand," she said, running her finger over the worn design. "What later need?"

"To sell it for bread, if necessary. It's made of good silver. Or..." He grinned wickedly. "In case I want to give it to a maiden. Ah, but she must be a very special maiden for me to part with that."

Elizabeth could feel another one of those hated blushes starting. She chose to ignore his last remark and quickly changed the subject. "Why is it in the shape of an *A?* For St. Thomas à Becket?"

"Nay—for *Amor. Amor vincit omnia.* It means—"

"'Love conquers all,'" Elizabeth easily translated.

Tarleton nodded his approval. "You know your Latin, I see."

"And French. The nuns educated me well," she added. She handed the hat back to him. "Your pin needs polishing."

"Why, then, prentice boy, you can do that this very evening. I have in mind a goodly house where we will spend this night."

"Is this house as goodly as last night's lodging?" Elizabeth arched her eyebrow at him. She was not going to be duped again.

"Nay, chuck." He laughed at her new worldly wisdom. "Truly, it is a fine house. Not as large as Esmond Manor, but a welcome one all the same. I have entertained there many a time. And, to while away the miles, I have in mind another song to teach you."

"Another one?" Elizabeth glared up at him, but he only laughed again.

"I should make you angry more often for, verily, your eyes flash a green lightning that is most wondrous to behold. But, in faith, the song is one that will please you. 'Tis called the 'Wooing of Robin Hood,' and we shall sing it in duet. You be Maid Marian while I am bold Robin! 'Tis a song we shall sing round the table tonight."

"We are to entertain again tonight, Tarleton?" Elizabeth felt the return of butterflies to the pit of her stomach.

"Aye, prentice, and every night if we want to eat and sleep in safety."

"But, Tarleton, you forget I *have* money. We could hire a carriage at the next inn we come to. There is no need for us to—"

Tarleton's eyes glittered darkly. Grabbing her roughly by the shoulders, he shook her hard. "There *is* need! You still don't realize all the dangers of traveling Her Majesty's highways. Who would ride as your protection? Me? I am but one man—and a coward to boot. I own no sword, only a dagger. Would you hire other men—ones who just happened to be loitering about this inn you speak of? What makes you think you could trust strangers you hire? Ha! They would take your fine carriage to a lonely stretch of the road."

Tarleton's eyes narrowed as he thrust his face into hers. "Can you guess what your protectors would do then, fair lady?" His voice sank into an icy whisper. "First, they would take all your money, then your jewelry, then they would strip you of your fine satins and velvets. And when they saw your sweet body, do you think it would end there? Nay! They would throw you to the ground. Two of them would hold you down while the third one would—"

All the color drained from Elizabeth's face. "Stop it!" She beat against his chest with her fists. Tears streamed down her face, making wide tracks through the dust from the road. "Stop tormenting me so! Please!" Her voice choked as great racking sobs engulfed her.

Gathering her into his arms, Tarleton held her snugly. "Hush, sweetling! That will not happen to you—not while I live." His lips brushed the top of her head. The soft silk of her hair set him afire. Torturing himself, he kissed her golden crown again. "You are safe in your dirty face and ragged shoes. Dry your eyes, chuck."

"You frightened me," she mumbled into the folds of his woolen jacket. He smelled of wood smoke, meadow grass and new-turned earth. She relaxed within the protective warmth of his arms.

"Aye! I meant to frighten you, and I won't apologize for it. 'Twas to make you understand the dangers, sweet one."

A hot fountain of desire boiled up from the deep well-spring inside him. Tarleton quickly released Elizabeth before she became aware of his body's need. "Methinks you should visit a pump. And there will be one anon, I promise." He coughed to cover the huskiness in his voice.

Once the jester and his slim apprentice turned onto the main highway between Oxford and Coventry, they encountered many fellow travelers from all classes of society.

A young couple, newly married, were journeying to the groom's father's house. The bride looked no more than sixteen, and she blushed shyly when Tarleton kissed her on the cheek, wishing them the blessing of many children. Elizabeth watched the newlyweds with an envious pang in her heart. Sir Robert La Faye had never once looked at Elizabeth like the boy did his bride. She sighed wistfully as the couple continued on their way, hand in hand.

"A penny for your thoughts, for they must be rich indeed," Tarleton asked.

"Did her father arrange her marriage?"

"That lass? Nay, 'tis a love match. There's not a dowry to be had of her, save her sweet smile. Why?" Though Tarleton suspected he knew the answer.

"I pray nightly for a husband who would make me as happy as that," she replied.

"And to that prayer I say amen," Tarleton replied softly.

A peddler was a welcome chance encounter in the early afternoon. Grizzled, with a steel gray beard and twinkling blue eyes, he hailed them as long-lost friends.

"Tarleton, you old rogue! The devil hasn't caught ye yet?" These were his first words of greeting, then he spied Elizabeth. "What changeling is this? Does he look any better when he's been washed?"

"Aye, Patch, he does. 'Tis my prentice, Robin. Mind your manners, boy, and give Master Patch here a pretty bow."

Elizabeth played her part as she was told. Tarleton's recent warning about the hazards of the road was still fresh in her mind.

"What's the news, old friend?" Tarleton asked him, when the three of them were comfortably settled behind a low stone wall in a nearby field. "Does the Queen still keep court at Hampton?"

"Aye, she was there a fortnight past, and I hear tell she will tarry there until after the harvest festival," Patch answered with a broad grin.

The peddler then recounted a long, rambling story concerning the latest gossip about the Queen and her favorite courtier, the Earl of Leicester. While he spoke, Patch shared with them some cold chicken. "Fresh killed yesterday," he added with a knowing wink.

Elizabeth wondered if that meant he had stolen the hen, but by now she had enough sense to keep quiet. The origin of the chicken was of no importance, as long as she could munch contentedly on a plump, tasty leg portion. Tarleton's wine was mellow, and she was glad of the opportunity to rest her weary feet, still tender from yesterday's barefoot walk. The grass beneath her was soft and sweet smelling, the sun warm, and soon Elizabeth drifted into a comfortable nap.

"Come, Robin Redbreast!" Tarleton's laughing voice intruded into her dreams, which were filled with luscious strawberries, rich cream, gardens full of sweet-smelling roses, and a tall man with merry eyes and brown curly hair who held her tightly in his arms.

Elizabeth stretched and wiggled her toes. "Was I asleep?"

"Aye, and snoring," said Patch, though his eyes regarded her kindly. "Be of good cheer, boy! Tarleton is a villain of the first and last degree, but there's no better man to be with on the road."

"So he keeps telling me, Master Patch," Elizabeth threw a wink at Tarleton, who rolled his eyes in surprise.

"Well, good day to ye then!" With that, the peddler leapt lightly over the wall, despite the heavy wooden case of wares he carried. "And, Tarleton," he called cheerily, "keep a good eye on that young scamp of yours. I prophesy that he will be a lion among the ladies yet!"

"That I will, Patch! Truly, that I will!" Tarleton promised with a rolling laugh.

Then the peddler struck off in the opposite direction, whistling a merry tune.

"What is the thing you most dearly wish to have?" queried Tarleton, cocking his head, looking like Puck, the faeries' jester.

"A good meal, a hot bath and a soft bed!" Elizabeth sighed wistfully.

"And what else?" he prodded, his eyes twinkling.

"Clean clothes, a horse, and...and—"

"Will this do in the meantime?" Tarleton held out his hand. Cradled in his palm was a plain wooden comb, decorated with a small painted rose.

"Oh, Tarleton!" Joy bubbled in her laughter as she took his gift.

"Don't cry! Tears are...unmanly, prentice!" Trying to sound stern, Tarleton was secretly pleased by her warm reaction. How Elizabeth's eyes sparkled like emeralds for just a simple comb!

"But where—?"

Tarleton grinned broadly. "Patch! He gave me a good bargain while you were off woolgathering."

Elizabeth turned pale, her laughter caught in her throat. "You didn't tell him that I'm a woman, did you?"

"Fret not! Old Patch knows I've an eye for a pretty face, and that I am always wasting my money on fripperies for them," he remarked with suppressed pride of his accomplishment.

Elizabeth eagerly used her new treasure. As she combed the tangles out of her hair, she sighed, realizing that her boyish guise hid whatever beauty she might claim. "I thank you for the gift, good Tarleton, though my face is far from pretty at this moment."

Roughly he shouldered his pack. "No more of this nonsense, prentice. They will have dined at Addison Hall afore we get there," he told her gruffly.

"Addison Hall?"

"Where we shall sleep tonight, if we do not linger here." Grasping Elizabeth around the waist, Tarleton swung her back over the wall. He marveled at how light she was and how easily his hands fit around her. How he longed to hold her in his embrace!

"By the book! 'Tis the finest goat that I've ever seen!"

Leaning over another low stone wall, Tarleton regarded a large shaggy goat, which stood placidly not ten paces away in a close-cropped field.

"Hmm?" Elizabeth glanced at the animal with a bored eye.

"I said, that is an exceedingly handsome goat." Tarleton put the pack down. "I am of a mind to ride him!"

"What? Now?" Looking at the sun, Elizabeth wondered the time, and how many more miles it was to the "goodly house." She thought longingly of a hot bath. "Why, in heaven's good name? It doesn't look very friendly."

Tarleton's brown eyes sparkled with devilment. "Because, sweet-faced youth, riding a goat is part of my act, and that animal there is an excellent specimen. Besides, I need the practice."

"Go on, then." Elizabeth tried to stifle a yawn. "I will mind the pack."

Tarleton swung his legs over the wall. "Be sure to watch me. You've never seen the like before!"

Advancing on the wary goat, Tarleton made odd clucking noises. The goat perked his ears. Bounding onto its back, Tarleton hooked his legs around the surprised animal's belly and gripped the horns in his hands. The goat took off at a trot, Tarleton encouraging it with whooping and arm waving.

Despite her resolve to ignore the jester's antics, Elizabeth could not keep a straight face. Each time the goat and his rider bounced past her, Elizabeth laughed even harder. After a few more circuits, Tarleton jumped easily off its back.

"Your turn!" He pulled the protesting goat over to the wall.

Horrified, Elizabeth retreated behind the pack. "You can't be serious!"

No, sweet lady, I'm not. Tarleton continued to smile charmingly at her while his mind whirled in a maddening confusion. He realized he was growing too fond of her. He needed the lady to put him firmly back where he belonged—in a roadside ditch.

Meanwhile, the goat, rolling his yellow eyes in a threatening manner, angrily pawed the soft ground. Tarleton cocked his head. A stray curl of brown hair fell across his forehead. "What's the matter, chuck? Afraid?" he taunted. "Isn't he fine enough for you?" Holding his breath, Tarleton waited for her just reproof.

Elizabeth wrinkled her nose. "I've never ridden a goat!"

"Ah! I knew your education had been sadly lacking in certain areas."

"And I am not about to start now!" She tilted up her chin defiantly.

Tarleton's eyes narrowed. All she needed was one more little push. He hoped she wouldn't slap his face—at least, not too hard. "Prentice, you misunderstood me. I am *telling* you to climb over that wall now, and get up on this fine steed's back!"

"You're addlepated!" The corner of her mouth twisted with exasperation. "Why?"

Tarleton noted with appreciation that Elizabeth's eyes darkened to a delightful shade of green. In spite of himself, he found he was quite enjoying this confrontation.

"For two reasons, because you are my apprentice and I am your master, and because we might be entertaining someplace where it will be expected of you to ride a goat. So hop to it! Besides . . ." His voice sank into a seductive whisper. "I'll wager you a whole shilling that you cannot remain on his back for more than a minute. You can pay me when we reach Hampton Court.''

Elizabeth stared at Tarleton, then at the goat. There was a definite challenge in both their eyes. Gritting her teeth, she tossed her head. ''Agreed! But I warn you, Master Tarleton, I may surprise you. One shilling it is—out of your wages!'' She clambered over the wall.

''I'll take my chances.'' He hid his surprise at her courage. ''All you have to do is hang on. Up you go!'' He swung her lightly on top of the uncooperative animal.

Unlike a horse, the goat's back sloped away from his rigid spine. It was more uncomfortable to sit astride him than to ride a sidesaddle.

''Hook your legs around him, and cross your ankles underneath,'' Tarleton instructed, biting back his laughter.

''My legs are not that long,'' Elizabeth muttered tersely.

''Then hug his sides with your knees. Get a firm grip around his horns.'' Tarleton wondered if he had overplayed this game. What if she fell and broke her neck? ''Are you sure you want to do this?''

''Aye,'' she answered. ''If you can do it, so can I!''

Tarleton let go and stepped back. For a split second the goat stood still, then he tried to shake the girl off his back. Setting her jaw, Elizabeth tightened her knees. The goat backed up several paces, then whirled away across the field, taking Elizabeth on the ride of her life.

Every tooth rattled in her head. She felt herself slipping to one side or the other. Elizabeth gripped the animal tighter. She heard Tarleton's voice encouraging her as they pranced past him. Or was he encouraging the goat?

Sweet Jesu! What heart and spirit! Tarleton was about to tell Elizabeth that her wager was won when a horse whinnied behind him.

As he turned his head, Tarleton's stomach lurched sickeningly. Four heavily armed men drew up to the wall where

Tarleton sat. Riding at their head, Tarleton recognized Sir Robert La Faye.

Four to one! The odds are not of my liking, but I will play this hand. The jester prayed that Elizabeth would stay at the other end of the field until he could get rid of Sir Robert. So far, Elizabeth had fooled everyone, but here was the one man who knew her. He might recognize her by her voice or by her brilliant golden hair. If he did, Tarleton's days as the Queen's favorite jester would be cut extremely short, and Elizabeth's days as an unhappily wedded wife would just begin.

Jumping off the wall, Tarleton swept the fat lord a deep bow. "God give you a good day, sir!"

"Good day." Sir Robert nodded curtly. Behind him, one of his men chortled.

"Look you yonder, m'lord! 'Tis a rare sight to be sure!"

Sir Robert swung his lazy gaze from Tarleton's face to the field beyond, where Elizabeth hung practically upside down on the racing goat.

Tarleton's throat tightened as he watched her. He licked his dry lips. "'Tis my apprentice, my lord. I am teaching him how to manage a goat." Seeking to draw their attention back to himself, Tarleton bantered on. "I am Tarleton, the Queen's own jester, so please your worship." He swept them another elegant bow in the dust.

"Did you say Tarleton?" Sir Robert's nasal voice whined. His piggish eyes narrowed at the player, then he grinned unpleasantly. "I saw your performance some days ago at Esmond Manor."

"Aye, your worship! 'Twas at your betrothal feast, as I recall."

Tarleton knew La Faye far better than a chance meeting at a manor home. For the past six months, this bloated peacock had been under the eye of the Queen's chief minister and spy master, Sir Francis Walsingham. Already the noose around the supporters of the imprisoned Queen of

Scots grew tighter. Not three weeks ago, John Ballard had been apprehended and confessed under torture to a plot to free Queen Mary under the leadership of one Anthony Babington, a close friend of Lord La Faye. Sir Robert, the younger son of a noble family, had gambled away most of his fortune early on. Though his part in the Catholic conspiracy was not obvious, Sir Robert's desperate need for money was. Under Walsingham's direction, Tarleton had been sent to ferret out La Faye's whereabouts and intentions. The jester's chance encounter with Elizabeth was an unforeseen roll of the dice. Then there was the matter of Sir Thomas Hayward's too-sudden death.

"My congratulations, your worship!" Tarleton bowed a third time with many an exaggerated flourish. *Keep looking at me and not at my apprentice, you hog in satin!*

"You remember well, jester," Sir Robert remarked unpleasantly. The man's voice made Tarleton's blood run cold. It was like holding a conversation with a loathsome toad.

Sir Robert leaned over his horse's neck, his little eyes boring into Tarleton. "Now, tell me, player, do you remember Lady Elizabeth Hayward, my betrothed?"

"Aye, sir, a most fair and beauteous lady!"

"Have you seen or heard of my lady?" La Faye's voice betrayed more anger than concern. "She has been lost these three days, and I do fear greatly for her safety."

So do I! "A beautiful lady lost?" The jester shook his head and made a show of sympathy. "I understand your concern, my lord, but, in truth, I've seen no lady upon this road. Wait! Earlier today, a fine carriage passed us, going to London, I think. The curtains were drawn, so I could not see who was inside, but it was accompanied by six or eight outriders."

"Was there a coat of arms on the door?" Sir Robert's eyes narrowed even more. He almost foamed at the mouth.

The sight of the nobleman's barely contained rage against the lady convinced Tarleton he was right to disguise Elizabeth. Never would he let her fall into this brute's grasp!

"I know not, sir," Tarleton answered innocently. "I was more anxious to leap out of its way. The carriage was traveling very fast. Perchance it held the lady whom you seek?"

Out of the corner of his eye, Tarleton saw Elizabeth losing her grip.

"Ho, Sir Robert!" the nearest horseman called to his employer. "The jester's lad is nearly under the hooves! I have not seen the like since the Bartholomew Fair!"

"I do not recall you had an apprentice, jester," Sir Robert remarked, looking over Tarleton's head at the two figures in the field.

A cold trickle of sweat coursed down Tarleton's neck. "He is new, your worship. He stayed in the stable at Esmond Manor. I am attempting to train him. Today's lesson is riding a goat." Tarleton gamboled an improvised jig to catch La Faye's attention. "Now it is one thing if the goat were experienced. It is another thing if the rider were experienced. But as you can see, neither this goat nor this boy has any experience at all."

"He's fallen off!" shouted one of the horsemen. "Ride him again, boy!" he called. "'Tis a rich diversion, eh, my lord?"

Elizabeth had not fallen off. The goat, growing tired of the sport, had dug its forefeet into the ground and bucked his hapless rider over his head. Elizabeth landed in the black muck of a large pig wallow with a resounding splat. Her head spinning, she dimly heard the voices by the wall. Wiping the thick, smelly mud out of her eyes and cursing Tarleton under her breath, she saw the jester with a group of horsemen who were waving and shouting.

How like Tarleton! she fumed, struggling to get a footing in the slippery mess. *No doubt he is passing the hat!*

Elizabeth had just regained her footing when the goat lowered his head and charged, butting her back into the mire. This elicited even more cheers from her distant audience.

"Robin!" Tarleton called to her. "Up, lad, and ride him again. Sir Robert La Faye finds your antics most amusing. Ride him again, I say, or 'twill be the worse for you this eventide!"

Sir Robert! Elizabeth's heart nearly stopped inside her. Squinting through her mud-tipped lashes, she gasped when she saw that it *was* he, and with a guard of wicked-looking villains! Immediately she understood Tarleton's ploy. She must play her part as if her life depended upon it—her life and Tarleton's. She glared at the goat, who pawed the ground nearby.

"Don't move, you vile brute," she ordered the creature.

Elizabeth slowly circled the wary animal. Every time she lunged to grab him around the neck, he danced out of her way. Slipping several more times, she completely coated herself with the foul mud. She heard the rough laughter of the men.

"Stop your shambling, you toad-wart!" Tarleton shouted at her. "The gentleman wants a good show. Ride that goat, or I'll whip you within an inch of your life!"

"Your lad had best lie with the pigs this night," Sir Robert remarked with an amused chuckle when he saw Elizabeth fall flat again.

"Aye, that he will, for I hope to lie with sweeter company," leered Tarleton, though his eyes remained fixed on Elizabeth. By now, she resembled a walking mud figure, her distinctive golden hair plastered with the black slime.

"Then we shall leave you to your... training, jester." Sir Robert tossed a coin to Tarleton. "Here's for a strop of ale. If you hear of my lady, leave word for me at the Rose and Crown in Woodstock."

"You are most generous, your worship!" Tarleton bowed deeply again, as the would-be husband and his minions rode off. "And may the devil take you down to hell!" he muttered after them.

"Come, Robin! Stop teasing that poor beast!" Tarleton called to his mud-caked charge. Elizabeth walked wearily back to the wall. Tarleton's eyes softened when he saw the streaks of tears on her face.

"Have they truly gone?" She shivered.

"Aye, my pet, but they left you with this!" He held out a silver shilling. "Sir Robert has covered my wager."

Numbly Elizabeth looked into Tarleton's liquid brown eyes. Giving her a mischievous wink, he burst into one of his deep, rolling laughs.

"You are a success, sweet Robin Redbreast!" He tossed his cap in the air. "Not even your sweet mother in heaven would recognize you!"

Elizabeth looked down at herself, then back at Tarleton, then at the large coin he flipped to her. His merry humor was infectious.

"What a supreme jest!" Tarleton capered up and down. "You made your dearest betrothed look a perfect ass. Sir Robert did not recognize his true love even when she was right under his nose! His *very* dainty nose!"

Slowly Elizabeth smiled as she thought of Sir Robert's unwitting mistake. How embarrassed that popinjay would be when she told her tale to the Queen and the court! Catching Tarleton's overflowing mirth, she gave herself up to gales of laughter.

"Oh, Tarleton, it *was* a goodly trick, wasn't it?" Her green eyes danced merrily. "But, Sir Jester, *you* still owe me a shilling of your own!"

"Aye, chuck, I will pay you my just debts anon," Tarleton agreed. *Jesu, how I would love to pay thee with kisses!* He jerked himself back to reality. "Now, my muddy prentice, we must get you to Addison Hall." Tarleton's eyes crinkled into a smile. "Be of good cheer, chuck! 'Tis just over that hill."

Under her layer of mud, Elizabeth sighed happily. A bath at last!

Chapter Five

"**B**y my troth, 'tis Dickon!"

A buxom woman, her face cherry red from bending over steaming pots, bounded down the stone steps of Addison Hall's kitchen. Grabbing Tarleton in her thick arms, she hugged him fiercely.

"'Tis a month of Sundays since you last showed your ugly face!" She gripped him even harder. "I thought ye had forgotten your Peg. Come now, give us a friendly greeting!" Shamelessly she planted a lusty kiss on Tarleton's grinning lips. He returned the salutation with equal force and ardor.

Elizabeth stared at the unlikely pair with surprise and some dismay. *She's old enough to be his mother!* Several scullery maids hung about the door, tittering at the couple. At last, the kiss ended, though the huge woman still clung to Tarleton's waist as if she owned him.

"And what company are ye keeping nowadays, Dickon my love?" Peg fastened her gaze on Elizabeth. "By the stars! He's black as an Ethiop."

Grinning, Tarleton disengaged himself from the rotund cook. "'Tis my new apprentice, Robin."

"Well, he'll not set foot in my kitchen until he's been washed." The woman shot an appraising look at Elizabeth, who wished she were miles away from the cook's critical stare.

Tarleton put his hand under Elizabeth's chin, forcing her to look up, though his touch was more of a caress than a manly grip. "When the boy is clean and fed, you shall see he has the sweetest face in the shire. Good Peg, do you think your master and mistress would care for a bit of song and story this eve?" He beguiled the woman with his winsome eyes.

Peg laughed, her whole body shaking with the effort. "Ye know they would, you rogue! Poor Sir William has been sore afflicted with pains in his joints of late. Your presence will glad his heart as it gladdens mine!"

Peg looked at Tarleton as if she would like to coat him in honey and eat him on the spot. Elizabeth's ire prickled in her throat. That woman was far too old for Tarleton and not at all pretty.

Tarleton grinned like a schoolboy. "Good! Then there is one more favor I'll ask of thee, sweetheart." He put his arm about her ample shoulders and nibbled on her ear.

Elizabeth pretended to be interested in a large orange cat that lounged nearby in the late afternoon sun. *Tarleton is making a lewd spectacle of himself.*

"And what is this favor?" Peg asked with a sly wink.

"My prentice is wearing the only clothes he owns which are not fit—"

"Not even for rags, I should say!" Peg sniffed.

"And he cannot appear in the hall in them."

"To be sure, he *will* not!" Peg pronounced with authority.

Does she mean to put me in the barn? Ha! I'd like to see her try it! Elizabeth tried to curb her annoyance.

Tarleton squeezed Peg's shoulder. "Take pity on my poor lad, for he is lately orphaned. Could you find him a suit of clothes, for sweet charity's sake, and for this?" He dropped a shilling down her ample bodice.

Peg shivered with pleasure. "Sweet Saint Ann, you are a merry rogue and no mistaking it, Dickon! Young Ned is about your boy's size. Tess!" She called over her shoulder to one of the gawking maids. "Fetch some of Ned's things quickly afore this lad catches his death of cold. Aye, and bring a towel!"

The maid, all giggles and black tresses, disappeared inside.

Elizabeth perked up at the mention of a towel. A bath! A hot, steaming bath with buckets of water, scented with oil of roses. And fine milled soap! Closing her eyes, she sighed pleasurably at the thought.

"And the rest of ye? What are ye staring at?" Peg bellowed at the kitchen staff. "Back to your work." The servants scattered like autumn leaves in a wind.

"Leave the lad to Tess, my sweet," Peg crooned to Tarleton, not even glancing at the filthy, fuming Elizabeth. "The minx will make him look like a Christian again, and perhaps teach him a few things in the bargain!"

Underneath her layers of dirt and mud, Elizabeth blanched. She flashed a beseeching look at Tarleton.

The jester chuckled. "Nay, Peg. Though Tess is a good girl, I think she'll frighten the boy." Tarleton wiggled his dark brows at Peg and smiled his best imp's grin. "Give him time though, and there will be no lass in England safe from him. Am I not his teacher—in all manner of skills?" Tarleton kissed Peg deeply again to stop any further conversation.

Elizabeth winced with envy. She could almost taste that kiss herself.

Tess, looking flushed and breathless, returned at that moment with a pair of gray breeches, black stockings, a clean white shirt and a brown woolen waistcoat. A piece of coarse toweling hung over her arm. Tarleton disengaged himself from Peg with a fond caress to her wide bottom.

Laughing at the cook's crude rejoinder, he led Elizabeth toward the stable.

"You are passing quiet, Robin Redbreast," he remarked cheerfully.

"I am amazed, and know not what to say!" Elizabeth stuttered. "Is Peg your mother or aunt?" she asked hopefully.

Tarleton exploded in laughter. "Nay, chuck! Peg is an old friend of mine. She took me in when I had nothing to my name except a ready wit. She was kind to me when I needed some kindness."

"And in return? You are . . . kind to her?" Elizabeth had not meant to sound so direct.

Tarleton raised his brow thoughtfully. "Aye, I am kind to her betimes," he answered coolly. He pointed at the horse trough. "Jump in!"

Elizabeth stared with horror at the cold, scummy water. Green slime coated the wooden sides.

"Surely you are jesting, Tarleton!"

He laughed at her confusion. "'Tis no jest. This is where we servants bathe. Did you think I was going to ask Peg to draw you a warm hip bath by the fire?"

Elizabeth bit her lower lip. She would never admit she had hoped for something exactly like that. She glared at him.

"I simply won't get into that dirty thing! You can't make me—!"

Before she could utter another word of protest, Tarleton picked her up around the waist. Snatching off her shoes, he threw her into the trough.

"How dare you!" Elizabeth sputtered when she rose to the surface, her green eyes blazing.

Tarleton only grinned as he held her down. "Hold your nose, or you'll regret it." He grabbed the top of her head firmly.

"No, knave! You are the one who will regre—'" The rest of her threat was drowned as Tarleton ducked her under the water again. He rubbed her hair vigorously. She surfaced coughing.

"Vile!" She spat out some of the water she had inhaled.

Tarleton stood back, regarding his sopping apprentice. Elizabeth's bright golden hair gleamed once more, and the chill water had brought a becoming pink to her cheeks. Her eyes, however, looked murderous, which only heightened the green color he found so enticing.

"Well, churl?" She glowered at him, shaking the water out of her eyes and hair. "Are you satisfied now? Have I given you enough entertainment for one afternoon?" She would not add anything more to his pleasure by letting him see how badly he had humiliated her.

"You look your proper self," he said approvingly. "Take my hand."

Elizabeth briefly considered pulling him into the water with her, and letting him have a taste of his own medicine. Then she sensibly realized that he had no other clothing save what was now clinging wetly around her. Instead, she grasped his hand and hauled herself carefully out of the trough.

Tarleton drew in his breath when he saw the wet shirt plastered transparently to Elizabeth. Her nipples, hardened by the cold water, jutted proudly against the fabric. Tarleton swallowed the knot in his throat as he felt a hot stirring within him. Under her boyish disguise, Lady Elizabeth was lush, ripe and ready for plucking. He itched to peel away her wet wrappings and savor her obvious charms. It would be so easy, here in the darkened barn, with an inviting bed of fresh hay just behind them.

Fool! the voice of sanity screamed inside him. *She's no wench to tumble in a barn, but the Queen's own goddaughter!* Averting his eyes with an unaccustomed burst of self-control, Tarleton roughly draped the towel around her.

"Cross your arms in front of you, or else you'll reveal your identity to all the world," he growled, his voice low and husky.

Elizabeth looked down at herself. Her ears burned with embarrassment.

"Where shall I change?" she asked in a muffled voice, not daring to raise her eyes to him.

Tarleton scooped up her shoes. "Follow me," he commanded gruffly as he led her to a small storage shed. "In here. Dress quickly, I'll keep a lookout for any prying eyes."

"Be sure you do, Master Tarleton!" Snatching Ned's clothes out of his hand, Elizabeth swept regally into the shadowy hut. "Watch especially your own!"

Tarleton laughed ruefully. Half-seriously, he considered throwing himself into the trough to douse the fire in his loins. How many more days of this sweet temptation could he stand?

"Do you still have my comb?" Elizabeth asked when she emerged from the shed.

Glancing over her, Tarleton grinned his approval. He could deal with her far better when she looked like a boy, than when she was revealed as a woman. "Aye, prentice." He cleared his throat. "Now let us rehearse for tonight's performance. Sir William and Lady Margaret Fairfax are good patrons of mine. If we please them, they will pay us right well." He spread out the wet breeches and shirt across a pile of hay to dry in the late afternoon's sun. Then, for the next hour, Tarleton schooled his apprentice in a bit of juggling, the verses of a new, witty song, and the punch lines for a few mildly bawdy jokes. Afterward they reappeared at the kitchen door.

"'Tis a transformation sure!" exclaimed Peg, beaming with pleasure at Elizabeth. "Who would have guessed what was hiding under all that mud!"

"Oh, he's a pretty lad!" Tess giggled and continued cutting up turnips and plopping them into a simmering pot.

Several of the other maids joined her, simpering and casting appreciative looks at Elizabeth.

"Leave off teasing the child and be about your business!" snapped Peg, her maternal instincts obviously aroused. "Here, my pet, sit down by the fire and have a cup of sweet cider. 'Tis fresh from the press."

"What's the news you've heard, Tarleton?" asked one of the lounging serving men.

Tarleton pulled up a stool to the trestle table. "Not much to tell, except that the Italians dress too loudly, the French eat too much, the Dutch belch rudely, and the Spanish are all whoresons!" he answered merrily.

Peg placed a bowl of hot water and a sliver of soap in front of Tarleton. He grinned with pleasure as he lathered his face generously.

Elizabeth stared enviously at the soap. She certainly could have used some of that, even in a horse trough.

"Shake a leg, Robin! Fetch my mirror from the pack." Tarleton spoke through the soapsuds. "Now, boy, hold it steady for me while I shave." Tarleton drew out his dagger with a flourish, and proceeded to scrape at his short, bristly whiskers.

Watching him carefully, Elizabeth winced when the dagger passed closely across his throat. The rasp of the blade against his tanned skin set her teeth on edge. The knife was so sharp that one little slip could spell disaster.

Noting her concern, Tarleton winked reassuringly at her. A bevy of maids cooed at his fresh, handsome appearance.

The merriment was cut short by the arrival of Master Brownlow, the steward, who solemnly greeted Tarleton as an equal, then announced that dinner was to be served up immediately in the hall.

"Come!" He beckoned to Tarleton. "His lordship wants you presently."

Tarleton nodded to Elizabeth. "Get my cap and motley, boy!" Snapping his fingers, he pointed to the pack.

Elizabeth blinked for a moment at his sudden command, then remembering her role, she returned his nod. She shook out Tarleton's multicolored jacket—its many brass bells jingled merrily as if they were glad to be released from their dark prison. Standing on a low stool, she held the coat open as Tarleton drew it over his wide shoulders. He winked mischievously at her as she tied the strings of his three-pointed coxcomb cap under his chin. His face was so close to hers she could have kissed his lips without moving. She was seized by a sudden desire to do so. Peg's round laughter brought Elizabeth to her senses.

"That's my Tarleton!" Peg beamed like a proud mother. "Her Majesty is fortunate that I let her borrow you now and then, my pretty duck!"

"Aye!" Tarleton bowed to the cook with a flourish. "Shall I tell the Queen you said so when I am next at court?"

"Get on with ye! And make the master laugh. He is much in need of good cheer these days!" She waved them out with a soup ladle.

Following the steward, the jester and his apprentice passed through a number of narrow, dark corridors and up a flight of stone stairs. After traversing several more passageways, they came to a thick, paneled door.

"Wait here until I call for you, Dickon," The steward vanished through the portal.

"How does Addison Hall look to you, prentice? Is it as grand as Esmond Manor?" Tarleton whispered to Elizabeth.

Elizabeth touched the nearby wall with her finger thoughtfully. "I am not sure. All these hallways look very mean, indeed. There are no tapestries, nor carved panels, nor pictures, nor any decoration on the walls. Perhaps Sir William has come upon hard times."

Tarleton chuckled quietly. "Nay, you have seen but the backstairs. Have you never been backstairs at Esmond?"

Embarrassed by the truth, Elizabeth bit her lower lip. "In sooth, I don't think I could locate the kitchens in my own house." She reddened a bit at the admission.

Tarleton looked down at her and stroked her smooth cheek with his knuckle. "Then, perhaps, you may want to find them when you return there," he said softly.

Elizabeth shivered. Tarleton's touch was so gentle, the merest whisper, yet the place on her cheek felt as if he had branded her.

Before she could sort out her distracted feelings, the door suddenly opened, and Brownlow poked his head through. "Ready?"

Casting a quick smile at Elizabeth, Tarleton nodded to the steward. "Bluff and bluster!" he whispered to her.

Brownlow threw open the door wider, and announced them in a majestic voice, "My lord and ladies, Tarleton, the Queen's own jester!"

Tarleton skipped into the great hall with a merry jingling of his bells. Elizabeth scampered behind him. In the center of the hall, Tarleton executed a deep court bow to the head table.

"Good my lord and you, most gracious lady, give me your leave to rhyme, for I've come to show activity upon this merry time—"

As Tarleton launched into his opening speech, Elizabeth quietly slipped into a shadowed recess, where she could observe the great hall of Addison. It was a fine room, richly paneled in polished wood with a high, vaulted ceiling of huge blackened beams. Large friendly fires roared in the monstrous stone fireplaces at each end, taking away the chill of the late summer evening. The upper servants, as well as members of Sir William's extended family, which seemed to include a number of elderly ladies, sat at two tables below the head table. Above them was Sir William Fairfax, an old, white-haired gentleman. His wife, Lady Margaret, looked twenty years his junior. Beside them were another elderly lady and a thin, reedy-looking cleric, who watched Tarleton's antics with his lips pursed in disapproval.

Elizabeth could see that Sir William did not look well, but he managed to smile weakly and thump his knife upon the table in appreciation of Tarleton's merry capers. Lady Margaret, though she smiled with her lips, was clearly bored even though Tarleton was being witty and highly amusing—a far cry from last night's performance at the disreputable Blue Boar.

"May I have your leave to present to your lordship my new apprentice?" Turning, Tarleton beckoned to Elizabeth.

Taking a deep breath to steady a sudden flash of nerves, she skipped lightly to the center of the room. Feeling the slight pressure of Tarleton's hand on her back, Elizabeth bowed in her best imitation of his court bow.

"This is young Robin Redbreast, for he sings like a bird. As I perceive you have been dining upon roast swan, perhaps you would care to hear the bird's side of the story?" Tarleton stepped back, leaving Elizabeth to sing the "Lament of the Roast Swan."

Elizabeth accompanied her verses with a great deal of comic mime, which Tarleton had taught her in the barn that afternoon. At the end, she again bowed to the warm applause of the company. Sir William seemed especially pleased. Even Lady Margaret looked interested. Tarleton bounded to her side.

"Well done!" he whispered to her under his breath. Then, to the audience, he continued, "Hast thou heard the story of the good wife of Kent?"

"Nay, Tarleton, tell us!" croaked one of the ancient ladies.

As the laughter and applause again echoed in the great hall, Elizabeth found that she was enjoying herself immensely. Their next few jokes amused the company even more. Tarleton gamboled around the tables snatching up an apple, a pear and a knife, which he immediately began to juggle while telling yet another funny tale. At the end of the story, he tossed the apple high into the air and caught it on the point of the knife. There were more cheers as he presented the fruit to Lady Margaret.

"I prithee, Tarleton, have your sweet bird sing again," she murmured.

"Your wish is ever my command, my lady." Tarleton addressed the hall. "Our play is done/All is well end if this suit be one/That you express content, but before we take our leave, sweet Robin will sing you to your rest."

Clearing her voice, Elizabeth began the opening lines of "The Greenwood Tree." The hall grew hushed again, even the serving men stood still, as Elizabeth's pure voice sang of springtime, green forests and true love.

Listening in the shadows, Tarleton's heart beat faster as again he felt the hot blood race through him. Images of Elizabeth, sitting beside his own fire in a cozy cottage on a cold winter's night, singing that very song for him alone, flickered through his mind. Afterward they would climb into their deep feather bed, and he would take her in his arms, feeling the full promise of that sweet song as his lips hungrily sought hers, and his hands stroked—

Shaking himself angrily, Tarleton pulled his gaze away from her. He gritted his teeth so tightly he could feel a vein throb at his temple and he cursed his fantasies. *Damn that song—and damn the little witch for working its spell on me! 'Tis time I put an end to this, for both our sakes.*

The ensuing applause at the end of Elizabeth's ballad roused Tarleton from his tormenting thoughts. Recovering himself, he capered to the center and bowed, roughly pushing Elizabeth into her bow, as well.

"As always, Tarleton, you have come in good time and have made us merry!" said Sir William in a high, weak voice, which was filled with warm affection. He held out a small purse in a frail, shaky hand. "You have richly de-

served this—you and your little birdling. When you next see
the Queen, I pray you give her our love and loyalty.''

''Thank you, Sir William.'' Taking the purse, Tarleton
bowed to both the master and mistress of the house. ''We
are on our way to Hampton Court, and it will be an honor
to give Her Grace your kind messages. Good night, my lord
and my ladies, and sweet dreams accompany you to bed!''
Tarleton danced out of the side door followed by Robin.

''That was wonderful!'' Elizabeth enthused when they
were once more in the narrow passage leading down to the
great kitchen. '' 'Tis more fun than I can remember having.
Didn't I sing well, Tarleton? Didn't they applaud so?'' She
looked up happily at him, expecting a smile or wink of approval, but Tarleton only hurried down the stairs ahead of
her without a backward glance.

His cool silence puzzled her. ''Did I do wrong? Did I give
offense?'' She tried to keep up with him as he pressed ahead
of her. She was out of breath by the time they reached the
warm, friendly kitchen.

''So you beguiled them all again, my charmer?'' Peg
laughed in greeting.

Tarleton pulled off his cap and ran his fingers through his
damp hair. ''Aye, and now a strop of your finest beer, Peg
of my heart, for jesting is thirsty work!'' He tossed his cap
over his shoulder at Elizabeth.

''And Robin?'' asked Tess shyly. ''Did Robin sing well?''

''Aye,'' Tarleton answered offhandedly. ''I believe he
thinks so.'' There was a definite chill in his voice.

He's jealous of my success! Elizabeth mulled that new
thought around in her mind as she packed away the colored
jacket that he had pulled off and flung at her. *What vanity!*

Peg set out heaping bowls of delicious-smelling stew on
the trestle table. ''Come now, and eat. Ye have earned it.''
On the side was a soft cheese garnished with mustard and
honey, a hot apple tart, cool beer, and warm brown bread
to sop up the gravy. Tarleton pulled up his stool to the table

and attacked the food wolfishly, praising Peg with every loud, smacking mouthful. Elizabeth found herself at the far end of the table next to a boy of nearly twelve years who introduced himself as Ned.

"Have you traveled far, Robin?" Ned asked in wide-eyed wonder. He was a pleasing lad with the exception of a face deeply scarred by a bout with smallpox.

"Aye." Elizabeth nibbled halfheartedly at her savory dinner and watched with an aching heart as Tarleton continued to make even bolder displays of affection toward the lusty Peg. Sipping a bit of her ale, she tried to concentrate on Ned's questions. "Aye, I came from above Kenilworth."

"And will you go to London?" Ned said the word as if the city's streets were paved with gold.

"By and by, I hope so," Elizabeth answered, trying to tear her gaze away from Tarleton. She noted he was drinking a great deal of Peg's strong beer. Shaking herself, she tried to be polite to the boy. "I thank you for your clothes. They fit right well."

Ned grinned. "Good! Now, I shall get a new suit at Christmastide!" He slapped Elizabeth between her shoulder blades in a friendly manner.

The action caught her unawares so that she choked on her ale. Pausing in his love play, Tarleton scowled at Elizabeth, then returned to Peg.

"Do you play chess?" Ned asked suddenly.

Elizabeth looked at the boy with surprise. "Do you?"

"Aye," he bragged, puffing out his cheeks a bit. "The deacon taught me, and I carved the pieces myself. If you would like, I can teach you how to play," the boy added gallantly.

"I know—a little," Elizabeth lied.

"Good! Then let us to it!" Leaping up from the table, Ned grabbed his mug of ale and jammed a large wedge of apple tart into his mouth.

Elizabeth took her mug and followed him into the ingle-nook, where the excited boy pulled a small bag out of the settle. Lying comfortably on his stomach, Ned took a piece of charcoal and drew a chessboard on the smooth field-stone of the hearth.

Elizabeth put her mug on the floor, then carefully stretched herself out, hoping she looked as boyish as pos-sible. She glanced up at Tarleton, who merely arched one eyebrow disdainfully at her. Confused and hurt, Elizabeth turned her attention to the game.

Tarleton stared moodily into his tankard. He saw how Elizabeth's golden hair glowed like a halo in the dancing firelight; the flames made her emerald eyes gleam with their own magic. *Damn her! Even lying in the cinders in bor-rowed clothing, she looks an angel. 'Twill be best to let her see how truly base I am.*

Tarleton slammed his tankard onto the table, rattling the crockery. "More beer, Peg mine own! I have in mind some lusty work that will raise a mighty thirst!" he announced loudly with a leer. The other servants chuckled good-na-turedly, while Peg burst into a peal of shrill giggles.

Elizabeth pretended to listen to Ned as he instructed her in the movements of the pieces, but her ears burned to hear Tarleton.

"Thou art a very knave, Dickon!" Peg chided him affec-tionately, then she kissed him loudly. He held her tightly and prolonged the kiss so that the others at the table banged their cups and knives with approval.

"You speak the truth, sweetheart, for I am the knave of hearts! Come, let me see what you are hiding in there." Tarleton began to undo the laces on Peg's bodice.

"As if he doesn't know already!" One of the serving men chuckled.

Peg shrieked with mock modesty as Tarleton began kiss-ing and caressing the huge mounds of florid flesh that strained at the weakened bodice.

"Hmm! Methinks there is more of ye than meets the eye!" Hungrily, Tarleton began pulling away the rest of the lacing.

Elizabeth bent her head lower over Ned's improvised board, blinking back tears. *Why should I care what he does? I shall be well rid of his company soon!*

"Come, sweet Peg! Let us make merry in private. I have in mind much sweet sport!" Tarleton stood up, swaying a little. He grasped the giggling Peg tightly around the waist. In the other hand, he held his mug.

"Robin!" he barked roughly.

Elizabeth lifted her head and drew her breath. Tarleton's eyes glittered unnaturally in the firelight. *He looks like the devil himself!* "Master?"

"Stir thy bones, and bring two full pots of beer for us." He prodded her with the toe of his shoe.

Biting back her anger and shame, Elizabeth got to her feet and accepted two brimming tankards from a smirking Tess.

"I won't make a move until you return," Ned promised her. Elizabeth nodded dully.

"Come, boy!" Tarleton snapped his fingers, as he and the cook made their squealing way down the dark passage. Balancing the beer, Elizabeth trudged shamefacedly behind them.

At the end of the hall, Tarleton kicked open the door to Peg's small bedchamber. Once inside, he pulled down Peg's shift, exposing an enormous pair of breasts, their nipples huge and engorged with desire. Elizabeth stared at the cook in unabashed amazement.

"Poor lad!" Peg sighed pleasurably as Tarleton loudly suckled the deep rose tips. "Methinks your boy has never seen a woman's teats before."

Looking up fiercely, Tarleton bared his teeth like a wolf hovering over its prey. "Oh, I think Robin has seen at least one pair of paps in his life, eh, boy?"

Elizabeth flushed hotly. What had she done to deserve this treatment?

"What shall I do with the beer—master?" She spat out the last word with contempt.

Peg merely laughed, but Tarleton's eyes glowed darker. Elizabeth was glad if she had angered him. What she really itched to do was to throw the brew over both of them and run. The problem was, she had no place to run to, and Tarleton, the villain, knew it. "Put the mugs down, dullard, then get out!" Tarleton growled hoarsely.

Elizabeth hastily placed the beer on a nearby chest, then fled, banging the door behind her.

I hate him! I hate him! I hate him! The refrain thudded in her brain as she ran down the passageway to the kitchen.

There was a good deal of ribald banter and eye-rolling from the other servants when she returned. Passing off the joking questions with a forced grin and a shrug, Elizabeth concentrated on Ned's chess game with a determined will— anything to blot out her thoughts of the activity that was happening at the far end of the corridor.

Elizabeth, who had played chess with her father since she was quite young, deliberately made false moves and stupid mistakes, so that Ned could beat her after a decent interval. When he finally checkmated her, Ned did his best not to crow with pride. Manfully, he shook her hand and declared that the game had been "passing fair." Elizabeth declined his companionable invitation to visit the privy with him, saying that she had to repack her master's things before she went to bed.

The other servants drifted out of the kitchen, leaving Elizabeth to wonder where on earth she was supposed to sleep. She prudently decided against joining Ned, and she certainly could not curl up with Tess and the other maids. Nor was she going to seek out Tarleton and ask him!

Once the house grew quiet, Elizabeth arranged herself in front of the fire, then knelt and said a quick prayer for her parents and for her safety. After a moment's hesitation, she included Tarleton in her intentions: his soul needed as much help as he could get. Then, wrapping her cloak around her and pillowing her head on the pack, Elizabeth fell immediately asleep.

Hidden in the dark passage, Tarleton silently watched her. Leaning against the wall for support, he swore at himself. Not only was his head spinning from too much strong drink, but he had managed to anger both the women in his life.

What sort of witch are you, lady? he silently asked the sleeper by the fire. *What spell have you cast upon my heart so that I had no desire for my own sweet Peg? I told her it was the drink, but 'twas you, in truth.*

Tarleton pressed his forehead against the cool stone wall. *What possessed you to drink so much, you fool? You know better than that. Old Walsingham would have your pounding head if he learned that one of his best informants could not control his thirst.*

Tarleton stared at Elizabeth's quiet form hungrily. *At least, my plan worked. The lady will count the moments until she is rid of me. 'Tis for the best, though I am in hell for it. Great Jove! I think my dinner is about to make a return trip!*

Clapping his hand to his mouth, Tarleton raced out the door to the courtyard just in time. When he returned a few minutes later, he saw Elizabeth had not moved.

"Sweet dreams, bright angel," he whispered. "Someday think well of me." Then he stumbled back to Peg's room, where the cook, though sorely disappointed, graciously allowed him to spend the rest of the night—to save his pride of manhood.

Chapter Six

"Boy! Wake up!"

Elizabeth's eyes flew open. By the light of the glowing embers in the kitchen hearth it was difficult for her to make out the face of the person who quietly shook her by the shoulder.

"Player boy, are you awake?" said the girl in a small, frightened voice.

"Aye, what is it?" Pulling herself up, Elizabeth rubbed the sleep from her eyes. The girl at her side appeared to be fourteen or fifteen and not dressed as a scullery maid.

"My mistress bade me bring you to her," the girl whispered urgently. "Please hurry!"

"Who is your mistress?" Elizabeth saw that the hand which held the candle was trembling.

"Lady Margaret. I am her maid, Catherine. Come, boy! My lady has summoned you, and she will grow angry with me if we tarry." Catherine plucked nervously at Elizabeth's sleeve.

The unexpected summons threw Elizabeth into a quandary. She wondered what a twelve-year-old boy would do in a situation like this.

"Is something amiss?" Elizabeth got slowly to her feet and stretched, easing the stiffness out of her muscles.

"I know not, only that I was bid to fetch you and to bring

you posthaste," Catherine whispered, looking fearfully
around the great empty kitchen. "Follow me!" She turned
and dashed into the passageway. Taking a deep breath,
Elizabeth scampered after the retreating point of light.

Addison Hall creaked and groaned in the night under the
weight of its advancing years, causing the fine hairs on the
back of Elizabeth's neck to rise and quiver with apprehension. Catherine did not slacken her pace, nor look back to
see if Elizabeth was following her. After ascending several
flights of stairs, they entered the long gallery. A large mullioned window cast a feeble light. Great hanging tapestries
trembled softly as the two hurried past them. Catherine led
Elizabeth to a handsomely carved door at the far end of the
wide hallway. A faint light shone under it. After rapping
softly, Catherine opened the door and pushed Elizabeth inside.

"The player boy, my lady," she murmured.

"You may go now," replied a silky voice from the curtained bed.

Catherine gave Elizabeth a nervous smile, then left, closing the door noiselessly behind her.

"Are you there, birdling?" The lady spoke again.

Elizabeth jumped. "Aye, my lady," she whispered,
glancing about the sumptuously appointed room. There was
no one else in attendance, not even a hound on the floor by
the hearth.

"Draw closer, sweet Robin Redbreast," commanded the
lady in sugared tones. "There is nothing to be afraid of."

Taking a deep breath, Elizabeth stepped into the center of
the chamber.

Lady Margaret sat in the middle of the magnificent canopied bed, surrounded by a number of embroidered pillows. The lady herself was dressed in a sheer chemise, a full
lace collar edging her low décolleté. Her long, unbound au-
burn hair drifted like a cloud across the pillows.

Elizabeth bowed low, feeling her face grow warm with her dratted blush. Her sixth sense found this unusual midnight visit highly disturbing.

"You wish me to sing for you, my lady?" Elizabeth asked, hoping her voice sounded naturally boyish.

"Aye, my sweet thrush. I wish you to sing, for I have a monstrous headache which keeps me from sleep." Lady Margaret's eyes glittered as her gaze swept over Elizabeth. She laughed low in her throat. "Come closer, boy, so I may see thee better."

Swallowing down her nervousness, Elizabeth advanced to the foot of the bed and stood there quietly, holding her hands behind her back to keep them from trembling. She cleared her throat. "What song would you like to hear, my lady?"

"A song of love," the woman in the bed whispered, reaching out a languid hand. "Come closer, sweet Robin. My eyesight is so poor." She patted the side of the bed. "Sit here, and we shall get to know each other much better."

Stunned by the request, Elizabeth edged along the side of the bed until she bumped into a low table that held a silver pitcher and two finely worked goblets.

"Ah, thou hast hit upon it." Lady Margaret giggled.

With a shock, Elizabeth realized the lady was slightly drunk.

"Pour us some wine, my chick." The lady giggled again.

Picking up the pitcher, Elizabeth splashed a little wine into each of the goblets, slopping some on the table.

"Your pardon, my lady," Elizabeth stammered, holding out the goblet to the older woman.

With a soft laugh, Lady Margaret took the cup, her fingers caressing the back of Elizabeth's hand. Her touch was reptilian.

The lady chuckled wickedly. "Thy hand is cold, pretty Robin. Come, get into bed with me, and I will warm you."

Elizabeth's eyes grew larger as she realized the full implication of Lady Margaret's invitation. Her mind worked
quickly. "Play the part," Tarleton had cautioned her. Very
well, she would—to the hilt.

Backing quickly away from the bedside, Elizabeth fell to
her knees and clasped her hands before her in supplication.

"Lady Margaret, you do not understand what you ask of
me!" Elizabeth made herself sound like a young, innocent
boy. "I have never known a woman, and I never shall. I am
promised to the church. Even now, I am on my way to Oxford, where I shall study for Holy Orders. I have taken a
vow of chastity."

Lady Margaret crawled out from under the coverings.
Appalled, Elizabeth watched as the woman inched, ser-
pentlike, across the bed. Her red lips parted in a seductive
smile, while her chemise fell off one shoulder, revealing her
full, rounded breasts. The lady's nipples were taut with desire.

"I knew you were better than a mere player boy," the lady
purred. "Come to me, sweet acolyte, and give me succor for
my sins."

"Lady Margaret, you do forget yourself." Jumping to her
feet, Elizabeth backed toward the door. "I belong to no one,
but to the Lord. Truly, I shall pray mightily for your soul.
Adieu!"

Grasping the door handle, Elizabeth wrenched it open
and fled down the darkened hall. She realized with sickening clarity that she could be accused of thievery or worse if
she were discovered above stairs. This was an absurd farce—
Lady Elizabeth Hayward, heiress of Esmond Manor, running like a hunted hare in the night.

Without daring to look back over her shoulder, Eliza-
beth tore down the wide main staircase. She half expected
Lady Margaret to set up a hue and cry at any moment.
Where in blazes was the kitchen?

At the foot of the stairs, she tripped over something soft that sent her sprawling amid the dusty rushes. Scrambling to her feet, Elizabeth saw it was the legs of one of the watchmen, who had fallen asleep.

"What in the devil's name?" he growled, half-awake.

Elizabeth dropped to her knees. "Please, sir, 'tis Robin, Tarleton's boy! I am lost and sore afraid!"

Closing a huge paw around Elizabeth's neck, the man shook her. "Lost, ye say?"

He peered closely into Elizabeth's face. She detected the strong smell of beer on his breath.

"Aye, I have a w-weakness to sleepwalk," she stammered. "And when I wakened, I did not know where I was. Please, sir, where is the kitchen? I must find my master, Tarleton, for...for I am frightened when I wake suddenly." Elizabeth licked her dry lips, and tried to look pathetic, hoping to win the varlet's sympathy.

The watchman stared at her with bleary eyes, shook her again, then dropped her. "Tarleton's boy, eh? The one with the sweet voice? Aye! I remember ye. Through that door, and down the stairs, you scamp!" he muttered. "And mind the stairs. 'Tis blacker than a bunghole in there."

Elizabeth breathed a sigh of relief. "Aye, sir, and good night to ye!" She bounded like a rabbit through the small door.

Once inside, the whole staircase was swallowed in thick darkness. Her heart pounded in her throat. She had always hated dark places. Putting one hand on the wall beside her, she inched her way down the steps, one at a time. At the bottom, she steadied herself for a moment, feeling for an opening in the wall. She nearly fell through the arch into the servants' lower passageway. At the far end, she was relieved to see the familiar glow from the kitchen's fireplace. Eagerly she started toward it, then stopped. If Lady Margaret came looking for her, surely she would seek her out in the kitchen. Elizabeth had to find another place to hide.

Tarleton! Without pausing to consider the consequences, Elizabeth dashed to the room where she knew he
lay with Peg. Trembling with fright and nervousness, Elizabeth pushed open the door to Peg's room, and tiptoed inside. By the light of a watery moon through a high small
window, she saw them both asleep. Tarleton lay on his
stomach, his arm flung over Peg, who was clothed in her
shift. Quietly stealing over to the bed, Elizabeth lightly
touched his shoulder.

Tarleton's reaction was both instantaneous and completely unexpected. Leaping up fully awake, he flashed a
dagger in his hand as he painfully grabbed a thick handful
of Elizabeth's hair with the other.

"God's teeth, varlet!" he swore as he yanked Elizabeth
to the floor beside the bed. "Make a move and I'll send you
to hell."

It felt as if he were tearing off the entire top of her head.
"Tarleton! 'Tis I!" she gasped. "For the love of God,
please don't slit my throat!"

"Robin?" Tarleton slowly released her, then he fumbled
at the table for the flint and tinder. "What jest is this? I've
a mind to whip you soundly," he growled while he lit a short
tallow candle.

He sounded as if he meant it. As shock of her experience
overtook her, Elizabeth began to shake uncontrollably.

"What is it?" Peg stirred sleepily.

"My prentice boy has in mind some mischief!" Tarleton
glared down at Elizabeth, who collapsed, sobbing and
trembling, on the bare floor. "Look at me, boy!"

"Hush, you fool! Can't you see the child is ill?" Peg
pulled back the sheet and heaved herself out of the bed.
"What ails you, Robin?"

"L-Lady M-Margaret," Elizabeth whimpered, her eyes
wide with remembrance. "She . . . she sent for me . . . and . . .
and when I went, she . . . she . . . wanted me to . . . to lie with
her!"

Tarleton swore again under his breath. "I forgot Lady Margaret's particular tastes," he whispered angrily. He knelt by Elizabeth, not knowing quite what to do with Peg standing nearby.

"The poor lambkin!" said Peg soothingly. "No wonder he shakes so."

Tarleton glanced quickly at Peg, knowing that her mothering nature would ferret out Elizabeth's secret. "'Tis no need for you to fret yourself, sweetheart. I shall deal with my apprentice."

"Deal with him gently, Dickon, for the lad has had a bad fright."

Tarleton had fully intended to treat Elizabeth as if she were truly a frightened boy, but when he saw the blank terror in her face, his resolve melted. Gently he gathered her into his arms, clasping her tightly to his chest. He rocked her softly in his embrace.

"Hush, hush, chuck. You are safe with us now."

"Why?" sobbed Elizabeth, pressing her wet face into the rich mat of Tarleton's dark chest hair. There was a faint aroma of wood smoke and leather about him. His strong arms promised her safe refuge. She was only dimly aware that Tarleton slept in another woman's bed clad modestly in his breeches. "What did Lady Margaret want of me?"

"Hush," soothed Tarleton, his fingers smoothing the spun gold of her cropped head. "'Tis nothing but the folly of a bored lady, and no matter to you, sweet Robin," he said softly, his heart filling with compassion for the terrified girl, and with anger toward the unhappy lecherous woman above stairs.

Peg regarded Tarleton and his apprentice with an appraising eye as Elizabeth grew quieter in his arms. "What that child needs is a hot posset!" She sniffed, wrapping a knit shawl over her shift. "I'll make him one. Put him in the bed, Dickon, and wrap him up warmly. The poor lad has been sorely frightened." Peg bustled out the door, closing it softly behind her.

"Come, ladybird," Tarleton whispered in Elizabeth's ear as he carried her to the bed, and placed her amid the tumbled sheets. " 'Tis a rough bed for a rough night, but you will be safer here than any other place in the house."

"Tarleton?" Elizabeth's green eyes were huge in the moonlight. "Lady Margaret thought I was a young boy, yet she wanted me to—"

He placed his finger lightly on her lips. "Lady Margaret is married to an old man who cannot satisfy her needs. She seeks out her fancy where she can find it. She prefers sweet-faced youths who are clean of the pox, and who are afraid to tell of her wickedness. The more fool I! I should have known!"

"But how could you?" Elizabeth whispered, nestling herself comfortably in the crook of his arm and listening to the strong, steady beat of his heart. She wished he would never let go of her.

"Did the lady ask you to draw near the bed because her eyesight was poor?" Tarleton questioned as he lightly stroked Elizabeth's face.

"Aye." Elizabeth sighed. His fingers smoothed away her fears.

"And did she ask you to pour wine to soothe her aching head?" Tarleton's thumb lightly traced down the bridge of her nose.

"Aye." Elizabeth shivered deliciously.

"And did she ask you to slip into bed to keep her warm?"

"Something like that." Elizabeth's green eyes flashed as she looked up at him. "Oh, Tarleton! You didn't!"

He chuckled wryly. "Aye, years ago, when I first came here. I was seventeen and hot-blooded to boot, with no more sense than a newborn pup. The lady was willing—nay, demanding—and she paid me well. But 'twas only once, sweetling, I swear. She frightened the very devil out of me.

I had no desire to be horsewhipped by Sir William's men. Like you, I ran to Peg, and she became my...my protection. We have been fast friends ever since. Ned is safe from Lady Margaret only because of his pockmarked face. I should have guessed she would seek you out as a bear seeks honey. Forgive me, chuck, but I was...was not myself tonight. Sometimes, I forget that you are not really a boy."

He swallowed and tried to ignore her gentle fingers resting over his heart and her soft curves molding to the contours of his lean body. Tarleton felt himself grow hot with his suppressed urges. He strove to banish them. Elizabeth needed his love and protection, not his selfish lust.

"How did you escape Lady Margaret's claws?" he asked gruffly.

"I played the part of a young cleric. I told her that I had taken the vow of chastity and that I was bound for the church. Then I ran!"

Tarleton chuckled as he hugged her tighter. "'Tis a pity you cannot act upon a stage."

"Nay." Elizabeth sighed. "I have no wish to do that. I only want to be safe at home, and to be a woman again. Being a boy is far too dangerous."

Peg returned with a steaming posset. Sitting on the bed next to Tarleton, she passed the cup to Elizabeth.

"Drink it up, my pet." Peg smiled kindly at her. "'Tis made with the master's good sack. 'Twill help ye sleep without another worry in the world."

Elizabeth smiled shyly at her, then drank the rich mixture down. The warm concoction of milk, cinnamon, honey and wine was comforting, as well as filling. Elizabeth felt its healing seep through her. Relaxing as the horror of the night's encounter faded, she fell asleep in Tarleton's arms.

"Such a pretty boy!" Peg remarked as she watched Tarleton tuck the covers around his apprentice. "And when her hair grows back, she will make an even prettier girl."

Tarleton looked up sharply at Peg, then he laughed lightly. "What do you mean, Peg? Have you been in the master's sack wine yourself?"

"Nay, good Dickon. 'Tis a sweet lass whom you counterfeit as a boy. Ye cannot fool old Peg, you rogue! What mischief are ye up to now?"

Looking unconcerned, Tarleton pulled on his shirt. "How did you come to this conclusion, pray tell?"

In answer, Peg smiled knowingly. "I suspected it when I watched her play at chess with young Ned. Though she is clever, I thought I spied the coy mistress underneath the breeches and waistcoat. She had poor Ned half-smitten with her, though he never realized it. Just now, when she came to us, all a-tremble, you took her into your arms and gentled her as if she were a kitten. La, if ye had seen the look in your eye!" Peg laughed merrily. "'Tis not the look a master gives a cowardly apprentice. Nay, I've seen that look afore, my sweet lad. I have seen it when you sing your songs of love."

"You amaze me, Peg." Tarleton smiled ruefully. "And I thank you for pointing out the chinks in our disguise. The next time she is frightened out of her wits, I will throw Robin against the wall, and tell her to act like a man!"

Peg patted his arm affectionately. "Now, now! Let there be no secrets between us, Dickon. Who is this young minx who has twined your heart around her little finger?"

Tarleton sighed as he regarded his exhausted employer. Her silky lashes rested on her cheeks like butterfly wings.

"She is no minx, but a fine lady, lately educated in France, who seeks to flee from a heartless marriage. I have been hired to take her in secret to Hampton Court. She is no passing fancy of mine, Peg. She is a goddaughter of our most Gracious Queen."

Peg whistled softly under her breath. "Poor sweet lady! And you, my fine friend, ought to be ashamed of yourself for what you have done to her! Now, harken to your Peg.

This time, you aim too far above yourself, and 'twill only lead to perdition.''

"Not so!" retorted Tarleton hotly, though he kept his voice low. "She thinks of me only as her guardian and escort. This time next week, God willing, her world will be in its proper place again."

Peg stared deeply into his eyes. "And what of your heart? For I spy it on your sleeve. Hide it away again, good Dickon, else it be badly bruised in good time."

"Aye," he answered shortly.

Peg changed her tone, becoming at once a co-conspirator. "Methinks it would be wise if you and your apprentice leave by early light before the good Lady Margaret is about."

Tarleton nodded in agreement.

Peg continued, "I will give you a goodly provender to see ye through a day or two. In faith, your lady looks as thin as a cony rabbit."

"You have a good heart, Peg, as ever!" Tarleton embraced her, kissing her on the cheek.

Peg smiled, then took up her candle. "Ye best stay here, lest she waken and take fright again. I am sure you have slept with her before," she added archly.

"As chastely as I would with the goddess Diana," Tarleton protested ruefully.

"For the rest of the night I'll be Tess's bedfellow, though that will take some explanation." Peg chuckled as she prepared to leave. "I shall have to tell her that you bite!" Still laughing to herself, Peg closed the door.

Tarleton smiled after her, then lay down on the bed next to Elizabeth. Though fast asleep, she sensed his warmth and snuggled again into his arms. Smoothing the covers over them both, he kissed her softly on her forehead.

Hampton Court seemed a world and a half away.

Chapter Seven

The next day dawned gray and dank. The wind blew an autumn chill from the north, heralding the end of summer and the promise of the cold winter months ahead. After a filling breakfast of pease porridge, coddled eggs with onion, and crusty bread dripping with butter and honey, Elizabeth and Tarleton made preparations for their departure from Addison Hall.

"Take good care of your charge, Dickon, then come home to me," Peg whispered fiercely in Tarleton's ear as she kissed him goodbye.

"I shall do the first, Peg. As to the other, only the Fates know for certain." Returning her kiss warmly, he looked at Elizabeth, who held a willow basket filled with generous provisions from Peg's larder. "And why are you standing there, boy? We've miles to cover before that storm catches us." Whistling a merry tune and snapping his fingers to his apprentice, he set a brisk pace down the lane toward the highway.

"Why does Peg call you Dickon?" Elizabeth asked Tarleton as they headed south once more.

"'Tis my name!" Tarleton grinned at his companion. "My Christian name is Richard—hence, Dickon. Did you think I had but one name?"

Elizabeth nodded ruefully. "I fear I did. I never thought of jesters having real names. Shall I call you Dickon?"

Tarleton's eyes grew narrow. Just hearing her say his familiar name made her seem far too accessible. He needed to maintain some distance lest they both regret it. "Tarleton is my professional name, and that is how you, as my apprentice, should address me. Dickon is the name my close friends call me," he answered stiffly.

"Oh." Miffed by his cool reply, Elizabeth shifted the food basket from one arm to the other. Of course Tarleton was right. She was not a close friend, merely his employer. But his obvious wish to stay aloof hurt—a feeling which both perplexed and disturbed Elizabeth.

Despite the ominous gathering of dark clouds in the northern sky, Tarleton and Elizabeth met with more travelers on the road. A pleasant morning's hour was spent with a chatty yeoman's wife, buxom Mistress Fletcher, who sat astride a small, laboring ass. She was on her way to the next village to sell the eggs she carried in her basket, exchange medicinal recipes with the village's wisewoman, and pass a long afternoon in gossip. It was clear to Elizabeth that gossip was the staff of life for Mistress Fletcher. Even Tarleton was hard-pressed to get in a word or two between the goodwife's rambling monologues.

"Plant rosemary, I says to her." Mistress Fletcher produced a small sprig of the herb, and thrust it under Elizabeth's nose. "Plant rosemary near the kitchen wall, and if it grows well, says I, then you will be the ruler of your household. That's what I tell every young bride, I do. So let that be a warning to you, young man. If your wife takes to planting rosemary, you've lost your place by the fire!" Mistress Fletcher rocked back and forth in her saddle at this witticism.

Tarleton, walking beside her wheezing animal, wiggled his eyebrows mischievously at Elizabeth. "Suppose, if I should have a wife, that I plant onions by the kitchen wall? What say you to that, Mistress Fletcher?" he asked innocently.

"I tell you true, you *are* a knave!" The goodwife laughed as she wagged a finger under his nose. "Onions, as you know full well, will arouse such manly desire in you that you would keep your poor wife in bed a week!" She laughed again, delighted with her answer.

If Tarleton thinks he can catch me blushing this day, he must bait his hook better, Elizabeth said to herself with a smile.

"And so, Master Player, what's the news from the north?" The goodwife looked encouragingly at Tarleton.

"Why, good mistress, the wind blows from the north and so brings the winter. The farmers near Warwick are afraid 'twill be a cold one. They say the signs show an early freeze, and they are hurrying the harvest."

"This is no news to me!" Mistress Fletcher snorted importantly. "I could have told you that a week ago! Nay, what news have you heard of the folk hereabouts? Forsooth, you've got a pair of handsome ears!"

"Aye, mistress," he replied thoughtfully, "there *is* a bit of news I heard bandied about up north."

"Tell! Tell!" she commanded, her eyes sparkling.

Elizabeth looked at Tarleton over the neck of the ass. Something in his tone made her wonder what jest he was going to loosen upon his unsuspecting audience. She recognized that impish grin.

"Have ye heard of the runaway wife?" he inquired.

At these unexpected words, Elizabeth's heart lurched. She glanced quickly at Tarleton. He, however, smiled innocently at Mistress Fletcher.

"Nay! Tell all!" cried the woman, her ears greedy for the tale.

"As I heard it, a nobleman, Sir Robert La Faye by name, has misplaced his betrothed. The Lady Elizabeth Hayward, who lives near Kenilworth, ran away last week, leaving her anxious bridegroom at the altar!'' The goodwife dissolved into rollicking laughter, for Tarleton told his story with a great deal of comic expression.

"'Tis true, upon my soul, mistress,'' he continued, improvising the details as he went along. "Left him flat in church, standing there in his new silken hose and silver-paned doublet. They say that when the preacher asked the lady 'Wilt thou take this man?' she cried out 'Nay! The devil can take him!' Then she picked up her skirts and petti-coats, bolted from the church as fleet as a hare, mounted Sir Robert's own black horse and rode away, still dressed in all her wedding finery!''

Mistress Fletcher slapped her thigh as tears of laughter rolled down her cheeks. Even Elizabeth was forced to smile at Tarleton's fictional recounting. How she wished she had the courage to do exactly that if ever she found herself before the altar with the odious Sir Robert by her side!

"And did Sir Robert catch her?'' Mistress Fletcher wiped her eyes.

"Nay! For the lady was a good rider. They do say that she left a trail of colored love knots all the way to Coventry. And that is where Sir Robert has gone to search for her—to Coventry.'' Tarleton emphasized the town's name.

"I pray the sweet lady gets clean away, if that marriage is so loathsome to her!'' said the goodwife, her eyes twinkling.

"Amen to that,'' Elizabeth whispered under her breath.

They parted company with the amiable Mistress Fletcher shortly thereafter, watching her sway contentedly down the lane toward the village of Little Rollright.

"Why on earth did you tell her that story about me?'' Elizabeth asked Tarleton, once they were alone again.

"There is method in my madness, chuck, or don't you trust me yet?'' He looked like Puck on a madcap spree. "That good woman will go into Little Rollright, and she will tell my story a dozen times, at least. No doubt she will elaborate upon it, so that if we heard it again tomorrow, we would scarcely recognize the details. But she will make sure to say that the poor runaway Lady Elizabeth was headed for Coventry—to the north, mind you—and far away from our true destination. If our luck holds, perhaps Sir Robert will hear this story himself, and he will turn his piggy snout toward Coventry, while we stroll merrily through the gates of Hampton Court!''

Elizabeth dimpled becomingly. ''Tarleton, you are a genius!''

The merry prankster basked happily in her warm approval. He would tell the tale of the runaway wife a thousand times if it rewarded him with such a smile from her. ''Haven't you heard the old saying 'Better a witty fool than a foolish wit for company'?''

''Nay, but I think I have the wittiest fool in England for my company.'' She smiled again. ''And I shall tell the Queen so.''

Tarleton's eyes danced. ''Good! Perhaps Her Grace will be moved to pay me more!''

Not all their encounters were so pleasant.

In the early afternoon, as the sky grew increasingly blacker, Tarleton and Elizabeth came upon a ragged girl by the side of the road. She was sobbing as she scooped out a small hole in the bank under a hawthorn hedgerow.

Approaching the distraught girl, Tarleton spoke kindly. ''What ails thee?''

She gazed up at him with her face tear streaked. ''Oh, sir, I beg you, for the sweet love of God, help me bury my child!''

She pointed to a tiny bundle that Elizabeth had not noticed before. It was pathetically wrapped in the coarse sacking used to carry grain. The young mother herself looked thin and sickly. She shivered in the rising wind, which blew through her tangled chestnut hair. Elizabeth felt a tight lump in her throat.

Tarleton knelt beside the grieving girl. His voice was soft and caressing. "Aye, my lass, let old Tarleton do this sad office for you. Sit back and rest." He drew his dagger and began to hack out large clods of the black earth. "Robin," he said over his shoulder, "give her something to eat. She looks half-starved."

Elizabeth, stunned by this unforeseen encounter, felt her own tears well up behind her eyes. Quickly busying herself with the basket, she drew out a thick wedge of yellow cheese and some of Peg's fine-milled white bread, which she offered to the girl.

"I am so very sorry for you. Was he ill?" Elizabeth whispered, watching the girl nibble at the food.

"Nay, he died a-borning. Poor little thing! He was unbaptized. It pains my heart to think him down in hell. 'Twas not his fault! The sin was mine!" She fell into a fresh round of heartrending tears.

Pausing in his labor, Tarleton again spoke comfortingly to the grieving young mother. "He's not in hell, lass. The angels have him for a playfellow in the heavenly kingdom."

"But the priest said he was damned!" the girl wailed.

"Then that priest should be burned in his own pulpit!" Tarleton stabbed the ground viciously.

"Drink some of this." Elizabeth offered a small bottle of cold cider. The girl took a long draft, then hiccuped. Elizabeth peeled a boiled egg and handed it to her. "'Twill give you strength," she murmured encouragingly.

"The hole is deep enough," said Tarleton gruffly, wiping his blade on his thigh. "Do you wish me to lay the babe in it?"

The girl nodded, her eyes huge and red rimmed with tears. "Do ye know a prayer to send him on his way?" she asked the player hopefully.

"I'm not a praying man," Tarleton answered shortly. "But my prentice prays daily. Say a prayer for the babe, Robin." Tarleton's brown eyes darkened as he gently laid the tiny corpse in the ground.

Elizabeth knelt beside the makeshift grave. She could not bring herself to look down at the still bundle.

"What was his name?" she asked the mother quietly.

"He came and went so fast, there was no time to name him," the girl said, and wept.

Elizabeth's lower lip trembled with pity for both mother and child. "Do you wish to name him now? I am sure his soul is not too far away. He will hear it." She swallowed back the lump in her throat.

"I would have called him Mark, had he lived," the girl whispered.

"Then I shall pray for Mark," Elizabeth said, and she composed her thoughts, hoping her prayer would ease the living, as well as the dead. "Dear Lord, look down upon this poor babe, Mark, who died before he could know you. As you loved children when you were on earth, take this little one to your heart and let him play forever in your heavenly fields. May his soul and the souls of all the faithful departed—" here Elizabeth gulped as she remembered her own recent loss "—rest in thy peace." Elizabeth scooped up a handful of earth and scattered it over the small wrapped form. "Ashes to ashes, dust to dust, until the day of resurrection. Amen."

"Amen," whispered the young mother, while Tarleton clutched his cap, his head bowed. The three of them knelt in silence for a moment while the wind added its own keening through the elms and beeches overhead.

"Distract her, while I cover him up," whispered Tarleton to Elizabeth.

Nodding, Elizabeth moved between the weeping mother and the shallow grave.

"Take a bit more of the cheese," Elizabeth urged. "Eat it. You are so pale."

"Ye are kind, lad," the girl said softly. "And ye said a fine prayer. I shall never forget this kindness."

Elizabeth's heart felt as if had been wrenched in two by the girl's whispered gratitude. *She looks to be my age, though the years have been more cruel to her.*

Tarleton stood, wiping the dirt from his hands. "'Tis done, young mistress. Now, you must be gone from this place," he told her somberly. "It will do you no good to be caught out in the storm that's brewing. Have you a place to stay?"

The girl nodded. "I have been living with an old woman nearby. They say she's a witch, but she has been good to me, when everyone else turned me out of doors."

"Go off then, and be of lighter heart. Thy babe is laid sweetly to rest." Tarleton took out Sir William's coin purse. Placing it in the girl's thin hand, he closed her fingers over it. "Take this. 'Tis not much. 'Twill not bring your babe back, but it will help you and your old woman find some comfort this winter."

"Oh, sir, I cannot—!" The girl's eyes were wide with amazement as she hefted the weight of the bag.

"Take it!" Tarleton gruffly ordered. "It pays a debt of mine. Now, go quickly, lass."

Without another word, the thin girl spun on her bare heels and dashed into the stubble field on the far side the road. Stopping for a moment, she turned back to them and dropped an awkward curtsy. Then, like a startled doe, she disappeared over the rise.

"Let us begone from here!" Tarleton heaved the pack on his back and hurried off. Elizabeth, disturbed by what had taken place, followed close behind him.

They walked on in silence, each with their own heavy thoughts. At length, Tarleton realized that his companion was weeping silently.

Stopping, he spoke gently to Elizabeth. "Have I set too fast a pace? Are you tired?" he inquired, throwing the pack down under a sheltering oak. "Sit down, ladybird, and tell me what is it? Are you hurt?"

Elizabeth shook her head. "That poor, poor girl!" she sobbed, burying her face in the crook of her elbow. "Why didn't she have a parson bury the child, and say prayers for his soul? Why did that sweet innocent babe have to be buried beside a highway in a d-ditch?" Elizabeth could not forget the sight of the young mother's haunted look, nor the utter degradation of the scene in which she had played a part.

"Because the child was born a bastard," snapped Tarleton angrily, though his anger was not directed at Elizabeth. "And that is why that whoreson pastor of hers told her it was damned. God's teeth, but I would like to put these hands around that sanctimonious neck!" He clenched his fist until his knuckles stood out white against his skin.

"It was kind of you to tell her that her baby would play with the angels, Tarleton," said Elizabeth, regarding him through teary lashes. "And it was good to give her the money, too. What did you mean when you said it paid a debt?"

She saw his jaw tighten. His eyes, usually so full of merriment, glowed with a cold fire. His new demeanor frightened her. She suddenly realized how very little she knew about the man she had entrusted herself with.

"That lass could have been my own mother," Tarleton said finally, his voice sounding as if it were pulled from the bottom of a deep, empty well. Turning his head, he stared at Elizabeth, locking her eyes with his penetrating stare. "But for God's grace, that babe could have been me. Does that shock you, Lady Elizabeth Hayward?"

Elizabeth shivered, not because of his admission, but because of the wholly different person he had suddenly become. "A little," she whispered truthfully. She could not read the look in his soul-searing eyes; they were dark and depthless. "You are telling me that you are a . . . a . . ."

"A bastard!" He spat the word out as if it were bitter bile. "'Tis all right to say the word, Lady Elizabeth. 'Tis what I am. I was born in a ditch by the side of a road such as this one, and I was left there to die, so I'm told."

"To die?" she gasped in horror. Tarleton usually seemed so cheerful, as if he had never known a care in the world. "Who found you?"

Tarleton's eyes sought a spot on the horizon while he continued in a hollow tone. "The steward of the household in which my mother had worked as a chambermaid—before the master dismissed her for her so-called loose morals. The steward guessed her time had come when she was missing one morning. There had been a heavy frost and he was able to follow her footsteps. By the time he got to the place, she was gone, but I remained, wailing for my life. He brought me back and the cook raised me. Perhaps that is why I am so fond of cooks!" There was no mirth in his voice.

Each word stabbed Elizabeth's heart like an icy dagger. She shuddered, thinking what a hardship it must have been for Tarleton's mother: alone, afraid, outcast and bearing a child in a frosty ditch. "And your mother?" she prodded gently.

Tarleton's lips curled back. "They found her body a week later. She drowned herself in the cow pond. Naturally, they buried her at a crossroads, because the priest said she was a suicide and therefore surely damned. I don't even know where she lies." His voice caught in his throat.

"I am so sorry, Tarleton," Elizabeth whispered.

She wanted to put her arms around him to ease away his pain and bitterness, but it was as if he had erected a great barrier between them—a barrier between her class and his, between the warm velvets of the manor house and the chill mud of the road. Finally he spoke again, though he still stared across the years of sorrow and abandonment.

"You have more compassion than the church, ladybird. I gave that girl our money in the hope she will not drown herself, but instead, will find courage for a new life."

"And so your debt is paid." Elizabeth sighed with understanding.

Turning on her angrily, his eyes blazed dark fire. "That debt will never be paid, Lady Elizabeth Hayward!" he told her bitterly. "There are not enough tears, not enough money, not enough prayers that will *ever* pay for my mother's shameful death, my father's cowardly sin, or the black mark of my birth!"

Elizabeth flinched at his words, each a blow to her face. She had no idea what she could do—or what he would permit her to do—to help him.

Snatching at the food basket, Tarleton rifled through it and took out a bottle of ale. Pulling the cork with his teeth, he tilted his head back and drained the brew in silence. Then he tossed the bottle into a tall clump of wayside grass.

Not knowing what to say, Elizabeth quietly retrieved the basket. Taking out two more boiled eggs, she peeled them, then offered one to Tarleton. He looked at her, then at the egg she held out to him with a trembling hand.

His face softened a little when he saw his pain mirrored in her dark green eyes, now glittering with unshed tears. "'Tis not your fault, chuck. Forgive my outburst. But 'tis best you know the truth about me. What did you expect when you plucked a protector from the side of the road? There are no more Knights of the Round Table in England, I fear. Only jesters with stained backgrounds. But, at least, I'm honest—in my own fashion." He wolfed down the egg.

"I didn't pick you as my protector," Elizabeth said quietly. "I believe my guardian angel did so. I'm glad. He chose very wisely."

Startled by her simplicity and her unquestioning faith, Tarleton looked at her for a long moment, then slowly his warm smile melted the icy contours of his face. It had been a long time since he had seen such a look in a woman's eye. He dared not hope it was one of love, and he did not want to think what else it might be.

"Well, prentice," he remarked lightly, though his heart pounded within his chest. "How long is it going to take you to unpack the rest of that food, or do you plan to starve us both to death?"

The storm, which had threatened all day, began with a spattering of fat raindrops. The blackened sky split asunder and a deluge poured down. The torrent caught Elizabeth and Tarleton traveling through open countryside. Shielding his eyes against the wind-lashed rain, Tarleton scanned the horizon in search of a deep forest, or, at the very least, a large haystack. A jagged fork of lightning leapt from the clouds to the receiving earth. The air was rent by an earsplitting clap of thunder. Jumping in fright, Elizabeth huddled closer to Tarleton.

"This way! Run!" he cried over the howl of the wind. Seizing Elizabeth by her hand, he plunged into the fallow meadow beside the road.

Muffled in her hooded cloak, Elizabeth could not see where they were running. Trustingly she hung on to Tarleton's strong hand and sloughed through the pelting rain. The sky lit up with another flash of lightning. The attending crash of thunder made Elizabeth's skin prickle and shiver. From her earliest childhood, she had feared thunderstorms.

"Almost there!" Tarleton called encouragingly over the wind.

The next flash of lightning revealed a stone building just ahead. Concentrating on keeping her footing in the wet grass and mud, Elizabeth raced after Tarleton.

The shelter proved to be an abandoned Norman church—a casualty of the late King Henry VIII's argument with the pope—now left to fall into quiet ruin. The roof had collapsed into the nave. The empty windows bore mute testimony of the stained glass they once held. Two of the walls had vanished to become hearths and chimneys of the local farmers. The round baptismal font stood like a stark sentinel in the exposed vestibule. Pulling Elizabeth under the gallery, Tarleton dropped his pack with a wry chuckle.

"Well, sweetling, I knew you would lure me into a church sooner or later, but I don't think you had this one in mind!"

Elizabeth was not in the mood to appreciate his humor. Instead she cringed as the thunder rolled over their heads. Despite her cloak, she was chilled and soaked to the skin. "Where are we?" she asked.

"Off the road and out of the wet. As for our exact location, I would say that tomorrow we should reach Woodstock, and from there it will be on to Oxford." Tarleton eased the rain-soaked cape from her shoulders, and shook the water off it. "For tonight, this will be our lodging."

"Here?" Looking dejectedly at the rubble on the cold stone floor, Elizabeth remembered Peg's warm, friendly kitchen.

Tarleton ran his fingers through his wet hair, squeezing the droplets from his thick curls. "I've slept in worse places, so don't turn up your pretty nose at this one, ladybird. Next time, you'll be thankful for a nice dry stable. Or perhaps you wish you were cozy in Lady Margaret's bed?" he added with a smirk.

"I'll take my chances here, thank you, Sir Jester!" she answered quickly, though her voice did not sound as convincing as her words.

Tarleton grinned. Illuminated by the lightning, he looked like a cheerful devil sprung from hell. "Gather up whatever dry wood you can find here, prentice, while I see what is at the other end. We shall have a fire going soon enough!"

With a wink at her, he darted along the remaining free-standing wall of the country church, stooping here and there amid the rubbish.

In the dry section, Elizabeth found a number of twigs and boughs lodged in a protected corner where they had been blown in through the gaping roof. Charred pieces of wood and a large black smudge on the stone floor gave evidence that the abandoned church had been a sanctuary for other travelers. At least, it was dry and out of the wind here. After sweeping the spot clear with her foot, Elizabeth knelt and began to snap the twigs into kindling. Tarleton returned, holding several large pieces of paneling.

"'Tis the pulpit, or what's left of it, but 'twill make a merry fire. We shall be warm and dry in no time!" Briskly Tarleton broke up the rotten wood and piled it on the makeshift hearth stone. Then he lit the kindling with a spark from his tinderbox. A small, cheerful blaze sprang up.

"Lay out your cloak so it will dry, my Robin." Tarleton undid his pack, pulling out his spare clothing that Peg had so recently brushed and packed for him. "Damp as a dungeon!" he snorted, shaking out his motley, its bells jingling softly. "If our bread is wet as well—"

A loud crash drowned out Tarleton's next words as a heavy branch from a nearby oak fell through the hole in the roof. Cowering against the back wall, Elizabeth screamed and covered her ears. Instantly Tarleton was by her side, his arms wrapped around her.

"'Twas only a bit of wind and thunder, sweetling!" he murmured, though he did not mind the chance to hold her close to his heart.

"Storms frighten me!" Elizabeth shivered, burying her head against his damp jerkin. The thick cloth smelled like a woolly sheep in spring. She jumped as the thunder rolled over them again.

"'Tis nothing but a great deal of bluster," Tarleton crooned softly in her ear. He noted how pink and perfectly formed it was. " 'Twill be gone soon, sweet lady, and we shall be none the worse for it, I swear."

"My nurse used to say the same thing." Elizabeth shut her eyes and clung to him, her fingers digging into the thick muscles of his arms.

"Then I shall hold you until it is over," Tarleton whispered comfortingly. Outside the church, the storm raged on while another brewed inside Tarleton's soul.

Her slim body pressing closer against him, Elizabeth wound her arms inside his jerkin and around his back. The sweetness of her hair held all the sunshine now driven away by the boiling mass of black clouds. *I could take her now, this moment,* Tarleton realized as her trembling limbs clung to him. He closed his eyes but could not blot out the vivid images that assailed his senses. He saw himself laying Elizabeth down on her cloak, his hands gently stripping the wet garments from her yielding body. His fingers stroked her downy cheek as he imagined kissing her sugared mouth, his warm tongue leading her in a dance of love and passion.

Another brilliant flash of lightning caused Elizabeth to bury her face against his throat. Tarleton felt her warm breath caress his skin, as she trembled like a frightened fawn in his arms. Gritting his teeth, he fought down the hot waves of passion that threatened to engulf him.

Elizabeth's arms tightened around his neck, bringing her full, ripe lips temptingly closer to his own. Her eyes closed in her terror, she didn't see the fires of lust that Tarleton knew blazed within him.

Madness! Feeling feverish, he fought against his natural urges which tightened his loins. His blood sang hotly through his veins. She's a virgin—and the Queen's own goddaughter! *If I harm her, or ruin her, I can count my brief remaining days as a guest in the Tower of London.*

Tarleton swallowed at the thought of the grisly fate that would be the inevitable end to such a pleasurable beginning. Roughly he pushed the cringing girl away from him and leapt to his feet. He stood with his back to the startled Elizabeth so she would not see the change she had worked upon his body.

"The storm is passing," he remarked, his voice raw with his desire and inner struggle. "Stop your sniveling, my lady. 'Twill only rain gently for the rest of this evening." Taking several deep breaths, he prodded the fire, willing his body to relax. He wondered if Elizabeth would think him mad if he went for a brisk, wet walk.

Elizabeth, stung by this sudden change in Tarleton's mood, wiped her face with her sleeve, then leaned back reflectively against the dry wall. What had she done wrong now? One minute Tarleton was kind and comforting. In fact, it was very pleasant to be held so closely in his arms, feeling the tingly sensations that danced a strange jig in her blood. Then, without warning, Tarleton acted as if she had the plague. Perhaps he didn't like women who cried in thunderstorms. Feeling a dull ache where only moments before there was such pleasure, Elizabeth watched the raindrops spatter into a large puddle in the center aisle.

"I am sorry if my fears annoy you, Master Tarleton," Elizabeth said coolly. "Please remember that I am not a man like you, but a woman. I am entitled to one or two womanly emotions."

Hearing the rebuke in her words, Tarleton clenched his teeth. "I do nothing *but* remember, Lady Elizabeth, and I am counting the moments until I can safely deposit you at Hampton Court!" He kept his face averted so she could not see the anguish on his face.

The unaccustomed sharpness of his reply was a sword thrust to her heart, but Elizabeth vowed not to show the pain he inflicted. "If my company has become burdensome to you, you are more than welcome to leave me at any time," she said bravely, praying her voice would not betray her whirling emotions. Drawing the money bag out of her shirt, Elizabeth extracted two gold angels.

Rising to her feet, she held the coins rigidly out to him. "Here is the payment I promised you, and I thank you for getting me this far. Just point me in the right direction to Woodstock, and I shall trouble you no further."

Turning slowly around, Tarleton stared at the tiny figure, her trembling chin tilted at a brave angle. Once again, his good resolutions slipped from his grasp.

"Put your money away, Lady Elizabeth," he muttered gruffly. "Are you truly thickheaded? You keep forgetting what I told you about flashing your coin in public. And sit down by that fire! 'Twill do neither of us any good if I must deliver you, shaking with a fever, to the Queen. And, for sweet Jesu's sake, stop sniveling! I know that I've landed you in a hard place, but, in a few days' time, you will be back with all your finery and comforts. In the meantime, let us make the best of this bargain. Now, what is there left to eat?"

Elizabeth's anger boiled inside her. By what right did this...this knave speak to her in such a manner? Tucking the coins away, the Queen's goddaughter took out her comb and began to carefully groom what was left of her hair.

"I have no idea what food there is," she remarked in an icy tone. "You have my leave to unpack the basket and prepare our supper, varlet." She stared into the fire with haughty pride, though she felt her heart cracking inside her. *He is only worried about what the Queen will do to him if I should come to any harm. I am nothing to him but a handful of gold angels.*

Tarleton, hearing the coldness in her voice, ground his teeth in anger against himself. Roughly he opened the basket and spread out the remains of Peg's feast. They ate apart with studied disdain.

Swallowing the last of his cheese-and-onion tart, Tarleton cleared his throat loudly. "If it pleases your ladyship, I think your cloak is dry enough. You can roll up in it and sleep close to the wall." He stood and made an elaborate bow to her. His tongue was heavy with sarcasm. "I shall sleep downwind so that my common presence will not disturb your dreams."

If he is going to continue to act like that, I shall ignore him completely, Elizabeth fumed. Inclining her head slightly, she pulled the heavy cloak around her, then walked regally to the darkest dry spot at the base of the belfry. She swept the area clear of the dust and other debris, then knelt to say her nightly prayer.

Tarleton watched her, the firelight casting its spell on the gold of her hair. His heart felt as if it were locked in hot iron bands. Flinging himself down on the other side of the fire, he pillowed his head on his pack. *God's teeth!* he swore as he drew himself up against the chill night air. *I let the minx keep the whole cloak to herself!*

Tarleton's bellow of rage startled Elizabeth out of a deep sleep. Every nerve in her body quivered. A violent crashing intermixed with low guttural sounds came from the darkness. Steeling herself to face a large dog or wolf, Elizabeth slowly rolled over and looked toward the fire. What she saw by the feeble light of the dying embers made her blood freeze.

A large bear of a man, his hair and beard matted with dirt, and dressed in flimsy rags, grappled with Tarleton. Both men fought for possession of Tarleton's dagger. Its naked blade gleamed dully in the dim light. Inadvertently Elizabeth uttered a small cry of alarm from her dark corner.

The intruder turned his head at the sound. " 'Tis a lass ye've got with ye?" the attacker snarled. "I'll sport with her once I've—"

But the man never finished his vile threat. Tarleton used the momentary distraction to wrench his hand free. Moving with the fluid speed born of practice in the service of Her Majesty's spy master, Tarleton sharply kicked his opponent's groin, then followed through with a heavy blow to his face. There was a sickening sound of bones crunching as the ruffian fell heavily to the stone floor and lay still. Tarleton sank down beside the brute.

"Tarleton!" Elizabeth ran to his side. Her protector panted heavily from his unexpected midnight exercise. She gingerly touched his bruised face. "Oh, sweet Dickon, are you hurt badly?"

"Water... to drink," he whispered in a raw croak. His head swam from the vagabond's first blow—a blow that was meant to kill.

Frantically looking around, Elizabeth saw the baptismal font, filled to the brim with fresh rainwater. Scooping up some in her cupped palms, Elizabeth offered her hands to Tarleton.

"I have no cup, Dickon," she apologized.

He smiled weakly at her as he steadied her hands with one of his. Then he guided her palms to his lips and sucked the rainwater noisily.

"More," he said, and coughed. His legs were weak and seemed to have little feeling in them.

"Oh, my sweet Dickon!" Elizabeth held out another handful of water to him. "I thought you had been killed! Are you badly hurt?" He again sipped from her hands, his lips brushing the delicate soft pads of her palms. A delicious spark ran through her fingers, and Elizabeth tightened them to keep from spilling the remaining water.

Tarleton gazed into her eyes, which glowed in the dark with the fire of emeralds. His answering smile was warm and loving. "I believe there is no finer cup in all this world than your sweet hands, ladybird. Fret not, chuck. I am in one piece, though my head is ringing a merry tune."

Sitting beside him, Elizabeth drew his head into her lap. Gently she massaged his temples with her cool, wet fingers. "Does it hurt mightily? Oh, sweet Dickon, I was sure he was going to kill you!"

Tarleton grunted with satisfaction. "I do believe I could lie on this hard floor all night long with your blessed nursing, my sweet." Tarleton kissed her hands, his lips softly caressing her fingers.

A warm current suffused her. Elizabeth's head felt light and momentarily dizzy. A delightful shiver of wanting ran through her. She completely forgot the vagabond who lay nearby. Closing her eyes as Tarleton's lips worked sweet magic on her palms, she moaned softly.

Her passionate sound jarred Tarleton back to their present predicament. With a regretful sigh, he sat up and eyed the inert form beside him. "I fear we must cease this pleasant pastime, my heart."

Tarleton crawled over to the unconscious man. The huge attacker lay on his stomach. Touching the man's scalp, Tarleton felt a large knot forming where he had struck the ruffian with the hilt of the dagger.

"Thank the good Lord, I'll not have this scum's death on my hands, but he will have a rare headache for the next few days," he observed. Tarleton struggled shakily to his feet, supporting himself against the font. Splashing more water across his face, he shook his head gingerly.

"Now, my sweet Elizabeth, we ourselves will become like thieves in the night. This one may have a confederate lurking nearby."

Elizabeth shivered as she looked out into the blackness surrounding the old church. "What if his friend should set up a hue and cry after us?" Never, in her wildest nightmares; did she think she would be running from the law officers of the parish for assault.

Noting her anxiety, Tarleton held her tightly by the arms and stared deeply in her frightened eyes. "Now listen to me, Elizabeth! No one is going to set up any hue and cry after us, lest it be this oaf here for his own purposes. Fear not, sweetling. You are under the protection of the best in the land."

"But you are only a player," she whimpered.

Tarleton allowed a brief smile play across his lips. "Aye, a player who happens to be in the service of Sir Francis Walsingham. Have you heard of him?"

"He's... he's one of the Queen's ministers, I think." Elizabeth licked her dry lips.

"Aye, he is her principal secretary. The Queen calls him her 'Moor,' for he is not only dark of face, but devious of mind, as well. He is the man who knows what is happening in the hidden corners throughout the land, and abroad, too. He is a master spider who sits in the middle of a large web of spies and informants. In short, he is a very powerful man, Elizabeth."

"How is he your friend?" Her voice cracked with nervousness.

"Because I... I gather information for him."

"You are a spy?" Elizabeth's eyes gleamed like a cat's in the night.

Tarleton's lips twitched into a rueful smile. " 'Tis not as bad as you make it sound. Let us say, I keep a finger on the pulse of the times. As a jester, I travel throughout the realm with my long ears and good memory. I have been in Sir Francis's employ for many years now. If need be, he will give us his protection. He has done so for me in the past."

"Have... have you ever...?"

"Aye," Tarleton answered her unspoken question curtly. "I've killed a man, but not for personal pleasure or revenge. 'Twas in my own defense. Now, my brave little one, let us be off and away from this place. We need to put miles between us and this devil's wrath, or, trust me, there will be nothing left of us for Sir Francis to protect. Do you understand, my sweet?"

Elizabeth nodded slowly. She gritted her teeth to keep them from chattering. "Aye, Tarleton."

"That is my brave ladybird! There is no moon to tell the time, but I think, by the smell of it, morning is only a scant hour away."

"Can you walk? Oh, Dickon, you are not well!" Elizabeth saw him wince as he moved away from the font. She put out her hands to steady him.

Tarleton smiled grimly into her pale face. "I can travel well enough, ladybird. With you by my side, I would gladly travel to hell and back. Come, gather your things."

Sidestepping around the large, still form, Elizabeth hastily packed up the food basket.

Tarleton stamped out the remains of the fire and scattered the ashes across the floor. He winced again as he hefted the pack onto his shoulder. Then he held out his hand to Elizabeth.

"We'll cut roundabout the fields. If this man and his friends come looking for revenge, they will search for us on the main road first. Our way to Oxford will be longer, but safer."

Without a backward glance at his assailant, Tarleton helped Elizabeth climb over the ruined wall of the church. Like two wandering spirits, they glided through the graveyard and melted into the rising mist.

Chapter Eight

The remaining hours of that dreadful night, and all the next dismal day, passed as a walking nightmare for Elizabeth. When Tarleton spoke of the perils of travel, she had only half believed him, thinking he exaggerated the evil that could befall her. But the brush with Sir Robert, then the horrific encounter with the robber had more than convinced her of the wisdom of her disguise. Even so, the vagabond's ear had caught the truth of her sex. Elizabeth realized how careful she must be in the future until she was safely at court. The jester and his frightened apprentice did not speak much that day, turning all their energies to their flight across the wet countryside.

Tarleton allowed them only a few rests. Though his head throbbed from the blow he had suffered at the thief's hands, he made no mention of it to his companion. His only concern was for Elizabeth's safety.

It was a blessing Elizabeth didn't realize what a near thing their encounter with that brute had been. If it wasn't for Tarleton's swift reflexes, both he and his sweet lady would be now lying in their own blood, their throats slit wide open. He shuddered to think of the hell Elizabeth would have suffered before that devil finally killed her. Tarleton closed his eyes momentarily and thanked God for Elizabeth's courage. Unlike most women of his experience, she had not screamed her fool head off, nor fainted on the spot. In fact, her one small cry had provided Tarleton with just the opening he needed to deal effectively with the blackguard.

Elizabeth was so tired her nerves ached, yet she did not complain of her fatigue. The energy engendered by the initial shock and horror of the encounter gave way to a near-stupor. Only Tarleton's solid, reassuring presence and his kind words softly spoken at her side encouraged her on.

Just when she thought she would faint from exhaustion, Tarleton found a field with several large haystacks still waiting to be gathered. Selecting the most solid-looking one, he scooped out a small nest for them. There they thankfully burrowed in for the night under her cloak.

"What will we do tomorrow, Tarleton?" Elizabeth's green eyes looked enormous with the dark circles under them.·

His face softened "We shall make for Banbury. 'Tis nearby."

"Oh, Tarleton!" She clutched at his arm. "Will it be safe to go there?"

His large hands framed her face, holding it gently. "Do you know what an actor does when he has forgotten his next line and the groundlings are pelting him with rotten cabbages?"

Elizabeth blinked, wondering what that had to do with their problem.

Tarleton continued. "He picks himself up with a grand display, and he makes his mistakes even bigger. When all else fails, bluff and bluster is the answer. It has gotten me out of many a scrape!"

"And at Banbury?" Her eyes burned dryly from sleeplessness.

"We are two players on the road, passing the time of day at a small, friendly alehouse where we can eat, drink and hear the news. That should tell us if the countryside has been raised against us. Which I highly doubt," he added with a smile. "Our would-be robber did not strike me as being a respectable law-abiding citizen himself." Tarleton did not mention the more likely threat—Sir Robert La Faye's minions could be there. No point in alarming Elizabeth any further.

Elizabeth did not answer him. She had fallen asleep, still clutching her meager supper.

Tarleton gently eased the bread out of her fingers. Then he gathered her into his arms, pulling the cloak snugly over them.

"You forgot to say your prayers tonight, my lady," he whispered in the hollow darkness of the sweet-smelling hay. "Though 'tis not my habit, I'll say them for you. Perchance that guardian angel of yours will listen to me."

Tarleton stumbled through a silent prayer for their safety. He did not remember falling asleep.

The next morning brought the welcome promise of better things to come. The day dawned chill, but a warming sun rose in a clear blue sky, signaling a fine harvest day. Tarleton smiled when he woke. Sunshine always put him in a good mood. Rising from their straw bed, he stretched happily in the welcoming rays, feeling much better after a sound night's sleep. He rubbed the tightness from the muscles of his shoulders and legs as he scanned their surroundings.

"'Wake, and see/The dew-bespangled herb and tree!'" He cheerfully shook Elizabeth awake.

Opening one eye, she blinked at him. "What was it you said?" she murmured, her voice still drowsy with sleep.

"A bit of poetry for your breakfast." Tarleton hopped lightly up and down, swinging his arms in the air.

Elizabeth watched him with amused interest. "What on earth are you doing, Tarleton? I'm not in the mood for a private performance." Yawning, she snuggled deeper into the sweet-smelling hay.

" 'Tis no jig, prentice boy. I need to loosen my muscles. How can I gimbal and gambol, if I am as stiff as a wooden Dutch doll?''

Elizabeth sat up with a start. "Do you mean to seek out a performance today?" she gasped.

"If we plan to eat anything, I think 'twould be a wise idea," he replied jauntily. "Come, up!" He held out his hand to her, smiling like an elf intent on whisking her off to faerie land. His syrupy-sweet voice dripped over her like honey. "I know you are still tired. So am I, but we must be off. I am sorry for it, chuck."

Sighing, Elizabeth took his hand. She was immediately aware of its strength and warmth. Tarleton pressed his lips lightly to her fingers, sending an unexpected tingling through her.

He cleared his throat loudly. "If I were a lady's maid, I would suggest that my mistress attend to the hay that is sprouting from her hair and clothing. As I am a man, I dare not take such liberties," he remarked, hoping he kept his true desire out of his voice.

Smiling at her companion's overflowing good spirits, Elizabeth took out her comb and carefully worked through the tangles that had crept into her hair during the night. She was glad Tarleton's good humor had returned. He had been so silent and serious the day before. Rubbing her face with her sleeve, Elizabeth thought longingly of a basin of warm, soapy water, clean clothes and a hot breakfast. She plucked out the odd bits of straw that had worked their way under her shirt.

Tarleton pretended not to watch Elizabeth. He gladly would have offered his assistance in removing the offending sprigs from their delightful nesting place between those milk white breasts of hers—breasts he had glimpsed often enough these past few days. To take his mind off such tempting thoughts and to relieve the sudden stiffness between his legs, Tarleton practiced several cartwheels and handsprings across the field.

"I'm ready," Elizabeth called after the whirling figure. "Which way?"

Tarleton stopped, spun comically around, then pointed. "There!"

Just on the other side of the haystack lay a broad highway. Even though the sun was barely above the horizon, the road was already full of traffic, all headed in one direction.

"Is it wise?" Elizabeth regarded the road with apprehension.

Tarleton grinned broadly. "Aye! The wisest thing we can do! Bluff and bluster, Robin." He handed her the pack. "Don't forget yourself today, my *boy*. Apprentices always carry their master's bag." His voice softened as he added, "Our fellow travelers would think it most strange if you didn't."

Elizabeth grasped the strap and tentatively hefted the heavy load. "I didn't have to carry it before," she muttered grumpily.

"We were on less-traveled roads before," he reminded her. "Now we must look natural as a master and his boy. Banbury is not far! Nor is breakfast!" he enticed seductively.

Taking a deep breath, Elizabeth slung the pack onto her back, shifting its weight into the best position across her slight shoulders.

A brief smile played over Tarleton's lips as he watched her struggle with the baggage. Then, squaring his own shoulders, Tarleton walked briskly toward the road, snapping his fingers at her to follow.

"Good morrow, mistress!" Tarleton addressed the farmer's wife, who had stopped to watch the jester and his boy climb over the stile.

"And to you," she answered, eyeing their dusty appearance and travel-worn clothes with some suspicion.

"Could you tell us which way Banbury is, for we lost our bearings in the dark last night?" Tarleton smiled beguilingly at her.

The woman allowed herself a small nod in return. " 'Tis this way. I, myself, am going there to help my husband with his stall. He took the wagon there last night to make ready for today."

Tarleton fell into step with the woman, leaving Elizabeth to follow along behind them. "And, I pray you, good mistress, what stall would that be? Perchance, I can give your good man some custom."

The woman grinned warmly at Tarleton. "Why, beer is his trade! We have six fine barrels to sell at the harvest fair. Thank St. Luke, 'twill be a warm day! Sunshine makes everyone more thirsty." Straightening her shawl, she cocked her head at Tarleton. "And what is your business, sir?"

"I am a teller of tall tales, a singer of sweet songs, a riddling rhymer, a punster of exceeding proportions! I jig and gibe, tumble and tickle your fancies with delight! In short, I am Tarleton, court jester to Her Most Gracious Majesty, and a traveling entertainer. That is my apprentice, Robin," he added, jerking his thumb over his shoulder.

He executed a short two-step down the road, then turned a cartwheel. The woman, clearly delighted with Tarleton's short performance, laughed with a high-pitched squeal.

"Well met, Master Player! And if your wit is as nimble as your tongue and feet, ye shall turn many a penny this day. Aye! And hearts, too!" she simpered.

Elizabeth shifted the pack to her other shoulder and snorted softly to herself. *That brazen woman is staring at Tarleton like some lovesick cow!*

"I am Mistress Johnson, though ye may call me Bess, seeing as I am named for the Queen ye serve!" The giggling woman gave Tarleton's arm a little squeeze.

Elizabeth made a face at the woman's back.

"Bess! Ah, sweet Bess! Did you know Elizabeth is a favorite name of mine?" The charmer shamelessly winked at the woman.

Bess giggled again, sounding like a cross between a schoolgirl and a stuck pig.

This is really too much on an empty stomach! Elizabeth glowered under the weight of the pack.

Over the crest of the next rise, the market town of Banbury spread out before them. Even from a distance, Elizabeth could see people hurrying to and fro. The morning breeze carried sounds of excited voices, cheerful music, and the warm smell of fresh-baked bread and roasting meat.

Banbury's streets were bedecked with colorful banners and pennants, as the local population prepared themselves for a day of buying and selling in celebration of the late summer harvest. Excited dogs and equally excited children were everywhere, especially underfoot. Stalls of every description lined the high street and crowded around the great stone cross in the town square. Geese and pigs hissed and squealed in their pens; their owners extolled their virtues of fatness and cheapness to everyone within earshot. Vendors hawked their wares in loud, singsong voices. After two days of rain, gray skies and numbing fear, the color and bustle of the marketplace was a gladsome sight to the jester's apprentice.

With many a promise to visit her booth and buy her beer later in the day, Tarleton and Mistress Bess parted company with a loud smacking kiss at the edge of town.

"Will we stay here, Tarleton?" Elizabeth asked him, as soon as the woman rounded the corner of the street with many a coquettish wave.

"Aye, Robin, and make our fortune!" Tarleton grinned broadly, his eyes sparkling in anticipation. "Don't look so solemn, chuck!"

"I thought we were in a hurry to get to Hampton Court," Elizabeth muttered, though she hoped they might stay long enough to get some breakfast. The delicious smells from the cook stalls made her stomach rumble in anticipation.

Tarleton cocked one eyebrow at her. "Aye, but it would look very strange if a traveling entertainer did not stop when there's a great fair to play. Think, my boy! What would people remember as suspicious, a jester who played in the marketplace, or one who pulled up his collar and hurried quickly out of town?"

Elizabeth sighed and nodded. She saw his point and, to be honest, the sounds and the color of the harvest fair were very tempting.

"First, we need to find the bailiff!" Tarleton started down the street, looking this way and that.

Elizabeth's heart stopped. Had Tarleton completely lost his wits? What if Sir Robert had lodged an inquiry about her? She was sure that he had. And what about that man they had left lying on the floor of the abandoned church? Suppose he had died from Tarleton's blow?

"Tarleton!" She pulled at his sleeve. "What about...you know?"

Grinning, he clapped his hand roughly between her shoulder blades.

"I *am* thinking, prentice! We cannot entertain without first registering with the bailiff and paying our license fee. Besides, we are safe enough. What is that devil's whelp going to do? Walk up, bold as you please, to the bailiff and say, 'I want to lodge a complaint against a jester who attempted to kill me as I tried to rob and kill him?'" Tarleton wiggled his thick brows at her, bringing a chuckle from his apprentice. "Good. I'm glad to see you are being sensible!"

Tarleton stopped the nearest man and asked directions to the town hall.

"No stall, you say?" The bailiff regarded the jester and his apprentice with an appraising eye.

"Nay." Tarleton grinned. "We need only a small pitch—and a goodly crowd to please."

"Have you letters patent? I brook no masterless vaga-bonds in Banbury." The bailiff stuck out his jaw and tried to look important.

Grinning even more broadly, Tarleton pulled an impressive-looking document from his pouch.

The parchment crackled as the bailiff unfolded it. He drew in a breath when he saw the royal seal. "Do you know what this says?" he inquired searchingly.

In answer, Tarleton took the letter from him, and began to read easily.

"Know ye by all men that the bearer of this letter patent is one Richard Tarleton, member of Her Most Gracious Majesty's company of players known hereafter as The Queen's Men. The said Master Tarleton has been a member of this company since its founding in the year of our Lord 1583, and, as such, he enjoys all rights and privileges thereto. Moreover, he hath, by divers jigs, songs, wit, swordplay and conversation, the particular patronage of Her Most Gracious Majesty, Elizabeth, and by Her Expressed Command is to receive all manners of courtesies wherever the said Master Tarleton may perform. Given under my Hand and Seal, Sir Christopher Hatton, Lord Chamberlain of the Royal Household, this eighth day of June in the year of Our Lord 1586."

Tarleton handed the letter back to the bailiff, whose face creased into a greasy grin. "This scamp is my apprentice, lately hired." Tarleton pointed toward Elizabeth.

The bailiff barely glanced at her. He was clearly awed by the arrival of such a celebrity as the Queen's own jester. "You do our fair honor, Master Tarleton. In faith, I have heard of ye!"

"And I trust your reports have been good?" Tarleton cocked his head.

"They say that none can make the Queen smile when she has a black mood upon her, except her fool, Tarleton. They say you can mend her body better than her physician, and her spirit better than a priest," the bailiff replied warmly, showing off his knowledge of court gossip.

"You are are too kind." Tarleton murmured with mock humility.

Elizabeth was most impressed by the bailiff's words. Up to now, she had only half believed Tarleton's boasting.

The bailiff took out a license from his desk. "The fee for entertainers is two shillings."

Tarleton sighed with a dramatic flourish. "Alas, sir, I have but one shilling about my person. Could you advance me the other shilling on my bond, and I will pay you at day's end?" Taking out the single coin, Tarleton placed it on the desk before the bailiff. "There would be, of course, a little extra in consideration of your charity," he added in a low voice.

The official quickly pocketed the shilling. "Seeing that you are the Queen's own man, so be it." Making a second notation on the license, the bailiff signed it and passed it across to Tarleton. "You may play by the market cross near the dancing bear."

Tarleton respectfully touched his cap, then he sailed out the door, Elizabeth following in his wake.

"'Twas a knavish cony-catcher to be sure," Tarleton muttered under his breath to Elizabeth as they made their way through the crowded streets "He knows full well that the fee is only a shilling."

"Shall sing the song about the roast swan, Tarleton?" Catching his infectious excitement, Elizabeth looked forward to performing.

Tarleton brushed his knuckle lightly down her nose. "Nay, chuck! Not today."

"Oh." Her face fell.

Surprised, Tarleton glanced at her, then his eyes softened with understanding. "Nay, 'tis not that I think you would do poorly," he said in a comforting voice. "But I fear that Sir Robert La Faye may have some of his hirelings about. The less seen of your fair face and bright hair, the better."

They entered the town square, which was filled with people bent on enjoying themselves. Enclosed in a shallow pit in one corner, the first of the day's cockfights was in progress, attracting a great many noisy patrons.

In the center of the square, a sad-faced scholar sat on the steps of the ancient market cross and penned simple love poems for country swains who hoped to catch the hearts of milkmaids. On the far side, a large brown bear shambled at the end of a chain held by a small black-haired man playing upon a reed pipe.

"'Tis a real beast!" Elizabeth breathed, looking at the lumbering animal with a mixture of apprehension and amazement.

Tarleton grinned at her childlike reaction. "He is old and toothless, and has had all his claws pulled out."

"How cruel!" Elizabeth protested.

"He could still squeeze you to death if he had a mind to, but he's used to being petted and fed on honeyed loaves."

Tarleton selected a spot on the opposite corner, between a stall selling spiced cakes, and one that was doing a brisk trade in trinkets and small household items. "We'll set up here."

"Tarleton, I'm so hungry," said Elizabeth wistfully, smelling the aroma of the cakes so near at hand. "Could we get one of those on credit?"

Tarleton cocked his eyebrow at her. "Credit is what the gentry use to put off their just debts until Judgment Day. There is no credit for poor, honest folk."

Her face turned down with disappointment.

Tarleton held out three pennies. "I trust these will buy you a wealth of spiced cakes, and some cider to wash them down."

"I thought we had no money!" Elizabeth looked into his mischievous eyes. "Oh, Tarleton, you didn't—?"

"Upon my honor—if I had any—I did not steal them. Let this be a lesson to you. Never let anyone know *exactly* how much money you have."

Grinning her thanks, Elizabeth snatched the pennies out of his hand before Tarleton had a chance to reconsider his offer. She bought a half-dozen cakes, studded with nuts and currants, and two brimming jack mugs of tangy cider. Seating herself comfortably on the ground and leaning against the pack bag, she happily regarded the colorful panorama before her.

Tarleton watched Elizabeth with amusement and warm pride. *We'd make a fine team, she and I. We could travel the highways together and—* Abruptly reminding himself of her true identity—and his—he silently cursed his idle fancy.

The sun edged toward noon when Tarleton finally decided the time was ripe for his first performance. Elizabeth helped him dress in his motley. In the glaring brightness of daylight, she saw how shabby his jacket of colored patches really was. Some of the green velvet diamonds were worn down to bare cloth. One red sleeve had a large moth hole in it. His gaudy purple and gold ribbons were badly frayed, and there was a faded wine stain on his soft white collar, which she knew would never come out in a week of washings. Several of his brass bells were missing from his points. To add insult to injury, the whole garment smelled foul.

I shall order a new motley for Tarleton when we get to court, Elizabeth vowed, as she tied his cap strings under his chin. *And I shall take great pleasure in personally burning this one.*

"Stand in the shade, and mind our pack," Tarleton whispered to her. "At the end of the show, be my gatherer.

Pass your hat among the crowd on your side. Be sure to let no one escape your sweet smile.''

Rattling a tambourine, Tarleton leapt into the center of the dusty square, where he proceeded to enchant the citizenry. He sang rollicking songs and danced his famous jigs. He juggled six colored balls at one time. Cartwheeling and tumbling, his body became a spinning, jingling, colorful blur. His jokes were outrageous, and the swelling crowd loved them, especially jests ridiculing tax collectors and lawyers. He danced a country reel, partnering many pretty, young farm maids and elderly dames alike.

Elizabeth felt a sharp prick of envy. How she wished *she* was the one he twirled in his hands! Watching his easy grace, his flashing smile and the nimble movements of his lithe body, her pulse skittered alarmingly. Every time Tarleton glanced over at her, Elizabeth's heart fluttered in response. *If he were a nobleman, I would—*

The thought froze in her brain. Elizabeth gave herself a shake. Tarleton wasn't the least bit interested in her. Didn't he openly flirt with every woman in sight? Besides, the man was a commoner. The whole idea was utterly ridiculous!

At the finale of his performance, Tarleton sang ''The Greenwood Tree,'' his rich baritone filling the square. '''Here shall he see/No enemy But winter and rough weather.''' As he sang the last lingering line, he looked directly at Elizabeth, his gaze as soft as a caress.

The very air around her seemed to sparkle. There was a thundering crash in her ears, which was a far cry from the applause that followed his last note. She felt she had been kissed by a white-hot bolt of lightning.

''Your hat, prentice!'' Tarleton's call broke the spell. He worked the crowd on the far side, shaking his tambourine as the coins fell into it. Laughing and flirting, the jester kissed many a blushing maid, and the not-so-innocent housewives, on the cheek.

Pulling herself together, Elizabeth cried, "Come, what say you for my master, Tarleton?" Holding out her cap, she waded into the nearest clutch of people, catching their silver tribute.

Tarleton jingled up to her, his face shiny with perspiration, and the tambourine full.

"We shall dine well this night, Robin Redbreast!" he chortled. "Come, help me out of this jacket, and we shall drink to our newfound fortune."

With trembling fingers, Elizabeth drew off his motley. She was afraid to look into his eyes. Did Tarleton feel the same flash of sensation when he looked at her?

"My throat is as parched as a preacher on Sunday." Tarleton ruffled his hair. "'Tis time we sample Mistress Bess's brew."

Elizabeth swallowed her disappointment. Her magic glow evaporated. It was only her imagination playing tricks in the noonday sun.

The beer-seller's wife was in a jovial mood, having liberally sampled some of her husband's wares. She eagerly shared the bits and pieces of the news she had already heard that morning. There was no report of any traveler being set upon by thieves, but only the hanging of some poor fellow in Warwickshire for beating his wife and mother-in-law to death.

Sipping her beer, Elizabeth shuddered quietly as she listened to the gruesome tale. Why did so many people take such pleasure in recounting others' pain, she wondered.

Spying Elizabeth's reaction, Tarleton flashed a broad smile at the beer seller. "Come now, Mistress Johnson. Surely you have a more amusing tale to tell." He thumped his mug for another round.

"Aye, Tarleton, though ye must promise not to steal my story for your own." Bess liberally poured him more beer from her large brown pitcher. "'Tis mine to tell, and that's the long and the short of it."

"What fine bit of gossip have you?" Tarleton grinned encouragingly.

Mistress Bess drew herself up importantly. "Marry, have ye heard of the runaway wife?"

Elizabeth almost choked on her drink, though she covered her dismay by lapsing into a coughing fit.

Tarleton's mischievous brown eyes opened wide. "Prithee, what is so interesting about this runaway wife?"

"Why, in faith, she is some grand lady from near Kenilworth. 'Tis said she left Sir Robert La Faye a-standing at the altar, calling him a rogue and a devil. It so scandalized the curate, that the poor man fell stone dead on the spot. But she, headstrong lass! She set not a fig for it, but she leapt over the body, and ran out of the church, whereupon she jumped on Sir Robert's huge black charger—astride, mind you—and away she rode."

"Such a lady of spirit!," Tarleton murmured. "And have they discovered where she went?" He noted with approval that Elizabeth managed to look interested without blushing.

"But no! You have not heard the whole telling of my story! The lady was met by her secret lover, a Scottish lord, they say. He whisked her up in his great coach and four and they made for the border, where they might be married at Gretna Green afore Sir Robert could find them. But he—Sir Robert, that is—he has set out after them, and 'tis said they have gone to ground near Sherwood Forest, just as Robin Hood and Maid Marian did of old. Now, what think you of that?"

Throwing back his head, Tarleton laughed richly. " 'Tis a worthy tale, and I'll not steal it. You do a better piece of work on it than I ever could. Here is for your fine beer, and for your fine story!" He handed Mistress Johnson four pennies.

She dimpled at him with gap-tooth pleasure. "You are a real gentleman, Master Tarleton, and there's no mistake!"

"Come, Robin, we have more work in hand. Ye cannot be listening to stories all day!" Tarleton snapped his fingers at Elizabeth.

"How your tale has grown!" Elizabeth marveled, running to keep up with him.

"Aye, Goodwife Fletcher did her work well, much better than I expected." Tarleton chuckled. "I hope, by tomorrow, we shall learn that the lady and her lover have crossed the border. It would be true justice if Sir Robert chased after them, and was met by the reavers."

"Who are they?" Elizabeth asked.

"Bandits of ill repute, who steal good English cattle and sell them for even better Scottish prices," Tarleton informed her.

Elizabeth smiled slowly at the thought. "And what would they do to Sir Robert, if they captured him?"

"Strip him of his clothes and money, then tie him backward on a goat, and send him on his way—if he is lucky. In any event, he must be miles from here. Come, Robin! We burn daylight! There is more money to be made!"

The afternoon's performance drew an even larger crowd, some of whom returned to see the Queen's jester a second time. As before, Tarleton capered, danced, juggled, told bawdy jokes and sang suggestive songs, all of which pleased the throng. Again he directed the last line of "The Greenwood Tree" to his apprentice.

Elizabeth's cheeks colored under the heat of his gaze. A tumble of confused thoughts and feelings assailed her, though outwardly she pretended not to notice his favor. This strange aching she felt for the Queen's favorite player bewildered her. Her common sense reminded her that she must not allow herself to fall under his spell. She was a lady, destined for a "good match," if not to the odious Sir Robert, then to some other lord. Tarleton's path led down the byways of England with merry disregard for dowries and marriage portions. Indeed, considering his past behavior, Tarleton had a merry disregard for marriage altogether.

And yet—

I would marry him, Elizabeth realized with a sudden fearful clarity, as she watched him flash his elfin smile at a shy little maid of ten. If Tarleton ever said, "Come away with me and we will wander the world together," Elizabeth knew deep in her heart, that all her sensible thoughts would disappear like an April shower.

"Ho, prentice!" Tarleton called to her. "Instead of gathering wool, gather pennies!"

Dragging herself roughly out of her daydream, Elizabeth moved among the crowd, holding out her hat as the silver pieces rained into it. The good nuns, who had taught her so carefully in France, would be shocked to the core if they could see her now. Surprisingly, Elizabeth found she didn't care a groat's worth. Here, in the warm afternoon sun of a late summer day, she could almost forget why she had started out on this improbable adventure. Sir Robert La Faye was as far from her care as Scotland, where, she fervently hoped, that vile lord might be even now riding his own goat, preferably backward.

"How now, Robin Redbreast?" Tarleton asked, pulling off his motley jacket and raking his fingers through his damp hair.

"Didn't we do well!" Elizabeth giggled as she began adding up the pile of groats, farthings, pennies and half-pennies.

Tarleton watched her, a smile playing over his lips. "Give you another week on the road, prentice, and you'll be able to estimate the take by the size of the crowd!" Then his face darkened as if a cloud blocked out the sun. "But I forget. In another week, the chill winds of autumn will be here, and you will be sitting in front of a roaring fire at Hampton Court."

"I pray we get there safely," she whispered, though her heart was not as eager as her voice.

"Amen to that," Tarleton answered gruffly. Then he cleared his throat. "By the looks of our goodly fortune, we shall be able to buy a fine dinner and a bed for the night, even after paying that shag-eared bailiff!"

"A bed?" Jesu! When had she last slept in a proper bed?

Tarleton grinned down at her surprised expression. "Yes, a bed, Robin Redbreast. I am sure you have heard of a bed before? Fine lords and ladies often sleep in them, I'm told. Of course, if you prefer a ticklish haystack, we could—"

"No, no!" Elizabeth stopped his banter with a giggle. "I would not deny you the pleasure of a bed!"

But I must deny myself the pleasures of sharing it with you the way I would wish, he thought bitterly. Tarleton roundly cursed the noble lord who would someday lay claim to Lady Elizabeth.

"Do you need some of my money?" Elizabeth started to reach for her bag, hidden under her shirt and vest.

Tarleton stayed her hand, holding her fingers for an extra moment. "Nay! That's not to be touched! We've earned enough here. Let us enjoy the rest of the fair before the sun sinks too low!"

While Tarleton went off to pay his debt to the bailiff, Elizabeth watched the great old bear dance one more time. A young couple strolled past her, the boy's arm about the girl's waist. He dangled a bunch of brightly colored ribbons before the girl's delighted eyes.

"For your wedding dress," the boy murmured, nuzzling her ear. "To tie into many love knots, for I love you many times over."

The girl blushed and laughed softly.

Elizabeth swallowed a hard lump in her throat. *Why can't I look forward to my wedding day as happily as she? I'm only chattel ready to be sold to the highest bidder! Will I never taste love like those two simple souls?*

"What a sad look of longing!" Tarleton's deep voice broke into her thoughts. "Here's something for you then." Reaching into his pouch, Tarleton pulled out a round object.

"A ball?" Elizabeth asked incredulously. Tarleton was carrying her disguise a little too far. "I think I am too old to play with a ball!"

Tarleton feigned a hurt look. Tossing the ball up in the air, he caught it with a quick flick of his wrist.

"Ah, well," he said with an exaggerated sigh. "Perhaps not. I wonder if that bear over there would be interested in my soap. No doubt, he'd try to eat it and—"

"Soap?" Elizabeth could scarcely believe her ears. "Oh, please, Tarleton! Is it truly soap?"

"I thought you said you were too old for a ball." He grinned, wiggling his brows playfully at her.

"It depends what the ball is made of," she answered pertly.

"Then you have learned another valuable lesson, prentice. Never be too quick to judge a thing by its outward appearance. Here." Tossing it lightly to her, he seemed pleasantly surprised when she caught it.

Soap! Her fingers caressed its waxy contours. She inhaled its sweet lavender fragrance—a lady's soap. She smiled shyly at Tarleton.

"Thank you, Dickon," she whispered, hoping he wouldn't mind her using his real name.

Tarleton cupped her chin between his thumb and fingers. For a moment, he looked as if he were going to bend down and kiss her on the lips. Her heart beat hopefully at the thought. She rose on tiptoe, not realizing that she had moistened her lips in expectation. He paused, as if he remembered something. Giving her a tight smile, he tapped her gently on the cheek.

"Take the pack, boy," he said hoarsely. " 'Tis time we find an inn before all the rooms have been taken."

As he turned away from her, Elizabeth felt as if she had been dropped from a high wall. Something had happened between them just now, but she wasn't sure what it was.

Within the half hour, Tarleton engaged a dormer room at The White Swan, a large, friendly inn off the highroad. Though the room was small, it had the advantage of privacy. There was only space for a single bed and a small table. For an extra halfpenny, one of the serving girls brought a bowl and a large pitcher of hot water. Giggling in sheer delight, Elizabeth rolled up her sleeves and gave herself over to the pure pleasure of washing her hair.

Tarleton sat on the bed, watching her. "I could have made a full bath and shaved with that water," he mused. "You have managed to use it all up in ten minutes." He tossed her the thin hucktoweling that the wench had also provided.

"Ah, but it was worth it." Elizabeth sighed, rubbing her head vigorously. "My hair was full of hay and dust."

She propped Tarleton's piece of mirror up against the pitcher, and regarded herself as she combed out the shining bob. Bending closer to the mirror, she rubbed her nose.

"By the book, I'm turning to freckles! And look how brown I've become! I shall stand out at court among all the ladies."

"You look healthy!" Tarleton snorted. "All those fine ladies at court cover themselves with a white paste. It makes them look like painted dolls."

"Even the Queen?" Elizabeth grinned wickedly over her shoulder.

"Especially the Queen, but don't you dare tell her I said so. In the mood she has been in these past few months, she'd have my head grinning from Tower Bridge!"

She would have my brains stewed and served up as a dog's breakfast if Her Majesty knew what thoughts I am having about her bewitching goddaughter, Tarleton added to himself.

Elizabeth, her toilette completed to the best of her ability, stood up and shook out her waistcoat before slipping it back on. She glanced at Tarleton through her lashes. Good Lord! He looked far too at home, stretched out on her bed.

"Tarleton, I have a question," she began, pretending to look again in the mirror so that he would not see the blush she knew stained her cheeks.

"What is your question this time, chuck?"

"There is only one bed. Where do you intend to sleep tonight?"

Tarleton pressed his lips tightly together to keep from blurting out the truth: *I wish to sleep in your arms tonight.* Instead, he stood up and smoothed the coverlet. Her simple question hurt him. She had slept in his arms before, what was the difference now? But he knew there *was* a difference. This afternoon, he had come far too close to kissing her.

"I will lie on the floor at your feet, my lady, like a good guard dog should," he answered coolly.

Elizabeth bit her lip when she realized she had offended him. "There is no need, Tarleton," she answered stiffly. "You bought and paid for it, the bed is yours. I shall make do with a pillow and my cloak on the floor."

He stared at her for a moment, his eyes glowing darkly in the gloaming of the twilight.

"So be it," he snapped. Then he opened the door and hurled himself down the narrow stairs.

"Tarleton where are you going?"

"To supper. If you wish, you may follow along, prentice boy!" he growled as he turned on the landing.

Elizabeth shut the door behind her with a bang and stomped after him. *Just who does he think I am? A doxy whose favors he can buy with soap, hot water and the promise of a night in a real bed?*

Yet, oddly enough, Elizabeth found herself wishing Tarleton *would* forget her noble birth, just once.

Chapter Nine

Good-natured clientele, warmed by a day of sunshine, profitable business and pleasure, filled the noisy taproom of The White Swan. Huge bowls of savory stew, trenchers of bread and assorted mugs of ale and beer covered the long, rough-hewn tables. The three serving girls and the tap boy ran back and forth under the scolding tongue of the hostess and the vigilant eye of the host. Many of the company were travelers from other parts of England, who had come to trade at the fair. A smattering of foreigners clustered in pockets among the gathering.

In a small corner booth away from the fire, Tarleton and Elizabeth ate their meal in silence. If it hadn't been for their sharp words earlier, Elizabeth would have enjoyed the meal spread before them: juicy hunks of beef, a cobbler of stewed apples, crusty wheat bread with a crock of melted cheddar and cool ale. As it was, she ate but tasted nothing: Tarleton's churlish behavior had taken away her appetite.

Whenever one of the serving girls passed by their table, Tarleton chatted warmly with her, pointedly ignoring Elizabeth opposite him. As the evening wore on and he consumed more beer, Tarleton put his arm around one of the wenches, pulling the tittering girl onto his lap, where he openly fondled her to her evident delight.

Keeping her head down, Elizabeth sipped her ale in embarrassed silence. Dimly through the babble round her, she overheard two men in the next booth quietly speaking French. Drawn to her mother's language, Elizabeth listened to their conversation.

"Do you understand their speech?" Tarleton quietly asked.

Elizabeth glanced up at him in surprise. It was the first civil thing he had said to her in nearly two hours. "Of course," she answered archly, trying to look superior. "Though their accent is horrid."

"They're not Frenchmen?" Tarleton's eyes narrowed. It would be of great interest to the Queen's spy master if there were those who pretended to be French when they were not. The Queen's imprisoned cousin, Mary of Scotland, was mustering many secret supporters in the realm who longed to depose Her Grace and put Catholic Mary on England's throne.

"Do they have the accent of a Scot?" Tarleton asked.

"Nay, they are French. What I meant was they are not from Paris," she explained with a show of studied patience.

"Most of the world is not from Paris," Tarleton testily reminded her. "What do they say?"

Elizabeth rolled her eyes. "One of them just remarked that no business can be done by the English without pots of beer to wash it down."

"Typical remark!" Tarleton snorted. "What else?"

Elizabeth suddenly blushed deeply. "They are talking about one of the wenches, the redheaded one."

Tarleton glanced across the room at the girl in question. A lively, pert creature, she looked seventeen in age and twenty-seven in experience.

"They have good taste in women," he observed knowingly. "Tell me what they say of her."

Elizabeth took a deep drink of her ale. "They...they are talking about her breasts, and her...oh, by the stars!"

"Her what?" Tarleton's eyes sparkled wickedly. "Tell me exactly what they say about her breasts and her...other parts."

"Please, Tarleton," Elizabeth begged him quietly. "It's very vulgar."

"Good!" Tarleton taunted. "I'm common enough for some good French vulgarity. Tell what they say of yon wench."

Banging her mug down on the table, Elizabeth glared at him. Her eyes flashed with a dangerous green fire. "I am sure you can understand their meaning, if you listen hard enough. They are not leaving much to the imagination." She slid out of the booth. "As for me, I will not stay here a minute longer, and entertain your shameful whims."

Elizabeth turned on her heel with her head held proudly high, pushed her way through the mob around the bar, then ran outside to the inn's privy. Fortunately, it was deserted. Afterward, she scampered up the stairs to their room. Wrapping herself in her cloak, she knelt by the small window, and gazed up at the stars that sparkled like ice chips in the sky.

"Dear Lord," she whispered. "Why is Tarleton so cruel to me? Please, Lord, deliver me soon to the Queen, and I pray you send me a good, true man to be my loving husband!"

With a heavy sigh, she pillowed her head on the pack and fell quickly into a deep sleep, worn out by the long day's activities.

Tarleton silently watched her through the crack of the door. His heart tightened with self-loathing when he saw her bed down on the rough floor. The rising moon caught her hair in its beams, turning it into a silver halo glowing around her head. Tarleton drew in his breath. Though he had seen this unearthly shine before, it never ceased to amaze him. Recalling her whispered prayer, he cursed himself for each bruising word he had uttered.

Pushing open the door softly, he tiptoed in and knelt by her side. A small crystal tear glistened on her cheek, its mute witness a searing firebrand to his soul. Gently he brushed it away with his fingertip. Scooping up her sleeping form in his arms, Tarleton held her for a moment close to his chest. Stirring slightly in her sleep, Elizabeth snuggled against him, instinctively seeking his warmth.

Though her weight was nothing in his arms, Tarleton trembled as he gazed on the sleeping innocent he held. Fierce waves of love and protection welled up inside him. He wanted to press her tightly against himself, to meld with her for eternity. His heart beat faster as if he had been running for his life. Fighting the natural urges within himself, Tarleton carried her to the bed, where he laid her head gently on the pillow, smoothing the wisps of her hair from her eyes. He covered her with the thick woolen blanket.

"I don't know if you are my salvation or my damnation, sweetling," he whispered into her ear. "If there is a voice that can fly to your heart, hear mine. I have not the strength to fight against the truth any longer. I love thee, Elizabeth Hayward, with every part of my being. I know I can never have thee, and that will be my penance for the life I have led. Be thou an angel to bless or a devil to tempt me, I will love thee forever."

He kissed her lingeringly on her warm, parted lips. In her sleep, Elizabeth softly responded, then she turned on her side. Shaking as if he burned with a fever, Tarleton rolled himself tightly in her cloak. It was still warm from Elizabeth's body, and smelled faintly of lavender soap.

Sleep finally came to Tarleton, relieving his tormenting thoughts.

When Elizabeth awoke the next morning, she was surprised to find herself tucked comfortably in the bed. Sitting up quickly, she looked around for Tarleton. She was alone, though the jumbled cloak on the floor gave evidence of where he had slept. She stretched luxuriously, like a cat in the sun. She felt new made after the first real night's sleep she had since her father's death. An early morning mist hovered over the cobbled streets below her dormer window, but she knew it would burn off soon. Through the ghostly air, a lone church bell rang, calling worshipers to service.

Slipping on her shoes, Elizabeth ran her comb through her hair. Then, wrapping the cloak around her to ward off the morning's chill, she made her way down to the pump in the courtyard. Only a few of the inn's patrons were stirring. Tarleton was nowhere to be seen.

"By my faith, Maude, 'tis the jester's pretty boy!"

Shaking the cold water out of her eyes, Elizabeth saw two of the inn's serving girls appraising her.

"Good morrow, pretty youth!" called Maude, the younger of the two.

The other, the redheaded wench, displayed a knowing grin as she sauntered closer to Elizabeth, who stood rooted to the spot.

"See, Maude? The boy blushes to hear you call him," the redhead teased. "Pray tell us, boy, have you never spoken to a girl before?"

Wiping her face on her sleeve, Elizabeth's mind desperately sought a way out of this latest encounter. God's teeth! Where the devil was Tarleton when she needed him?

"Aye, mistress, I speak often to girls." Elizabeth assumed her best boyish voice. "But never so early in the morning." Elizabeth began walking briskly toward the inn's back door.

The redheaded girl and Maude dashed ahead of her, blocking the way.

"Where are you going so quickly, pretty lad?" the redhead crooned.

Elizabeth licked her lips as she regarded the forward maid.

"I must find my master to wait upon him," Elizabeth replied, looking quickly around for another escape route.

"He is in the taproom at breakfast," Maude informed her shyly.

"We shall let you by if you pay us a forfeit," the redhead teased.

"I fear I have no money about me." Elizabeth backed up a step. Though she was tempted to push both girls into the mud, Elizabeth knew that was *not* how a boy was supposed to act.

"Then a kiss, sweet lad. One each! By my troth, you look to have sweet lips and I've not tasted fresh kisses since midsummer's eve!"

Giggling, the redhead advanced toward Elizabeth, while Maude circled around, cutting off her retreat.

At that moment, Tarleton appeared at the doorway. Taking one look at his apprentice's latest scrape, he chuckled.

"Nay, sweethearts!" he called to the girls, striding into the yard. "Robin is not for the likes of ye!"

Slipping his arms around the girls, Tarleton gave them each a squeeze. "My prentice is for the church," he told them, nibbling the redhead on her ear. "I am to see him safely as far as Oxford, where he will spend his days shut up with heavy books of religion." Grinning impishly, Tarleton wiggled his brows at Elizabeth.

"Don't waste your temptations on fair Robin! But, sweet ducks, please tempt me, for I gave away my soul long ago."

He kissed the redhead lustfully on the mouth, followed by another, more chaste kiss for Maude. His hands crept up from their waists until he held a breast in each, gently playing with them through the thin fabric of their bodices. The girls giggled with pleasure as Tarleton dipped his head, peppering their necks with his kisses.

Swallowing back a tight, hard lump that had crept into her throat, Elizabeth dashed around the threesome to the safety of the cool dark taproom. She tried to eat the cheese, bread and hot ale that the tap boy set before her. She refused to look up when Tarleton sat down on the bench across from her.

"Well, Robin Redbreast, what do you have to say for yourself? It seems I cannot leave you alone for two minutes without you getting into trouble."

"I trust you enjoyed getting me out of my trouble," she muttered into her ale pot. She dared not look up into those dancing eyes of his. She wanted to nurse her anger at him, not fall under his spell like every country maid.

Tarleton chuckled. "A kiss, a tickle—and a penny each."

"Is that all? I am surprised you didn't take . . . take what was so plainly offered, especially from the redheaded wench." Elizabeth tried to sound unconcerned. A mass of conflicting emotions seethed within her.

Tarleton answered softly. "'Twas money that they chiefly wanted—that, and a little kindness. Besides, they were too young for my tastes."

"Oh!" Elizabeth felt her cheeks grow hot, and she was thankful for the dimness of the room. If the redhead was too young for him, so was she. No doubt Tarleton considered Elizabeth only a heartbeat out of the schoolroom. That thought was singularly disappointing!

Abruptly Tarleton stood up. "Finish your breakfast, my lad. The day grows apace and we must be gone."

"Why do you do it?" Walking briskly down the road to Oxford, Elizabeth suddenly blurted out the question.

"Do what?" The jester cocked his head as he regarded the girl by his side. Obviously she had been mulling over something important ever since they left Banbury, but Tarleton hadn't a notion what she meant.

Elizabeth stared straight ahead with a determined set to her chin. "Back there at the inn—at the fair—on the road—

in kitchens. Why did you always kiss and touch serving girls as if they were your..." Her voice trailed off in confusion.

"As if they were my lovers?" Tarleton finished the sentence for her, a smile creeping to the corners of his mouth. Did he detect a little green worm of jealousy sitting on her shoulder?

"Well . . . yes. Everywhere we go, you pay all manner of personal attention to women—to women of all ages." *Except to me!* she wanted to scream.

Tarleton chuckled. "Why not? A kiss, a hug, the feel of a willing wench pressed against me—there's no harm done, only a bit of pleasure. Great Jove, my Lady, you are turning a deep shade of scarlet!" he added with amusement in his voice.

"But how can you love those women? You hardly know them!" Elizabeth protested.

"I tell them I love them, and that is enough. 'Tis all a game. Why? What ails you, Robin Redcheeks?" he asked casually, glancing at her out of the corner of his eye. He could not let her suspect what he truly desired.

"But that's so cruel! You are no better than Sir Robert!" A festering anger rose in her throat.

"Nay, ladybird, Sir Robert is more of a knave, by far," Tarleton said evenly. "He loves your money. I love a merry wench to suit my pleasure—and hers. If I pass her a coin or two for her time and company, at least mine has been an honest bargain. We both know the rules of the game."

"Love should not be so lightly taken nor given," said Elizabeth quietly. "Don't you dream of a wife and family, Tarleton?" Looking up at him, her green eyes were huge.

"My trade keeps me from a home," he replied shortly.

"You could settle down, find a new trade."

"At my age?" He chuckled at the thought. "Nay, I have too much of the wanderlust and love of adventure in me yet. It takes all my time and skill to please the Queen and her subjects. The Queen, especially, is a jealous mistress. She wants her Tarleton's heart to pine only for her."

"And does it?" Elizabeth asked carefully. Why did his answer matter so much to her?

"When I am at court, the Queen is my lodestar and my affection turns only to her. That is true for all her male courtiers. Her Majesty seldom allows wives to stay at Court except on rare occasions. She wants all the attention herself."

"Really?" Elizabeth was surprised. "You mean the court is full of husbands without wives? But that must be very difficult—for the husbands, I mean. And for their poor wives who are left at home."

Tarleton's brown eyes twinkled with mischief. "Oh, it *is!* That's why there are so many short tempers at court, and why there are so many anxious wives in the country. Perhaps you can understand why some of them become like Lady Margaret Fairfax."

Elizabeth shuddered at the recollection. Never would she sink as low as that! "But don't you...? Haven't you ever truly loved someone?"

Tarleton turned away from her. It was so easy to whisper his heartfelt words of love into her sleeping ear. Now, by the day's bright sun, he had to hide the truth, lest it prove the ruin of them both.

"I do love a lady—a very great lady," he finally replied in a guarded manner, "but she is too far above my station. And, she is promised to a wealthy lord of high esteem."

Elizabeth suddenly felt very hollow inside. "Does this lady know you love her?"

"Nay, what good would that do? If I fell on my knee and professed my love, she'd laugh and think I was jesting. Or she would grow angry at my boldness, and banish me forever. I dare not risk that." Tarleton gazed deeply into her eyes. "There are some things, chuck, which are best left unspoken." Let Elizabeth think his tale was true. It was, but not in the telling of it.

"Who is this lady?" Elizabeth could barely voice the question.

"She can be found at court when we get there, but I won't tell you her name, chuck. So don't ask."

Tarleton looked so grim that Elizabeth wished she had not brought the subject up. It was obvious she had hit some raw nerve. She sighed. What would it be like to be loved by Tarleton? It was true he was a rogue, and lived only a little bit within the law, but at least, he was honest about his character. Elizabeth knew in her heart that if he ever loved truly, his passion would be deep and abiding.

"Are you tired?" Tarleton asked, hearing her sigh.

Angry at herself for giving in to wishful thinking, Elizabeth tossed her head. "I am no simpering fine lady in silks and satins, Master Jester. I can walk as far as you can, and as well as you can. If you are not tired, then neither am I. And I am most anxious to reach my destination." She skipped a few steps ahead to prove her point.

Tarleton hid his amusement at her show of spirit. "Very well then, prentice. We'll walk another hour—or two."

In the midafternoon, they passed by a large stone gateway, marking the entrance to a manor estate. The house itself was hidden from view by a long avenue of oak and conifer trees. Elizabeth was surprised when Tarleton hurried past it, his eyes averted.

"Tarleton, wait!" She stopped before the imposing stone lions that guarded the portals.

"What?" He looked over his shoulder at her. "Don't tarry there, prentice, or they will set the hounds upon you."

"This looks like a goodly place to spend the night. We could go round to the kitchen like we did before, and perhaps the master of the house—"

Tarleton didn't allow her to finish. Grabbing her by the arm, he nearly jerked her off her feet as he pulled her away from the gate.

"The master of this house is a white-livered dog!" he hissed. "And I'll be damned to the lowest circle of hell if I cast my shadow across his threshold!" Tarleton's eyes darkened alarmingly. Under his tan, his face grew white with anger; his mouth was tight and grim. He strode quickly down the highway, dragging Elizabeth behind him. His fingers bit painfully into her arm.

"Let go of me!" she panted. "You are hurting me!" As if she had suddenly caught fire, he released her, though he did not stop. "Tarleton, please wait!"

At the crest of the hill, he finally drew to a halt and waited for her to catch up. Below them, the manor house nestled in the crook of the valley. Its many mullioned windows sparkled like the facets of a diamond in the rays of the afternoon sun. Tarleton stared at the place as if he could will its instant destruction.

"What is it? I didn't know—"

"You couldn't know," Tarleton spoke quietly, his voice coming from a dark cavern deep inside him

"You've been there before?" she whispered

Tarleton glared at her with a blood-chilling eye. "Been there? Aye, my fine lady! I was raised in its kitchen!" He laughed bitterly

"*That's* where you were born?" Elizabeth stared at the grand building incredulously.

Tarleton bared his teeth "Nay, have you forgotten my story already? I was born somewhere along this road. For all I know, we could be standing on the very spot."

Elizabeth looked around at the countryside. It seemed inviting and pleasant enough in the warm sunshine, but what had it looked like to Tarleton's young mother as she struggled in a frosty ditch, suffering alone the pains of childbirth? Elizabeth shuddered.

"I'm sorry," she whispered, placing her hand in his.

Visibly softening under her gentle pressure, Tarleton's thunderous eyes cleared when he looked down at her. "'Twas long ago, chuck," he whispered hoarsely.

"Then the master of the house took you in?" Elizabeth prodded.

"He had little choice." Tarleton snorted. "When he discovered me mewling by the kitchen fireside, he was of a mind to toss me out with the slops, but the local curate told him it was his Christian duty to keep me. Christian duty! Ha! At the age of five I was tending the pigs." Tarleton's lips curled back with distaste. "Have you ever met a pig? Mean-spirited, devil-ridden beasts. They terrified me. They bit me more than once. I think the good master of the house hoped the pigs would make a dinner of me, instead of the other way around!"

"The master?" Elizabeth arched her eyebrow. "I think you mean your father," she added quietly.

Tarleton's eyes widened at her perception, then he nodded. "Aye. Richard, Earl of Fawkland, indeed sired me. The biggest jest is that I am his only surviving child. Three wives, innumerable mistresses, God knows how many children, and only I lived to adulthood. That grand house down tnere, Breden Hall, should have been mine someday, but my... father did not see fit to make an honest woman of my mother." He laughed mirthlessly.

"Because she was his servant," Elizabeth murmured understandingly

Tarleton nodded. ' And she was reputed to be a Gypsy. The master claimed she bewitched him with a love potion. That was his excuse to turn her out when he discovered my impending debut. He made my childhood a merry hell in payment!'

It wrung Elizabeth's heart to hear the pain in Tarleton's voice. She laid her head against his shoulder. "That frightened little boy grew up to become a very brave man."

Elizabeth's soft voice and gentle touch acted as a sooth-ing oil poured over the open raw wounds of Tarleton's soul. All the poisonous pent-up anger of the years drained away from him, as he recounted his story for the first time.

He put his arm around Elizabeth, drawing her closer to him. "I wasn't as brave as you may think. I ran away—of-ten. Each time, I was caught by one of the gamekeepers and brought back, trussed up like a maddened dog. Aye, and beaten well for it, too. When I was twelve years, I set out on my own."

"Twelve?" Elizabeth gasped. "Like I—"

"I was the guttersnipe you only pretend to be, and I tell you truly, sweetling, you lead the life of a prince compared to me."

Elizabeth squeezed his hand and tried to think of some-thing comforting to say. "Your mother must have been very pretty and had a sweet temperament," she observed after a short silence. "For you have survived a harsh life with no marks of cruelty upon you, and everyone finds you . . . very pleasing to look upon." She cleared her throat as his hand closed warmly around her own.

"There are marks, Elizabeth," he said huskily, "but I keep them hidden. I thank you for your kind words about my mother. Though I never knew her, it pleases me to think well of her."

"I never knew my mother, either," Elizabeth said gently. "She died of a fever when I was quite young. My father of-ten told me that I resembled her."

"Then she must have been very beautiful, indeed." Rais-ing her hand to his lips, he kissed it fervently.

Elizabeth blushed at his compliment, but she did not pull her hand away from his. The print of his warm lips burned on her skin.

Tarleton cleared his throat. Any moment now he might confess his love for her. If he read the signs correctly, Elizabeth was more than half in love with him. It wouldn't take too much to push her over the edge.

"Hungry, chuck?" he asked abruptly. When she nodded, he withdrew his hand from her gentle fingers. "Then we are in luck, for over there I spy a thick bramble of bushes loaded down with blackberries. They will go right well with our bread and cheese. So let us pick a capful or two."

Laughing happily, Elizabeth plunged into the thicket. Soon she was stuffing more blackberries into her mouth than in her hat.

Tarleton, his black mood lifted by Elizabeth's loving spirit, grinned as he joined her.

They spent the night in another friendly haystack, Elizabeth nestled once again in Tarleton's protective arms. She awakened just after midnight, whimpering from a nightmare.

"There, there, chuck," Tarleton said drowsily. "'Tis only a dream." He held the trembling girl tightly, stroking her cheek with the edge of his thumb.

"I dreamt of him—that man." She shivered.

"What man, sweetling?" Tarleton murmured.

"The one who tried to...kill you." Gulping down a sob, she buried her face in Tarleton's vest. His heart beat in a steady, comforting rhythm under his shirt. "We were back in that church, and I tried to knock him out but he didn't fall! Instead he started walking toward me, pointing his finger at me and saying he was going to murder me. He just kept coming at me, and I couldn't move. I wanted to run, but I couldn't. And I couldn't find you!"

Tarleton continued to smooth the worry lines from her soft face, wishing he could kiss her fears away. Elizabeth was not used to the violence Tarleton had known since childhood. How long would this specter haunt her dreams?

"Try to put him out of your mind, sweetling," he whispered.

"But we just left him lying there. Suppose he died! I'd be a…an accomplice to murder! And you? Oh, sweet Dickon, they would hang you!" Elizabeth's tears renewed. "I shall burn in hell for it," she whispered fearfully. "I am not sorry for what you did. Indeed, I would have done it myself, had I the strength. That's a very wicked thought, isn't it?"

Tarleton brushed his lips lightly through her silky hair. "There are a lot more evil people in hell already, Elizabeth. The devil has no time for the likes of you."

"Truly?" She looked up at him; her eyes were huge and moist in the darkness of the night.

Tarleton's throat tightened. "Truly, my dove, now go to sleep for we still have a long way to go before the end of our journey."

Comforted by his words and the warmth of his embrace, Elizabeth soon drifted back to sleep. Cradling her tenderly, Tarleton looked up at the stars twinkling through the loose covering of straw. Of all the women he had known in his life—and admittedly there were a great many whose names and faces ran together—why was he so shaken by this fragile blossom from a noble family tree? She belonged in a tapestry, seated under a spreading oak, with the mysterious white unicorn bowing at her feet. Elizabeth was brave and kind and so innocent. Yet she had stolen Tarleton's heart when he wasn't looking.

He lay awake a long time, musing over the Fates who had cast Elizabeth into his life.

Chapter Ten

The next morning dawned warm and very humid.

"Odd weather for this late in August," Tarleton remarked, stretching and brushing off the hay that had crept down his collar. "First, 'tis cool and the leaves begin to turn, now this!"

Elizabeth ran her fingers through her hair, pulling out the prickly hay. She wriggled her shoulders "Ugh! I feel itchy all over!" What she desperately wanted was a bath. It seemed like a lifetime ago when she last had a proper one.

Taking her by the hand, Tarleton pulled her out of the haystack. "Come, ladybird! Let us be off before the good farmer finds us in his field. We'll look for a brook or a pump along the way where we can wash."

By late morning, sticky perspiration rolled down Elizabeth's face in great droplets. The sky had a sickly cast about it, and the still air was hung thick with heat and moisture. Elizabeth was relieved when the road ducked into a shaded wood.

"Listen!" Putting the pack down in the middle of the road, Tarleton cocked his head.

"Horsemen?" Elizabeth looked down the empty byway apprehensively. Were Sir Robert's men still searching for her?

"Nay, chuck!" Tarleton's mouth curled into an elfin grin.

" 'Tis a pleasing sound, a cooling sound, a watery sound!''

Turning off the track, he plunged through the brambles, Elizabeth close at his heels. She, too, heard the unmistakable bubbling sounds of a river.

The bright clear water tumbled over smooth stones as it wove its merry way to the south. Though the river was not wide, it was deep in places and its current ran along swiftly. Graceful weeping willows hung over the bank, their branches delicately trailing in the crystal water. Just where the stream curved away, a small clearing of meadow grass beckoned.

Throwing his pack and cap to the ground, Tarleton stretched out over the bank and splashed the refreshing water onto his face.

Elizabeth was quick to follow suit. The cool river ran deliciously through her fingers. Cupping her hands, she laved her hot skin.

''Perchance I could borrow a bit of your sweet soap?'' Pulling out his dagger, Tarleton tested its edge with his thumb. ''My face is in sore need of a scraping.''

''Of course.'' Elizabeth wiped the water out of her eyes. ''It's in the pack.'' Pulling off her shoes and stockings, she dipped her burning feet in the rushing stream. The icy water massaged her soles like a thousand little fingers.

Whistling to himself, Tarleton stripped off his jerkin, then pulled his shirt over his head. Gazing at his muscular chest covered with curly brown hair, Elizabeth felt her cheeks grow warm. The only times she had seen him with his shirt off was at their first memorable meeting, and that night when she found him with Peg. On both occasions, she had been too overwrought to take much notice of Tarleton's finely shaped form. Now secretly watching him on this sun-dappled day, she was forced to admit that Tarleton was even more handsome than she imagined. Her fingers ached to touch his broad shoulders and feel the muscles that rippled beneath his skin.

Elizabeth's heart pounded an erratic rhythm. A wave of light-headedness washed over her. Wrenching her gaze from him, she lay back, looking innocently up at the sky, waiting until her quickened pulse had quieted.

Unmindful of his appreciative audience, Tarleton again lay down by the river's edge, this time dipping his whole head into the water. Shaking out his brown curls with a cheerful whoop, he began to lather up his face with the soap. Turning his back to Elizabeth, Tarleton propped his piece of mirror against the bole of the nearby willow. Still whistling, he applied the dagger's edge and his concentration to his shaving.

Elizabeth listened to his cheerful music as she idlly watched the waving tree branches that framed the small patch of sky above her. *I'd be cheerful too, if I could doff my clothes and take a dip in this cool water. I wonder if—*

Excited by this tempting possibility, Elizabeth sat up and glanced at her companion. "Tarleton, I would like to..." The rest of her words died on her lips. She choked back a cry of distress.

"What is it?" Tarleton, his face half-lathered, spun around, his dagger now poised for defense. A small trickle of blood ran down his cheek where he had nicked himself.

Her hands covering her mouth and her eyes filling with tears, Elizabeth could only mutely shake her head.

"What ails you, sweetling?" he asked tenderly. Elizabeth was obviously upset over something, yet the forest seemed peaceful enough with only the occasional rook's call and the babbling of the river. "Did you brush against a clump of stinging nettles?"

Her gorge rose in her throat. "What happened to your back?"

Tarleton's lips pressed tightly together. Turning again to the mirror, he observed her carefully in its reflection as he quickly finished his shaving. The horrified look in her deep green eyes was more than he could bear.

"It happened a long time ago," he muttered grimly. He saw her creep forward, her gaze riveted to the shame that was written into his flesh.

Thick, long scars crisscrossed his shoulders and snaked down the length of his spine, disappearing below the waistband of his breeches. The ugly welts stood out white against the golden tan of his skin. Elizabeth shuddered involuntarily.

"You were beaten like this for running away?" she barely whispered.

"Nay." Tarleton paused while he ran the dagger up the side of his throat. He wiped off the soap on his thigh. "They only beat me with a birch rod then. These marks were made with a whip." He stared at her in the glass, waiting tensely to see her reaction.

Elizabeth paled and bit her knuckles to stifle another cry. "Who? Why?" She tried to blink back her tears.

Tarleton snorted. "The law-abiding bailiffs of Abington, that's who." Turning, he studied her intently. His eyes dulled to a muddy brown. "Didn't I mention that you were in the company and protection of a known felon? Does that shock you, Lady Elizabeth?" He steeled himself for her revulsion.

Swallowing the hard lump that had risen in her throat, Elizabeth spoke softly. "No one would beat a horse or a dog as cruelly as that. What offense was it?"

Releasing his breath slowly, Tarleton dared to hope that he heard nothing but sweet compassion in her voice.

"Vagrancy, my lady. For performing in a public place without a license. I was near sixteen then, and knew nothing of letters patent. All I knew was how to toss three balls in the air, how to pipe a pleasing tune, and how to tell a good story."

"This is against the law?" Elizabeth's chin trembled.

"Aye, Lady Elizabeth, if a player has no master. 'Tis a law enacted by our good Parliament in 1572 called the Act for the Punishment of Vagabonds. 'Tis now engraved upon my brain, as well as on my back. I was tried before some wizened old justice who never laughed a day in his life. Do you know what the prescribed punishment is for a first offence?''

Elizabeth could only mutely shake her head. How young he must have looked at sixteen!

Tarleton's cold eyes bored into her. "The act states that a convicted player should be stripped, grievously whipped and burnt through the gristle of the right ear.''

Elizabeth felt weak in her knees. A wave of nausea swept over her.

Tarleton continued stoically. "For adults, 'tis twelve lashes, for children, only six.''

"Children are punished, too?" Elizabeth's stifled tears rolled unchecked down her cheeks.

"Aye." Tarleton wanted to reach out and wipe them away, but he resisted the impulse. No doubt she would loathe his touch. Curling his fingers into a tight ball, he dug his nails into his palm.

"I was judged as an adult so I received twelve stripes. I fainted before the rest of the sentence could be carried out. The constable must have had some spark of kindness in him. He let me go without setting a hot poker through my ear.''

"Did the constable take care of you?" Elizabeth could only imagine the bloody mess Tarleton must have looked. She shuddered.

Tarleton shook his head. "Nay. He turned me loose. I fainted again by the side of the road, and remember nothing until I awoke and found myself—in a convent!''

"A convent?''

"Aye!" Tarleton laughed wryly at her surprise. "Oh, not a Catholic one, to be sure. Once it had been a nunnery. Now 'tis a home for pious women who pray a good deal and tend the sick. Someone found me and brought me to them. 'Tis thanks to their healing arts that I am alive and can still tumble cartwheels today.''

Elizabeth said nothing. Circling around Tarleton, she looked again at the brutal marks of the Queen's justice upon her most favorite jester. Hesitantly she ran her finger along the ridge of a scar. She felt him stiffen at her touch.

"Oh, I'm sorry! Do they hurt still?" she asked fearfully.

"Nay, ladybird," he said thickly. He was on fire.

"I meant no harm," she continued, stroking him lightly. She could tell the cuts had been deep.

He sucked in his breath sharply. "My Lady Elizabeth, you are tormenting me more now than any lashing could do." His voice took on a steely edge. "Please remove your hand and do not presume to touch me again!"

Digging his nails deeper into his palms, Tarleton fought down the shocks of fire and ice that sang through his blood at each soft caress. Beads of sweat stood out on his forehead as he forced back his aching need. He felt himself grow hard and tight as flames raged in his loins.

Stung by his rebuff, Elizabeth backed away, brusquely wiping her tears on her sleeve. Only moments before, she had nearly pressed her lips against the vile marks. What had she done to unleash his sudden anger?

Kneeling down by the bank, Tarleton splashed more water on his burning face. He didn't trust himself to look at her.

Elizabeth squared her shoulders. If Tarleton wanted to be angry, so be it. But it was not fair to turn on her because she was born of a noble family and would never be lashed in the street. "If you are finished with the soap, Tarleton, I would like to use it. I intend to take a bath!" she announced, pleased at how nonchalant she sounded.

Jerking his head up, Tarleton blinked at her through droplets of water.

"A bath?" he echoed as if he hadn't understood what she said.

"Aye," she replied evenly. "A bath. The day is hot, and I am filthy. My hair is a mat of dust and straw, my skin itches all over. I intend to take a bath, Tarleton! I expect you to sit over there—" she pointed to a place under an oak ten yards into the forest "—and watch to make sure I am not disturbed. You are not to watch *me*. Do you mark my words?"

"Perfectly, my lady." His expression clouded with anger. A bath? Damn the minx! Didn't she realize what she had done to him already? Now she intended to take off her clothes, while he was supposed to remain calm and not look?

Tarleton tossed her the ball of soap. Elizabeth deftly caught it, even though it was slippery.

He glowered at her, then turned away. Two could play this scene. "With your kind permission, my lady, I too shall bathe," he continued. *I need to drown myself.*

"What?" Elizabeth's eyes flashed emerald sparks.

"Your honor will be protected, my lady." Tarleton yanked off his shoes and stockings. "If I recall, you are paying me right well to do so. Go around the bend over there, and you may soak yourself to your heart's content. You will be safe from all prying eyes, especially mine. I will swim here. I trust I will be safe from your curiosity." He looked at her with a sardonic lift of his eyebrow, which sent her temper soaring.

Turning on her heel, Elizabeth disappeared behind a thick clump of holly bushes.

"Can you swim?" he called after her.

"I don't intend to swim." Her answer shot back through the waxy green leaves. "The good nuns in France did not seem to think swimming was part of a proper lady's education."

"Stay near the bank," Tarleton warned her. "Don't step anywhere unless you can see the bottom. Do you hear me?"

"Go soak your head," was her reply. A passing rook echoed her words.

Tarleton ground his teeth as he pulled off his breeches. Splashing noisily into the water, he plunged headfirst into the deeper middle channel. The icy coldness quickly cooled his heated ardor, though her seductive image still throbbed in his brain.

Around the bend, Elizabeth heard him splashing about, making a great deal of noise. Banishing the knave from her thoughts, she unlaced the waistcoat and pulled off her shirt. The warm air kissed her bare skin, making her feel delightfully free—and a little wanton. Lifting the small money pouch from around her neck, she stuffed it into one of the pockets of her breeches before wiggling out of them. Clutching her precious soap, Elizabeth stepped gingerly into the river.

Its icy chill brought goose bumps to her skin. For the first few moments, her toes felt numb. Easing herself a little deeper into the water, she tingled with pleasure as the current swirled around her. Cocking her head, she distinctly heard Tarleton's noisy ablutions. He sang a ribald song; its earthy lyrics hung clearly in the heavy air. Obviously he was trying to annoy her. Ignoring his rich baritone, Elizabeth crouched down, allowing the water to flow over her shoulders. Holding her breath, she ducked her head.

Once her hair was thoroughly wet, Elizabeth worked the soap through it, reveling in the sweet lavender smell. Rinsing, she experienced pure pleasure as the lather washed away downstream. Snaking the water out of her eyes, she listened again to Tarleton. His distant song continued its vulgar pace. Wrinkling her nose at the content of the lyrics, she soaped up the rest of herself.

The warm air, cold water and the scent of lavender surrounding her were sinfully delicious. Her skin and spirits felt renewed, fresh and invigorated. The lavender fragrance clung to her skin and hair, making her feel more like a woman instead of a grimy street urchin. Looking with disdain at her filthy, wretched clothes on the bank, Elizabeth wished she could wash them, as well, but she realized it would take the rest of the day to dry them out. She hated the thought of putting them on again. Swaying with the current, she closed her eyes, basking in the warmth of the sun.

Dreaming of the clean clothes she would wear at Hampton Court, Elizabeth allowed herself to drift a little farther downstream. This day was such a nice one, after all, despite the fact that Tarleton was out of sorts again. Tarleton! Elizabeth could not stop herself from thinking of him: he was such a puzzle. One minute he was kind, even tender. The next he was rough and coarse, acting like a randy rooster. Which one was the *real* Tarleton?

Lost in her musings, Elizabeth stepped forward to steady herself against the pull of the current. To her horror, she discovered there was nothing underfoot. Before she could find the shallows, she was swept underwater.

Chapter Eleven

For one terrifying moment, Elizabeth froze. Then, kicking and thrashing blindly, she rose to the surface of the swirling, rushing river. She screamed as the current pulled her under a second time. *I am going to die!* The thought wrapped itself icily around her heart. Fighting against the surge, she bobbed to the surface again. Once more, the waters closed over her.

Something wrapped itself around her waist. Though she could not see what it was, Elizabeth remembered the long, drooping willows. She twisted and beat against their entangling branches. She felt herself being pulled up into the air.

"I've got you!" Tarleton's voice was close to her ear.

Panicked, Elizabeth knew he was dragging her down. Trying to break free, she dug her nails into his arm, which gripped her tightly around her middle.

"Calm down, Elizabeth!" he yelled at her.

Not heeding him, she struggled to draw a clean breath of air.

"Stop kicking, or you'll drown us both!" Tarleton growled.

Something hard thumped her on the back of her head; the water and sky spun in a rainbow whirligig. Her limbs felt heavy and refused her command. She closed her eyes, too spent to fight whatever was happening to her. *If this is death, be swift,* Elizabeth prayed. Then everything went black.

Please, God, don't let her die! Tarleton pulled Elizabeth's still body onto the grassy bank. Scrambling to her side, he pressed down on her back with his strong hands, willing the life force back into her. His lips uttered a heartfelt prayer.

Coughing, Elizabeth spewed out a small gush of water. With a cry of relief, Tarleton kneaded her back harder as her eyelids fluttered open. She gasped raggedly for air.

As the color seeped slowly back into her pale cheeks, Tarleton felt his own tears fill his eyes. "All's well, sweetling," he crooned, pushing her hair out of her face.

Coughing again, Elizabeth tried to pull herself into a sitting position. Her body trembled with the shock of her terrifying experience.

"C-cold." Her teeth chattered.

Tarleton bounded to the pack and pulled out her warm cloak. Gathering her into his arms, he held her snugly against him, rocking her gently. "Just breathe quietly, sweet dove. Lean against me. You are safe now."

Elizabeth gulped the humid air. Closing her eyes, she tilted back against his warm chest. She could feel his heart racing. "Head hurts," she mumbled.

Tarleton chuckled softly. "Forgive me, ladybird. I gave you a small tap to quiet you."

Elizabeth's eyes flew open. "You...you hit me? How dare you!" she sputtered, then fell into a coughing fit.

Smiling, Tarleton turned her over and thumped her soundly between her shoulder blades. "Would you have preferred it if I let you float down to Oxford?" he asked with warm amusement. "You would have caused quite a stir among the lusty university students, when your fair, naked body was dragged ashore. Of course, you would have been quite dead, so you could not have enjoyed all the admiring attention." Propping her upright, his dark brown eyes softened at the sight of her. Her face was still very pale.

"You are a knave!" Huddling deeper into the cape's folds, Elizabeth tried to control the shivering that racked her body.

"Thank you for your kind words, my lady," said Tarleton lightly, though his arms tightened around her. "I much appreciate your boundless gratitude toward me for having saved you from such an embarrassing end."

Ignoring his gentle rebuke, Elizabeth took a few more deep breaths. As she laid her head against Tarleton's chest, his rough curly hairs tickled her cheek. She drank in the comfort of his nearness. His deep voice wrapped around her like a warm blanket.

"Thank you, Tarleton," she murmured, inhaling his manly scent. "I am forgetting my manners."

"And I am trying to remember mine," he answered thickly.

Aware that his heart was racing, Tarleton knew he should put Elizabeth down and tell her to get dressed. He felt her relax, her sweet body nestling against him. Her wet golden hair spread like a damp butterfly's wings across his chest. Her hands still clutched his, her fingers instinctively entwining around his own. Underneath the thickness of the cloak, he saw the rise and fall of her breasts. Her nipples, hardened by the cold water, jutted against the woolen fabric. Her slim legs pressed against his own, the smooth softness of her thigh brushing against his hair-roughened one.

Looking up at the blue vault of the sky, Tarleton breathed deeply, hoping to check the hot flush of his pent-up desires, which surged through him like wildfire. His loins ached, torturing him. Elizabeth chose this moment to look up at him. A small smile of enchantment wreathed her lips. Her eyes were fathomless pools of green. Tarleton felt himself drowning. Lowering his head, he brushed his lips against hers, caressing her mouth more than kissing it. Surprised by his own boldness, he pulled back quickly. Parting her moist, pink lips, Elizabeth raised herself to meet his kiss. Her sweet invitation was one he could neither resist nor control. Kneeling, he pulled her up with him. His arms encircling her slim waist, his mouth took hers hungrily, devouring its softness.

Tarleton's first feathery kiss left Elizabeth's lips burning with fire. As his arms enfolded her, she felt the cloak slip from her shoulders. The cool dampness of his skin pressed against hers as he drew her to him. Then his mouth delved into hers with the jolt of lightning, its current jumping through her skin, igniting a hundred fiery sparks. Stealing her arms around his neck, she buried her hands in the tangle of his thick hair as a maelstrom of new, raw emotions gripped her.

Elizabeth was shocked at her own eager response to the touch of his lips, yet she throbbed for more. His tongue darted between her teeth, searching for hers. Fireworks exploded behind her closed lids as her tongue answered his quest. She could barely breathe.

The suddenness and urgency of her response surprised Tarleton. Her firm breasts flattened against his chest, her hardened nipples pressing into him. His manhood throbbed with sweet, hard agony as he grasped her rounded hips, pulling her hungrily to himself. His mind swam in a colorful confusion. One small part of his sanity shrieked a warning. Even as Elizabeth clutched him greedily, he knew he was sealing their eventual doom. It wasn't too late—not yet. Growling deep in his throat, he wrenched himself away from her. Surprised, Elizabeth collapsed onto the grass.

"Why did you do that?" She panted, her body throbbing in a hundred different places. "Is something wrong?"

Tarleton turned away from her. His scars stood out in silent, screaming testimony. The muscles of his trim buttocks tightened visibly.

"I didn't mean to offend you," she continued, trying to understand the strange vibrations that sent a thousand shocks through her body.

Tarleton's shoulders slumped; he emitted a low groan.

"Did I hurt you?" She stood, pulling the cape about her. "Where does it hurt?"

"In my heart, fair lady," he whispered, still not looking at her. "You have mortally wounded my heart."

"What?" she asked, not daring to believe what he said.

Tarleton glanced around. Seeing her standing by the river, his eyes burned like living coals in his sockets. With her nakedness only partially covered by the damp cloak, she looked like a water sprite come to seduce him.

He cleared his throat. "You are beautiful, brave and extremely desirable," he said, slowly picking his words. His gaze wandered down from her enormous eyes, to her soft shoulders, finally resting on her barely concealed breasts. She moved toward him and the cloak parted, revealing one silky thigh and the sweet secret place above.

Licking his dry lips, Tarleton sought her eyes again. Jesu! They were emerald green with passion. "The truth of the matter is, I want to take you in my arms and never let you go. I want to explore your body, to taste your sweetness, and to teach you what it is to be truly loved by a man."

He tore himself away from the bewitching apparition before him. Instead, he stared at the rushing river. "But you are a lady of property, as well as the Queen's goddaughter. You are meant for the bed of some fine lord, and he will not want . . . damaged goods. I have sworn to protect your virtue—not to take it!"

Scooping up a handful of pebbles, he flung one with his considerable strength into the water. "So, I beg you, Lady Elizabeth, please get dressed, and let us forget this madness. I was wrong to kiss you as if you were some country wench. The fault is mine." He pitched another stone; it glanced off the willow tree on the opposite shore.

Elizabeth was not sure if she could move. Her mind blazed with half-formed questions, half-expressed emotions. She felt awake and alive, yet powerless at the same time.

"I have been kissed before," she began slowly. "Sir Robert kissed me once or twice when my betrothal contract was signed. But his kiss was not like yours."

Again Tarleton looked over his shoulder. The sunlight played in the white fire of her golden hair. He felt the magnetism of her deep, entrancing eyes. At the sight of the lush creamy curves of her ripe body, the sword between his legs rose stiffly to attention.

"Sir Robert's kisses were dead," Elizabeth continued. "His lips were those of a wet, slimy fish. It was all I could do to kiss him back."

Tarleton clenched the remaining pebbles in his fist, the stones biting into his palm. He prayed the pain would help keep his perspective.

The tip of Elizabeth's pink tongue ran over her lips. "I thought I would get used to his kisses. After all, what do I know what happens between a man and a woman? It wasn't until I met you, and I saw the way the serving wenches and Peg acted, that I realized there was something more to love. But I didn't know what it was. I only knew they found pleasure in your kisses, while I... I did not take any pleasure in Sir Robert's."

Tarleton gritted his teeth. "You are not a serving wench in some beggarly inn, nor even sweet Peg in her kitchen," he said hoarsely. "You are Lady Elizabeth Hayward of Esmond Manor. You do not take a tumble in some hayloft for a sixpence!"

"No!" she snapped. A bitter smile cut across her mouth. "I take a tumble in a canopied bed! I am property, bought and sold to the highest noble bidder. You sing sweet words of love under the greenwood tree, but those songs are not for me. Love doesn't enter into marriage negotiations. After I am wedded and bedded, my estates will become my husband's. Then I am expected to produce children, who will inherit my fine estate, and who will make advantageous marriages—for even more money!'' She muffled a sob.

Tarleton turned, the full glory of his manhood displayed without shame before her.

As she gazed at his golden body, Elizabeth's heart lurched wildly. She could not suppress an exclamation of admiration. He stood so close to her, she could feel the heat of his desire.

''There is nothing I can do, my lady,'' Tarleton said. His voice sounded as if it were lost in the wind, though his hard body played false with his words.

Their eyes locked as their breathing came in unison. The blood coursed through Elizabeth's veins like an awakened river plunging heedlessly toward a precipice. Tarleton was a forest god, his face filled with expressions of love and pain as he stood proudly among the greenwood trees. Greedily filling her vision with his magnificent body, she saw how much he wanted her. His need and her overwhelming response to him gave her the courage to continue.

''There *is* something,'' she answered softly. ''Do what you said you wanted to do. Take me in your arms, and teach me what love is.''

Tarleton expelled all the air from his lungs. ''Sweet lady! I dare not—'' Though his eyes dared a great deal more as he drank in her beauty.

Elizabeth took a step closer to him. ''Harken to me, Tarleton...Dickon. When we arrive at Hampton Court, you will hand me up to the bidding block. For the rest of my life, I will have no choice whose lips claim mine, whose body lies next to mine. But I vow I will not become another Lady Margaret who takes young boys for comfort.'' A sense of urgency drove Elizabeth on. ''Until we come to court, I am as free as any maiden on a May Day. Take my virtue, Dickon. I give it to you willingly. I want, for one time in my life, to be held and kissed and loved for myself—not for my estates. Give me something I can dream about when I am in the depths of a wintry marriage.''

Elizabeth's pleading eyes caught his, drowning him in their emerald depths. The hammering of his heart roared in his ears, blotting out the voice of reason.

''Fair Elizabeth, think of what you are asking me.'' The sweetness of her lavender soap, mingling with her stronger female musk, assailed his nostrils like an intoxicating perfume. Her warm invitation was irresistible; he ached for fulfillment. ''You will be disgraced forever.'' His voice broke with huskiness. ''And I will dance my last jig on a gibbet for debauching you.''

''No one will ever know,'' she whispered. Reaching out to him, she let the cloak slip to the ground.

He stifled a low groan. The mere touch of her fingers on his arm sent a bolt of fire through him.

Elizabeth continued in a low musical tone. ''I will say I was taken when I was in France by a member of the King's court. I will tell my husband that I was but a girl and too frightened to know what to do. I will say I never dared tell anyone, save my confessor.'' Tilting her head, she smiled provocatively at Tarleton.

''And where did you learn to weave such a tale?'' Every one of his nerve endings quivered. She was a witch!

''It happened to a close friend of mine at school.'' Elizabeth's eyes grew misty. ''She was thirteen, and she cried in my lap when she whispered the story to me. She was so terrified. Oh, Dickon, I don't want to be terrified! Please, help me.'' Her searching fingers lightly brushed his cheek. ''Teach me how to love you.''

He could barely speak. His cheek burned where she touched it. A nerve throbbed against his temple. His shaft was a firebrand. '' 'Twill hurt you, ladybird.''

''I know,'' she answered softly, still stroking his smooth cheek.

"There will be blood."

"I know." As if poised on tiptoe, her whole being ached for him. The prolonged anticipation was unbearable. "Please, Dickon?" she whispered.

Tarleton's heart exploded in his chest. Sweeping her into his arms, he smothered her lips with his fevered kisses. Moaning in the back of her throat, she quivered at the passion of his embrace.

"I will try to be gentle," he whispered, his breath hot against her cheek.

"I know." Twining her arms around his neck, Elizabeth returned his kisses with joyful abandon.

Gently Tarleton eased her down onto the flattened grass. In wonder, he traced his finger over the line of her neck to the sweet hollow where her shoulder met. Moaning softly, she grew limp and yielding as his fingertips outlined the circles of her breasts. She gasped his name as his thumb caressed the underside of the soft mounds.

"Are you sure you want this, my darling?" he murmured, praying that she did, for he didn't think he could stop himself now.

"Oh yes, Dickon!" she breathed.

"I love you—" he began, but she placed her hand gently across his lips.

"Don't say it," she whispered. "It is enough that you are here with me now. Some things are best left unspoken, remember?"

He closed his eyes for a moment to blot out her indictment. Taking his hand in hers, she brought it to her lips. Slowly she kissed each of his fingers in turn. The touch of her mouth hurled him to the pinnacle of abandonment.

"But for me, you are my only love, Dickon," she continued. "Now and forever." Her tongue laved the palm of his hand.

Tarleton's gaze tenderly caressed her. Elizabeth loved him! The shock of her admission sent his blood racing through him at a breakneck speed. There could be no holding back now.

"May God help us both, my darling!" Reclaiming her lips, he crushed her to him, drinking deeply of her nectar.

Elizabeth couldn't get enough of him. His kisses sent new spirals of ecstasy through her. When their lips finally broke apart, she felt as if she were drifting on a misty cloud. She drew in her breath as his fingers glided over her breasts. With each exquisite stroke, quivers of fiery arrows ricocheted through her body. Taking a rosy bud between his thumb and forefinger, Tarleton gently rolled it. Her nipples firmed instantly under his touch. The mixture of pain and pleasure was almost more than she could bear. A deep warmth spread up from her loins. Bending his head, his lips touched the hardened peak with tantalizing possessiveness. Playfully he suckled her. Gasping in sweet agony, Elizabeth dug her fingers into his thick curls, pulling him closer to her. She writhed in response to his exquisite love play. There was no escape from his sweet torture. Her legs parted, leaving her open, moist and throbbing.

"My sweet lady," he whispered. Lying down beside her, he slipped a supporting hand under the small of her back.

Gently he massaged her silken belly in slow, languid circles, each rotation edging closer to the golden fleecy triangle of her essence. With each movement her world spun and careened on its axis.

Tarleton's lips explored her soft, ivory flesh. When he lifted her to himself, the hardened peaks of her breasts crushed against the curly hair of his chest. Slowly his hand slid down her taut stomach to the swell of her hips. She shivered when his hardness brushed against her thigh. Elizabeth whispered his name over and over. The sound of it sang like sweetest music in his ears.

"Not yet, my darling," he murmured, nibbling on her earlobe. "Not until you're ready."

As he spoke, his hand skimmed along her thighs, then dipped between them. Elizabeth reacted as if she had been stung. Raining feathery kisses on her ear, her cheek, her eyes, her neck, Tarleton continued to caress her intimately. As he aroused her, Elizabeth's body instinctively arched to meet his. The cloud she drifted on soared, dipped, then soared again under his masterful stroking. Opening like a rose in the warm rays of a summer sun, her petals unfolded for him. A passion gripped her, banishing her thoughts. His fingers were a conjurer's, commanding her to the dance of love. His expert touch sent her up to the blazing sun.

Suddenly, unexpectedly, she shattered into a million glowing stars. The descent afterward was steep and delicious. She whimpered in sweet ecstasy. Each silvery quiver was a delightful aftershock. Through the soft haze in her mind, she heard his low laugh, like the purr of a large cat.

"Now let us go together, my love" Tarleton whispered. He lowered his body on top of her, tucking her curves neatly into his own contours. He kissed her lingeringly, his tongue gliding in and out of her mouth in slow strokes while his hands caressed the softness of her thighs.

Half freezing, half aflame, Elizabeth cried out for release. Then she knew he was at her portal—tense, tight, yet wet. Her eyes flew open. Tarleton's face was mere inches from her own. His deep brown eyes smoldered with passion, though he smiled tenderly at her.

"'Tis time for both of us," he whispered. She trembled under his fingers. "A few seconds more, then there will never be pain again."

Elizabeth nodded, then held her breath. This was what she had asked for, what she feared and wanted at the same time. Whispering his name, she moaned as she welcomed him into her body. Tarleton's mouth sought Elizabeth's as he moved quickly within her.

White-hot, searing fire ripped through her. Whimpering, she dug her nails into his skin and buried her face in his neck. Every muscle in his back tensed under her fingertips. He moved more slowly again and again. With each stroke, the pain faded as her passion grew to explosive proportions. Fiery tingling surged through her, soaring higher and higher until the peak of delight was reached. Tarleton was true to his word: he took her with him to paradise.

Again Elizabeth's world exploded in a star-burst, engulfing her in a shower of fiery sensations. Tarleton cried out in joyful triumph as his love flowed into her like warm honey. He kissed her face, her eyes, the tip of her nose, whispering her name over and over as if it were his own private prayer. Elizabeth was filled with an amazing sense of completeness. Sighing with pleasant exhaustion, she pillowed her head on his shoulder.

"Are you all right?" he asked her quietly.

Slowly opening her eyes, Elizabeth felt as if she had been very far away and was now being pulled back to reality. Taking a deep, soul-drenching breath, she nodded.

"Good." He brushed a gentle kiss across her forehead. "Let's see what damage is done." He eased himself off her.

Elizabeth flushed crimson when she felt the warm trickle of blood ooze down her leg. Suddenly shy, she was embarrassed that Tarleton should see her vulnerability. She threw her arm over her eyes to shield herself from his gaze.

"You were right." He chuckled. "You were undoubtedly a virgin." Cupping some water from the river, Tarleton gently washed her.

As she tried to hold back her tears, a sob escaped Elizabeth's lips. Tarleton lifted her into his arms, as if she were a small child who had fallen and skinned her knee.

"Darling, darling Elizabeth, please don't cry." He rocked her gently, stroking her cheeks. "Does it still hurt? Oh, sweetling, forgive me. I wish I had been more skilled."

"What do you mean—more skilled?" Elizabeth asked tremulously.

Tarleton smiled a little crookedly. "I mean, I wish I knew the art of deflowering virgins. I fear you were my first."

"First?" She blinked at him through her tears. He looked like a small boy who had been caught stealing sweetmeats.

"Yes, my first virgin. I...umm...never met a forsworn virgin before—at least, not intimately. All of my other... ah...the others were more experienced." Tarleton turned a little red about the ears.

Elizabeth found his discomfort oddly endearing. "Then we are a matched pair. You are my first lover and I am your first virgin."

He kissed her on the nose. "They say you never forget your first time."

The corners of Elizabeth's mouth turned upward. "Really?" She ran her fingers lightly through his chest hair. Curling one of the tendrils around her finger, she tugged gently. "Tell me about yours."

"Oh, no, ladybird! It was highly embarrassing!"

"Tell me," she softly commanded, still playing with the wiry curls.

He shivered at her teasing touch. "I was fifteen, and soundly drunk. 'Twas the only way I could muster the courage. Even so, the wench had to guide me. Afterward, I threw up in the straw. It wasn't the girl, 'twas the sack wine. Rotten stuff, sack wine." He kissed her maddening fingers.

Elizabeth rested quietly in his arms, then she giggled. "Remember when you made me sing at that wretched Blue Boar?"

"Aye." Tarleton glanced at her with an amused eye.

"You told me that my first performance would be like losing my virginity—I'd be scared to death and not enjoy it. Well, you were only half-right. I was frightened, but I enjoyed it immensely!"

She suppressed another giggle when she saw a slow, proud smile curl his lips. Her fingers continued their lazy play, lightly scraping his skin with her nails.

He shivered. "My sweet Lady Elizabeth. Do you know what you are doing to me?"

"My sweet Richard Tarleton. Do you think we could do it again?" She smiled up at him with a look that was both innocent and feline.

"So soon?" He quivered as she continued her stroking. When her finger grazed one of his nipples, he groaned.

"I haven't much time to call my own," she replied quietly. "I want to be in your arms as much as possible until...until then."

His lips pressed against hers, then gently covered her mouth. As he stoked her passion, his own grew stronger. When they drew slowly apart, Tarleton cradled her face between his warm hands.

"When you first fell into my life, I wasn't sure if you were an angel or a devil. I'm still not sure."

"Neither." She smiled, brushing an errant lock of brown hair off his forehead. "I'm a woman, sweet Dickon."

Chapter Twelve

In a private upper room in the Mitre Inn at Oxford, Sir Robert La Faye poured himself another cupful of canary wine. Though it was only two in the afternoon, Sir Robert was well into his fourth bottle of the expensive import. His small eyes were sunk into slits above the florid folds of his fleshy cheeks, accentuating his porcine look. To his companion, a garishly dressed woman of doubtful breeding and reputation, Sir Robert resembled a great hairy hog in a peascod jacket and plumed hat. Regarding him cautiously over the rim of her cup, Nan Quincy pretended to sip her wine. As each day dragged by with no trace of the elusive Lady Elizabeth, Sir Robert's vindictiveness lashed out in all directions. Nan knew from painful experience that he hated being thwarted, or having his dignity insulted.

"A pox on the bitch!" Sir Robert slurred, downing the sweet wine in one ferocious gulp. "She's made me the laughingstock in two—nay, three—counties. But she'll pay for it, Nan. By all that's in hell, she'll pay for it tenfold!" He slammed the pewter vessel down on the table. It skipped along the boards, then fell to the floor.

Quietly Nan leaned over and picked it up.

"No one is laughing at—" she began.

The man across from her interrupted loudly. "Silence, woman! Did I seek your opinion? I tell you, I have been made a fool by that bitch! Now they are writing ballads about Sir Robert La Faye's runaway wife who bolted from the church door on his big black horse! That foul piece of doggerel leaves me—*me,* the wronged husband—without a shred of respect! All the countryside is singing of the sweet Lady Elizabeth, and her handsome Scottish lover. The chorus calls me a merry cuckold!''

"Nay, Sir Robert, I think—"

"Don't think!" He pounded his fist on the table.

Nan remained outwardly unperturbed, willing herself to stay calm. Once, in the days when Sir Robert was younger and slimmer, Nan loved him, content to be his bedmate. But over the past few years, as his girth became larger and his fortunes smaller from gambling and bad investments, Sir Robert's caresses grew more harsh, his lovemaking more cruel. Now Nan dared not leave him. She knew he would pursue her as savagely as he chased after Lady Elizabeth. His revenge against Nan's perceived injury to his bloated vanity would be brutal and she did not enjoy the protection of a noble birth.

"More!" Sir Robert waved a shaky finger at the bottle. Nan poured another cupful. "And tell that poxy landlord **we** want two more bottles of this bog water!''

"Perhaps he has run out," Nan murmured as she placed the cup in front of the drunken lord. She wished fervently that Sir Robert would succumb to the fumes of the wine and give her a few hours of peace.

"Don't cross me, Nan! I've been crossed enough by women!" Sir Robert slurped greedily.

Going to the door, Nan motioned to the tap boy, who waited in attendance just outside.

"Two more bottles of wine," she quietly told the wide-eyed lad.

A few hot tears of self-pity ran down Sir Robert's puffy cheeks. "Only this morning I heard some onion-eyed student singing the praises of Lady Elizabeth Hayward under my window! I dumped the entire chamber pot over his head. Aye! And threw the pot after him for good measure. Knocked him into the gutter. 'Tis a lesson he'll not soon forget!''

"Aye, my lord." Nan remembered the incident only too clearly. The student's cap and gown were ruined beyond repair. It took a gold noble to cool the singer's wrath.

Sir Robert wiped his runny nose on the burgundy velvet of his slashed sleeve. "Handsome Scottish lover! Ha! If there is a lover—which I doubt—he isn't taking her to Scotland. The chit is headed straight for her godmother. The wench is somewhere on this road. When I find her, I will whip her within an inch of her miserable life! Aye, and take my pleasure in it, too!''

"You'll have to marry her first," Nan said smoothly, feeling more than a little sorry for the Lady Elizabeth.

"Aye, by the first bumbling cleric I can find. Then I'll make her dance to my tune!''

"Why waste your time on her?" Nan suggested smoothly. "Surely there are other fish in the sea who would leap at your . . . hook." She arched her brow meaningfully.

Sir Robert glared at his paramour. "Because the baggage has a fortune I could well use, you dolt! And she has connections to both political camps. If Mary of Scotland is freed and comes to her rightful power, the Hayward estates are safe from confiscation. The little bitch is a Catholic. If Elizabeth remains where she is, I will stand in good stead as the husband of her goddaughter. I care not if the Scots whore or the English bastard sits on the throne. So long as the Hayward wench is in my pocket, my fortune is secure." He drained the bottle, wiping the back of his hand across his thick lips.

Shuddering at his treasonous words, Nan prayed the walls of the Mitre did not have ears.

There was a gentle rap on the door. Sir Robert answered by hurling his empty cup at it. "Come in, damn you!''

Trembling, the pale tap boy crept inside, clutching two fresh bottles of canary.

"Don't stare at me, you sniveling cony! Put the wine on the sideboard, then get your miserable hide out of here!"

"Yes, s-sir!" Scampering the length of the room, the boy set down the bottles. Quickly picking up the three empties, he raced for the door. Sir Robert drew a small dagger from his belt and threw it after him. Striking the doorjamb, the blade quivered just inches from the terrified boy's face.

"Have you heard of a ballad called 'The Runaway Wife'?" Sir Robert bellowed at him.

The boy looked first at the man, then at the woman, who slowly shook her head at him. "No, sir, not I! I have no time for songs, s-sir!"

"Get you gone!"

The tap boy flew out the door and down the stairs. He didn't stop trembling until he reached the cool cellar, where he placed the empties in a barrel. Running outside across the inn yard, he barely made it to the privy before his bowels turned to water. The shivering lad heartily wished the fat lord to hell, taking his custom with him.

Upstairs, Nan pried the dagger out of the wood then pocketed the weapon. If Sir Robert had injured or, worse, killed the lad— Behind her, she heard a low snore. Her prayers were temporarily answered. Sir Robert slumped across the table, the cup still gripped in his hand. He would stay that way until his hirelings returned from their latest search. Crossing her arms over her breasts, Nan hugged herself. *God help that poor Lady. And God help me!*

"Sweet ladybird!" Tarleton nuzzled the sleeping girl curled in the crook of his arm.

"Hmm?"

"Wake up, slugabed!" He tickled her nose with a blade of grass.

"Do we have to?" Elizabeth snuggled closer to him.

Tarleton kissed her lightly on top of her head. "I fear so, my darling. Clouds have come up, and we must find some sort of shelter before the storm."

Elizabeth reluctantly opened her eyes, her body warm and moist from the afternoon's lovemaking. Sniffing the air like a terrier, she sensed a definite change in the weather. A small breeze ruffled through the leaves, carrying the heavy scent of rain. Stretching, she watched Tarleton pull on his breeches.

"I wish—" she began.

Glancing over his shoulder, Tarleton attempted to assume a stern look. "Not again, my lady! You'll wear me out!"

Elizabeth laughed. "I wish today would never end." Running her fingers through her hair, she pulled out a few stray leaves and twigs. "I wish you and I could forget about Hampton Court." She grew serious. "Could we do that, Dickon? Just keep going on our way? I wouldn't mind it— not with you by my side."

Tarleton felt his heart crack at the thought of her tempting suggestion. If he thought they could get away with it, he would go to the ends of the earth with her—and the devil take Sir Robert! Instead, he shook his head slowly.

"Nay, Elizabeth, I must get thee to the Queen."

Elizabeth glared at him with burning, reproachful eyes. "I see your game, Sir Jester!" Rising, she shook the last remnants of sleep from her joints. She looked a young goddess, clothed only in her indignation. "You have played your sport well with me. Next week, when I'm safely tucked up with the Queen, you are free to go on your merry way and break some other girl's heart!"

Stalking down to the river's edge, Elizabeth waded up to her knees, splashing its chill water over her flushed face and trembling body.

" 'Tis is not what I meant, ladybird!'' Tarleton protested as he watched her closely, in case she decided to take another unplanned swim.

Elizabeth flounced back to the bank, then disappeared through the bushes where she had left her clothes.

"Truly?" Her voice sliced through the verdant curtain. "I suppose you think you are not good enough for me. Or, perchance, I am not good enough for you!"

Tarleton groped for the right words to soothe her.

After a short silence, she reappeared, dressed in her travel-stained breeches and the once-white shirt. The rosy tips of her nipples peeked saucily through the neck opening, which was not yet tied shut. Looking away, Tarleton tried to collect his thoughts. He had not bargained for such a sudden shift in her mood after so sweet a bout of love play.

His throat ached with the torment of regret. "What you or I want is not the point, Lady Elizabeth," he said stiffly, pretending to take great care in the lacing of his jerkin. "The fact of the matter is this, you are expected at Hampton Court within this fortnight, and I am expected to deliver you there in one piece."

Grumbling over her filthy stockings, Elizabeth paused and looked at him, amazed at his words. "Expected? How can the Queen expect me? She doesn't even know I've run away. And how does she know you are delivering me like a New Year's gift?" Her eyes flashed a dangerous green.

Tarleton gingerly sat down beside her, his own shoes and stockings in his hands. "Because I sent a message, telling Her Majesty we were coming," he replied evenly.

"A message?" She snorted. "Oh, that's a good jest, Tarleton! Did you find a friendly jackrabbit to carry it for you?"

"No," he replied quietly. "A friendly peddler."

Elizabeth stopped fuming, and thought back across the days. "Patch? You sent a message by Patch?"

Tarleton nodded.

Elizabeth knotted her brow. "But he was going north. And how can you trust him, anyway?" she persisted, not wanting to believe him.

"Because, like myself, Master Patch is also a spy in the service of Sir Francis Walsingham."

"Oh," said Elizabeth in a very small voice. She saw by the expression in Tarleton's eyes that his words were true and he wished they weren't.

"I told Patch the whole story while you slept that afternoon. I felt it best that Sir Francis be aware of what was afoot. Patch planned to meet with one of the Queen's couriers in Stratford. With fast post-horses, that courier should be at Hampton by now. If we don't appear within a reasonable amount of time, the Queen will send her soldiers looking for us."

"Oh." Elizabeth's voice held a tear.

Tarleton wanted to reach out to her, but he was unsure of her reaction. Instead, he waited, watching her out of the corner of his eye. "I thought it was for the best, Elizabeth," he added softly.

"And now?" Her eyes were those of an injured fawn.

Tarleton laid his hand over hers. "I wish with all my heart that we could travel together, singing silly songs to simpering housewives, eating stale bread and cheese and whatever else we could steal. I would have us wandering the roads in summer, and curled together before a fire in winter. That is what I wish, but wishes . . ." His voice trailed off.

Brusquely wiping a stray tear with her sleeve, Elizabeth glowered at the stocking in her hand. "And I wish... I wish I could have at least one pair of clean stockings with no holes!"

Tarleton could stand it no longer. Pulling her into his arms, he held her tightly. Elizabeth quietly lay in his embrace, her head against his chest.

"I can hear your heart," she murmured.

"Good." He kissed her hair, which smelled of lavender and sunshine. "I'm glad to know I am still alive. I wondered about that awhile ago."

Elizabeth looked up at him. "Oh?"

He grinned impishly. "For a while there, methought I had died and gone to heaven, for I was in the company of an angel."

"Not so." She laid her head back on his chest. "But it is nice of you to think that."

"Nay, sweet angel, I see now I was mistaken."

"How so?"

"I've never seen an angel wear such a beggarly, reeky pair of stockings and those shoes! Why, their soles are the ones who need saving—not mine!"

A small smile lit up Elizabeth's face.

Wiggling his brows at her, Tarleton flashed his best, most devilish, grin. "'Tis time I wave my magic wand and turn you once again into a prentice boy. We need food, my lad, and shelter, too. I doubt you'll want to spend another night in a hayrick."

Elizabeth cocked her head at him. "Not so," she bantered. "I've heard lovemaking is very pleasurable in hayricks!"

"Lady Elizabeth! I am surprised!" Tarleton assumed the expression of a prim cleric. "What would all your good nuns say if they heard you?"

"No doubt, it would shock them into silence!" Elizabeth grinned wickedly.

Gathering their few belongings together, they worked their way back through the underbrush to the road. Following behind Tarleton, Elizabeth paused for a moment, looking over her shoulder at the glistening river, the waving willows and the flattened patch of grass. Her gaze took in all the colors of the place, trying to imprint the scene in her mind forever. She knew she would never hear a rook's cry or smell a blade of meadow grass without remembering this one magical afternoon.

"We burn daylight, Robin Redbreast!" Tarleton called to her.

"Aye!" Elizabeth answered. Whispering a heartfelt adieu, she scrambled after him.

A short time later, they rejoined the main highway. Staring in disbelief at the milepost, Tarleton threw back his head, roaring with laughter. "We are closer than I thought! Had we not dallied, we could have been in Oxford by now!"

"I did not mind the dallying." Her eyes twinkling, Elizabeth's lips curled in a secret smile. "So, where are we?"

"Two miles from Godstow and none too soon, by the looks of that sky!" Tarleton turned down the hard-packed road, whistling happily.

"Do you know of an inn at Godstow?" Elizabeth panted, trying to keep up with him.

Tarleton chuckled. "Nay, sweetling, no inn, but a safe place to be sure. In fact, 'tis the safest place in England, except inside a church."

"What then?"

"The Priory of St. Aloysius. The good ladies there know me well. We shall find a dry bed and a plain but filling meal." Glancing down at Elizabeth, Tarleton smiled crookedly. "Though I think the mother abbess will disapprove if I asked her for only one bed!"

Elizabeth wrinkled her nose. "Why? She'll think I'm a boy." Elizabeth looked forward to spending the night wrapped in Tarleton's love.

The jester cocked one eyebrow. "Don't be too sure about that. Mother Catherine may be as old as the hills, but her eye is sharper than a hound's tooth. If anyone can see through your disguise, she will."

Suddenly the thought of spending the night in the Priory of St. Aloysius did not sound at all appealing to Elizabeth.

Only the threat of the gathering black clouds hurried her steps after Tarleton's, quashing any objections on her lips.

The first raindrops fell as Tarleton pulled the bell rope hanging by the stout wooden door of the old priory. A small hatchway opened, and a soft voice chirped, "Peace be with you!"

"And with you, Sister Agnes!" Tarleton laughed. "Please! Open this door before we drown."

"Richard! Praise be!" the cheerful voice replied.

Elizabeth heard the bolt slide back. The door swung open on its well-oiled hinges.

As round as she was tall, Sister Agnes greeted Tarleton like a long-lost son, then warmly smiled at Elizabeth.

"'Tis my new apprentice, Robin." Tarleton indicated his wet companion.

Playing her role to the hilt, Elizabeth swept a deep bow to Sister Agnes. The cheerful nun chuckled at the apprentice's good manners.

"By my troth, you are a gift from heaven this stormy evening, Richard" she twittered merrily to Tarleton as she led them down a cool, dim corridor.

A wave of nostalgia swept over Elizabeth as she followed behind the jester and his plain-garbed admirer. The priory was like the convent in France where she had spent six happy years. An aura of peace and orderliness, mixed with the scent of beeswax, dried herbs and lye soap, seeped out from the old stone walls. Light footfalls, a tinkle of distant laughter and the chime of a bell made Elizabeth feel at home, despite her borrowed identity.

"A gift, you say?" Tarleton wiggled his eyebrows at the diminutive nun. "And next you'll tell me that God sent this storm especially, so I would be sure to stop at your door."

Sister Agnes laughed merrily. "God works in mysterious ways, Richard. Oh, won't Mother Abbess be happy to see you!"

"Is she well?" he asked in an undertone.

Sister Agnes's fresh laughter answered his question. "She enjoys the best of health, thank the Lord. And you, you scamp, will be a tonic for us all."

"Does that mean I shall have to sing for my supper?" Tarleton asked, winking broadly at her.

"Only if you remember where you are, and don't sing any of your tavern ballads." By the twinkle in her eye, Elizabeth suspected Sister Agnes might have a number of worldly interests.

Halting outside a beautifully carved door, Sister Agnes knocked twice, then entered.

"I don't suppose I have to tell you how to act in pious company, Robin Redbreast," Tarleton muttered as they waited for admittance.

"I shall be a credit to you, master." Elizabeth lifted her eyebrow. "But I had no idea you were so close to the bosom of the Church."

He chuckled softly. "Nay, chuck. There are other bosoms I would rather be closer to!"

Elizabeth felt her cheeks flame. But before she could answer him, the door swung open and they were ushered into the presence of the Reverend Mother Catherine, Abbess of the Priory of St. Aloysius.

Mother Catherine was tiny and she appeared to be made up of bones held together by a thin covering of pale, translucent skin. *One good puff of wind would blow her away,* Elizabeth thought. Then she looked into the abbess's bright blue eyes. Elizabeth had the uncomfortable feeling that they could read her very soul.

"Richard, my son!" Mother Catherine's voice was as clear as a bell on a crisp winter's morning. "It gladdens my heart to see you again."

Bending one knee by the old nun's padded chair, Tarleton removed his cap. Gently he kissed her frail-looking hand. Elizabeth stared at him in wide-eyed wonder. Never had she seen Tarleton so respectfully humble. Elizabeth stared down at her feet, hoping she looked like a shy boy.

"Good Mother, it gladdens me to see you looking well," Tarleton answered tenderly.

The mother abbess cocked her head. "Sister Agnes informs me you've now taken on the added responsibility of an apprentice. I am surprised, Richard. Responsibility is not one of your virtues."

Through her lashes, Elizabeth saw Tarleton redden slightly. She suppressed a smile.

"My apprentice, Robin," he muttered.

"Come closer, Robin," Mother Catherine said gently. "Step into the light."

Keeping her eyes on her shoes, Elizabeth inched forward a few paces, then executed one of her best sweeping bows.

"Very pretty, my child," complimented Mother Catherine.

"Thank you, Mother Abbess," Elizabeth said softly, not daring to look into those all-knowing eyes.

"Tell me, is Tarleton a good master to you?" the little woman inquired.

"Aye, Mother Abbess. He does not beat me often." Elizabeth responded guilelessly.

Tarleton rolled his eyes heavenward. "The lad jests, Mother Catherine. I have had no cause to beat him—as yet."

"Give me your hand, child." Mother Catherine gestured to Elizabeth.

Quaking inwardly, Elizabeth crept forward, knelt as Tarleton did, and placed her hand in the older woman's. Mother Catherine's skin felt like cool silk.

"Your fingers are cold, child," mused Mother Catherine.

"The boy is shy, Mother," said Tarleton quickly. "He is not used to being in the company of nuns."

"Just so," murmured the Reverend Mother. "And your parents, Robin? Do they approve of your choice of occupation?"

"My parents are both dead." Elizabeth's lower lip trembled. "My father died very recently."

"May his soul rest in eternal peace, my child, I am sorry to hear of it. How recently?"

Though the old woman's tone remained kind and soothing, Elizabeth detected a shrewdness underneath.

"Within this fortnight." A sharp pain squeezed Elizabeth's heart. *Please, dear Lord, don't let me cry now!*

"We shall remember him in our prayers." Releasing Elizabeth's hand, Mother Catherine stroked her cropped hair.

"Thank you, good Mother," Elizabeth mumbled. "'Tis a comfort."

Tarleton cleared his voice loudly.

Leaning against the high back of her chair, Mother Catherine turned once more toward him.

"Sister Agnes tells me you would like to entertain us after our supper, Richard," she remarked, speculatively eyeing the handsome young man.

"At your pleasure and mine, good Mother!" He grinned.

"I trust you have a few songs in your repertory that are suitable?" Mother Catherine's eyes twinkled.

"Most chaste songs, and a jig, if you would like," he answered humbly.

"I am sure your jig would be most entertaining for my sisters, provided, of course, that it has no lewd movements."

"None, I assure you. Why, I would even dance this jig for Her Majesty in her private apartments!" Tarleton chuckled.

"I trust you are never *in* the Queen's private apartments, whatever the reason, Richard. Your company there would be most unseemly."

Tarleton coughed. "I only meant that, if the Queen invited me—and her other favored entertainers—to her private apartments to amuse her ladies while they were sewing—or some such—why then, my jig would be so tame as not to bring a maidenly blush to any cheek."

Elizabeth noted that Tarleton's own cheek seemed stained with an unusually ruddy color as he stumbled out his explanation. She wondered how often Tarleton had seen the inside of the Queen's private apartments.

"I see," Mother Catherine smiled as she ruffled his hair. "Someday, my son, you will go too far, then you'll hang for it."

"I pray that day will not come too soon," he answered easily.

"Amen," Elizabeth whispered to herself.

"So, Richard, how long will you stay with us this time?" Mother Catherine cocked her head like an inquisitive wren.

"We ask only lodging for the night, and some food," he replied. "We journey to Oxford on the morrow, and, from there to court, where we shall dance attendance upon the Queen."

"Please give to Her Grace our most loving loyalty, and tell her that we pray daily for her," intoned the ancient lady.

"That will give her much good cheer," Tarleton acknowledged.

"The supper hour comes apace, my children. You may refresh yourselves at the pump. I presume you remember the way, Richard?" She smiled as he rose and stood tall before her.

"In my sleep, good Mother." He bowed to her.

"Oh, Richard! I have two new novices since you were here last. They are quite young and still given to giddiness. Please keep those dancing eyes of yours... on your apprentice." The mother abbess smiled sweetly at him.

"You have my word upon it, Mother Catherine." Opening the door, Tarleton motioned for Elizabeth to make her bow.

"Thank you for your kindness and your hospitality." Elizabeth bobbed, then turned to leave.

"Thank you, child. *Dominus vobiscum.*" Mother Catherine added softly.

"Et cum spiritu tuo." It wasn't until after Tarleton had closed the door behind her that Elizabeth realized she had answered Mother Catherine's blessing in flawless Latin.

"'He doesn't beat me often!'" Tarleton mimicked as he applied himself to the pump handle. "Don't give me any ideas, prentice boy!"

Elizabeth giggled softly, rolling up her sleeves as the cold water gushed out. "The devil prompted me!"

"In the words of an associate of mine, 'go soak your head!'"

As Tarleton predicted, the food was plain but nourishing. The soup swam with vegetables and a few pieces of chicken. Sweet butter thickly coated slices of fresh crusty bread. Elizabeth attacked her dinner with all the gusto of a normal twelve-year-old boy.

"You are making a spectacle of yourself," Tarleton hissed as a young, bright-eyed novice served Elizabeth a second portion.

"Have patience, master," Elizabeth said between mouthfuls of bread and soup. "This is the first hot meal we have had in two days. Besides, you forget I'm a growing boy!" She winked at him.

"Pig!" Tarleton muttered, though he smiled when he said it. It was good to see Elizabeth look so happy. Her eyes shone and her skin glowed with health and vigor. *No matter what happens in the future, I have this one day to hold in my heart.*

After supper and thanksgiving prayers, the long refectory tables were quickly cleared. Then Tarleton, clad in his tattered motley, capered to the center of the room and bowed to the gowned and wimpled assembly.

"Mother Catherine and good sisters, 'tis good to be home again!"

His simple words brought a warm round of applause.

Taking out his penny whistle, Tarleton played a sweet sprightly tune. This was followed by juggling an apple, a pear and Sister Agnes's ring of keys. Unlike the rowdy audiences at the Banbury fair, the holy sisters were silently appreciative. Tarleton next told a story about a hen who couldn't keep track of the number of eggs she laid, which sent some of the younger nuns into fits of giggles. Tarleton danced his promised jig while everyone clapped in time. Elizabeth noticed that he restrained himself from leaping onto the tables.

"My prentice, Robin, has the voice of an angel, if I may be so bold as to say that. He knows a sweet song, which I trust will not offend."

Tarleton stepped to one side and played the first few notes of "The Greenwood Tree." Lifting her voice, Elizabeth gave herself over to the beautiful lyrics which Tarleton had taught her.

"Under the greenwood tree/Who loves to lie with me/ And turn his merry note/Unto the sweet bird's throat?/ Come hither, come hither, come hither, come hither/Here shall he see/No enemy/But winter and rough weather."

The words, as she sang them, took on a whole new meaning for Elizabeth as she recalled that afternoon, under the greenwood trees of the enchanted glade. She colored at the remembrance. As her last note died away, she smiled at Tarleton.

The nuns were clearly enchanted. Mother Catherine never took her birdlike eyes off the couple as they took their final bows.

As Tarleton pulled off his motley, one of the younger novices came up to them. "Mother Abbess wishes to speak with you, Master Tarleton, after evensong."

"Tell the good mother that I will wait upon her pleasure." He smiled at the rosy fresh face.

"Mother Abbess also instructed me to tell you to be sure to *attend* evensong. She said you were in most need of praying. Oh, your pardon!" The young nun caught herself when she realized she had probably delivered far more than the intended message.

Tarleton chuckled gently. "Tell Mother Catherine my prentice and I will be there."

"Thank you, Master Tarleton." The novice bobbed her head, then she glanced shyly at Elizabeth. "You sang most sweetly, Master Robin," she whispered. Blushing an alarming shade of red, she bolted like a deer.

Tarleton shook his head, laughing heartily. "I do believe you have stolen that young girl's heart, Master Robin!" He clapped Elizabeth soundly on the back.

"But... but she's a nun!" Elizabeth sputtered in shock.

"Aye, but she is also a female," he answered knowingly. "And a pretty one, too, despite all that sackcloth she's covered in."

The small chapel of the priory with its honeyed smell of the beeswax candles and the soft chanting of the holy women reminded Elizabeth even more of the far-off days in France. Kneeling quietly in the back, Elizabeth gave herself up to the well-remembered Latin prayers and the comfort they brought to her soul. Lingering at the end of the service until the last of the good ladies left, Elizabeth timidly ventured up to the altar railing. There, in the solitude lit by a single sanctuary candle in its red glass globe, Elizabeth prayed for the souls of her parents—and for forgiveness.

"I love Dickon truly, and I would gladly marry him, if it were possible. If what we did today was sinful, then I am sorry it was wrong. But, sweet Lord, it didn't feel wrong."

There was a soft scraping sound as Tarleton knelt by her side. Surprised to see him, Elizabeth forgot the rest of her prayers. Smiling, Tarleton put his finger to his lips, then he bowed his head.

Elizabeth felt a lurch of excitement within her as his elbow lightly touched hers. It was if some strange glow surrounded them.

Tarleton nudged her arm, smiled and signaled her to watch him. Elaborately pointing to his jerkin, he reached inside it and appeared to be wrestling with something lodged there. Then he slowly withdrew his hand and held it out. His fingers were curled gently around—nothing.

Yet that nothing was real. Elizabeth could see it, pulsating as his fingers opened and closed in steady rhythm. He held it gently, lovingly, for a moment. Then, turning to her, he offered to Elizabeth—his heart.

"Oh!" she gasped in understanding.

Tarleton put his finger to his lips again as he held out his beating heart to her. His eyes pleaded her acceptance.

Bowing her head in acknowledgment, Elizabeth cupped her hands as Tarleton placed his inside, then closed her hands around his invisible offering. Bringing her hands to her lips, Elizabeth kissed his gift of love, then she folded her hands against her breast.

Smiling with satisfaction, Tarleton bowed his head.

Inspired, Elizabeth reached inside her own waistcoat. Imitating Tarleton's action, she withdrew her heart and held it out to him. Tarleton bowed gravely as if she had just presented him with the most precious jewel on earth. He accepted her hands with a kiss on her palms. The touch of his soft lips against her burning skin sent shivers down her spine. She leaned against the marble railing for support.

After carefully concealing her heart in his jerkin, Tarleton touched Elizabeth's sleeve again, signaling her to watch him once more. He pointed to the pouch at his belt. Opening it, he withdrew—nothing.

Yet that nothing was also real. Elizabeth could see its outline in the light of the single candle. Round, smooth and golden, it was his ring of promise and of love. A tear prickled behind her eyes.

Gently taking her left hand in his, Tarleton slipped his ring onto her fourth finger. He pretended it stuck on her knuckle, before he pushed home his gift of imagination.

Hardly daring to breathe, Elizabeth pointed to her pocket where her comb lay. She pulled out—nothing, curling her fingers to show the round golden contours of her ring. Tarleton's smile widened with approval and he held out his left hand. Elizabeth slipped her ring down his fourth finger. Bowing her head, she kissed his hand. She felt him tremble at her touch.

Tarleton placed her right hand within his, their fingers twining and interlocking. Resting his left hand on top of the two, he held them firmly for a moment. Cupping Elizabeth's chin between his fingers, he gently drew her face near to his. His lips touched hers like a whispered vow in the holy silence of the chapel.

Elizabeth felt as if her heart had burst from her mouth and was sailing on wings above them.

Still clasping her hand, Tarleton rose, taking her with him. Seeing nothing but the light shining in each other's eyes, they walked slowly, hand in hand down the empty aisle. At the door, the cold night air jolted them back to reality. Tarleton gently withdrew his hand from hers.

"Dickon, does this—?" she began.

Tarleton smiled, a secret promise smoldered in the depths of his dark eyes. He again placed a finger to his lips. "There are some things that are best left unspoken, my love," he whispered.

The moment was shattered by the light, hurrying footsteps of Sister Agnes. "There you are!" She laughed, holding her candle higher. "Mother Abbess wondered if you had fallen down the well. Run along, Richard. I'll tend to your Robin."

Flashing a crooked smile to Elizabeth over his shoulder, Tarleton walked quickly down the arched corridor.

Sister Agnes turned her full, undivided attention on Elizabeth. "Now, you dear boy, come along with me."

Sister Agnes moved with surprising speed for someone of her girth. Before Elizabeth knew what was happening, she was firmly propelled in the opposite direction from Tarleton's receding footsteps. Stopping midway in her flight down an inner hallway, Sister Agnes threw open a door.

"I'm sure you will find this much more comfortable than some smelly hayloft at an inn!" She beamed proudly.

Inside the small room was a cot covered with a thin straw mattress, linen sheets and a woven wool blanket. A basin and a pitcher of fresh water waited on a small table by the bed. Beside the bowl lay a folded piece of huck toweling. A wooden cross hung over the bed. Everything in the room, including the stone floor, was painfully clean.

"Aye, good Sister," Elizabeth replied in her best boy's voice. "'Tis a damn sight better. Oh, I beg your pardon!" She hoped she sounded convincing.

Sister Agnes shook with laughter. "Just like a boy! Now, Mother Abbess says your clothing is a disgrace, and, I must confess, I heartily agree with her. What they need is a good cleaning and a bit of mending, by the look of them. So, my Robin, you just hop like a bird right out of those things, and I shall set you to rights."

Within a few efficient minutes, Sister Agnes left Elizabeth cowering naked behind the door. Her filthy clothes disappeared down the hall over the arm of the clucking good lady, who was none the wiser of Elizabeth's secret. Feeling her way carefully to the bed, Elizabeth pulled back the covers and slipped gratefully in between the clean sheets. She wondered when Tarleton would come to join her. The bed was a bit narrow for the two of them, but Elizabeth was sure they could manage. She certainly wouldn't mind if she had to lie on top of him. Elizabeth fell asleep, dreaming of Tarleton's warm smile and sweet lovemaking.

"Come in, Richard," responded Mother Catherine pleasantly when Tarleton rapped softly on her door. "I was wondering if you had forgotten my message."

"Never, good Mother." Tarleton respectfully kissed her hand. "I was in the chapel, saying my prayers. Surprised?"

A small lift of her eyebrows was the only outward sign of Mother Catherine's amazement. "Nothing you do surprises me, Richard. It is merely a matter of the degree, which is interesting."

Shifting his feet, Tarleton waited for her to offer him a seat. There were only two women in the world he respected—the Queen and Mother Catherine. No—three. Now there was Elizabeth.

Mother Catherine pointed to her desk. "There is some malmsey wine on the table. Be so good as to pour two glasses, Richard. And, Richard, mind the glasses. They are from Venice and extremely costly."

"Malmsey?" Tarleton lifted his brows in surprise.

"They tell me that a glassful after supper does wonders for one's digestion and aids one's sleep." Mother Catherine folded her hands comfortably over her stomach.

"They do, do they?" Tarleton grinned. "Whoever 'they' are must be very generous. Malmsey and Venetian glass?" He handed her one of the slim, gold-flecked goblets.

"Part of the dowry from one of our new novices. Now, sit down, you rogue. I have in mind some serious talk with you." She pointed to the low footstool. Nodding, Tarleton seated himself.

"Good!" Mother Catherine sipped a little of her wine, then looked directly into Tarleton's eyes. "Now, Richard, tell me why, in God's holy name, did you cut off that beautiful girl's lovely hair, and what is she doing dressed as a boy and running around the countryside with you?"

Chapter Thirteen

Tarleton's stomach lurched, though his smile never faltered.

"A girl?" he asked smoothly. "You mean Robin?"

"Do not play the fool with me, Master Jester. I am far better at it than you are. Who is she?"

Twirling the delicate glass in his hand, Tarleton watched the ruby liquid shimmer within the golden-flaked crystal. "She's a lass who—" he began, but Mother Catherine's chuckle stopped him.

"Oh, no, my son. She is no lass. She is gentle-born. Those hands of hers have seen nothing harder than plying a needle, though I noticed some recent blisters and cuts. What has she been doing?"

"Riding a goat." Tarleton smiled at the recollection.

"Oh, Richard!" The ancient abbess took a large sip of wine before she continued. "She is obviously wellborn and well educated, too." Pausing, she waited for some response from her favorite "black sheep."

The sheep, however, said nothing.

Mother Catherine continued placidly. "Shall I tell you who she is, Master Trickster? Has she donned that shameful garb to hide her true identity? Perhaps she is fleeing from an unwanted marriage?"

Tarleton poked at the fire.

Mother Catherine nodded to herself. "Is your Robin the spirited Lady Elizabeth who is fleeing from Sir Robert La Faye?"

A slow grin spread across Tarleton's face as he continued to regard the leaping flames. "So you've heard that story, good Mother?" he asked softly.

"Our walls are not as thick as some people's heads, Richard. The whole county has heard the tale. But I must confess you don't quite fit the description of a Scottish lord with a coach and four. I want the truth, Richard. All of it!" Sitting back, Mother Catherine sipped her wine and waited.

Tarleton sighed. He should have known better than to try to bluff his way with the Reverend Mother Catherine. She had him pegged from the first day he arrived at her door— a half-dead, sixteen-year-old scarecrow with his back laid open by a whip. In the twelve years since then, she had doctored his brawling wounds, scolded his morals, given him sound advice that he usually ignored, and prayed unceasingly for his soul. He, in turn, adored her as the mother he had never known.

"If I did not know you to be a saintly woman, Mother, I would think you a witch!" His white teeth flashed in the firelight.

"Saints have been soothsayers in their time," she observed.

Tarleton drank deeply; the wine coursed warmly through his veins.

"You are right, as usual. My humble apprentice is the Lady Elizabeth Hayward of Esmond Manor and goddaughter to the Queen. Yes, she is the runaway wife, though, in truth, she was never married to Sir Robert, who, incidentally, is a foul . . . hedgepig." Checking his language, Tarleton continued. "The lady was on her way to court when her horse bolted. She found me—" remembering, he chuckled "—and she asked for my protection and assistance. In faith, we are on our way to the Queen."

"And her father is, in fact, dead?"

A muscle in Tarleton's jaw tightened. "Aye, and by foul play, I suspect. I'll take the matter to Sir Francis Walsingham by and by."

"Yes, I thought her sorrow was genuine," mused Mother Catherine. "How long have you dragged this poor lady around the countryside on your way to Hampton Court?"

"Six—seven days." Tarleton suddenly felt uncomfortable as her eyes sliced into his soul.

"All that time, and you are only halfway there?" she murmured.

"There have been...complications along the way." Taking a deep breath, Tarleton recounted their adventures, including their accidental meeting with Sir Robert. He voiced his fear that Sir Robert's hirelings would discover them.

Mother Catherine sipped her wine reflectively. "There is one more reason, sweet Richard. You do not wish your journey to end."

"Not wish it to end?" Tarleton looked at her with amazement. "God's teeth! Every day we spend out on the road we are in danger. Elizabeth has nightmares. She is tired, dirty, hungry—"

"And she is desperately in love with you, my son." Mother Catherine finished quietly.

Tarleton gaped at her. How could Mother Catherine know that? Tarleton only half believed it himself.

The wise woman chuckled. "Don't look like a landed trout, Richard. It is as plain as the nose on your face."

"How...how do you know she loves me?" he flustered. "I am merely her servant. She is a noble lady."

"And she loves you, poor little thing. One only has to see her smile at you. What is worse, my fine jackanapes, you are equally besotted with her!"

Laughing nervously, Tarleton drained the remains of the malmsey. "You know me, Mother. I have a love in every village and town. In haylofts, under hedgerows, by kitchen fires—''

''Enough, Richard! I am well aware of your history. This time, it is different. I can see it, and if you refuse to admit it, at least to yourself, then you are the biggest fool the good Lord ever created!''

''I do love her,'' he whispered. ''God help me, Mother, but I do.''

''How much?'' Mother Catherine leaned forward to read his face.

''I love her more than my own life.''

There was a heavy silence in the room. Only the fire, sinking into embers, gave an occasional hiss and pop.

''Does she know this?'' the mother abbess probed.

Tarleton nodded slowly. ''I think so. I have tried to show her.''

''Have you taken your obvious advantage?'' she asked directly.

Tarleton gazed unflinchingly into her bright eyes. ''Elizabeth came to me and lay willingly with me. I won't deny it. I would, by all that is holy, make her my wife!''

''Ha! The Queen will have you hung, drawn and quartered. You know how she feels about marriage and virginity. She is obsessed with the second and despises the first. And I speak no treason within these walls, Master Spy, so don't start taking notes. You have gotten yourself into a pretty pickle this time. Pour us more wine, Richard. I fear I will not sleep well this night.''

Tarleton generously refilled their glasses from the bottle on the table. He could almost hear the humming inside Mother Catherine's head as she examined his problem from every angle. It was actually a relief that she had forced his story out of him.

''Well, good Mother?'' Handing her the goblet, he sat again at her feet. ''Can you give me absolution?''

"I will give you several pieces of good advice. Like bird shot, I will fire them forth all in one volley. You decide which will strike home." She sipped her wine thoughtfully before continuing.

"The most practical thing would be to leave the lady in my care. I could have her safely to Hampton Court within two days' time, while you can continue on your merry way. I understand York has very nice weather this time of year," she suggested.

"York is damned cold this time of year." Tarleton dismissed her first idea with a shrug of his shoulders. "Next?"

"You say she rides? I could loan you both good horses. You would be at Hampton by this time tomorrow night."

"Horses have a particular dislike for my hide. The feeling is mutual." Tarleton grinned ruefully. "I do better on goats."

Mother Catherine sighed. "Very well. Continue in your disguise as master and apprentice, but not by the back lanes. You must travel with all speed on the main road. I can provide you with funds. You could be at Hampton Court in less than three days—two, if the weather holds."

Tarleton shook his head. "Elizabeth has the courage that would shame half the Queen's guard, but she tires faster than I do, though she hates to admit it. We shall reach Hampton Court in four, possibly five more days."

"Five days? What can you hope will happen in five days?"

Tarleton spoke with quiet determination. "A miracle might happen in five days. You always told me I should put my fate in God's hands."

The old lady sighed. "Why do you always take the right advice, and use it at the wrong time?"

"Because I'm a fool?" Tarleton teased.

Smiling sadly at him, she ran her fingers through his dark hair.

"I shall ask that your body be buried here," she told him half-seriously.

He grinned. "Please don't forget my head. It will be hanging around on London Bridge."

"Finish your wine, Richard," Mother Catherine snapped. "Then go to bed. I've put you out in the gatehouse, as usual."

"I know—to keep the rooster away from the hens." He wiggled his brows at her. "And where have you hidden my sweet chick?"

"I think the rooster has had quite enough excitement for one day," Mother Catherine remarked archly.

"Point taken, good Mother!" Tarleton tossed back the rest of his malmsey, then replaced the glass carefully on the table. "My thanks for your wine—and for your good advice. I shall sleep like a babe. Good night, Mother." Bowing, he winked at her.

"God give you good rest, my son," she answered as he closed the door behind him.

Staring into the dying embers for a long time, Mother Catherine slowly sipped her malmsey and thought on Tarleton's latest scrape. Finally she rose, rubbed her hands together to warm her stiff joints, then moved to her desk. Drawing the candle close to her eyes, she took out her writing materials. Dipping her quill into the thick ink, she began a letter to another one of her "black sheep."

"To Sir Walter Raleigh at the Queen's court, Hampton. My dear boy, I am in most urgent need of your aid and influence..." she began.

The clock in the courtyard struck half past midnight when she snuffed out her candle.

The next morning dawned chill and wet, with rain falling intermittently. After a good breakfast of porridge, bread slathered with marmalade, and hot ale, Tarleton and Elizabeth made ready their goodbyes to the ladies of St. Aloysius.

Mother Catherine drew Tarleton aside and pretended to adjust the lacing of his jerkin. "I have heard some news this morning, just after matins, which I need to tell you, my son."

Looking down into Mother's Catherine's eyes, Tarleton saw an unaccustomed fear in them. "What news, Mother?" He licked his dry lips.

"The miller, when he delivered our flour this morning, told Sister Agnes that Sir Robert La Faye is offering a reward for the return of Lady Elizabeth."

"A reward?" Tarleton felt as if someone had punched him hard in the stomach.

"Aye, one that would tempt St. Michael himself," the mother abbess emphasized. "Twenty golden angels."

Tarleton whistled softly through his teeth. "I see." For such a sum, most of the countryside would sell their souls to the devil.

"Your apprentice will be most diligently sought..." Mother Catherine let the rest of her thought hang in the air. For such a sum, Tarleton knew his life was not worth a farthing if he came between Elizabeth and a fortune seeker.

The jester glanced over to Elizabeth, who spoke in deep conversation with the animated Sister Agnes. Elizabeth's face shone from good food, and a secure night's sleep. He had half a mind to take Mother Catherine's advice, and leave her in the care of the good sisters. Mother Catherine's warnings had given him a restless night, despite the malmsey. This new piece of information made his blood run cold. Just then, Elizabeth smiled at him, which pierced his heart with a ray of sunshine. In that moment, he knew Elizabeth would fight to stay with him, no matter what the future held. For his part, he was equally adamant that he would keep her by his side for as long as possible. Hampton Court would loom on the horizon soon enough.

"Sir Robert has raised the stakes, good Mother," Tarleton said with a rueful grin. "It makes the game more interesting."

"And dangerous," she added.

"Life is dangerous, Mother. And I've never been able to resist a good wager."

"May God be with you and your lady." Mother Catherine blessed him.

"Amen to that, good Mother!" Tarleton kissed her hand. "Perhaps he'll have an ace or two up his sleeve for me!"

"I missed you last night." Elizabeth's silver voice broke into Tarleton's thoughts as they slogged down the muddy road toward Oxford. "Sister Agnes took all my clothes to wash them, and I had to keep to my bed for decency's sake. I waited for you," she added reproachfully, "but I must have fallen asleep."

Tarleton smiled. Twenty angels? Elizabeth was worth a hundredfold. "'Tis not from lack of wanting, sweetling. Indeed, I spent a restless night wishing to hold thee in my arms."

"Why did you not come to me, then?"

"Because Mother Catherine put me far away in the gatehouse."

Elizabeth furrowed her brows. "Did she think I was there?"

Laughing, Tarleton touched her cheek lightly. "Nay, my love. She knew exactly where you were—and exactly *who* you are."

Elizabeth drew in her breath sharply. "She *knew* I was not a boy?"

"Aye, and she knows you are Lady Elizabeth Hayward."

"How?"

"Because she is the wisest woman in England—and because she heard the tale of the runaway wife."

"Oh!" A brilliant blush stole into her cheeks. "Did she guess that we . . . that is, that you and I are . . . I mean . . . ?"

Tarleton laughed softly at her confusion. "That we are lovers? Aye, my lady, she did. She put a large flea in my ear for that! That is why you were hidden deep in the cloister, and I was banished to the gatehouse."

Elizabeth arched her brow. "I am surprised that the mother abbess let you take me away from her protection."

"Oh, she suggested strongly that she keep you," Tarleton replied with a twinkle in his eye. "But I said you weren't cut out to be a nun."

"What ho! If you have a Christian charity about you, help me!"

The unusual greeting halted Tarleton and Elizabeth less than a mile from the outskirts of the great university town. The distressed voice of a young man was clear enough, but the speaker was nowhere to be seen.

"Who goes there?" Tossing the pack to Elizabeth, Tarleton quietly drew his dagger. Though they were within sight of civilization, the jester took no chances. Mother Catherine's warning made Tarleton doubly cautious.

"In the tree! I've been hung up here the whole sottish night, and I am half-dead with cold."

Looking up, Tarleton made out a dark shape caught against the black bark of an ancient oak beside the road. As the jester approached the base of the tree, a large, gray animal rose up, growling menacingly. "God's nightshirt, 'tis a wolf!" Gripping his dagger tighter, Tarleton crouched, ready if the beast sprang.

"Down, Toby!" the voice in the tree commanded.

"Oh, the poor thing!" Brushing past Tarleton, Elizabeth crouched down by the animal. "He's been tied up on a short lead!"

"Eliz . . . Robin!" Tarleton moved toward her, but the huge beast growled at his approach.

" 'Tis only a dog, master.'' Elizabeth fumbled with the stout rope that the hairy brute pulled taut. "He's a beautiful, beautiful wolfhound!'' Making soft, cooing noises, she untied the animal from the tree. She led him to a puddle of muddy water, which the dog lapped up greedily.

"He's all bluff," said the voice above them. "That is why I'm up here. For sweet Jesu's sake, get me down!"

Sheathing his knife, Tarleton stepped up to the oak for a closer inspection. A young man, extremely red in the face, hung by the nape of his student gown on a thick branch. His feet dangled a good six feet above the ground.

Casting a wary glance at the dog, Tarleton swung himself up into the tree. "Get ready for a drop," he warned the student, then he cut him free. Jumping lightly down, Tarleton helped the unfortunate boy to stand.

"I am in your honor's service forever!" the student gasped, rubbing the back of his neck. "Jonathan Biggs, of Christ Church." Jonathan tried to bow but found himself too stiff. Tarleton caught him before he tumbled over.

"Tarleton, roving player and jester. Yon wolf-tamer is my prentice, Robin." Tarleton regarded Elizabeth and the dog with open amazement. The animal far outweighed her, and should the beast take it into its head to stand on its hind legs, it would tower over her. Yet, both the girl and Toby seemed perfectly at ease with each other.

"You have no idea how pleased I am to make your acquaintance." Jonathan beamed. Then he shivered. "Brr! This foul weather is not conducive for idle conversation. Pray accompany me to my humble lodgings, where we may dry ourselves by a goodly fire, and partake of some much-needed refreshment."

Jonathan relieved Elizabeth from the thrall of the excited Toby, who practically leapt into his master's arms for joy. For the next few moments there was a great deal of flailing limbs and paws, until man and beast had sorted themselves into their proper order.

Tarleton bowed to the student. "We accept, with pleasure your kind invitation, for methinks my boy has fallen in
love with your... dog. As for myself, I am wet to the skin."

Snapping his fingers at Elizabeth to take up the pack,
Tarleton and Jonathan, with the noble Toby striding ahead,
made their way toward the city of a hundred steepled bells.
With a small sigh of resignation, Elizabeth shouldered the
bulging sack and trudged after them. At least, the promise
of a fire and food was in the offing. Since leaving Godstow,
she and the jester had gotten miserably cold and wet. Elizabeth fervently hoped that Tarleton would decide to spend
the rest of the day at Oxford. The wet weather did not bode
well for a day of travel.

The College of Christ Church proved to be a magnificent
collection of buildings around three sides of a grassy quad-
rangle. On the right was a high-roofed, mullion-windowed
building that was, Jonathan proudly informed his guests,
the Dining Hall. "And there, my fine fellows, you may entrance, enchant, and otherwise entertain us poor slaving
students with your many talents."

The gregarious student hurried them up a narrow stone
staircase nearby. Throwing open his door, he ushered his
guests into a small, drafty room that was sparsely and
plainly furnished.

"Smith!" Jonathan bellowed down the staircase. "A
plague on that varlet. What ho! Smith, I say!"

A thin boy of thirteen or so scrambled up the stairs, carrying an armload of wood. "Master Biggs, sir! I did not
expect ye back so soon." The boy quickly began laying a fire
in the small hearth, while Toby hung over his shoulder,
watching every move. The fire leapt up in the grate and began to crackle cheerfully.

"Back so soon? Nay, come too late, you snipe. This is my
bed maker and general thorn in my side, Roger Smith,"
Jonathan said, introducing the serving boy to Tarleton and
Elizabeth. "Now, Smith, scamper to the buttery, and take

whatever you can lay your hands on. Bring it back within two ticks of the clock, for we are famished. D'ye hear me, Smith? Perishing with hunger!''

As the boy raced out the door, Jonathan's cheerful voice followed him. ''Give my compliments to Master Robinson and tell him to wait upon me directly!''

Slamming the door, Jonathan turned to his newfound friends with a grin. ''Make yourselves at home. You are my most honored guests for the fine service you have done me and my faithful hound this day.''

While Jonathan disappeared into the bedchamber to change, the faithful hound settled himself comfortably on the floor in front of the fire. He put his great shaggy head in Elizabeth's lap, allowing her to rub his ears. Tarleton watched the pair with an envious smile. How he would love to lie where that flea-bitten beast was, and have sweet Elizabeth ply her fingers through *his* hair!

Reappearing in dry garb, Jonathan pulled a stool and chair nearer to the fire, waving Tarleton into the better of the two. ''No doubt you have been wondering what was I doing up that infernal tree,'' the student began, easing off his shoes and wiggling his toes pleasurably toward the warming grate.

''The question had occurred in my mind,'' Tarleton conceded.

''And so you shall be answered. I am, as you may have surmised, a scholar in the eternal quest for knowledge. I am also, in my lesser moments, a songster of no mean repute,'' Jonathan added modestly.

''A most mean meaning!'' interrupted a pleasant voice at the doorway.

''Philip! You come apace and in good time!'' Jonathan summoned his friend inside. ''Close the door, man, or you will kill us all with cold. This is my soul mate, boon companion, and friend in need, Philip Robinson, aspiring student of the medical arts. These two fine fellows are my saviors. They are also—players!'' Jonathan ended triumphantly.

Philip grinned good-naturedly. "I spy some sport in this. Hell's bells, Jonathan! Where have you been? We missed you at supper last night.''

"Trussed up and hung out to drown by two of the vilest villains it has ever been my misfortune to meet. And, by my troth, should I ever meet them again, I shall serve them with a suit so enormous, 'twill make them weep whole onions for a month," Jonathan replied with a show of outrage.

"In case you have not noticed it, good players, my friend is a lawyer-to-be.'' Stretching his long frame out before the fire, Philip pillowed his head on Toby's rump. He nodded to Elizabeth. "I see Toby's affections are as fickle as ever.''

"If he were of a more bloodthirsty nature, I would not have been set upon in such a rude and ungodly manner.'' By his tone, it was plain Jonathan was most anxious to continue the tale of his misadventure.

"And what, pray tell, was your offense?'' Philip yawned.

"Why, for the singing of my latest composition!'' Jonathan blustered.

Tarleton suppressed a smile. "Was your song so badly rhymed, Master Biggs?''

"Nay, 'tis one of my best compositions!'' Jonathan blustered.

Philip winked at Tarleton. "Jonathan's good father thinks his son is here at Oxford studying the law. What he doesn't know is that my fine friend spends most of his time in alehouses drinking beer, falling in love and writing ballads about his disasters of the heart.'' Closing his eyes, Philip looked as if he was going to take a nap.

Elizabeth bent her head low over Toby to hid her grin.

Jonathan ignored Philip's last gibe. "Yesterday afternoon I took Toby for a small stroll along the country lanes, singing to my heart's content. We were practically home when I was set upon by two burly varlets!''

"Bandits?" Tarleton asked casually. He wondered if Jonathan's assailants were in search of a reward of twenty golden angels.

"I had no time to inquire their exact occupation. They seized me in a most uncomfortable fashion, and they asked where I had learned such a vile song. ''Tis mine own work!' I told them proudly. Whereupon one of them offered to cut out my tongue!"

Philip's eyes snapped open. "By all the angels, what song of yours so offended them?"

"The one I sang for you the other night. You remember, 'The Runaway Wife'!" Jonathan announced with a flourish.

Elizabeth gasped softly. Tarleton's story seemed to be traveling faster than they were. She wondered what would Jonathan say if he knew the runaway wife was sitting on the floor by his hearth scratching his dog's chin?

Tarleton assumed an amused expression. "What is so offensive about a runaway wife, unless, of course, you are the abandoned husband?" he inquired lazily.

Jonathan snorted loudly. "Thereby hangs the tale—and me along with it! It seems these two ruffians are in the service of one Sir Robert La Faye—the same Sir Robert who was left at the altar by his less-than-blushing bride, the lady of my song. I heard the tale last week, and it cried out to be set to rhyme and music."

"''Tis become a popular ballad at the Bulldog," Philip informed Tarleton. "Yester eve I heard the young choristers of Magdalen singing it on their way to practice. They did it right well a cappella in three-part harmony."

Jonathan smiled ruefully. "These whoresons had no taste for my music. They hung me up on a tree to teach me to sing a better tune, as they told me. They tied up poor Toby within an inch of his life, though he never sang a note!"

"What are Sir Robert's men doing so near Oxford?" Tarleton innocently inquired, though his heart pounded heavily within his chest. "The story of the runaway wife, as I heard it in Banbury, told of the Lady Elizabeth going north with her Scottish lover."

Elizabeth felt her cheeks begin to burn, and she was glad she sat so near to the fire, ignored by the others. If they only knew! A Scottish lover? Oh no! Her one true love was only a heartbeat away from them. She stole a quick glance at Tarleton, who returned her look with a conspiratorial wink.

"I asked them that selfsame question as they hung me up. The blackguards said they sought the Lady Elizabeth Hayward on the southern roads. They said she is goddaughter to the Queen and that Sir Robert is not deceived by the tale of a lover in kilts. I'll tell you true, good friends. If the master is anything like his men, I hope to heaven that sweet lady is never apprehended." Jonathan paused and sighed theatrically. "Would I could meet her! I hear tell she is fair of face, and she can ride a horse like Diana the Huntress. Oh, what a ballad I would compose in her honor!"

Tarleton laughed in a deep, jovial way. With a knowing look at Elizabeth, he observed, "It sounds as if you've fallen in love with the lady sight unseen, Master Biggs."

"Jonathan falls in love at the drop of a hat," remarked Philip calmly.

The young lawyer drew himself up. "I have already suffered grievous bodily injury on her account, my friend, and I would do it again if I had but one sweet look from such a lady!" Jonathan's face softened into a dreamy state.

"I would hold out for a kiss, myself," Philip argued. "A loving look is well enough, but, if I am going to suffer for it, I'd prefer a kiss for my pains."

"But she is a noble lady!" Jonathan looked a little hurt that his romantic ideal was being questioned. "She does not offer kisses to poor students. I would settle for a kind look."

Philip snorted. "I would settle for the kiss and—perhaps, a glove to remember her by."

Elizabeth could tell that Philip took pleasure in baiting his lovesick friend. No doubt the two scholars would have debated the issue for the next hour had it not been for the timely arrival of Smith, loaded with heaping trenchers of purloined food from the college buttery.

As Tarleton's apprentice, Elizabeth went immediately to work, toasting slabs of bread on a poker and watching over the warming wine. Young Roger clattered noisily as he arranged cups, plates and knives on the table. Sniffing the food, Toby roused himself to take his place under the board, there to await the inevitable scraps.

Eating quietly by the fire, Elizabeth enjoyed watching and listening as the two youthful students dined with Tarleton. *I shall remember all of this,* she promised herself as she bit contentedly into a thick wedge of onion tart. *In the years to come...*

She did not want to think about the bleakness of the years to come without Tarleton's rich, merry voice in her ear, without his strong arms around her holding her nightmares at bay, without his fiery love to light up her heart. No, she would live fully each of these golden moments, and store them, like a treasure horde, in the velvet-lined box of her memory.

At the end of the meal, Jonathan rocked back on his stool. "Now, let us turn our dull and sluggish brains to merrier pastimes!" he waxed warmly, fortified by a cup of Madeira wine. "We have among our company a famous player—Master Tarleton! The question that I put to you, good Philip, is this, do we share our guest with the rest of our dronelike company? Or do we keep his merry wit entirely to ourselves?"

Philip pretended to ponder the question deeply.

Glancing over to Elizabeth, Tarleton gave her an encouraging wink. Thank the stars they had met Jonathan, he thought. Unknowingly, Tarleton and Elizabeth could have walked right into the arms of Sir Robert's minions. Here, within the golden walls of Christ Church, the jester and his charge were safe, dry and well fed thanks to Jonathan's gratitude. Tarleton was beginning to believe in Elizabeth's guardian angel riding on her shoulder. He just hoped the angel wouldn't fall off before the end of the journey.

Philip cleared his throat. "Ah, Jonathan, let us share the wealth. Our sniveling companions struggling with parchment and quill could use a bit of amusement. Good Master Tarleton, would you grace our humble Hall with your wit and witticisms?" Philip toasted Tarleton with his brimming cup. "I fear we cannot pay you with coin, only food and our good audience."

"My pleasure is yours, masters." Tarleton affably returned the toast. "Let us be merry this day and the devil take tomorrow!"

"May the devil take Sir Robert, too!" Elizabeth whispered into Toby's friendly ear.

Chapter Fourteen

"'Tis a goodly room!" Tarleton's deep voice filled the empty hall. "By my head, sweet Robin, you are getting spoiled. After playing in such a fine place, you will think yourself too grand to sing for pennies at an inn."

"I will sing wherever you are ... master," Elizabeth answered softly.

Crossing the polished floor, Tarleton leaned over her so that only she could hear his words. "I would have you sing by my side forever, sweetling."

Elizabeth dimpled with pleasure as his honeyed voice filled her ear.

Leaving Jonathan and Philip to themselves for an hour or two, the jester and his apprentice rehearsed for their evening's performance in the middle of the great vaulted Dining Hall built by Cardinal Wolsey in King Henry VIII's time. The magnificence of the carvings and stained glass matched anything Elizabeth had seen in France.

"Ah! But wait until you see Hampton Court! Wolsey built that one, too." Tarleton rolled his eyes in appreciation.

"Yes ... Hampton Court ..." murmured Elizabeth quietly. Hampton Court meant the end of her time with this wonderful man who stood close beside her, his arm flung companionably around her shoulders.

"Aye, I know, chuck," he whispered, understanding her hesitation. "But let us put that distant palace out of our minds. We are *here* now."

"So long as Sir Robert is not here, I am content." Elizabeth smiled crookedly.

Tarleton noticed that one of the serving men strained to overhear their conversation. *He is probably thinking that we are plotting to steal the students blind, and take the college silver plate, as well.* Whirling away from Elizabeth's side, Tarleton executed several handsprings in succession, ending with a spinning leap.

"I shall start with that to warm things up," he announced in a loud voice. "Now, let us practice a little juggling."

He handed Elizabeth his six colored balls. "Toss them to me, one at a time, when I call for them. When I have finished, I will toss them back to you, one at time. Ready, boy?"

"Aye, master!" Assuming her best manly stance, Elizabeth pitched the balls to Tarleton.

In a few moments, he had them all in the air, his hands whipping effortlessly about them.

What clever hands he has! Elizabeth admired. *And what wonderful things he can do to me with those supple fingers!* The memory of yesterday's tender lovemaking filled her with a warm glow. Tarleton's cheerful voice broke into her sweet daydream.

"Now, Robin Redbreast, catch!" He flipped the balls back to her. She dropped the last one and it went bouncing away under the benches by the wall.

"If that happens tonight, pretend it is part of the act," Tarleton told her. "Remember, play the part always. Bluff and bluster! Now, try out your voice with the love song."

She is a bewitching nymph! Tarleton's heart beat faster as he listened to her sing "The Greenwood Tree." When he spied her secret smile, he knew she sang the words just for him. *I would take you back to that greenwood glen, if I had no honor at all.*

The sounds of several hands clapping startled Elizabeth as she ended her song. Two serving men, a few scullions from the kitchen, and the steward himself stood at the far end of the vast room, smiling at her. She bowed gracefully to them.

"Ye have a sweet-voiced boy, Master Jester," remarked the steward to Tarleton. "After you have entertained the young gentlemen tonight, we would appreciate a song or two in the pantry. You will find the college's beer is the best in Oxford," he added by way of enticement.

Tarleton grinned. "Robin and I would be honored, sir, to enjoy both your company and your beer."

Nodding, the steward waved his minions back to their duties.

Tarleton clapped Elizabeth soundly on the back. "I vow I have had better luck with you by my side, Robin, than I ever did alone." His voice sank into a whisper. "And I am not only referring to the offers of free beer!"

Elizabeth blushed as her soul sang.

Formal dinner in the Hall that evening was everything Jonathan had promised it would be. Tarleton and Elizabeth waited in the anteroom while the stately dons and their robed students ate their noisy way through huge slabs of beef, thick wedges of cheese, buckets of beer, round loaves of crusty bread, and dishes of stewed apples and pears served in a sweet cinnamon sauce. Elizabeth's mouth watered at the delicious savory smells that wafted through the crack of the door.

"Patience, sweetling," said Tarleton, adjusting his cap. "Our dinner will be just as good anon. And Jonathan has offered us a place by his fire tonight. What more could we ask?"

Elizabeth arched her eyebrow mischievously. "A little privacy?"

Tarleton brushed her cheek with his finger. "In a college full of young men whose every thought is turned toward the fairer sex?"

The urge to kiss her seized Tarleton. Her tempting lips, glistening and pink, hovered near his. His desire for her swept over him like a sudden hot wind. It was all he could do to remember where they were, and that the steward would summon them at any moment. To distract himself, Tarleton fiddled with the ragged ribbons on his motley coat.

"I wish I had a needle and thread," Elizabeth muttered, trying to take her mind off the exciting nearness of her love. Just now she thought he was going to kiss her. She was sure she had spied that intent dancing in Tarleton's brown eyes. But the moment disappointingly passed. "Your tunic becomes more and more a shambles every time you put it on," she grumbled.

Tarleton nodded. "Aye, it has seen hard wear these past two months. I must get a new one when I return to court."

"In bright satins and gaudy velvets?" Elizabeth asked innocently, thinking of the new motley she planned as a surprise for him.

Tarleton snorted. "Nay, sweetling! I am no courtier! Can you see me in such a fine array?"

Yes, Elizabeth thought as she watched him practice a few notes on his penny whistle. *I can see you in a doublet of silver satin and black velvet. You would make a finer gentleman than many who strut about in such clothing—like Sir Robert La Faye.*

Poking his head through the double doors, the steward announced that the company awaited the players. Tarleton tossed the whistle to Elizabeth, winked broadly at her, then he bounded into the Dining Hall. Elizabeth followed close behind him.

Unlike the sedate audience of the priory of the night before, the Dining Hall of Christ Church was a roaring mass of high spirits, fueled by beer and youth. The budding physicians, mathematicians, lawyers, clergymen, philosophers and courtly gentlemen were in constant movement about the long trestle tables and benches. Leaping fires roared in the two large fireplaces opposite each other in the center of the chamber. At one end, on a raised platform, the dean and his dons quietly dined at the high table, as if the chaos below them was a mere figment of their imagination.

The entire company greeted Tarleton's jingling appearance with loud cheers and stamping feet, since their hands were full of bread and mugs.

Throwing back his shoulders, Tarleton flexed his knees and tumbled the length of the hall between the two rows of tables. This feat was greeted with more cheers and stamping.

In midflight, Elizabeth saw another one of his bells fly off. Quietly moving down the side of the room, she retrieved it among the forest of feet. *I vow I will find a needle and thread this night,* she promised herself as she pocketed the brass trinket.

Tarleton's performance continued its rollicking pace. He juggled the colored balls higher than he had at rehearsal. Elizabeth managed to catch everything thrown at her, including someone's cap. Grinning, she tossed it back into the cheerfully rowdy mob. She good-naturedly ducked airborne rolls and greasy rib bones. Everyone, including a noisy pack of college dogs under the tables, had a rousing good time.

Grabbing her around her waist, Tarleton heaved her on top of a table.

"My prentice may look the angel, but he has a song which will please the devil in you," announced Tarleton with a sly smile. "Sing the one about the wench with the rolling eye!" he whispered to her.

Elizabeth gaped at him. "But that's not what we practiced this afternoon!" she protested under her breath.

"But that is what they want to hear, Robin Redbreast!" Though his lips were curved in a wide smile, Tarleton's eyes pleaded. "Play the part." His dark brows wiggled at her.

Elizabeth cleared her throat and began the first verse. As Tarleton predicted, it was exactly what the students wanted. After the third rendition, Elizabeth gratefully got off the table while Tarleton launched into a few of his bawdy stories and jokes, all with brilliant puns and wordplay, which delighted the student audience.

At the end of their performance, Tarleton held his hands out for silence. "Sweet Robin has a love song to sing you to your rest, good gentlemen, and I pray you give a careful ear to it." Bowing, Tarleton turned to Elizabeth, who walked quietly to the center of the vast room.

"'Under the greenwood tree...'" she began, lifting her voice as if it were on a dove's wings, flying over the heads of the scholars.

Her eyes closed; she again envisioned the magic glade by the swift-flowing stream, as she sang of love on a summer's afternoon. There was utter silence as her last note died away, then the Hall erupted into a frenzy of banging, stamping, cheers and cries for more.

Tarleton's brown eyes glistened as he took her hand, and together they bowed before the high table. Even the venerable dean seemed pleased.

"Now, *that* is a love song, Biggs!" Philip called out, as Elizabeth and Tarleton made their exit toward the pantry.

Elizabeth grinned. She knew poor Jonathan would spend the next hour disputing the point.

In the darkened passageway between the hall and the kitchens, Tarleton's hand sought hers. Lifting it to his lips, he kissed her fingers, grazing her skin with his teeth and tongue. Her heart dancing, she shamelessly wished there was some discreet alcove nearby.

"I have never heard you sing that song as well as you did this night," Tarleton whispered.

"I sang it for you only," she responded softly.

His lips caressed the tender pulse point on her wrist. "I know."

The depth of his love, and his desire for her hung upon those simple two words. A delicious tremor inside her heated her thighs and the secret garden above them. After giving her hand a final squeeze, Tarleton dropped it as they entered the kitchens.

"Old Wolsey knew what he was doing when he planned these glorious rooms!" Tarleton enthused warmly over a mug of the promised "best beer in Oxford."

The Queen's favorite jester and his apprentice had sung a few songs, juggled a number of kitchen implements and told several ribald jokes for the appreciative kitchen staff. Comfortably seated on low stools in front of one of the massive fireplaces, the players tucked into a well-deserved supper.

"This is the king of all kitchens!" Tarleton continued, waving a bone in the air. "I am a collector of kitchens, my friends. In my humble opinion, 'tis the best in all England. Why, I do believe you can roast a whole ox in that fireplace!"

The cook beamed with greasy appreciation. "Two, if they are not above average in size," he boasted proudly.

While Tarleton and the cook waxed warmer over the comparative merits and sizes of the kitchens at Westminster Palace and Christ Church, Elizabeth sipped her beer and gazed dreamily into the fire. Filled with a good dinner, and secure in her love, Elizabeth allowed her fancy to wander. She imagined herself and Tarleton playing before the Queen at Hampton Court, not revealing Elizabeth's true identity until after the Queen had applauded their performance. *Surely, Her Majesty will see how much in love we*

*are, and she will grant me my dearest wish—to marry where
my heart is!*

She felt a sharp kick against her stool's leg. Yawning,
Elizabeth rubbed her eyes.

Tarleton pulled her to her feet. "'Tis time I put this scamp
to bed. We have many miles to go on the morrow. Our
thanks for the fine beer and supper!" Bowing, he pushed his
apprentice out the door and down the stone staircase to the
cloister below.

Kneeling on the cold flagged floor of the tiny Cathedral
of Christ Church, Elizabeth whispered her night prayers.
They had chanced upon this hidden church at the bottom of
the hall's staircase, and Elizabeth begged to slip inside for
her evening's devotions. Originally part of the Priory of St.
Frideswide upon whose foundations Cardinal Wolsey had
laid out his new institution of learning, the smallest cathedral in England was now completely surrounded by the college.

Finishing her prayers with a plea for the husband of her
choice, Elizabeth rose and looked for Tarleton. She heard
the soft tinkling of the belled coat that he still wore. Stepping out of the shadows, Tarleton went down on his knees
before her.

"Since I know you were praying for forgiveness, I pray
for yours, sweet lady," he whispered thickly. Taking both
her hands in his, he gazed up into her surprised eyes.

Elizabeth's lips trembled. "You have no need to ask me
for forgiveness, Dickon," she assured him, hoping he didn't
regret his lovemaking.

"There *is* need, lady," he responded softly. "I beg your
forgiveness for all the hardships I have brought upon you.
For cutting your fair hair, for dressing you in shameful rags,
and for thrusting you amid rough company." He grinned
sheepishly. "I am particularly sorry about the goat. That
was for my own amusement."

"And it spared meeting Sir Robert face-to-face," Elizabeth reminded him. She ran her fingers through the unruly tangles of his dark hair.

Tarleton continued doggedly. "Most of all, I beg your forgiveness for my failure to do what you asked of me. We should have been at Hampton Court by now. Instead I have pulled you hither and yon about the countryside."

"That has not been your fault, Dickon." Her throat felt dry. Was he planning on leaving her now? "There has been the weather, and avoiding Sir Robert's men—"

Tarleton shook his head. "Nay, dear heart! 'Tis because I was loath to part from you. Mother Catherine saw it clearly. And she reminded me of my place," he added bitterly.

Elizabeth's hands continued to softly stroke his hair. Her tender touch sent hot rivulets of liquid fire through him. Still kneeling, he wrapped his arms around her waist and buried his head in the folds of her shirt.

"I wish that your place was with me always, Dickon," Elizabeth murmured. "Are you asking my forgiveness for loving me?"

Tarleton smiled, his teeth shone in the dim light. "Nay, never that, sweetling. But I ask your forgiveness for desiring you...as I am far below your station." He placed a finger against her lips to stop her protest. "Nay, hear me out. That I will love you all my life, you know. That I wish to hide you away with me, I think you know. That the Queen would seek us out, and end this folly for both of us— that is a certainty. Forgive me, dearest Elizabeth, for putting us both in such an impossible position!" Bending his head, he kissed her hands, caressing the soft pads of her palms.

As his lips sweetly drained all her doubts and fears, a flood of overwhelming joy washed over Elizabeth. "I will never regret—nor forget—this time I have had with you, no matter what the future holds for either of us," she told him, barely able to speak. "There is nothing to forgive." She kissed his hair, inhaling the scent of fire smoke and a hint of lavender.

When he looked up at her, the light of desire illuminated his liquid brown eyes. "I have kept you in harm's way because of my own selfishness. Sir Robert is close, by all accounts." He started to tell her of the huge reward for her, then checked himself. Elizabeth had enough to worry her. "We should not have tarried here in Oxford today."

Elizabeth lightly pressed her lips against his. "I would not have had it any other way."

Rising and pulling her into the deepest shadow behind a thick pillar, Tarleton clasped her body to him. Hungrily his mouth covered hers with a long, lingering kiss as if he had been thirsty for many days and now drank from a cool mountain stream. His tongue delved into the sweetness of her mouth. A low growl rose deep from within his throat.

Clinging to him, Elizabeth was conscious of where his warm skin touched hers. She could feel his uneven breathing against her cheek as he held her in the darkness. His hard-muscled thigh brushed against her hip. The heat and fullness of his desire pressed against her as he took her mouth again. His nearness sent her senses spinning; she held wildfire in her arms. His little brass bells betrayed their presence, but no one heard them in that still, holy place.

Tarleton drew in a ragged breath. "If this were not a church, my love, I would lay you down right here on this cold stone, and show you again the depth of my love." Again he sought her honeyed lips.

"Perhaps Jonathan and Philip have gone out," suggested Elizabeth. A hot ache grew in her throat. "We could make use of their room for a bit."

Tarleton's eyes drank in her upturned face. "Perhaps," he answered briefly. Reluctantly they parted, though he was loath to let her go. Elizabeth intoxicated him like a strong, heady brew. There was not a spot in all of Christ Church where they wouldn't run some risk of discovery by one of the lusty students or their puritan masters. 'Twas as bad as the priory, Tarleton cursed to himself. Now that he had tasted of Elizabeth's sweet body, he craved her all the more. "Let us leave this place, sweetling," he growled. "And, by all that's holy, let's both try to remember that you are a boy!"

Turning abruptly on his heel, he strode out the church door, snapping his fingers for her to follow.

Elizabeth waited until her quickened pulse subsided, then she padded after him. *What I wouldn't give for a nice, cozy haystack just now!*

"What, ho, Tarleton!" Jonathan's voice echoed across the dark quad as the jester and Elizabeth emerged from the gloom of the cloister. "We thought you had gone up in smoke but then we heard your bells!"

Damn! Elizabeth fumed silently.

"My prentice was saying his bedtime prayers in your chapel," replied Tarleton easily, joining Jonathan and Philip near the college's gate.

"Bedtime? Nay, the evening has just begun." Jonathan wrapped his arms around each of their shoulders. "Your fame has traveled rapidly since dinner. There have been requests for your immediate appearance at the Bulldog yonder, where the sluggards of our sister colleges eagerly await your coming. Lighten their hearts—as well as their purses, Tarleton."

"Surely your apprentice can stay up an hour longer," Philip added good-naturedly. "No one in Oxford should miss hearing his sweet voice."

Tarleton nodded, secretly glad of the diversion the students offered. Had he and Elizabeth returned to Jonathan's room and found no one there, he knew he would have given in to his heart's desire, without a second thought to the danger of discovery. Tarleton hated to think what would happen to Elizabeth should the young men of Christ Church suspect there was a "doxy" in Jonathan's room.

"I would not deny the students of this great university the chance to throw away their money," Tarleton acquiesced.

Looking up at the few stars that peeped between the clouds, Elizabeth heartily wished Jonathan and Philip at the bottom of a well.

"Aye, that's the spirit!" Jonathan proclaimed loudly, as he and Philip propelled their guests across the rutted street and into a small, noisy alehouse that was crammed to overflowing with boisterous students.

Following closely behind Tarleton, Elizabeth silently cursed Jonathan's ill timing. *Tomorrow, the very first spot that looks inviting, I will seduce Tarleton no matter how many miles he insists we must travel!*

Leaping up on a long table in the middle of the warm, smoky room, Jonathan banged two pewter mugs together for silence. When his command for attention went unnoticed, Tarleton joined him. The sight of the broadshouldered man standing tall in a coat of motley and bells, grinning like Robin Goodfellow, reduced the clamor to a manageable level.

"Oyez! Oyez! Oyez!" Jonathan began in his most pompous manner. "At great *personal* expense, we have with us this evening the finest songster and punster of the land. The Queen's own favored player—"

"Here's to good Queen Bess!" cried a voice in the back. There was a general cheer, while Jonathan struggled to regain the fragile order.

"As I was saying, for your pleasure and his profit, sponsored by the gentlemen scholars of Christ Church—"

"Merton College forever!" sang out a slightly tipsy voice. His cry was immediately drowned by representatives of the other colleges.

"Here's to the lions of Oriel!"

"Balliol men, to me!"

"Magdalen!"

"Brasenose!"

Before a friendly riot could develop, Tarleton smilingly pushed Jonathan down to the floor. Picking up three wooden trenchers, the jester began to juggle them. Abandoning their partisan bickering, the students gave their noisy approval to the entertainment.

From juggling, Tarleton moved to a bawdy song concerning a fat friar and a thin widow, which was particularly well received.

"I hear tell you are partial to love songs," Tarleton began.

"We may as well sing about it, as there is nothing else we can do about it!" answered one wag near the door.

Tarleton laughed with sympathetic understanding. "Then allow my apprentice to join me, and we will sing of Robin Hood and Maid Marian."

Holding out his hand to Elizabeth, Tarleton pulled her up onto the tabletop beside him. Her white-gold hair caught the light from the lanterns.

"Ignore the noise and sing for me," he whispered into her ear, then he began the first verse.

When Elizabeth's soaring soprano joined the chorus, the room fell appreciatively silent. The students did not stir through the next five verses as Robin Hood sang of his prowess with a bow, and Marian asked if he had shot an arrow into her heart. The applause was thunderous at the conclusion.

"If they are as liberal with their pennies as they are with their enthusiasm, we shall make a fortune here tonight!" Tarleton whispered to Elizabeth as they bowed.

"Do you know the ballad of the runaway wife?" bellowed an older voice from a dim corner of the taproom.

Elizabeth's heart froze midbeat. The voice was her nightmare come true. She felt Tarleton tense beside her, though his smile remained in place.

"Nay, sir! I have not heard it," he answered smoothly. Inwardly Tarleton's mind moved quickly, assessing the possibilities of this unwelcome encounter. He cursed that he had left his dagger in Jonathan's room.

Sir Robert La Faye pushed his way through the press of students. His face flushed with drink and anger.

"Hast not heard it, Master Tarleton?" Sir Robert sneered, standing at the foot of the table. "Why, every whey-faced, pimpled ass in this room knows the song of the man who could not keep his bride!"

A shrill voice began to sing "Oh, hast thou heard of the lady fair..." but the words died in his throat when one of Sir Robert's men drew his sword, pointing it toward the offending youth.

A tense silence enveloped the taproom. Behind the counter, the landlord paled when he saw the black look in Sir Robert's eye. In an undertone, the proprietor told one of the tap boys to ease out the back door, and run for the town watch. Nodding, the youth wriggled through the crowd like an eel and was gone.

Stepping behind Tarleton's protective form, Elizabeth tried to control the spasmodic trembling within her. Sheer black fright swept through her. *Jesu, don't let me faint now!*

"Perchance you would like another ditty? 'The Fox and the Hens'?" Tarleton began to sing, but he was stopped by the rasp of metal against metal as Sir Robert drew his sword.

"No, you fool!" the man snarled. "I wish to hear your apprentice sing. Let's hear your sweet voice again, apprentice!" Sir Robert's little pig's eyes glinted dangerously.

Keeping in Tarleton's shadow, Elizabeth cleared her throat. "'She had a dark and rolling eye/And her hair hung down in ring-a-lets—"

Sir Robert's fist smashed down on the the tabletop. "For shame, Master Tarleton, to teach your young apprentice such a lewd song as that! What would the Queen say?"

"We will not sing it for the Queen," replied Tarleton evenly. "Since we have displeased your worship with our sport, we will be gone." He leaped lightly off the table, pulling Elizabeth with him.

With speed that was surprising for a man of his bulk, Sir Robert overturned the table, blocking their exit. The assembly quickly backed out of the way of the razor-sharp rapier.

Sir Robert leveled his sword's point within an inch of Tarleton's throat. "Do not move, apprentice, if you value this churl's life," he cautioned Elizabeth silkily.

"Leave the boy alone, Sir Robert!" Tarleton growled. Knotting his fists, the player watched for an opening to fling himself upon the drunken lord. All he needed was one moment's distraction.

"Aye, knave! But I threaten no boy." Moving the point of his rapier closer to Tarleton, he nicked the sensitive skin on the jester's neck, causing a thin trickle of blood to run down into his collar.

"Run along, Robin," Tarleton crisply ordered the tiny figure behind him. "The gentlemen is clearly in his cups. Go back to our lodgings." *Keep your head, sweet Elizabeth!* he prayed.

"Don't move!" Sir Robert cautioned her. Again he pricked Tarleton's neck.

"Do as I bid thee, Robin!" Tarleton licked his dry lips as he stared down the wicked blade into the red eyes of the man who held it.

"Show yourself, apprentice, or my next cut to his throat will be deeper. Aye! 'Twill leave this fool speechless!" Sir Robert giggled at his pun, though his eyes never wavered from the jester.

Quaking, Elizabeth stepped between the two men. She gasped in horror when she saw Tarleton's bloodied neck. With his free hand, Sir Robert grasped her firmly around her wrist. His rings bit painfully into her flesh.

"Call her Robin? For shame! She is the Lady Elizabeth Hayward!" Sir Robert smirked his triumph.

At her name, a buzz ran round the room like a fire in a stable. Pressing closer, the excited students narrowed the circle around the threesome. Jonathan exchanged a startled look with Philip who nodded. The two friends quietly edged closer to Elizabeth.

Elizabeth flinched as La Faye tightened his grip on her. "I don't know what you mean, my lord..." she began, hoping to bluff her way out of his grasp. *Play the part,* Tarleton's eyes begged.

Wrenching her arm, Sir Robert brought Elizabeth to her knees. Tarleton leapt to her defense but the sword's point scratched deeply across his chest.

"You don't know what I mean?" mimicked Sir Robert nastily. "Then let me instruct you, you lying wench! I wondered when I saw you covered in mud. There was something that seemed familiar to me, but I put it out of my mind. I could not imagine my pretty little bride riding a goat! But when you opened those sweet lips and sang tonight, I knew who you were. In good time you will sing another tune, Lady Elizabeth."

"Sir, you have had too much to drink," Elizabeth blustered. Letting go of her arm, Sir Robert backhanded her viciously across her face.

Blood gushing from her nose and torn lip, Elizabeth lost all sense of place. Only the sticky floor of the alehouse seemed stable. Her head droned with a loud buzzing and she tasted the salt of her own blood. Dimly she heard Sir Robert's voice screaming at her.

"Get up, you bitch, or I will run your lover through!"

Seeing Elizabeth fall at his feet, Tarleton's heart hammered. Though his blood seethed and his raw nerves screamed in protest, he willed himself to remain still. The rapier in Sir Robert's hand held steady at his throat.

"Run, Robin!" Tarleton sharply ordered her as he glared with cold fury at La Faye. *Turn your eye away one moment, you bastard, and I'll have my hands around your fat neck!*

"Robin?" Sir Robert screeched into Tarleton's face. "She is my own precious wife!"

"I am no man's wife!" Elizabeth rose shakily to her feet. The room spun crazily around her, yet she was determined to play the part to the last.

Sir Robert's face turned reddish purple; his eyes were almost lost in the folds of fat. "You are mine in all but wedding and bedding!" he shrieked at her. "The ceremony itself is a mere formality. As to the bedding, we shall do that here and now!"

Grabbing a handful of her shirt, Sir Robert ripped it open from neck to waist, bearing her lush breasts in the firelight. There was a general intake of breath at the surprising sight. Finally turning away from Tarelton, Sir Robert ogled Elizabeth hungrily.

"Dickon!" Elizabeth's anguished cry pierced the rafters of the alehouse.

At her stricken cry, pandemonium erupted on all sides. The students, with cries of "for the lady's honor!" fell upon Sir Robert's hirelings in a seething mass.

Tarleton catapulted onto Sir Robert; his momentum sent them both crashing to the floor. Elizabeth backed away as the two men scrambled quickly to their feet. Sir Robert, his sword still in his hand, glanced first at Tarleton, then at Elizabeth.

"If I can't have you, my pet, no one else will, I swear!" he screeched.

Elizabeth turned toward the safety of the crowd. At the same instant, Sir Robert lunged at her heart, while Tarleton grabbed him from behind, one arm locked around Sir Robert's neck, the other hand closed over the wrist holding the sword, deflecting its thrust. The two men spun away, fighting for possession of the weapon.

Elizabeth felt a sudden flash of fire sear through left shoulder. Before she knew what happened, someone lifted her from behind and dragged her toward the rear of the Bulldog. Elizabeth fought her unknown abductor.

"Lady Elizabeth! 'Tis Philip!" he said in her ear.

The lanky medical student carried her out the back door into the comparative safety of the cold alleyway behind the alehouse. When he set Elizabeth on her feet, she swayed.

Philip caught her before she hit the cobblestones. "Sweet Jesu!" he breathed. "You've been cut!" Her warm blood gushed over his hand. Supporting her, he wrapped her in his student gown.

"Dickon," she murmured. Growing more dizzy, she heard a rushing sound in her ears.

"He is in good company, my lady. I'll get you back to Jonathan's, and tend your wounds."

"Tell ... Dickon ..." Elizabeth fainted.

Philip swept her into his arms.

The porter at the gate of Christ Church only shook his head in disgust as he nodded to Philip. The noise at the Bulldog was more boisterous than usual. It wasn't fitting for the young gentlemen to be out at all hours, carousing and drinking. At least, Philip Robinson was sober enough to carry home one of the younger boys, the porter thought, as he watched Philip weave unsteadily across the quad. The unconscious fresher was tossed over Philip's shoulder like a sack of meal.

The tap boy of the Bulldog had a devil of a time finding the night watch. The proctors of Oxford were unusually busy that evening, and the tap boy was always one step behind them. He caught up with the officers as they took a quick pot of beer at the Golden Cross.

"My master at the Bulldog begs you come at once!" The boy was panting as he spoke to the dark-gowned official. "There's a riot breaking out there, and methinks the jester will be killed!"

The chief proctor blinked wearily. Rat-baiting, wenching and now—a jester? "A plague on higher education!" he swore as he downed the rest of his beer.

Chapter Fifteen

A blinding, murderous rage gripped Tarleton. Curses spewed from his lips as the two men struggled over possession of La Faye's rapier. Though Sir Robert was both taller and heavier than his adversary, he did not possess the expert skills that Tarleton had acquired over the years in the service of Sir Francis Walsingham. Using La Faye's weight against him, Tarleton tripped his bulky opponent, wresting the sword from his attacker's grip. Sir Robert rolled into a group of brawling students who were beating one of his henchmen into a pulp.

His face contorted with scalding fury, Tarleton bore down on the scrambling butterball before him. The thought of Elizabeth being touched by this piece of offal inflamed his brain.

Snatching a dagger from the belt of a startled onlooker, Sir Robert faced his vengeful opponent.

"Cut me, varlet, and you'll hang for it, I promise you!" Sir Robert threatened, circling the overturned table.

Tarleton bared his teeth. "I have no intention of cutting you, Sir Robert. I mean to kill you!" Tarleton executed a series of lightning parries that were barely deflected by La Faye's frantic use of the dagger.

Widening his eyes with surprise at Tarleton's ability with the sword, Sir Robert backed away from the flashing blade.

Tarleton's lips curled with contempt as he pressed his advantage. His savage attack ripped open one of Sir Robert's expensive sleeves. Only the padded wings on La Faye's shoulders protected him from a bloody injury.

Finding himself outfought and outmaneuvered, Sir Robert looked frantically for a means of escape. Tarleton knew if that happened, there might never be another chance to face down the pompous lord. Lunging, the jester felt his point sink into Sir Robert's thigh. The nobleman fell to the floor, screaming like a skewered pig, as he called for his minions to save him.

"The watch! The watch!" One of the younger students, stationed near the door, gave warning above the din. The discordant rasping of the proctor's whirling alarm rattles could be heard coming from the street.

Suddenly mindful of their studies and other pressing engagements, many of the collegers bolted through the back door. Running upstairs, a few others climbed out the windows, seeking the safety of Oxford's roofs.

Seeing that his quarry still lived, Tarleton damned his lost opportunity. Bowing to prudence, the wily player sent Sir Robert's sword skittering under stools and benches, far away from the scene of the fray.

When the proctors found them a few moments later, Sir Robert was being supported by one of his men, who was trying to staunch the flow of blood from the graze in the fat lord's leg. Tarleton coolly leaned against the counter, drinking deeply from an abandoned jug of beer. Though most of the students had vanished, Jonathan remained, lounging near the jester.

His brow furrowed, Tarleton scanned the emptying room for Elizabeth.

"Philip took the lady," Jonathan murmured quietly. "She is safe."

Tarleton allowed himself a tight smile. Relieved she was out of danger, the player turned his full attention to the matter at hand.

"I have been most foully attacked!" shrieked Sir Robert, pointing his dagger at Tarleton. "That pernicious knave has killed me!"

The proctor glanced from the armed lord at his feet to the unarmed Tarleton at the counter.

"I see no weapon about the player," remarked the proctor slowly. "What was the cause of this brawl?"

"I am Sir Robert La Faye!" the injured man screamed. "I was escorting my wife home, when this villain attacked me!"

"What wife?" The proctor looked around the alehouse, littered with broken furniture and crockery. "Forsooth, sir, I see no lady here."

The reek of beer hung heavy about the room. The proctor glanced at Sir Robert, convinced that the fat lord had fallen victim to its spirits.

"She was here! I swear to it!" Sir Robert's little pig eyes glinted at Tarleton. "And that smiling rogue kidnapped her!"

"Know you his meaning?" The proctor stared sharply at Tarleton.

"The gentleman took a liking to my young apprentice, sir," replied Tarleton with a shrug of his shoulders. "I admit Robin is fair of face, but I am not a panderer to any man's perverted pleasures. I sent my prentice back to our lodgings."

"Liar!" Sir Robert's face purpled with rage. "That smooth-talking whoreson has wounded me most grievously. Look you! I bleed!"

"You will note I am unarmed, sir." Tarleton smiled, though his eyes glittered like ice chips. "The floor is slippery with beer, and, as you can see, things did get out of hand. Perhaps the gentleman tripped upon his own dagger," he suggested innocently.

"Your name, jester?" The proctor did not like players in general, but the officer of the law decided that he liked Sir Robert even less.

"I am Tarleton, a member of The Queen's Men." Fumbling in his pouch under his motley, he pulled out his letter of patent. "I also have the pleasure of Her Majesty's particular favor. As a matter of fact, I am on my way to Hampton Court at her command."

Reading the paper by the lantern light, the proctor scrutinized the lord chamberlain's seal. Tarleton's credentials were impressive, while Sir Robert's claim was only the angered ravings of a drunkard. The proctor decided against waking the justice of the peace at this ungodly hour.

"I need not detain you, Sir Robert, as I perceive you are in sore need of a physician. Please present yourself at the town hall tomorrow morning at nine. The justice will give you his full attention then," promised the proctor.

"But that varlet tried to kill me!" sputtered Sir Robert.

"I see no life-threatening wound, and I see no weapon in the player's hand. I see no witnesses against him..." The proctor paused, while his gaze swept around the room.

Sir Robert's henchmen, seeing that the lady had slipped away, held their tongues.

"Who drew his weapon first?" the proctor asked the assembly.

"The gentleman." Jonathan spoke up clearly. "And so say all of us!" The few remaining students nodded their assent.

"And the lady?" asked the proctor.

"We saw the player's apprentice only," said Jonathan, relishing the opportunity to split legalistic hairs.

The proctor nodded again.

Sir Robert struggled to his feet, his eyes blazing. "What about my wife?"

The proctor groaned inwardly. *Fie upon all drunken lords! And people wonder why the youth of Oxford run so wild.*

"As there is no lady present, I cannot attest to your wife, my lord. I suggest you tend to your wound, lest it fester. I promise you, my lord, you will be served full justice in the morning."

With a final glare at Tarleton, Sir Robert gave himself up to wailing over his injury. His henchmen quickly escorted him from the scene.

Sighing, the proctor turned back to the player. "And you, jester, must be gone from Oxford by first light. If Sir Robert decides to press charges once he is before the justice, I will be forced to seek you out. Do you understand my meaning, player?"

Tarleton nodded. "By first light, I shall be but a memory, good sir."

The chief proctor merely grunted and left. Drawing a ragged breath of relief, Tarleton tossed a few pennies on the counter to pay for the beer he had quaffed. Then he strode out into the night, followed by a grinning Jonathan.

Elizabeth floated up from a sickening haze of pain. When she opened her eyes, she discovered she was lying in a bed, the rough sheeting tucked tightly across her breasts and under her arms. Her body felt heavy as lead, and she burned with an incredible thirst.

"Water..." she whispered weakly.

Holding a cup in his hand, Philip leaned over her. "Try not to move, Lady Elizabeth," he said gently. "Or you will start bleeding again. Just a sip, now." Slipping his hand under her head, he held her carefully.

"Dickon..." she murmured. Where was he? And where was she?

Philip smiled. "I believe he had some unfinished business with Lord La Faye. He'll be here directly, lady. 'Tis you who is in danger. You've lost a lot of blood."

"You . . . ?" Elizabeth felt strangely giddy. She had trouble forming complete thoughts.

"Did you forget I am in Oxford to study medicine?" Philip touched the strip of cloth bandaging that wound around around her shoulder and under her arm. "I am right glad you were unconscious," he continued. "I had to cauterize the wound to stop the bleeding. Then I sewed you up with some fine silk thread—black, I'm afraid." Philip grew more serious. "You will carry that scar for the rest of your life, Lady Elizabeth. For that I am sorry."

"Water, please . . ." Elizabeth's tongue flicked across her lips.

"Only sip a little. I shall give you a draft to help you sleep." Pressing his hand against her forehead, Philip found it warm. A frown knotted his brow. As he had feared, she was already running a temperature.

"I want to see Dickon," his patient protested in a shallow voice.

"In good time," Philip soothed. Then he turned to the pale Smith, who lingered at the door. "Warm some wine and bring it directly. Also, get me some rose water in a basin and a piece of toweling. Hop to it, Smith!" The boy scampered out of sight. Philip grinned at Elizabeth. "Smith is a good servant, but a poor physician's assistant. I fear he lost his dinner while I was tending you."

Realizing she was naked under the covers, Elizabeth tried to draw the sheet higher. She winced with the effort.

"My clothes . . ." she mumbled.

Philip nodded understandingly. "I had to cut you out of them, I fear."

A look of horror crossed her face.

Philip pretended to ignore it as he busied himself with his bottles and powders. "I am a doctor, Lady. Well . . . almost.

I have been at study here for the past six years, and before that, I learned much from the local midwife. I have seen men, women and children in every state of undress. I've delivered babies, on occasion. I've even doctored horses, cows, and dogs in my time. Once, I mended a rabbit's torn ear. You are a just a patient to me."

He dabbed some ointment on to a cloth. "This is camphor. 'Twill promote healing the cut on your lip. I fear 'twill sting badly."

Looking into Philip's gray eyes, Elizabeth knew she could trust him. She nodded. Gently he applied the strong-smelling medicine to her injured mouth. He understated the pain. It felt as if he had touched her lips with a live coal.

Philip stroked her forehead. Though the medical student considered himself the most peace-loving person in the world, he would have cheerfully cut out Sir Robert's heart for the injuries done to the lady. Her white skin would be bruised and swollen for days.

Smith returned with the wine and rose water. Philip mixed some powder into the wine, then supported Elizabeth's head as he urged her to drink.

"'Twill ease your pain, and bring you blessed sleep," he cajoled.

"I want to see Dickon," Elizabeth whispered as she sipped the comforting brew. Its warmth immediately flowed through her.

"He will come soon, my lady, and when he does, he will want to see you fast asleep." Philip handed the cup back to the awed bed maker.

After soaking a cloth in the basin of rose water, the student doctor wiped Elizabeth's burning forehead with it. The sweet smell reminded her of the gardens at Esmond Manor. She felt herself slipping into a mindless drowsy state.

"Wake me... when Dickon comes..." she murmured.

"Aye, my lady," Philip whispered.

* * *

Sunlight streamed through the streaked windows when Elizabeth woke again. Disoriented, she could not remember where she was. The reality of her injury returned with a sudden, blinding pain as she struggled to sit up.

Hearing her cry out, Tarleton rushed into the room. Brokenly murmuring incoherent endearments, he knelt beside the bed. He had not slept since returning from the Bulldog to find Elizabeth wounded and running a fever. Throughout the long hours of the night, Tarleton paced the adjacent sitting room, frantic with worry for Elizabeth and furious at both Sir Robert and himself for her condition. Would she ever forgive him for all the trouble he had brought upon her?

"Feeling better, sweetling?" he managed to croak as he stoftly stroked her brow. It was still very warm.

"Much." She licked her cracked lips and tried to smile at him. "You are here."

Tarleton winced when he heard how frail she sounded.

Blinking, Elizabeth tried to clear her head. The pain in her shoulder settled into a dull ache and her fingers felt stiff.

"Philip has gone to get you something from the kitchens." Tarleton tried to sound cheerful. He slopped some water into a cup. "I'm afraid I make a terrible nursemaid. Philip said you would probably be thirsty. Here, let me help you," he urged. He brought the cup to her lips. His hand trembled as he held her. Elizabeth seemed to weigh almost nothing.

Weakened from her exertion, Elizabeth sank against the pillow. Gingerly she touched her lips and bruised cheek.

Tarleton took her hand in his, caressing her fingers as he spoke. "Forgive me for saying so, chuck, but it looks as if you've been in a schoolyard brawl," he bantered, praying for Philip's swift return. "If you were a boy, you would be very proud of those marks on your face."

"Do I look very ugly?" Elizabeth whispered.

Tarleton kissed her fingers. "Ugly? Nay, my sweet, you have the face of an angel—though I must admit, I've never seen an angel with such a black eye before. You are the envy of every young colleger here." Tarleton smiled impishly, though his heart was full sore. Elizabeth looked as if she might fly up to heaven at any moment—black eye and all. *How long can I keep up this jesting? This is the hardest performance of my career. Blast you, Robinson! Where are you?*

Fortunately, Philip arrived at that moment, bearing a covered bowl.

"You took your sweet time, prentice physician!" Tarleton growled.

Instead of being offended, Philip smiled as he crossed to Elizabeth's bedside. "You look less feverish this morning," he told her, feeling her forehead. "How are you?"

"Weak," she answered.

Drawing up a stool beside her, Philip held out the bowl of soup. Its aroma stirred even Elizabeth's peckish appetite. Joining them in the cramped sickroom, Jonathan stood nearby, holding a cup of watered wine. Tarleton supported Elizabeth's head as Philip endeavored to get some nourishment into her.

" 'Tis your doctor's prescription that you eat all of this, my lady," intoned Philip as he spooned the hot, savory soup into her. "I had to promise a great number of things to the undercook to give me this beef broth."

"Surely not your virtue," joked Jonathan halfheartedly.

"Nay, I gave that away long ago," Philip remarked. "And watch your language, Jonathan. We are entertaining a lady here."

"And what of yesterday?" Jonathan defended himself.

Philip flushed. "I plead ignorance," he said, holding out another spoonful to Elizabeth.

During this exchange, Tarleton, the master of puns and quips, remained strangely silent. He could not trust himself to say anything; too many emotions rubbed his heart raw. Instead, he cradled Elizabeth's golden head gently while he gazed at her as if she might disappear from his grasp at any moment. After taking each spoonful of broth, Elizabeth smiled weakly at Tarleton. Her luminous green eyes spoke volumes of her love.

Watching Tarleton and Elizabeth exchange their silent dialogue, Jonathan sighed. Exactly what was the jester to the lady, the student lawyer wondered enviously. In the Bulldog the night before, Tarleton fought like a madman— or perhaps a knight of old defending his lady. In fact, Jonathan concluded, Tarleton had acted exactly like Elizabeth's lover.

After several more mouthfuls, Elizabeth waved away the broth. "Last night...what happened?"

"I fear I lost my temper with that swine," Tarleton murmured gently. "Unfortunately, I could only give him a little nick, instead of a sound thrust to the heart—if the whoreson possesses a heart."

Elizabeth clutched his hand. "Sir Robert is hurt? Oh, my love! 'Tis a hanging offence to strike a nobleman!"

Looking at the marks on the face of his beloved put there by La Faye, Tarleton gritted his teeth. "Have no fear, sweet Elizabeth. I'll not hang yet. If I ever do, 'twill be for killing Sir Robert La Faye, not for scratching him."

Elizabeth went very white.

"You jackass!" Philip swore under his breath at Tarleton. The young doctor's fingers closed over Elizabeth's pulse; her heartbeat was racing. "There is no need to go into all the details at the moment."

"We must flee this place!" Elizabeth tried to rise. "You will be arrested!"

Tarleton eased her back against the pillow. "Fret not, my dove."

"Nay, lady! 'Tis dangerous for you to move now," protested Philip, placing his hand on her forehead. He shot a worried look to Tarleton. Elizabeth felt much warmer.

"And no one must know you exist," added Jonathan softly from his place near the doorway.

Taking the wine cup from his friend, Philip mixed in white powder.

"Why?" Elizabeth held Tarleton's hand tighter, as if she could keep him from being dragged away to the gallows.

Ignoring Philip's angry looks, Jonathan continued in a quiet tone. "Sir Robert's men are combing Oxford for you even now. There is a huge reward for your whereabouts. Lord La Faye swore before the justice this morning that Tarleton had stolen his wife, and that he, Sir Robert, was in the act of reclaiming her when Tarleton attacked him."

Elizabeth gasped at the accusation. She looked from one to the other of them in turn. By their grim expressions, she knew Jonathan spoke the truth. Tarleton tried to grin at her, but his usual imp's smile came out lopsided. Philip silently offered her the drugged wine. She sipped it, not realizing it would make her sleep again.

"But if no wife can be found, then Sir Robert's story holds no water," Jonathan continued. "And there isn't a man in Oxford who will swear that any person, other than the jester's apprentice, was at the Bulldog last night."

Jonathan was pleased with himself. He had spent most of the night going from college to college making sure that his fellow students understood his legal logic. To a man, everyone vowed they would remain true to the lady's secret, despite the lure of Sir Robert's gold.

"And what about Dickon?" Elizabeth whispered, large tears forming in her deep green eyes as she glanced up at him.

Tarleton pressed her fingers to his lips once again, wishing he could suck her fever from them. "We are safe enough now, and when you are stronger, we shall be on our merry way, singing for pennies, my sweetest Robin, until we reach the Queen.''

''How... long... will... that... be?'' Elizabeth's eyelids grew heavy as Philip's sleeping potion began to take effect.

''By and by, my love. By and by,'' Tarleton whispered, watching her drift back into oblivion.

''Methinks I should give you a cup of my brew, as well, good player,'' Philip remarked after the three of them withdrew to Jonathan's sitting room, leaving the faithful Toby asleep at Elizabeth's feet. ''You look in sore need of rest yourself.''

''In good time, Philip.'' Tarleton stared out the dirty window.

''The Lady Elizabeth was right to fear for you, Tarleton,'' Jonathan observed after a prolonged silence. ''You should have left at the crack of dawn as the proctor warned you. I heard the complaint Lord La Faye lodged against you. I think 'twill be only a matter of time before 'tis discovered you are still in Oxford. The proctor cannot be so lenient again, even if you are under the patronage of the lord chamberlain. Sir Robert has set out a hue and cry against you.'' Jonathan burst into a surprising laughter. ''Especially after he was ordered to pay for all the damages due the landlord of the Bulldog. 'Twas a most expensive evening for him.''

''You could leave the lady with us,'' Philip suggested carefully, not at all sure how Tarleton would react to this suggestion. ''You could make all speed for London. Jonathan and I will care for her and will see that she arrives safely to the Queen when she is well.''

Turning from the window, Tarleton fixed both students with a hollow-eyed glare. ''Would you abandon your heart to another to save your own neck?'' he asked heatedly. ''If you were me, would you leave such a lady? Would you?" he snapped at Jonathan. "Could you?" he questioned Philip.

Philip gazed at the feeble fire burning in the grate. Tarleton sounded like a man who was on the brink of losing all reason. "Nay," the student doctor at last admitted. "For such a lady, I would stay by her side come rack, or fire, or doomsday."

Chapter Sixteen

The sun sank low in the western sky as the bells of Oxford's many towers tolled six o'clock. Waking, Elizabeth found herself looking into the enchanted eyes of the young bed maker, Roger Smith. The boy had spent the past two and a half hours staring at the sleeping girl—and falling in love with her. When Elizabeth weakly returned his smile, his heart turned a cartwheel inside his rib cage.

"Don't move, Lady! Master Philip will box my ears sore a-plenty, if you but move a muscle. And Master Tarleton would flay me alive!" Smith chattered, falling over the stool in his haste to search out the young doctor.

"Water, please," Elizabeth whispered. "My mouth feels as if I have been eating wool."

Grabbing the jug, Smith overfilled the cup. Stiffly he held it out to her. When he realized that he had to put his arm around her to help her drink, his mind reeled. Quaking a little, he slipped his hand under her head, and brought the cup carefully to her lips. She steadied his hand with hers. He nearly died with pleasure at her gentle touch on his skin. Trying not to stare at her bare shoulders, he accidently sloshed some water onto her neck. It ran down the hollow between her breasts, hidden under the sheeting. The journey of that rivulet mesmerized Smith.

"Thank you," said Elizabeth, her voice a little stronger.

Her brilliant smile flustered the poor boy even more.

"I'll get Master Philip and try to wake Master Tarleton," the lovesick Smith burbled, backing toward the door. "Master Philip gave your... ah... friend a powerful sleeping draft, so I may not be able to stir him yet. I will be back anon!" Then the boy bolted into the outer room.

Lying back against the pillow, Elizabeth gazed meditatively at a crack in the ceiling. Her head was clearer now. She remembered Jonathan had said something about the need for Tarleton to leave Oxford immediately. If Dickon was asleep nearby, it was obvious he had no intention of going without her. *Fool!* she thought fondly, *you will bring yourself into ruin because of me—if I let you.*

Very well! Elizabeth would insist they must quit Oxford without delay. Tarleton was more in danger than she was. His freedom and possibly his life hung in the balance. Closing her eyes, Elizabeth considered her tactics. Walsingham! The Queen's chief minister would protect Dickon.

Entering the room quietly, Philip knelt by the bed. "It seems you've frightened the wits out of Smith," he remarked. "I've never heard him deliver so disjointed a message. He said something about drowning you."

Elizabeth grinned crookedly through her swollen lip. "He helped me to take some water."

Philip nodded, wiser than Elizabeth. The student doctor diagnosed Smith to be suffering from an acute case of first love. Philip didn't blame the lad one bit.

"I have sent the boy to beg some tender meat for you," Philip told her. He felt her pulse for a moment, then put his hand to her cool brow. "Your heartbeat is stronger," he observed with satisfaction.

"Tarleton? Is he... is he well?" Elizabeth searched Philip's face. "Smith said you had to give him a potion."

The budding doctor arched his eyebrow wryly. "Tarleton was worn-out with worry over you, my lady." As he spoke, Philip carefully examined her wound under the bandage. "I grew tired of watching him pace a furrow in the floorboards, so I drugged his wine. He's a stubborn man, so it took a lot to knock him out." Pausing in his ministrations, Philip grinned. "He's curled up by the fire in the other room with his arm thrown lovingly over Toby."

Elizabeth giggled, though the effort hurt her bruised lip. "That must be a rare sight, Philip."

"Aye," he agreed. "But you will have to take my word on it. You are not to stir from this bed. By the way, do you need to use the chamber pot?" he asked in a more professional tone.

Elizabeth nodded. After Philip had handed it to her, he discreetly withdrew for a moment. Though Elizabeth had grown used to telling Tarleton when she needed to pause behind a bush, it was an entirely different matter in her present condition. Once her need had been taken care of, Philip continued his work, applying a salve to her lip and a poultice to her blackened eye.

Elizabeth took a deep breath. "Tarleton must leave Oxford."

"I know that, my lady, and so does he." Philip avoided her eyes. "Tarleton likes to play a dangerous game, my lady. Perhaps you can persuade him. Jonathan and I have tried, but he won't listen to us."

Elizabeth studied the young doctor. "Then we will both go in the morning," she announced firmly.

Philip stopped mixing the poultice and stared at her, the muscles in his jaw working furiously. "Sweet lady! You don't know what—"

"Philip," Elizabeth interrupted him determinedly. "I *do* know. I have money...or did have, in the pocket of my breeches."

Philip mutely picked up the small money bag from the meager pile of her belongings on the table.

Elizabeth nodded. "Aye. You will find enough to hire the fastest post-horses in Oxford. Do this for me, Philip. Please?"

Philip pressed his lips tightly together. The only man who could talk some sense into her was sound asleep with a dog. "If you ride a horse tomorrow, you will die, my lady," he told her brusquely.

"If I don't, Tarleton will be discovered, arrested, and perhaps executed under false testimony. That would kill me all the same," she answered in an unwavering tone.

"I'll engage a coach," Philip suggested desperately. "You could travel in some comfort, at least."

"Post-horses, Philip." Her voice brooked no argument. "Saddled and ready by morning's first light." Her eyes gleamed with an unearthly glow.

"Lady Elizabeth, I beg you..." he began.

Gripping the sheet tightly around her, Elizabeth got slowly out of the bed. Holding on to the side table, she steadied herself. "If you don't hire them, Philip, I will this minute!"

She is moonstruck, Philip thought, as he watched her struggle to stay upright.

He ran his hands through his light brown hair. "If you insist on this, I will hire three horses, not two, my lady. I will not let you travel that road without me."

They stared at each other for a moment, then her face relaxed. Elizabeth sank gratefully down on the bed again, smiling a little to herself. At least, her ruse had worked. She wasn't sure how long she could have remained standing.

"Thank you, Philip," she murmured quietly.

"I hope I am not signing your death warrant, my lady," he replied grimly. "I will get you to Hampton Court, but you must promise me you will do exactly as I say." He was surprised when she nodded meekly. "Rest. When Smith comes with your dinner, you are to eat every bite of it. I'll go to the stables and see what I can find for us."

Philip felt himself slipping under the spell of her huge green eyes. *This is madness!* he thought, gripping her money bag.

"Feed her!" he snapped at Smith, who entered the room bearing a full tray. Philip threw on his cape and stomped out the door, leaving the stunned boy with the smiling girl.

"What?" Rubbing the sleep from his eyes, Tarleton wondered if he had heard Philip correctly. He looked first at the student, who grimly tied up a small bag of medicines and bandages, then at Elizabeth, who calmly sipped a cup of warmed wine. "Have you both taken leave of your wits? I forbid it!" He glared at Elizabeth again. He didn't like the steely expression in her eyes.

"Don't rail so, Dickon," she purred sweetly, looking as demure as possible, considering she was lying naked in a bed with only a sheet tucked under her arms. "You have no right to forbid me. I am not your wife. Indeed, you are my hireling—or has that fact slipped through the cracks of your brain? I will ride to the Queen tomorrow morning. You may do what you please!" Leaning back against the pillow, she grinned triumphantly at him.

Tarleton turned on Philip. "God's teeth! 'Twill kill her! Tell her that, prentice healer!" he raged. "Elizabeth, you are too weak to travel. And certainly not at dawn tomorrow!"

Elizabeth clucked her tongue at him. "My, my, you *do* make a great deal of noise when you don't get your own way, Dickon. I don't believe I have seen this side of you before," she added archly. "I intend to go to my loving godmother, and Philip will see that I get there in one piece."

"Pray God that you do, doctor of physic," hissed Tarleton, clenching his teeth in frustration. "Pray God, we *both* do. And someone find Mistress Hardhead a nightshirt! 'Tis indecent!"

* * *

Thanks to Philip's sleeping potion, Elizabeth enjoyed a dreamless night. In the cold morning's dawn, she felt the best she had been since her injury. Young Smith willingly gave up the only spare set of clothing he owned for his new-found goddess. Elizabeth promised him she would send a new set when she got to court. Smith's joy knew no bounds when she kissed him lightly on the cheek.

"That's done it!" Jonathan tried to hide his apprehension under a layer of banter. "The little beggar will be completely worthless for a month."

Standing on tiptoe, Elizabeth kissed the law student on the cheek, as well. Her eyes sparkled. "As I recall, Jonathan, you once said you would gladly suffer for a kind look from me. There is my kiss instead. Are you paid in full?"

For once, the lawyer-to-be found himself speechless.

In the college's stable yard, Tarleton lifted Elizabeth gently onto the saddle of her white palfrey; their eyes locked—his pleading, hers encouraging. "Minx!" he growled under his breath as he adjusted her stirrups, though his eyes spoke in a different tone.

"Don't sulk!" she softly admonished him before bending over and kissing him on the ear.

Behind them, Philip cleared his voice. "Remember, my lady, I am holding out for a glove, as well as a kiss." He tried to sound lighthearted.

"Get us to Hampton Court, Philip, and I shall reward you as best I can!" Elizabeth chirped bravely. The fresh morning air was bracing. She prayed she could last out the day.

"If you don't get her to the Queen, you can count your life span in minutes," Tarleton rumbled at the lanky young doctor.

Elizabeth gathered her mount's reins in her good hand. Philip had bound her other arm in a sling tight against her chest to take some strain off her injured shoulder. She settled herself into a comfortable position. Deep in her pocket, she felt her wooden comb, her scissors case and Tarleton's brass bell. These were her only worldly possessions now, save for the few shillings left over from the rental of their three fine-looking mounts.

Tarleton glowered at his horse. He hated riding and this particular trip promised to be grim for a number of different reasons. Growling dire threats to the chestnut gelding, Tarleton mounted and tried to get comfortable in his saddle.

As Elizabeth walked her horse past his, she playfully wiggled her brows. *Play the part* she signaled to Tarleton.

In turn, he doffed his cap to her. "Lady Elizabeth, shall we ride into the jaws of hell?" he asked with studied politeness.

She dimpled. "I go only as far as Hampton Court myself," Elizabeth answered innocently.

Tarleton snapped his fingers impatiently. "Come, Robin Redbreast! We burn daylight!" Angrily he kneed his horse into a walk.

Shaking his head at the two of them, Philip swung easily into his own saddle. With a curt nod of farewell to Jonathan, he followed the others into the quiet highroad. When the three of them crested the hill at Shotover, they paused, looking back upon the still-dreaming university town.

Elizabeth smiled at her worried companions. "Now let us ride with a purpose, good masters!"

Spurring their horses into an easy canter, they ate up the miles before them.

By midmorning, Elizabeth's arm throbbed like a firebrand. Seeing her sway in the saddle, Tarleton called a halt. Helping her off the horse, he gently laid her under a beech tree while Philip tethered their mounts.

"Sweet Elizabeth! This madcap plan is foolhardy." Tarleton smoothed stray golden strands of her short hair away from her face. Her fair skin seemed almost translucent.

Sweet Jesu! Why was she doing this to herself? Why was she doing it to him? Her courage was tearing his heart in twain.

Taking out his bag, Philip mixed a concoction of herbs and wine, which he offered Elizabeth.

She shook her head. "No, Philip, I can't sleep now."

" 'Twill ease some of the pain," he told her tightly.

Peering down the open neck of her shirt, he checked the bandage. There was some seepage of blood, though most of his sutures looked as if they were holding. Taking a sweet-smelling herb from his bag, he bound the crushed leaves over the wound with a fresh piece of linen.

"A wisewoman once told me this helps to stop the bleeding. It usually works." He offered her the water bag. " 'Tis safe to drink, I promise you."

Smiling her thanks, Elizabeth lay back and closed her eyes for a moment, hoping Philip's herbs would soon take effect. She couldn't let either man know how weak she felt. They would whisk her straight back to Oxford, and she would have accomplished nothing for her suffering.

Tarleton wandered over to the horses. "Philip, my harness strap needs attending, and I am not skilled in such matters."

"I'm a mender of bodies, not leather, Master Tarleton," Philip grumbled as he joined him. "What is the matter?"

"Nothing with the harness, Philip," whispered Tarleton, "but there is a world of wrong with my lady."

"What would you have me do?" Philip looked over his shoulder at the dozing Elizabeth. "Knock her over the head?"

"That thought had crossed my mind," Tarleton responded grimly. "But I dare not. How long can she last at this rate?"

Philip shook his head. "In sooth, I cannot say. To see her you would think a middling wind would blow her away, yet she has the heart of a lioness—and a love surpassing all my experience," he added, looking enviously at the older man.

"Has the fever returned?" Tarleton watched a stray breeze ruffling Elizabeth's downy fine hair as she dozed.

"Not yet, but 'tis not far away," Philip answered quietly.

"The moment she falls into a faint, this fool's quest is done." Tarleton clenched and unclenched his fists in frustration. "We will take her to the nearest inn, manor house, village or whatever we can find. Are we agreed?"

"Aye!" Philip was relieved that Tarleton made the decision.

"Couldn't you give her something that will hasten this plan?"

"Nay, Tarleton. She made me swear a solemn oath not to drug her. Besides, I think by now she recognizes my poppy elixir when she tastes it, even in wine."

Tarleton swore softly. "So be it then. Let us continue while the sky holds back the rain, and pray, prentice doctor. Pray!"

"I have, Tarleton. I have said more prayers this morning than in the past twelvemonth together!"

They stopped at noon, and again an hour later. Philip grew more and more agitated as he noted heavier bleeding through the bandages and the return of her fever. To make matters even worse, the sky turned darker and a chill wind blew out of the northwest.

"How far are we now?" Elizabeth asked Tarleton, her voice broken by pain and fatigue.

"We shall be turning toward Slough soon," he answered stiffly, trying to keep his anguish out of his voice. "There I will find us a decent inn for the night."

"No!" Elizabeth clutched at him, her leaf green eyes bright with fever. "We'll go on! Every hour brings us closer to safety." She knew they could not stop, or she would never be able to go on again.

Tarleton ground his teeth. "Philip! Reason with the wench!" he snarled.

The jester had never felt more out of control of his life as he did now. He was the one who outwitted enemies to the crown. He was the one who had a thousand tricks up his sleeve for every occasion. His was the voice that could beguile a maiden out of her petticoats or quell a brawl in an alehouse. Yet in the face of one fevered slip of a girl, he was helpless.

"Lady Elizabeth . . ." Philip protested, casting a worried glance at the player. Tarleton looked as haggard as she. At this alarming rate, Philip could find himself on a highway with *two* patients on his young hands.

Without waiting to hear the rest of Philip's admonitions, Elizabeth rose unsteadily to her feet, and walked over to her palfrey. Pulling herself painfully into the saddle, she glared defiantly at her two shocked companions.

"Then I shall go on alone, masters. You needn't assume any more responsibility for me. Philip, you are free to return to Oxford. Dickon—you can go to the devil!" Putting a strip of cloth between her teeth, she bit down hard upon it, then she wheeled her horse southward.

Dumbfounded, the two men stared with disbelief at each other, then they hastily gathered up their things, mounting their surprised horses with all speed. When Tarleton drew abreast of Elizabeth, he saw her tears rolling down her cheeks, though she stared straight ahead. The cloth was still clamped tightly in her teeth. The image of another time flashed unbidden into Tarleton's memory. She had been tired and crying in the loft of the Blue Boar when Tarleton first handed her the pack strap while he removed her splinter. How much had changed since then—for both of them!

"You are mad!" Tarleton shouted at her. Elizabeth acted as if she were not even aware of his presence. "Damn you, Elizabeth! And damn me too for following you! All right!

You win this hand! But I warn you, the game isn't over yet! We'll go down the primrose path to perdition together!''

She smiled at him through her tears.

The rains began in midafternoon, as the storm overtook them. Elizabeth refused to seek shelter despite the shouting from both her escorts. The rain felt cool to her fevered brow, and she willingly let herself get drenched.

Swearing to himself, Philip muttered "chill and lung fever." Tarleton fingered the hilt of his dagger, seriously rethinking his threat to knock her out, as he gamely kept pace with her. All the while, he prayed for a miracle.

Are you there, Lord? How long must this act play before you ring the curtain down? 'Tis the worst scene of my life. Must my lady suffer longer in this farce? Let me take the catcalls and gibes of the groundlings. Jesu, what prompt book are you using?

As if in answer to his unorthodox prayer, Elizabeth suddenly slumped in the saddle. Riding by her side, Tarleton caught her, pulling his horse to a stop. Elizabeth's palfrey, feeling no weight on its back, halted several yards ahead. Elizabeth had thankfully fainted. Gently lifting her down, Tarleton laid her on a wet grassy bank under the dubious shelter of a thick hedgerow, while Philip retrieved her horse. The rain settled into a fine mist.

Looking up and down the deserted highway, Tarleton swore colorfully. All day long, they had passed many travelers. Now, when they could have used some help, there was no one to be seen in either direction. The lowering weather and the coming of nightfall had hurried most people off the roads.

Opening his smelling salts, Philip waved them under Elizabeth's nose. Slowly she revived. Philip poured her some of his drugged wine.

"How far?" she whispered, taking the cup.

"Soon," Tarleton lied. He exchanged a meaningful look with Philip, who quickly nodded assent. They would stop at the next likely place.

"Where are we?" Elizabeth murmured groggily.

"Under a hedge," the jester answered glibly.

"Let's go on. " Her head lolled against Tarleton's arm.

"Do you know where we are in truth?" Philip whispered to him. Now that the murky twilight was upon them, Philip was unsure of his bearings, and more than a little afraid. He had no wish to encounter strangers after dark, especially on such a moonless night as this.

"Aye." Tarleton cradled Elizabeth in his arms. "Near Windsor. The White Hart is there, I know the landlord well. It should only be a few more miles down the road."

"Thank God!" Philip breathed with relief.

"Hold your thanks, my young friend. We are not there yet."

Drifting in and out of consciousness, Elizabeth no longer felt any pain. She heard Tarleton and Philip speaking, but their words were garbled in her ear. She made no sound, when Philip gently lifted her up to Tarleton as he held his horse steady. Gratefully she lay back against his chest, cushioned by the warmth of his body and his steadily beating heart.

"Sweet Dickon," she murmured.

Tarleton winced at her blessing. "Close your eyes, my only love, and I will take you home," he whispered. He draped Elizabeth's cloak over his shoulders, drawing its folds around her, so that she was sheltered warmly within. Then, humming "The Greenwood Tree" to lull her, he urged his horse into a gentle walk. Philip followed with Elizabeth's horse.

Just as darkness closed in about them, they were accosted by a party of armed horsemen. Philip moved closer to Tarleton's flank side. Quietly drawing his dagger with one hand, Tarleton held the half-awake Elizabeth tighter against him.

"Stop in the name of the Queen!" one of the horsemen cried as they thundering down upon them.

Philip looked to Tarleton, who nodded assent. Both men reined in their horses and waited, though neither relaxed despite hearing the Queen's name invoked.

The horsemen, two of them bearing sputtering torches, surrounded the jester's party. The tallest, wearing a bright breastplate with a soggy white plume in his polished helmet, leaned forward.

"Who goes there?" the man demanded. "State your name and business!"

"Philip Robinson, a student of Christ Church, so please you, sir," Philip croaked.

"You are far from Oxford this night," the man mused, his carefully groomed mustaches visible in the light. "Who is with you?"

Recognizing the leader, Tarleton relaxed. "I was taking him for a bit of skylarking, but alas, the sky turned black!"

"By the mass! Tarleton, you blackguard!" The tall stranger laughed loudly, the sound echoing in the darkness. "The Queen sends her regards and desires your feet upon her hearth immediately. I trust you have not managed to lose your apprentice, Master Jester, or you will have the devil to pay!"

Tarleton grew serious. "Nay, Raleigh. She is here, close to my heart." Tarleton parted the folds of the sodden cape. Elizabeth's wan face shone palely in the sputtering light of the outriders' torches. "I have been praying for help. It seems the Lord sent you."

Sir Walter Raleigh snorted. "The Queen sent me. The abbess of St. Aloysius sent me. The Lord had nothing to do with it. We are not on speaking terms these days," he answered lightly. Leaning over his saddle, he peered closely at Elizabeth. "God's nightgown, man! What ails her?"

"A sword wound, which my young friend here is tending with great skill. Though I did not do it, I am to blame," Tarleton admitted, gripping Elizabeth fiercely under the cloak.

Raleigh whistled through his teeth. "You'd best make a good speech with the Almighty, you fool. The Queen was livid when she received a report that you dressed the lady as a boy and were taking her unchaperoned through the countryside. I tremble to think what she will say to you now."

"Best leave that to later, Raleigh. Lady Elizabeth burns with a fever," replied Tarleton quietly.

"Hell's bells, man! Ride on! We will speak more of this in good time—that is, if you still have a tongue in your head and your head on your shoulders!" Wheeling his stallion about, Sir Walter set a quick pace back down the road.

"'Tis too fast for the lady, Tarleton," Philip protested as they cantered behind the lead outriders. "How is she faring?"

"She's fainted dead away, and that's the best news of this shag-eared journey," Tarleton answered grimly. The worst news, he knew, was waiting for him with right royal ire at Hampton Court.

Chapter Seventeen

The reddish silhouette of the palace at Hampton Court loomed in the predawn. For every mile Tarleton rode that wet, grim night, cradling the unconscious Elizabeth close to him, he cursed himself a thousand times for his selfishness, his cockiness and, most of all, for his stubbornness. Why didn't he let Mother Catherine take Elizabeth when he had the chance? Instead of arriving half-dead on a cold, gray morn, Elizabeth would be cozily asleep now in a soft bed. And Tarleton would be back in the kitchen where he belonged. At least, the kitchens of Hampton Court were far preferable to the place he expected would be his new, temporary home—the Tower of London.

I regret nothing, and I shall take the memory of our love with me to the grave—and beyond, he promised himself, as they rode through the Clock Tower gate and into the cobbled courtyard of Hampton Court.

Many torches burned away the gloom, except in Tarleton's heart. Having heard of the lady's arrival from one of the soldiers sent ahead, people thronged the doorways. Eager hands reached up to Tarleton, ready to bear Elizabeth away from him.

"Nay," he growled hoarsely. "I promised my lady to deliver her to Hampton Court, and, by God, I will see her to her door!"

Carefully cradling Elizabeth, Tarleton swung one leg over his winded horse and slid nimbly to the ground. Following Raleigh's lead, Tarleton, with an aching heart, carried his beloved inside the great palace. The hovering servants, guards and courtiers parted to let the silent procession pass through. Each step Tarleton took down the polished corridors felt like a lead weight clamped around his ankle.

On the second floor, they were met by Dr. John Dee, the Queen's personal physician, and Lady Mary Sidney, one of the Queen's closest friends.

"Show me where to take my lady," Tarleton said tightly, afraid to display any emotion. "I have brought her this far. Permit me the honor of carrying her to the end."

Tarleton's eyes looked so determined, Lady Mary nodded understandingly. She led him into a small, comfortably appointed room where a cheerful fire blazed in the hearth. The covers of a canopied bed were pulled back, waiting to receive their sweet occupant. Tenderly Tarleton laid Elizabeth amid the lace, satin, linen and goose down where he knew she belonged. Caring not who saw him, he leaned over her, kissed her lightly on her fevered brow, then pressed a lingering kiss on her dry lips.

"I love thee, sweetest Robin. Pray remember me with kindness," he whispered into her ear, hoping deep within her sleep, she heard him.

Stirring slightly, Elizabeth's fingers opened as if they sought his hand. "Dickon..." she said, and sighed, though only Tarleton heard her.

A lump welled up in his throat. He would have kissed her again, but he was pulled away from the bedside.

"The Lady Elizabeth is in good hands, my friend," Raleigh told the stoic jester gently. "You have done right well." With a firm push the courtier guided Tarleton out into the hall where a weary Philip waited anxiously.

"Wait!" Tarleton called back into Elizabeth's room. "This young man has tended my lady's wounds. She would be comforted if he were here with her now. 'Tis Master Philip Robinson of Oxford," he said, introducing the boy.

Dr. Dee made a face but politely motioned the tall student inside.

"Watch over her for me, good Philip," Tarleton whispered as Philip passed him. "Don't let her die!"

Philip tried to speak some word of encouragement but he didn't know what to say. Instead, he merely nodded.

The click of the door lock behind him was the deadliest sound Tarleton had ever heard.

"The Queen commanded that you wait upon her immediately," remarked Raleigh, as they crossed the Long Gallery. "But, methinks 'twould be best for all concerned if you got some sleep, and some cleaner clothes, before your audience."

"Amen to that!" Yawning, Tarleton stretched his stiff muscles.

"And take a bath, man!" continued the tall knight, wrinkling his nose. "You stink to high heaven, and the Queen dislikes foul air!"

Tarleton smiled without humor. "I will shame every flower in the garden when I see her."

Raleigh clapped the jester on the back. "I suggest you sleep in the stables until you can get a wash."

With those parting words of cold comfort, the tall courtier strode off.

Tarleton looked after him ruefully, then he made his way down to the mews. Outside, he passed the wing wherein he knew Elizabeth lay. Slowly he scanned along the many windows of Wolsey's rambling pleasure dome. *So, we are back to where we were at the beginning: the lady in her perfumed chamber, and the jester in the stable.*

Giving himself a shake, he stumbled toward a much-needed rest in the hayloft.

Tarleton slept round the clock. As evening of the second day came on, he awoke with a start, wondered briefly where he was, then remembered the royal command. With his stomach growling for food, he presented himself at the kitchen door, where the cooks welcomed him with a hot tub, clean clothing and a hearty dinner. The scullery maids and undercooks were particularly interested in hearing of his adventures, but Tarleton begged off, saying he must speak with the Queen first.

"Well, you rascal! You've taken your sweet time in answering my summons!" Queen Elizabeth attempted to sound stern when her tardy jester finally made his appearance. Tarleton could always bring a smile to her lips, and a lift to her weary heart, made heavier these days by the constant threat of a Catholic rebellion.

"Had I come earlier, Your Grace, you would have sent me back to the pigsty," he defended himself, going down on one knee. "But here I am, as sweet smelling as any rose, and so I hope I am forgiven for taking my sweet time to sweeten the air around me." He bowed his freshly washed curly head.

The Queen burst into laughter; her ladies joined in her merriment.

"'Tis good to have you back at court, you foolish wit!" she said, beckoning him to rise.

"Ah, better a witty fool, than ever a foolish wit, Your Grace. For methinks you are surrounded with more of the latter, than the former." This remark brought another round of laughter.

Tarleton was relieved that he made a good impression. He knew he had much to answer for, and the Queen's moods were like a weathercock—constantly changing.

Her Grace settled herself on a deep cushioned chair, fanning out her ivory satin skirts about her. With every move, Elizabeth of England sparkled like a thousand stars. The candlelight reflected in the brilliant jewels she wore on her dress, in her hair and on her fingers.

The Queen arched one carefully drawn eyebrow. "Now, then, my scamp! What have you been up to this past fortnight?"

Drawing a deep breath, Tarleton recounted most of his travels with the Lady Elizabeth Hayward, embellishing his story with wit and mimicry. Only the memory of that golden afternoon under the greenwood trees did he lock in his heart.

When he finished, the Queen said nothing, despite the fact that she had been laughing only moments before. Opening the reticule at her waist, she extracted a piece of marchpane, which she popped into her mouth. Nervously, her ladies waited for her response.

The Queen's amber eyes bored into Tarleton. "You have told us a pleasant tale. I suppose you think I should now applaud this fool, who cut my goddaughter's hair so short, and who dressed her like a beggar boy?" The Queen feigned mild surprise. Abruptly her tone changed, becoming cold as the wind that howled around the palace's hundred chimneys.

"God's teeth, you knave! If you had cut my hair in such a manner, and dressed me in such mean fashion, I think I would have encouraged the villain in the ruined church to finish you off! Aye! And paid him well in the bargain, too!" The ladies behind the Queen tittered.

Tarleton flushed. "Fortunately, my Lady Elizabeth did not pause to think of it at the time, Your Grace. Indeed, the event upset her mightily. She has suffered nightmares because of it. Pray tell me, Your Grace, does she still have these nightmares?" Tarleton's eyes pleaded to his Queen. He knew nothing of Elizabeth's present condition.

The Queen eyed him shrewdly. "Sir Robert La Faye arrived at court yesterday, bringing a serious charge against you, Tarleton. He says you stole his bride, then attacked him when he pressed his rightful claim. How do you answer to that?'' The Queen appeared to study a particular ring on her finger, but Tarleton knew from long association that she was giving him her fullest attention.

He chose to defend himself by attack. ''Lady Elizabeth is not yet La Faye's wife, as I understand it. Nor did I steal her.'' His voice changed, becoming more seductive. ''She literally fell my way, begging me to escort her to you, her most royal godmother, who loves her and will protect her from a marriage contract which the lady despises.''

''Are you presuming to tell me my duty toward my god-daughter, jester?'' asked the Queen in a dangerous under-tone.

Tarleton gulped inwardly, though he presented a smiling exterior. ''Never, Your Grace. I am but a prattling fool. But in faith, Sir Robert is angry because I have helped to make him a bigger fool than even I am. Indeed, his vanity is as puffed up as his doublet!''

''Then we pray God he does not explode—at least, not at court.'' The Queen smiled at her jester. She leaned closer to him. ''Speak to me, sweet Tarleton. I see there is another thing to be said. You have no fear of losing your tongue. It will last as long as you have your wit!''

Taking heart from her words, Tarleton continued. ''The Lady Elizabeth is most distressed over her match with Sir Robert, Your Grace. She fears him, and with good reason.''

''Oh?'' The Queen peered closely at him. ''How so?''

Tarleton licked his lips. A commoner rarely accused a nobleman of a capital crime. Tarleton knew he was tread-ing on thin ice.

''The night I performed at Esmond Manor was in cele-bration of the lady's betrothal to Lord La Faye. Though I had never met Lady Elizabeth before that evening, I could see she was most unhappy. She told me later she knew she could not go though with the marriage. Sir Thomas agreed with her decision. That next morning, Lord La Faye gave a basket of fresh-picked mushrooms to Sir Thomas. Shortly after eating them, the old lord was taken suddenly ill, and died before nightfall.''

The room was very quiet. The ladies looked to see what the Queen would say.

''There are some poisonous mushrooms in the woods,'' she remarked carefully. ''Sir Robert is not a qualified botanist. A mistake, perhaps?''

''A convenient mistake, Your Grace,'' Tarleton replied vehemently. ''The lady's father died before any change could be made to the contract. Lord La Faye showed no grief at his host's sudden departure from this life. Instead, he wanted the lady wedded and bedded before her father was even cold in the ground! When Eliz... the lady delayed, Sir Robert shut her up in her room and swore he would force himself upon her. How is my lady, Your Grace?''

''She is still unconscious, Tarleton. Indeed, the doctors fear for her life.'' The Queen saw the color drain from Tarleton's face at this news, though he struggled against his emotions.

''May I see her?'' he finally whispered.

The Queen sniffed loudly with haughty disapproval. ''She is in my private apartments and is being well taken care of by my maids. No one may disturb her, by her doctor's orders—and by mine!''

Bowing his head, Tarleton hid the pain he knew was in his eyes. ''You are my Queen and I obey your commands, Your Grace,'' he murmured.

''We were speaking of Sir Robert La Faye, Tarleton. Do you accuse him of murder?'' Her words stood out sharply in the perfumed air of the overheated room.

Tarleton's eyes glittered with hatred. ''I do, so please Your Grace. Furthermore, I accuse him of attempted murder.

Had I not stopped him, Lord La Faye would have run Elizabeth through!''

The Queen nodded thoughtfully. "So I was told by the young physician who attended her. Apparently he was a witness to this tavern brawl.''

"Philip Robinson? Aye, he is as good a man as ever I have met.''

The Queen nodded her head in agreement; the rubies entwined in her hair twinkled in the firelight. "The same. He is a very skilled one, as well.''

"Is he still here?'' Tarleton's hopes lifted. Perhaps Philip could smuggle him in to see Elizabeth.

The Queen dabbed the corner of her lips with her lace handkerchief. "He returned to Oxford this afternoon. 'Tis a pity. I found the medical discussions he waged with our Dr. Dee to be most interesting. Philip will make a fine physician in due time.''

Tarleton hid his disappointment. "In any event, he is a reliable witness to what I have just said, Your Grace. Lord La Faye is—''

The Queen tapped her foot. "Sir Robert attends me here at court. He is no concern of yours. Do you understand me, Tarleton?'' The Queen's pale eyes narrowed. "You are discharged of your responsibilities toward my goddaughter. I suppose you expect to be paid for your services.''

"Nay, Your Grace, I did not—'' Tarleton realized the conversation had taken a more dangerous turn.

"You did very little as far as I can see, except to dress Elizabeth shamefully, teach her to swear and sing bawdy songs, make a fool of her on the back of a goat—a goat, mind you!—put her through the discomforts of sleeping outside in wet weather, throw her amongst the foulest of company, thrust her into bodily danger, then send her to me half-dead. What payment do you think you deserve for all this goodly care, Master Fool?''

Dropping to his knees again, Tarleton bowed his head. It racked him with guilt to hear his offenses so brutally outlined. "No payment, Your Grace. As you so often point out, I am the biggest fool in the kingdom."

When he looked up at her, the Queen saw his eyes shining with unshed tears. The sight unnerved her.

"You have been punished enough, you jackanapes," she muttered gruffly. "But I command one thing more—you are never to see, nor speak to, Lady Elizabeth again. Do you understand this plainly, Tarleton? The lady has suffered enough at your hands."

If the Queen had taken up a dagger and stabbed him in the heart, she could not have hurt him more. Tarleton knew by the set of her jaw that she meant every word she spoke. The implication was clear: he was lucky to be let off so lightly. After all, what was he but a gypsy player, and a bastard? For ten glorious days he had forgotten himself. Now, he must force himself to forget the lady.

The Queen tapped him on the chin with her fan. "Put away that long face, jester, and sing something merry for us!"

Swallowing down his heavy heart, Tarleton rose and sang "Pastimes in Good Company," a composition written by the Queen's great father, King Henry VIII. Hearing it always pleased Her Grace.

Tarleton's interview with Sir Francis Walsingham was more candid.

"Sir Robert La Faye's name has appeared in many dispatches recently," the Queen's chief minister observed. "There is talk he is in sympathy with the Scots Queen. And your charges against him are most interesting." Sitting back in his chair, Sir Francis eyed his informant with hooded speculation. "The evidence concerning Sir Thomas Hayward's death is circumstantial, though suspicious."

"Speak with some of the servants at Esmond Manor, Sir Francis. They will bear out the tale. Jane, one of the cooks, is especially forthright."

Sir Francis pursed his lips. "And I presume you have tested her...honesty?"

Tarleton flushed, though he did not look away. "Aye, after my own fashion, my lord. But more to the point, there is the matter of La Faye's attempted murder of my Lady Elizabeth. That was done within sight of half the students at Oxford."

"Who had drunk a great deal of beer, I presume?" Sir Francis twirled his quill pen between his fingers.

"Two were reasonably sober at the time, whose testimony will ring true—Philip Robinson and Jonathan Biggs, both of Christ Church."

"Ah, yes, Philip Robinson," Sir Francis mused. "I understand he has the makings of a fine doctor, despite our good John Dee's envious opinion. I agree. I shall speak with your young friend anon."

Tarleton licked his lips as he brought up the subject closest to his heart. "How does the Lady Elizabeth?"

"I hear she is mending," the minister replied mildly.

"The Queen has forbidden me to see or speak with her." Tarleton tried to keep his voice level.

Sir Francis nodded. "But not to speak *about* her, I see. Her Grace feels you have become too close to her goddaughter. Is that true?"

Staring at the minister, Tarleton wondered if Walsingham could read men's minds. "Aye! We grew...very close," he conceded.

"The lady comes with a vast estate," Walsingham mused.

"The lady comes with a loving heart that surpasses all earthly wealth," Tarleton responded quietly.

The small office grew quiet as each man contemplated his own thoughts. The only sounds were the popping and hissing of the fire that danced brightly, lighting up the rich linenfold carving on the paneled walls. At last, Sir Francis spoke softly.

"I have in mind to go a-hunting, Tarleton. There is a particularly loathsome rat at court which needs to be destroyed."

Tarleton's face creased into a slow grin. "Would that rat be quite large and wear costly garments worth far more than he can afford, my lord?"

"Just so." Sir Francis inclined his head. "But to catch so great a rat, we must bait the trap with an especially delicate morsel."

Tarleton felt a cold shiver run down his spine. "The Lady Elizabeth."

"That is the nut and core of it. And you, my wise fool, must play the most dangerous game of your career."

"And the stakes, my lord? I like to know the wager before I play my hand."

Sir Francis smiled warmly for the first time. "Why, the Lady Elizabeth, of course. Isn't that what we have been discussing?"

Tarleton drew himself up. "I am your man, my lord."

"And the lady's too, I warrant." Sir Francis knitted his brows together "Take heed, Tarleton. What I have in mind could fail utterly and lead to your death."

"For such fair stakes, I would wrestle with Lucifer himself." Tarleton's eyes glowed with anticipation.

"You may have to, player. Now bend your ear to me, then give me your good counsel, for your mind has more twists and turns to it than a garden maze."

Tarleton grinned at Sir Francis's compliment, for no man in the kingdom had so devious a mind as the Queen's spy master.

Chapter Eighteen

Elizabeth hovered in a feverish limbo. Sometimes floating near the surface of consciousness, she heard voices around her. An older man argued with a younger one. A girlish voice murmured snatches of the psalms. Cool hands bathed Elizabeth's hot skin. Once, someone smelling strongly of musk and roses kissed her brow. Most of the time Elizabeth drifted amid fanciful hallucinations.

She dreamed of green glades and gurgling rivers, of meadow grass and the call of black rooks in the forest. Most of all, she dreamed of a laughing, dark-haired man clasping her in his arms, his lips kissing hers, inflaming her with a glorious passion. Other visions crowded around her: smoky inns and wanton wenches, floors sticky with spilled ale and trodden food, a flashing sword pointed toward her heart. Screaming in fright, she awoke, chilled with sweat.

"There, there, my sweet." A richly gowned young woman dabbed Elizabeth's face with a damp cloth that smelled faintly of roses.

"Tarleton?" Elizabeth whispered hoarsely, trying to focus her eyes.

"Do you dream of the jester again?" the lady crooned. "Hush, now."

"Water, please," Elizabeth begged weakly. Her throat felt parched.

Widening her eyes with delighted surprise, the lady stopped her ministrations. "Why, Elizabeth, you truly *are* awake! Thanks be to the good Lord!" Quickly she poured a cupful from the silver pitcher on the bedside candle stand. Gently she supported Elizabeth, who sipped the cold water gratefully. "For a moment, I thought you were having another dream."

Feeling weak, Elizabeth rejoiced that her fever was gone. "Tell me..." she began.

The young woman laughed pleasantly. "In due time. Let me send for something to eat, then I shall talk so much that you will hold your ears and plead leave to sleep again. In good faith, Elizabeth, I am glad you are better."

Opening the door a crack, the lady spoke to someone unseen, then she returned to the bedside. "I am Lady Anne Bacon, one of the Queen's handmaids. I have been with you these last three days."

"Three?" Her mind reeling, Elizabeth signed for more water.

Lady Anne held the cup to her lips. "Aye, my dearest dear. For a time we feared we would lose you entirely. But that young doctor of yours, Philip—so handsome, that one!—he refused to believe Dr. Dee. Imagine! The Queen's own physician! And here this young man, not even out of university, told our good Dr. Dee—in no uncertain terms, mind you!—exactly how outdated his medical practices were! Oh, my dear! What a blow to the great man's vanity! As you can see, your Philip Robinson was right!"

"Philip? Is he here?" Dimly the memories of their hellish journey flowed back to her.

"Bless you, no! As soon as he had done as much as he could for you, he jumped on his horse and raced pell-mell back to Oxford. It seems he had been tardy from his books and feared expulsion."

"Tarleton?" Elizabeth cast her chatty nurse a beseeching look. "Is he well?"

"The jester?" Lady Anne laughed merrily. "Aye, you called for him often enough in your fever. His antics must have pleased you well."

"Then he *is* safe!" Elizabeth thought her heart would burst from happiness. At least, her ordeal had been worth it.

"Safe? Why, I should hope so! Only last night, he set the whole court to merriment by pouring a full jug of Rhenish wine over some poor lord's brand-new doublet. The Queen wept with mirth. 'Tis good to see her merry, now that Tarleton has returned. Even that old sourpuss, Sir Francis Walsingham, laughed upon that occasion! And what could the drenched victim do, but smile? Forsooth, Elizabeth, if looks could kill, Tarleton would have died on the very spot!" Lady Anne erupted into gales of laughter.

Elizabeth's lips curved in a weak smile. "Whose doublet was so ruined?" she asked.

Lady Anne shook her hands in frustration. "Oh, dear! I am trying to remember his name. 'Twas some preening popinjay. Terribly fat, though he fancies he cuts a fine figure! In sooth, he has no wit about him at all."

"Sir Robert La Faye?" Elizabeth ventured with a chill in her heart.

"Aye! The very name! You know of this lord?"

Elizabeth shuddered. "I was betrothed to him—once." Good for Tarleton! How she would have enjoyed to see Sir Robert's face and the expensive, dripping doublet!

"Betrothed? Poor you!" Lady Anne shook her head, then giggled. " 'Twas a most marvelous jest!"

"When can I see Tarleton?" Elizabeth longed to feel his strong arms around her again; to see that wonderful imp's expression creep into his brown eyes; to hear his soothing voice caress her name softly; to feel his kisses on her hungry mouth. "Please tell him to come to me with all speed!"

"The jester?" Lady Anne looked puzzled. "Nay, you are not strong enough for such lively entertainment. By and by, you will be down in the Hall with the Court and you can laugh at him then.''

"But I want to see him now!" Elizabeth's lower lip began to tremble.

Lady Anne patted her arm. "Oh, sweet Elizabeth, be of good cheer! You must rest first. Now that Tarleton has returned from his summer wandering over hill and dale, the Queen cannot bear to have him out of her sight. She says she is sick of sad-faced men, and she craves his merriment."

"Has...has he asked after me?" Elizabeth prayed he had visited her.

Lady Anne regarded her patient with open surprise. "Asked for you? Why on earth? Nay! 'Twould be unseemly to allow a common player in your bedchamber. The only men the Queen has permitted to see you are Dr. Dee, and, of course, the delightful Dr. Robinson. Such a man! Oh, my!" It was obvious that the Lady Anne was much taken with Elizabeth's makeshift physician.

"And Sir Robert La Faye?" Elizabeth could barely speak the man's name. Just thinking of him made her teeth ache. "Did *he* ask after me?"

Cocking her head, Lady Anne thought for a moment. "I believe he did—once. He wanted to know if you would live. When I told her aye, he just grunted—such a pig!—and went on his way, without so much as a message of cheer. In sooth, he looks the very swine, as well!"

Elizabeth felt empty inside. After that hellish ride she made for him, had Tarleton so quickly forgotten her? Turning her head away, Elizabeth swallowed back a tear.

Lady Anne spied her troubled look. "Forgive me, dear. I've tired you out. I warned you I would talk your ear off."

Elizabeth mustered a smile. "I am deeply grateful to you for your kind patience. I will be glad to hear as much of your chat as you wish, for I have been in rough company of late."

"Aye, so your Dr. Robinson told us."

"Philip?" Elizabeth blushed. "What *else* did he say?" She prayed Philip had been discreet in his tale-telling.

Lady Anne rolled her eyes. "Alackaday! He didn't say much. Imagine our surprise to see you with your hair cut so short and you dressed in a poor boy's clothes!"

"Oh!" Elizabeth remembered young Smith and Ned of Addison Hall. "I borrowed clothing from two poor boys, and I promised them new things."

Lady Anne clapped her hands. "And so you shall! Oh, what fun it will be to order a wonderful new wardrobe for them—and for you, as well! Outside of that shift you are wearing, you've not a stitch to your name."

Elizabeth experienced a sinking sensation. "What happened to my things?"

"By the stars, Elizabeth! You couldn't possibly have wanted those smelly clothes! Lady Mary Sidney ordered everything burned, even the shoes."

Elizabeth almost sobbed. Was there nothing left to remind her of her few short days of freedom—and of love?

Lady Anne clapped her hand to her brow. "Oh, my mind runs apace! There were some items in the pocket of the breeches. I saved them. Also, Philip left your purse with some shillings. He is such a nice, honest man—that Philip." She sighed, smiling dreamily.

"Where are they?"

Elizabeth looked so stricken that Lady Anne thought it best to humor her, though she couldn't understand what all the fuss was about. She mustn't excite Elizabeth any more than necessary; it might bring on her fever again. Opening the clothes chest, Lady Anne took out a small carved box, which she placed in Elizabeth's outstretched hands.

"As you can see your money is safe and sound," Lady Anne remarked.

Elizabeth didn't care about her purse. In one hand she held her dear wooden comb, treasuring Tarleton's thoughtful gift. In the other, she clutched the brass bell from his motley tunic. The only other items in the box were her faithful embroidery scissors, which lay primly in their case.

Elizabeth gazed at the bell with tears welling in her eyes. It was more precious than any gold to her. With a bittersweet tug to her heart, she remembered how she planned to sew it back on—but there had been no time. Lovingly she kissed the brass trinket.

Elizabeth tried not to condemn the jester. After all, Tarleton had been perfectly straightforward with her. Hadn't he said plainly that he took his pleasures when and where he could? Why should Elizabeth think she was going to be any different to him? In sooth, it was she who had seduced him, not the other way around. Elizabeth had only herself to blame for the fact that she had fallen in love with Tarleton. Now she was at Hampton Court, as he promised. Though he had obviously put her out of his mind, Elizabeth knew she would never forget the Queen's royal fool, nor would she ever love another man.

A fortnight later, the Queen, together with her enormous retinue of three thousand souls, packed up their chests, state papers, household goods, hunting falcons, clothing, silver plate and other sundries. Down the great river Thames they sailed in overloaded barges to Her Majesty's favorite palace at Greenwich. During these two weeks, Elizabeth saw no one except the servants, Lady Anne, Lady Mary and grumpy Dr. Dee. The Queen sent her goddaughter kind messages and tempting tidbits from the kitchens. Gallant Sir Walter Raleigh sent gillyflowers. Sir Robert La Faye sent a note saying that he was looking forward to their next meeting. Elizabeth hurled his curt missive into the fire accompanying it with a colorful oath, which much amused Lady Anne.

From Tarleton, there was nothing.

Though still very weak, Elizabeth looked forward to the trip to Greenwich. Dr. Dee made short work of Elizabeth's pleasure by giving her a potion so that the invalid slept most of the way downriver, sheltered inside the curtained pavilion on one of the royal barges.

Just before the boat cast off from the water gate at Hampton Court, Tarleton leapt aboard. With a smug grin, he settled himself amidships between the oarsmen. As the barge followed the current to Greenwich, Tarleton entertained the courtiers and crew with a wide selection of songs and tunes played on his whistle. Though his music pleased all who heard it, for Tarleton there was only one special audience—the sleeping lady behind the drawn curtains. Lady Mary Sidney looked archly at the grinning jester.

"How now, Tarleton! I thought the Queen was most clear when she told you her pleasure concerning yon Lady Elizabeth."

Tarleton flashed a beguiling smile. "Aye, she did, Lady Mary, and, as you are my witness, I obey Her Grace to every jot and tittle of her command."

"Oh?" Lady Mary cocked her head. Tarleton was exceedingly charming when he chose. "Then why you are here, and not with the baggage, where you usually travel?"

Tarleton cocked his head in imitation of Lady Mary. "Her Grace commanded me not to see, or to speak to, my Lady Elizabeth. Tell me true, Lady Mary, have I set eyes on her?"

"Nay." Lady Mary tried to keep a straight face.

"And have I spoken to her?"

"Nay, Tarleton."

"I do not recall that the Queen mentioned anything about not singing or whistling for the lady, but perhaps my mind misgives. What say you, Lady Mary?" He smiled his most impish grin at her.

She giggled. "I say you are a rogue, Tarleton, but a clever one."

Hours later, when Elizabeth awoke in her new apartments at Greenwich Palace, many of the songs that Tarleton had taught her danced through her mind.

The trees had not yet turned their riotous shades of red and gold when Elizabeth had slipped out of her father's home and fled down the road to Hampton Court. Now, as she made a slow recovery, those selfsame leaves were gone and the bare, skeletal branches groaned in protest as the icy breath of the promised early winter blew through them. Though she was living amid one of the most glittering courts of Europe, Elizabeth found herself a virtual prisoner. By royal command, she was not allowed to stir outside her apartment, and she saw very few people. No one around Elizabeth would speak to her of Tarleton, nor would anyone take a message to him. The knowledge that Tarleton lived under the same large roof was almost more than she could bear at times. There was one blessing: so far, she had not been forced to see Sir Robert La Faye, whom she knew lurked about the Queen.

In the second week of October, Elizabeth's French maid, Charlotte, finally arrived with her mistress's wardrobe from Esmond Manor. The faithful retainer had taken over a month to pack up Elizabeth's extensive possessions, as well as her own, smaller ensemble, and to make the long journey to Greenwich south of London. Initially shocked to see how thin her young mistress was, Charlotte happily fell in with Lady Anne's nursing.

"*Mon Dieu!* Your wrists hang out of your sleeve like…like those of a scarecrow!" The little maid shook her head as she made alterations to Elizabeth's gowns. "You must eat more."

"I try but, for once, I have no appetite." Elizabeth sighed ruefully.

In fact, Elizabeth was having trouble keeping down the little food she did eat. Her unexpected attacks of nausea disturbed her. She planned to mention the matter the next time she saw Philip. As her first doctor, he was the only outsider allowed to attend her. She much preferred Philip's visits to those of Dr. John Dee. That doddering quack spoke in a high, reedy voice, and he had nothing but horrible things to say about Philip.

Getting dressed in her gowns proved very tiring for Elizabeth. During the past six weeks, she had forgotten how confining high fashion was. Charlotte's prodding fingers stuffed her mistress into whalebone corsets, lacing them up tightly. The huge farthingale hoops, heavy stiffened stomachers, a half-dozen petticoats, and double padded sleeves further weighed her down.

"This is just too much, Charlotte!" Elizabeth gasped as her maid adjusted a wide lace ruff around her neck. "I can barely breathe!"

"*Non, ma petite!*" Charlotte soothed. "You have been so ill. Now you are getting better, and soon you will outshine all the ladies of fashion, *oui?*"

"*Non!*" Elizabeth fanned herself. "Please untie the laces. I'm going to faint!" With that, she crumpled to the floor in a heap of brocade and velvet.

"I had the pleasure of meeting Sir Francis Walsingham today," Philip mentioned casually, when next he visited Elizabeth. Outside, the cold October rain drummed against the windowpanes.

"And how fares Sir Francis?" Elizabeth asked, having yet to meet the man she had heard so much about.

Lifting her double ruff, Philip inspected the scar tissue on her shoulder. "He suffers from stones in his gall bladder, caused from overwork, no doubt. We had a very interesting conversation. Ah! You have healed nicely," observed Philip with a certain pride, "but 'twill take much longer for your muscles to regain their former use. Please make a fist for me, my lady."

"I've tried, Philip!" Elizabeth's fingers of her left hand quivered as she tried to ball them together.

He looked at her with sympathy. "Does it pain you?" he asked quietly.

"It tingles, as if my arm has gone to sleep," she answered, rubbing the affected area carefully.

Philip nodded. "That's to be expected."

"Dr. Dee suggests that I drink powdered rhinoceros horn in vinegar. He says 'twill give me strength." Elizabeth wrinkled her nose with distaste at the thought.

Philip snorted in derision. "Dr. Dee thinks he is God in a nightgown, and you'll do no such thing, Lady Elizabeth. It doesn't work, and 'twill make you sick."

"I already am," Elizabeth told him quietly.

The medical student regarded her steadily. "When?" he asked softly.

"Nearly every day."

"In the mornings?"

"Usually." Elizabeth eyed him through her lashes.

"And how do you feel afterward?"

"Fine, though I still seem to tire easily." Why was Philip looking at her so oddly?

Philip crossed to the window, staring out at the rain-lashed garden. Then, he took a deep breath. "I must ask you something of a personal nature, my lady, and I beg you to answer me. I ask it as your doctor, not out of idle curiosity."

"What is it?" Elizabeth felt a small stab of fear.

"Did you ever . . . lie with Tarleton? I mean, as a wife lies with her husband?" Philip did not look at Elizabeth, but, instead, he continued to stare at the last few blossoms on the rosebushes below.

"Aye," Elizabeth confessed softly. That golden afternoon under the greenwood trees burned in her memory. In a clearer voice she asked, "Does my admission shock you, Philip?"

Philip gazed at her, so fragile by the fireside, then he swore under his breath. Crossing to her side and kneeling before her, he took her hands in his.

"Nay. I know how much you loved him." Philip gently placed one hand over her stiff beaded stomacher. "But you have *got* to stop wearing things like this, my lady. 'Twill not bode well for the little one you carry."

"Little one . . . ?" Elizabeth gasped, then blushed deeply, as the full impact of Philip's words engulfed her. "Oh, Philip! Are you sure?"

"When did you last have your monthly courses?" he asked quietly.

Elizabeth chewed on her lip as her thoughts filtered back to the day she'd first met Tarleton. "I have always been a bit irregular," she murmured. "I think 'twas a week or two before my father died."

Philip nodded. "Then I *am* sure," he replied quietly. "You will have a sweet babe in early May."

Elizabeth had half suspected her condition, but she tried to tell herself that it was not possible. She thought she was merely suffering the aftereffects of her fever. Now Philip confirmed her fears. Feeling light-headed, she gripped his arm for support. The vision of the thin, ragged peasant girl burying her bastard baby in a ditch swam before Elizabeth's eyes. No! She'd never let that happen to her.

"You had no idea?" asked Philip gently.

Elizabeth could only shake her head mutely. Philip quickly poured a little wine into a cup.

"Drink this," he said, as he removed the choking ruff from around her neck.

"Tell no one," Elizabeth begged him.

"Not even Tarleton?" Philip cocked his eyebrow in surprise.

"Tarleton?" She shook her head. "Oh, Philip, he has forgotten me!"

She looked at the student with such sadness that Philip felt a knife twist in his stomach. "Nay, not so, sweet lady," he said soothingly.

Tears stung behind her eyelids. "Not two days ago, I saw him just below my window in the garden, Philip. He was singing..." She bit her lip as she recalled the scene. "He was singing the Robin Hood duet with...Lady Catherine Germaine, one of the Queen's maids. And when the song was over, he chased her about the rosebushes, saying that she owed him a...kiss for the song! I heard them plainly, even through the glass." Elizabeth wiped her tears away with the back of her hand. She did not want Philip to see how deeply Tarleton's betrayal had wounded her. "They were both laughing quite merrily, and never once did he look up to see me at my window." Avoiding Philip's searching eyes, she stared into the fire.

"Perhaps you mistook..." he suggested halfheartedly.

Elizabeth expelled a short, bitter laugh. "I think not. He once told me he had a lady love here at court. At least, he was honest about that. Nay, I was...convenient, and, in truth, 'tis all my fault. As to telling him about...about the child, I want to do that myself. Have you seen him since we came to Greenwich?" Elizabeth tried to keep her voice level.

"Nay," said Philip, nurturing black thoughts against the faithless jester. "I have not spoken to him." He pressed his lips tightly together.

"I must think of what to do," Elizabeth murmured beside him.

"You must rest, eat lightly five or six times a day. You must drink plenty of milk and take walks in the air when the days are fair. You must wear your gowns a trifle looser. Most of all, you must not fret, my lady." Philip tried his best to soothe her concerns, though he knew his words were merely feathers in the wind.

"Philip, I owe you so much, but may I ask you one more service?" Elizabeth held his hand tightly.

"I am ever yours to command, my lady," Philip answered with heartfelt sincerity. It was on the tip of his tongue to ask her to marry him on the spot, but he knew she was not his for the asking, nor would her heart ever be his for the taking, no matter how injured it was.

Elizabeth's green eyes looked deeply into his. "When my time comes, no matter where they hide me away, will you deliver my child?"

Smiling warmly, Philip kissed her hand. "I wouldn't miss it for all the world, my lady. I will be there," he promised.

And I will damn Tarleton with every labor pain she suffers, he promised himself grimly.

As luck would have it, Philip met Tarleton face-to-face in the stable as the medical student saddled his horse. It had been a difficult day, first questioned at length by the enigmatic Walsingham, then his equally nerve-racking time with Lady Elizabeth. The young doctor was almost out of patience, especially with the man who now stood before him.

"No smile for an old comrade-in-arms, Philip?" Tarleton greeted him, looking warily over his shoulder.

The jester had been keeping company with Philip's deuced horse for nearly two hours, and it had not been a pleasant experience for either man or beast. Tarleton knew he was taking a chance to even speak with Philip, but the weeks of enforced silence had nearly driven him mad.

"'Tis been a hard day and I am tired," replied Philip shortly, cinching the gelding's girth strap. He avoided looking at the jester.

"How does the fair lady?" Tarleton asked softly.

"Well enough," Philip replied coolly. "I am much surprised you are asking me. Surely, you could find that out yourself. Have you thought of walking up to her door and knocking?"

"God's blood, man! Don't you think I've wanted to?" Tarleton's heartfelt outburst took Philip aback. "There is not a day that passes in this blasted place that I don't think of her, watch for her, listen for the sound of her sweet voice. At night, she haunts my dreams.''

''Then why, in the name of heaven, haven't you sought her out before this?'' Philip knew he was dangerously close to losing his temper. *She needs you more than ever, you blackguard!*

Tarleton nodded with understanding at the wrath he spied in the student's face. ''Because I am forbidden by the Queen's express command to speak her name. I cannot ask for her, nor inquire her health of anyone in the palace. I am treading upon eggs even to speak to you. The Queen has locked away my Robin Redbreast like a lark in a cage. She has been here almost a month, and I have yet to catch a glimpse of her, though I loiter near her gallery as often as I dare. I see the disgust in your eyes, good Philip. Believe me, no one is as disgusted with me as myself!''

Philip felt his anger drain away as Tarleton spoke. He sought for something comforting to say to the player.

''Would it make you feel any better to know that my lady asks after you?'' Philip was tempted to tell Tarleton of his impending fatherhood, but he feared the consequences. That fire storm would come down soon enough. Besides, it was Elizabeth's choice to tell whom she pleased, not Philip's.

Tarleton raised his head as if Philip had just given pure water to a man dying of thirst. A soft glow lit up his brown eyes. ''She has?''

''Do I tell her that you miss her company so much that you must chase the Queen's maids around the rose gardens?''

Tarleton smiled grimly at Philip's rebuke. How could he tell the student that scene was played as broad farce to hide the real truth? No, Tarleton had sworn an oath to silence on that score. ''You saw that? 'Twas my own physic, prentice doctor. I thought perchance I could chase away my memories by dallying with others.''

"And?" Philip observed Tarleton carefully. He divined some inner struggle, but what it was Philip could not fathom.

"I found my remedy for naught, so I have taken a great deal of beer instead."

"Truly? Then do I tell Lady Elizabeth that you are lying around a stable, drunk as a sailor on leave? That news will cheer her marvelously well."

"Am I as bad as that, my friend?" Tarleton smiled crookedly. Better to let Philip think he was drinking in the stable than to suspect he had lain in wait for the boy.

Philip nodded. "Aye. Is that my report to the lady?"

"Nay." Tarleton ran his fingers through his hair. "'Tis a false medicine I have been taking. Please tell my lady that I love her, and that my love is true. Will you tell her those words for me?"

"I will, whenever I see her again. Now, I must be off before the rain comes. Fare thee well, friend jester." He paused, then tossed Tarleton a crumb of comfort. "Believe me when I tell you, you are close to the lady. In faith, you are under her heart." Not trusting himself to say another word, Philip hastily saluted Tarleton, then mounted his horse.

"God speed you, doctor of hearts!" Tarleton called after him.

Chapter Nineteen

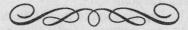

Two days after Tarleton's meeting with Philip, Sir Francis sent for the jester.

"My lord?" Tarleton inquired politely, when the two were alone in Walsingham's neat office.

"Help yourself to some wine. It has just arrived from Beaujolais," Sir Francis offered. "I perceive this past month has been a trial for you?"

Nodding his thanks at Walsingham's unusual hospitality, Tarleton poured himself a large goblet. "In sooth, I have been in hell, Sir Francis. 'Tis not a gladsome place." He drank down the new wine in one ferocious gulp.

"Perhaps I can make it more merry for you, Tarleton." Sir Francis leaned across his desk, his black eyes glowing. " 'Tis time to set our trap."

Tarleton's fingers tightened around the goblet's stem. "Does Her Grace know?"

Sir Francis chuckled. "There is nothing under her roof that the Queen does not know."

"And . . . she approves?"

Sir Francis inclined his head. "Wholeheartedly. 'Twill be soon."

"Not soon enough for me," Tarleton poured himself more wine, though this time, he was content to sip it. "And . . . my Lady Elizabeth?" He uttered her name softly.

"She is the golden pawn."

Tarleton shot his patron a pleading look. "She will find her role most distressing. Surely, it would ease her mind if we told..."

Sir Francis shook his head. "Nay. Her reactions must be natural. We agreed upon this point, if you recall."

"Aye." Tarleton winced when he considered how distressed Elizabeth was going to be.

Sir Francis held up his hand to stop all further protests. "Screw up your great courage, Master Player. The lady—and ourselves—will need all your skill if we are to catch our rat, who grows fatter with self-importance by the day."

"I will not fail you, my lord. I have waited too long for this!" Tarleton drained the goblet.

At last, Elizabeth was summoned to wait upon the Queen. After weeks of confinement in her few rooms while she supposedly recuperated, Elizabeth sparkled with anticipation at the thought of finally seeing more of her surroundings—and meeting with her illustrious godmother. She was bubbling with nervousness and excitement when Sir Walter Raleigh presented himself as her escort.

"You are looking much better than when I last saw you, Lady Elizabeth," complimented the tall gentlemen as he bowed over her hand.

"I am feeling much better, Sir Walter," Elizabeth replied, sweeping him a curtsy. "I am not feverish, nor on horseback, nor dressed unusually."

"So I observe, my lady." Raleigh's eyes twinkled as he regarded the golden pawn whose name was spoken in certain quarters of the great palace. Now that he could observe her in the daylight, Raleigh agreed completely with everything he had heard. Lady Elizabeth was, indeed, a most unique young woman.

"La! Let us be gone," exclaimed Lady Anne. "Her Grace does not like anyone to be late. *She* never is!"

To Elizabeth's awestruck eyes, Greenwich Palace was far more magnificent than what she had seen of Hampton Court. Brightly colored flags waved from its many white towers, announcing the presence of the Queen. A thousand panes of glass glinted from its many windows. Its halls and galleries were a rabbit warren of confusion. People arrayed in jewel-colored clothing rushed importantly about the polished galleries. The two ladies stayed close to Raleigh's heels as he conducted them to the Queen.

As she scurried after the tall knight, Elizabeth glanced about her, hoping she would spy Tarleton among the courtiers. She knew she must tell him about the baby soon, before her condition became obvious and she was banished in disgrace. She prayed she could go home to Esmond Manor and have the child there, instead of the forbidding Tower where another young mother, Lady Catherine Grey, spent some very unpleasant months for the crime of marrying without the Queen's approval. Since Philip's diagnosis, Elizabeth had done a great deal of thinking. No matter the cost, she vowed to keep the child. He would be the living reminder of the man who ensnared her heart.

Though Elizabeth hopefully searched amid the hundreds of faces in the halls and galleries of Greenwich, none was the one she pined for. The only bell she heard was the battered brass one she wore on a red ribbon at her waist. It jingled softly as she moved.

"My dearest godchild!"

Rising slowly from her deep curtsy, Elizabeth gazed at the Queen for the first time. *She looks old,* was Elizabeth's candid impression, which she quickly squelched.

Elizabeth smoothed down the simple pale blue gown she had chosen for this first important meeting. Compared to the Queen and her ladies, Elizabeth felt like a small homely dove who had landed among a flock of stately peacocks.

"Please excuse my poor attire, Your Grace. I am not used to being in such glittering company."

"You are a glad sight for these old eyes of mine, my child!" said the Queen kindly. "Come, sit down here beside me." She pointed to a low padded footstool. The air around the Queen was heavy with musk rose.

Elizabeth gratefully sank down on the offered seat, spreading her silken skirts out around her. "Your Grace looks younger than I remember," she complimented, hoping she said the right thing. The Queen's obsession with youth was well-known.

The Queen glowed. "And you, my dear, have obviously grown up since we last met." The Queen took one of Elizabeth's hands in hers. "I am very sorry to learn of your father's sudden death. He was a gentleman of the old school—not like the brash young upstarts we have at court these days."

Elizabeth bowed her head. "Thank you, Your Grace is most kind."

Cupping Elizabeth's chin in her hand, the Queen peered into the girl's face. "And I trust you are recovered from your ordeal? Yes, you certainly seem better than when I last saw you looking like a drowned kitten. Rest assured, I have taken Tarleton to task for it."

At his name, Elizabeth felt a warm glow flow through her. Dropping her gaze to her lap, she spoke carefully, hoping that her true feelings would not be betrayed by her voice.

"I am most grateful to Master Tarleton for helping me . . ." she began, but the Queen snorted.

"A fine lot of help he gave! At least, your hair is growing back, no thanks to that jackanapes! But let us speak of more pleasant topics. Advent will soon be upon us, and after that—the Christmas season! And I have devised a special happiness for you, my dearest child."

"What is that, Your Grace?" A little warning jangled inside her head. There was something in the Queen's pale eyes that looked out of tune with the Queen's cheerful voice.

"Your marriage, child! That is what your father wanted before he died, and, as the guardian of your estates, that is now my concern."

"You are most kind," said Elizabeth, her mind a-whirl with a mixture of happiness and apprehension. *This could be my salvation and the baby's!* Grasping her little bell with her good hand, she smiled up at the Queen.

"I have given much thought to the matter," continued the Queen easily. "Your scandalous roaming about the countryside with such a rogue as Tarleton has made it difficult for me to match you."

Elizabeth swallowed. For Tarleton's sake, she was glad the Queen had no idea how "damaged" the goods were.

"I am so very sorry to have caused you inconvenience, Your Grace," she murmured. "But I was frightened. You see..."

The Queen waved her hand; her many rings flashed in the firelight. "Yes, yes, yes! I've heard your story from several sources. I will not tire you to repeat it to me again. I trust you have learned much since you decided to strike out on your own?"

"Oh, aye, Your Grace! Indeed I have." Elizabeth hung her head so that the Queen would not see the blush her goddaughter felt creeping into her cheeks. The best of all her lessons were the ones in Tarleton's arms.

Though she noticed Elizabeth's secret smile, the Queen continued as if she had not. "The long and the short of it is this, my dear girl. Thanks to your gadding about unchaperoned, there is only one gentleman who is willing to accept you as his wife—Sir Robert La Faye!"

The color draining from her face, a cold knot formed in Elizabeth's stomach. Feeling faint, Elizabeth gritted her teeth to keep from falling over.

Unwittingly she gripped the Queen's hand fiercely. "Your Grace, I would rather not marry at all. Please, I beg of you. Send me to a nunnery somewhere. But, please, not marriage with Sir Robert! He is . . ."

"Ungrateful wretch!" The Queen snatched her hand out of Elizabeth's moist grasp. "How dare you question my decisions! Sir Robert is whom your father picked, and who is still willing to take you!"

Elizabeth numbly shook her head. "All he wants is my estates, Your Grace. He hates me!" Elizabeth could not control her sobs.

Rising, the Queen moved away from the abject girl at her feet. "That's all any man wants, my fine headstrong miss! What did you think marriage was about? Love? Bah!" She spat out the word. " 'Tis property and heirs! In time, perhaps Sir Robert will come to like you."

"But, Your Grace . . ." The walls, heavily hung with thick tapestries, closed around Elizabeth. The room grew stiflingly hot.

The Queen stamped one of her golden slippers. "Silence! I will hear no more whining from you! I have decided you shall marry Sir Robert on All Saints' Day in the evening, and that is that! Set your mind to it! You have a week to prepare yourself. Now, you may go!" The Queen's harsh words rang in her ear long after Elizabeth was escorted in silence from the chamber.

Property and heirs, Elizabeth thought as she lay on her bed in the early evening darkness, without so much as a fire to cheer her spirits. She gritted her teeth and called up from deep inside her a wellspring of courage and determination. *If that is the name of the game, then I shall play it to the end.* Elizabeth rolled the little bell around her palm, willing Tarleton's spirit into her own. *Sir Robert will have my property, and good riddance to him! As for me, I already have the heir. That will be my revenge!*

She fell asleep, clasping the bell tightly in her left fist.

Though he knew what to expect, when Tarleton heard the formal announcement of the Lady Elizabeth Hayward's impending nuptials, he disappeared into the stews and ale-houses of Bankside for two days. When he returned, red eyed, everyone noticed that the imp was gone from his smile.

"So, my drunken fool! Have you finally decided to stop sulking?" Queen Elizabeth affectionately cocked one carefully drawn eyebrow at the bowed head of her wayward player.

"Aye, Your Grace, I have been a fool beyond fools, but I have purged myself of such foolishness." Tarleton looked up at his Queen.

His hair was washed and trimmed; his cheeks clean shaven and his brown eyes clear. Only around the corners of his mouth did the Queen detect a new hardness.

"Good! I am glad to hear it. I am planning a small supper to be served in my apartments on All Hallows' Eve. It will be in honor of Sir Robert La Faye and Lady Elizabeth, who are to be married the following night—as you well know." Her lips twitched, watching for his reaction. Tarleton's face remained impassive. *He's a good actor,* applauded the Queen to herself.

"Aye, Your Grace?" Tarleton asked politely.

"I trust you will devise some entertainment for us—something that will please the company?" The Queen looked deeply into her fool's eyes. Yes, the spark was there, just waiting for the moment to ignite.

"I strive always to please my Queen," Tarleton spoke lightly, though his eyes glowed a darker, dangerous hue. A subtle look of understanding passed between the Queen and her loyal servant—a look that was not caught by any of the ladies attending Her Majesty.

"I wish especially to please Sir Robert La Faye. As the bridegroom of my beloved goddaughter, he is my honored guest."

A small muscle throbbed at Tarleton's temple, but he managed to keep his voice even. "I have in mind just the thing, Your Grace. I have been preparing for just this occasion. 'Twill be a surprise."

With satisfaction, the Queen noted a devilish light creep into Tarleton's eyes and a slow smile curl his lips. The imp had returned! "I do so dote on surprises, my clever fool," she said warmly.

After dispatching new clothes to Smith and Ned, as well as a lute for Jonathan and green riding gloves for Philip, there remained only one more piece of business before her detested wedding. For Tarleton, Elizabeth engaged the services of one of the tailors at court to fashion him a new coat of motley.

"In red and green satin with cloth of silver sleeves," Elizabeth instructed the little man. "Make the breeches gold velvet with silver bells on all the points. Be sure to double-stitch the bells as he tends to lose them."

"Satin and velvet?" Tarleton bellowed at the tailor, when the man came to measure him. "Cloth of silver sleeves? Are you *sure* you've got the right man?"

"Aye, Master Tarleton. The lady specifically requested it."

"What lady? The court is full of ladies these days!" Was this some whim of the Queen's, he wondered.

The tailor drew himself up primly. "I am not at liberty to say which lady has commissioned your suit, but she also requested silver bells. And she told me to double-stitch them! As if I didn't already know that! She said you lose your bells."

With an understanding grin, Tarleton snapped his fingers under the tailor's nose. "Well, about it, man! Measure me for this fool's finery!" How often had Elizabeth moaned over his loose bells?

All Hallows' Eve arrived far too quickly for Elizabeth. The Queen's private supper would be the first time she had to face her bloated intended since he had wounded her in Oxford. Elizabeth was not looking forward to the encounter.

As she dressed for the evening's festivities, one of the younger pages knocked at her door. He clutched a small tussy-mussy bouquet of rosemary, dried herbs and lavender.

"The gentleman said to regard the lavender especially," repeated the boy earnestly.

"And who is this gentleman?" Elizabeth smiled warmly into the child's wide blue eyes.

"I cannot say, Lady Elizabeth." Then he bolted out the door.

Charlotte giggled as she adjusted Elizabeth's ruff. "I think you have a secret admirer, *ma petite*."

"Perhaps," mused Elizabeth, poking her fingers among the lavender sprigs.

Nestled there, she found a pilgrim's badge, the silver letter *A*. On a small card were scrawled the words, "Play the play."

He's remembered me after all! Elizabeth's heart sang with delight, betraying her true feelings for the fickle jester. Slipping the card under her pillow, she pinned the trinket to her satin-and-pearl bodice, just above her heart. His comforting message brought a becoming glow to her cheeks, as she was escorted down the wide oaken staircase to the Queen's private apartments.

Sir Robert La Faye smiled into the mirror as he adjusted his dangling jeweled earring. *You have done well,* he congratulated himself with satisfaction. *You have won the favor of this Queen, and you are safe from Babington's mess.* He shuddered as he remembered the grisly executions of Ballard, Babington and five other friends which took place a month ago. *By this time tomorrow night, you will be married to the wench. Then, my headstrong Lady Elizabeth, I shall take the greatest pleasure in instructing you who is the master of my house!* Fluffing his ruff and flicking a small speck from his golden velvet sleeve, Sir Robert La Faye strutted down the gallery to sup with the Queen. The thought of Elizabeth's vast estates brought a greedy look to his swinelike features.

Elizabeth's escort left her at the door to the private supper chamber. Inside she heard a lute being softly strummed.

"Under the greenwood tree/Who loves to lie with me?"

Elizabeth froze, her heart beating wildly. That deep beautiful voice sang to her nightly in her dreams.

"And sing a merry note . . ." He suddenly quavered, then went flat.

How odd! Elizabeth listened with surprise.

After attempting a few more stumbling words, Tarleton stopped singing altogether, though the lute continued to play the melody in a sad cadence.

Her mind a tumbling mixture of hope and fear, Elizabeth took a deep breath to steady her nerves. She must not betray herself in front of the Queen . . . or to Tarleton. She must greet him as she would greet any other servant and she must find a way to speak with him. Just a few whispered words about the babe was all she craved. She hoped the news would please him. Tarleton must still have some small regard for her. Elizabeth touched the silver token pinned to her bodice. *I will not let him know how much his coldness has hurt me. Remember: play the play.*

Taking a deep breath, Elizabeth entered the room. Surprisingly, it was empty, though she saw that the table was laid for supper. The musician and his lute had vanished. A low fire burned in the hearth and a single candle on the sideboard shed its feeble light. Elizabeth wondered if there was some mistake. Perhaps the page had misunderstood the time and had come too early. She turned to go.

"Good evening, my Lady Elizabeth." Behind her, Tarleton spoke in an odd yet gentle tone.

"Dickon!" she answered quickly over her choking, beating heart. Stepping out of a shadowed corner, he swept her a deep bow. His movement was fluid and full of easy grace.

How devilishly handsome he looked in the firelight, even more stunningly virile than Elizabeth remembered! The rich outlines of his shoulders strained against a soft white shirt of finest lawn. His muscular legs were clad in a pair of tight black breeches. His dark eyes glowed with a savage inner fire and an errant brown curl fell bewitchingly across his forehead.

"Dickon! It's been so long!" Elizabeth took several steps toward him, before she remembered her resolve to remain in control of herself. "Too long," she added coolly.

Tarleton noted her hesitation and the determined set of her chin. Her sudden aloofness clawed at his soul. Well, what should he expect when he had not visited her in weeks? Their enforced separation was certainly not his idea. A muscle pulsed angrily at his jaw. "Aye, long enough for you to become a fine lady dressed in pearls again," he observed with a trace of sarcasm.

Bewildered by his unusual tone, Elizabeth flinched. She had hoped for some sort of an apology for his prolonged absence. So, the scene she had witnessed in the rose garden must be true! Turning away, she fought back her desire to throw herself into his arms. She would not stoop to such an indignity with a man who plainly found her company an unwelcome surprise. Perhaps he had been waiting for someone else? Her finger crept to the silver pin over her heart.

"I overheard you singing just now—you were out of tune. Most unlike you, Tarleton," she observed, fighting to keep her features composed..

"I was . . . distracted."

Her eyebrow flickered upward. "Oh?"

"That is the last time I shall ever sing that song, my lady," he answered with a hint of sadness.

Elizabeth tried to read his face, but he deliberately remained in the shadows.

She tossed her head. "I have not had the opportunity to thank you, nor to pay you what I owe for your services." She spoke with a light bitterness. Why was he standing so far away from her?

"I have been paid well enough," he said stiffly. "The Queen put a flea in my ear, and you have dressed me in outrageous finery."

"You were in sore need of a new suit of motley," she snapped at him, surprised at her own vehemence. "'Tis certainly a welcome change from those rags you wore on the road!" *This is not what I meant to say to him.*

He snorted with disdain. "Can you see me on the road in that foppish coat? Silver bells, my lady? My throat would be slit ear to ear for those alone!"

"So, save it for court!" she retorted hotly, then bit her tongue at the sound of her own shrill voice.

"I intend to leave the court as soon as the Queen releases me." Tarleton's dark eyes searched hers. He wondered why they were nipping at each other like two pack hounds. It was not how he had envisioned this scene to be played. He wasn't prepared for Elizabeth to be so cold. He knew he had to hurry. The Queen was due at any moment.

Suddenly Elizabeth stifled a small sob. "Why, Dickon? Why must you go?" she asked so quietly he almost didn't hear her.

"Tomorrow you are to be married and I have no desire to take part in your happiness." His mellow baritone was edged with bitterness.

"Happiness?" Elizabeth ground the word out between her teeth. Her resolve flew up the chimney with the smoke. "How dare you call my marriage to that…that shag-eared, overfed whoreson my happiness!" Her eyes blazed green fire. "And where have you been, you…you cony-catching, lack-witted heartbreaker to leave me to this fate?"

A slow, incredulous smile crept over Tarleton's face as he marveled both at Elizabeth's fiery eyes and at her prodigious use of her new vocabulary. "Do not rail at me, sweet chuck. I was royally commanded never to see or speak with you again."

The mention of royal command brought Elizabeth back to her senses. "And I was commanded to forget you," she told him quietly.

Tarleton took a step nearer. "They said you were ashamed to have been with me."

Elizabeth's eyes blurred with tears. "I thought you had forgotten me."

The air between them crackled with the emotions they dared not utter. The silver *A* on her bodice gleamed in the dancing light. Tenderly Tarleton's eyes melted into hers.

"'Tis no matter now, chuck," he said, managing no more than a hoarse whisper. Did he think he had been in hell before? Not even at the lych-gate compared to this moment—and what he knew was to come. For both their sakes, he had to play this wretched scene to the end. "Our short time together was for naught. Tomorrow night you will be married to Sir Robert La Faye!" He spat the words out as if they would poison him.

"Yes," she said firmly, clutching the brass bell for courage. "Tomorrow night Lord La Faye will get what he wants—my estates. But come May, I shall get what I want—a child."

"A child . . . ?" Tarleton repeated, his liquid brown eyes widened with astonishment. This was an unexpected roll of the dice.

"Aye, Dickon." There was a gentle softness in her voice. "The heir to my estates—but not Sir Robert's son."

"You are . . . with child?" There was a tinge of wonder in his question.

A smile trembled over her lips. "And I pray that he will have his father's brown curls and laughing eyes. I shall teach him to sing 'The Greenwood Tree' as his father once taught me."

"Sweetest Elizabeth!" Closing the gap between them, Tarleton swung her into the circle of his arms, kissing her devouringly.

With a purr deep in her throat, Elizabeth gave herself to the passion of his kiss, tasting the sweet salt of him. His lips, firm and demanding, searched for hers again, taking them hungrily. Elizabeth felt herself lifted from the floor as he pulled her to him. He smelled deliciously of wood smoke and mint—not the heavy, cloying perfume of a courtier. His steel arms held her possessively. She abandoned herself to the whirl of sensation.

"'Tis true! Oh, my darling Dickon!" Elizabeth gasped, her eyes shining with drops of happiness. "Then you *do* love me still!"

"Sweetling!" His lips brushed against hers as he spoke. "I never stopped loving you! Didn't Philip tell you?"

"When?" She panted, gripping him tighter, her body craving his.

"Two weeks ago. I asked him to tell you that I loved you." Tarleton's voice was laced with anguish and anger. Tearing her lace ruff away, his lips burned a path down her neck to her shoulder, tenderly caressing the angry, red scar there.

Nearly swooning with the sensation, Elizabeth struggled to speak clearly. "I have not seen Philip since then. He promised to return before Christmas. I have asked him to attend me when . . . when our child is born.''

Gently smoothing her hair back from her forehead, Tarleton tried to imprint in his memory every feature of her face. He traced her trembling lips with his finger. "Good! Then I am content to know you are in his skilled hands—should I not see you again. Oh, my sweet, sweet Elizabeth!''

Crushing her to him, his mouth swooped down to recapture hers. Tearing her seed pearl cap from her head, he wove his fingers through her bright hair, now more entrancing than ever. In that breathless instant, the world stood still. All plots and intrigues were driven from his mind. Only Elizabeth and the precious secret she carried mattered now.

''Hold, villain!'' The Queen's chill voice of outrage shattered the sweetness of the moment.

Rough hands seized Tarleton, wrenching him away from Elizabeth's arms. The Queen stepped out from behind one of the long arras. Accompanying her was Sir Walter Raleigh with a number of the guards—and Sir Robert La Faye. The Queen's face mottled with anger under her white powder, as she glared at the flushed couple. Elizabeth, trembling violently, sank to the floor in a deep curtsy.

The royal eyes sparked amber lightning. "This is a fine kettle of fish, indeed! You can see, Sir Walter, I was right to keep these two apart! As I had feared, this miscreant has wantonly made free with my impressionable goddaughter's good virtue! You gentlemen are witnesses to this shameful scene! This . . . this commoner has abused my goodwill, disobeyed my direct commands, and has sullied the reputation of this foolish piece of baggage!''

Stung by every word the Queen uttered, Elizabeth did not dare to look up. She shivered with fear, not so much for herself, but for the man whose kisses were still warm on her love-swollen lips.

"So it would seem, Your Grace," Sir Walter remarked agreeably.

Turning to Lord La Faye, the Queen continued. "And, Sir Robert, I am at loss what to say to you! Here, before your eyes on the very eve of your wedding, this shameless creature has abused your good name and intentions by this unholy and unlawful behavior. How can I, in good conscience, give her to you as your wife?"

Sir Robert paled in the firelight. "But, Your Grace," he stammered, "I knew her to be a wanton when I agreed to marry her. Under my loving hand, she will mature into an upright wife!" He licked his lips nervously.

Tarleton heaved against the burly guard who held him. "That sot is only interested in the lady's fortune, not the lady, Your Grace!" Tarleton raged. "The blackguard doesn't want to see her money slip through his fat fingers. He doesn't care a farthing for—"

"Silence!" The Queen stamped her foot at Tarleton.

"Your Grace, I must have Elizabeth as my wife!" Sir Robert was visibly perspiring. "The contract is valid."

"Your Grace, a word, I beg you!" Tarleton shot the Queen a desperate look.

"I do not want to hear your voice again, fool! You have displeased me mightily, Tarleton, and you shall pay most dearly for it, that I promise you! Sir Walter, I command you to convene the Star Chamber this very night, and to try this man—for treason!"

"Treason!" Elizabeth gasped, her tears spilling down her face. "No!"

The Queen turned her scornful eye on her shivering goddaughter. "Yes, mistress, treason for disobedience to me and for ravishing you, who are supposed to be under my protection."

"But he did not ravish me!" she protested.

"Your Grace, but one word!" Tarleton's eyes grew darker.

"Must I bind up both your tongues? Am I not the mistress in my own house?" roared the Queen, displaying the frightening Tudor temper. "Take the churl away—and dispatch him with all speed! And you, goddaughter, shall be kept close confined until you are safely married and off my hands!"

Elizabeth heard no more. As Tarleton was led away under the gloating smirk of Sir Robert La Faye, she fainted in a heap of pearls and white satin.

Chapter Twenty

Throughout that endless night, Elizabeth lay sleepless in her bed alternately crying and praying. Somewhere else in that vast palace, her only love was on trial for his life. If it were not for the babe growing under her heart, she would have considered taking her own life before she was joined to Lord La Faye.

"Sweet Jesu, forgive me," she prayed through her tears. "I cannot forgive myself for the wrong I have done to Dickon. This misadventure has all been my fault!"

Elizabeth buried her head in the pillow. As the gray dawn glimmered over the spires of Greenwich she fell into a fitful, unsatisfying sleep.

After coaxing Elizabeth to taste her breakfast, Charlotte could not put off her onerous task any longer. "I have been commanded to tell you, *ma chérie,* that . . . that . . ." The little maid's eyes grew round with tears. "The jester has been found guilty. He is to die on Tower Hill this afternoon."

"No!" Elizabeth gasped. She clutched the little brass bell as if it had the power to save its former owner's life.

Charlotte bit her lip painfully before continuing. Her mistress's eyes were so bright she feared Elizabeth's fever might return. "And the Queen has commanded that you are to be one of the witnesses at his execution."

Elizabeth gaped at Charlotte in horror. "She would not be so cruel!"

Charlotte nodded sadly. "I fear this was Sir Robert La Faye's doing. Nevertheless, I am to have you dressed, and ready, when he arrives at two."

"Sir Robert?" Elizabeth's voice broke miserably.

"*Oui*. He begged to accompany you on this most sad duty."

Elizabeth's lips curled back, baring her teeth like a cornered animal. "Oh, 'twill not be a sad duty for Sir Robert La Faye! I am sure he is looking forward to it with the greatest of pleasure!"

Shutting her ear to Charlotte's sympathetic chatter, Elizabeth pondered what she must do. Hugging the pillow for comfort, her fingers touched a small scrap of paper hidden there. Drawing it out into the light, Elizabeth again read Tarleton's message, "Play the play." Very well, that was exactly what she intended to do.

"Lay out my black velvet gown, Charlotte, then find me every bright colored ribbon you can," she instructed her startled maid. "Get Lady Anne to help us, for we have much work to do before two o'clock!"

Sir Robert La Faye looked forward to Tarleton's execution with relish. It was the perfect wedding present. He could not wait to see the tearstained face of his bride as she beheld the grisly end of her lover. It had taken him a bit of wheedling for the Queen to grant his request that Elizabeth be present at Tarleton's end. Sir Robert smiled at himself smugly in his looking glass. Once he was married to the Queen's little hellcat, Sir Robert was safe forever and his possibilities at court were boundless.

Sir Robert arrived at the door of Elizabeth's apartments a few minutes before the appointed hour. To his surprise, she was already waiting for him. When he saw her, his jaw dropped in astonishment.

"You cannot wear that!" he bristled angrily at her.

Elizabeth lifted her chin, meeting his furious gaze straight on. "I was commanded to wait upon you at two o'clock. I was not told what I may wear."

"I forbid you to go out in that...that fashion!" His eyes narrowed into red slits.

Elizabeth eyed him with cold triumph. "I am my own mistress until six o'clock tonight. I will do exactly what I please until then. Come, my lord, we burn daylight!" Sweeping regally past him, she snapped her fingers for him to follow.

Sir Robert glowered as he went down the stairs after her. *But after six this evening, you will dance another tune, mistress!*

All heads turned to stare as Elizabeth walked toward the waiting coach. From ruff to hem, her black gown was festooned with hundreds of colorful ribbons tied in love knots. The ends fluttered gaily in the breeze like so many brave flags. Pinned among the ribbons were clusters of tiny bells that jingled as she moved. Her treasured brass bell hung from her waist; its richer tone was heard above the rest. The silver *A*, newly polished, blazed on her breast.

In his desire to humiliate her, Sir Robert had ordered an open carriage so that his grief-stricken betrothed would make a fool of herself, when she cried in public for her convicted lover. Now, as they were helped into the coach, Sir Robert cursed his overweening vanity.

Dry-eyed, Elizabeth held herself like a queen; her unfettered white-golden hair flew about her head in the cold November wind. The stinging air brought a bright color to her cheeks, making her all the more beautiful to behold.

Three figures watched from an upstairs gallery window as the carriage pulled out of the courtyard.

"My goddaughter makes a brave show," remarked the Queen. "With a few ribbons, she outshines all my jewels."

"Even if you were in your petticoat, you are always Gloriana," replied Sir Walter with the smoothness of a seasoned courtier. Secretly he concurred with the Queen's assessment.

Sir Francis Walsingham said nothing, but he permitted himself a wintry smile.

The gathered crowd on Tower Hill was larger than Elizabeth had expected. Word spread like wildfire among the citizens of London that the popular member of The Queen's Men, Tarleton, was to be executed. Sir Robert's carriage was hemmed in by the pressing mob.

A wooden platform had been erected on the highest point of ground. A stout crosstree loomed over it. There was a festival air about the place as the people watched the arrival of other dignitaries. The burly executioner, with his black mask concealing his face, drew special applause.

Elizabeth shuddered at the sights around her. She prayed that Sir Robert wouldn't notice the true state of her emotions.

"'Twas thoughtful of Her Majesty to provide a bit of spectacle for this otherwise drab day," mocked Sir Robert. He fully intended to make the most out of this occasion, no matter how outrageously Elizabeth chose to display herself. He was not going to be cheated of his revenge upon the man who dared to thwart his plans. "Look, my dear! Someone is selling hot nuts. Over there, I spy cider and sweetmeats. Would you like something to eat?"

Ignoring him, Elizabeth concentrated on the empty place of execution, willing herself to remain strong. *I must play this part to the end. I will grieve later.*

A roll of drums announced the arrival of the prisoner. Elizabeth felt momentarily dizzy. She took a deep breath as she saw the crowds part, allowing two rows of pikemen to pass through them. In the middle of the armed guard, she could just make out Tarleton's white shirt and his bare dark head. The crowd grew more excited as they watched the escort and condemned man mount the stairs of the gallows.

A soft gasp escaped Elizabeth's lips. *How magnificent he looks!* His shirt, open at the throat, displayed his broad chest and rippling muscles. His face freshly shaved, Tarleton laughed as he walked through the crowd—now talking with one of his guards—now throwing a jest to some of the bystanders. In fact, Tarleton looked exactly as he did before a performance.

"That rogue has no sense of decency," muttered La Faye, disappointed that the jester was not groveling. "Ah, well, just wait until they put the rope around his neck!"

With another drumroll, the captain of the guard stepped forward to read the charge and sentence. While he intoned the legal language, Tarleton scanned the crowd. Startled when he first spied Elizabeth, his dark brown eyes softened at the sight of her. Though his hands were tied behind his back, he managed a small bow in her direction. His eyes widened in surprise and his whole face spread into a smile when he saw her proudly stand up in the carriage. Her rainbow-hued ribbons made a cheerful display as she publicly acknowledged her love for him.

"Sit down, damn you!" Sir Robert hissed, feeling extremely annoyed, as all eyes turned to look at Elizabeth.

"I have a knife in my hand," she said calmly, clutching the fruit knife she had secreted within the folds of her skirt. "If you put a finger on me, I will cut it off!"

Sir Robert stared at her, complete surprise on his face. Then he drew back when he caught sight of the blade.

A loud cheer from the crowd greeted the captain of the guard when he announced that Tarleton would not suffer a traitor's death. By the Queen's mercy, he was to be merely hung by the neck, escaping disembowelment. Afterward, his body would be permitted a Christian burial, instead of being carved into pieces with his head affixed atop a pike on London Bridge.

Closing her eyes momentarily, Elizabeth thanked both God and the Queen. At least, her beloved would not suffer too much.

The drum rolled a third time, then Tarleton stepped forward to make the customary speech from the gallows. The crowd grew quiet. A scrivener, leaning against the base of the platform, poised with a lead pencil to jot down Tarleton's last words. By evening, those words would be printed on souvenir broadsides, and sold all over London town.

Elizabeth clenched her fists. In one hand she held her knife; in the other was the brass bell.

"Good people, I thank you for coming to see my farewell performance." Tarleton's infectious grin and witty words brought a roar of approval from the crowd. They especially enjoyed it when the condemned made a good show, and Tarleton was a master at showmanship. "Though this stage is not as large as I would have liked, at least today I am to play the leading part in a tragedy."

Elizabeth could scarcely believe her ears and eyes. Her sweet Dickon was laughing and jesting only a few short moments before his death! The fire of his smile lit up his handsome face. The chill wind ruffled through his thick brown curls. Glowing with her pride of him, Elizabeth stood motionless in the carriage, her eyes drinking in his every gesture. Fuming, Lord La Faye sank lower into the seat.

"Dance a jig for us, Tarleton," a man in the crowd called out.

Tarleton's smile deepened into laughter. "Aye, ye shall see me dance by and by. 'Tis called the 'Hangman's Jig.' You'll have to be the judge if I do it right well, for I hope to be singing with an angel by then. And I pray to the good Lord that she's a fair-haired angel." The crowd cheered these courageous words. Tarleton stared directly at Elizabeth; his gaze spoke poetry to her. "Aye, an angel with golden hair and green eyes and dressed in the colors of the rainbow. *That* is heaven, my friends!"

The captain of the guard spoke in a low tone to Tarleton. Nodding, his expressive face changed and became more sober.

"I am told to be brief. 'Tis hard, when I have a captive audience." A grin tempted the corners of his mouth. "The matter is this—they say my crime is treason, and, as my judges are wittier than I, I bow to their opinion. But 'tis more true to say that I am to die this afternoon for the love of a lady."

His gaze caught Elizabeth's face and held it, promising her his love. Many faces turned in her direction. A murmur of appreciation rippled through the crowd.

"If I offended Her Majesty, then I am heartily sorry for it. If my act offended the lady, then I am most sorry for that, as well." His voice grew stronger, carrying over the heads of the throng. "But I am not sorry that I loved the lady. I would give my heart away to her again, if she did not have it already."

Hot tears stung Elizabeth's lashes. Vowing not to cry, she returned Tarleton's smile. *I cannot let his last look at me be one of sorrow.* Lifting her fingers to her lips, she kissed their tips, then sent her kiss winging toward the bound man standing so bravely in the shadow of the gallows tree.

A collective sigh carried on the wind. Some of the women actually sniffled at the sight.

"Sit down, Elizabeth!" growled Sir Robert behind her. "You have shamed us both with your bold behavior."

Elizabeth did not acknowledge that she had heard him.

Tarleton threw back his shoulders. "And so, my friends, here is my epilogue—live well each day, for each day is a gift. Love God, and love your Queen as I have tried to do, for Her Grace is the most loving, the most wise, and the most merciful of rulers. God bless you all this cold day, for coming to see me off. God save our good Queen Bess!" He lifted his rich voice to the heavens. "And may the Lord love and protect my sweet Robin Redbreast!" Across the sea of faces that separated them, Tarleton sent his message to Elizabeth with eyes that bespoke of his eternal love.

The executioner pulled Tarleton to the center of the platform, under the crosstree, where a sturdy rope had been flung over the top. Stepping forward, a shivering clergyman muttered a blessing over Tarleton's bowed head. Then the hangman placed the noose around the player's neck. For one last instant, Tarleton looked back at Elizabeth, flashing her a brilliant smile. In that split second, he wiggled his brows in their familiar signal—play the part!

The drums began a long, ominous roll. Elizabeth gripped the bell tighter, its metal digging into her flesh.

With a quick jerk, the executioner released the trapdoor and Tarleton's body swung freely in the air. His face went very red as his legs thrashed about, seeking the foothold that was no longer there.

Rising, La Faye gripped the stricken Elizabeth firmly by the shoulders. "Don't turn your pretty head away now, my dear," he purred, observing Tarleton's death throes with a wicked gleam of pleasure. "This is the best part!" Pinching Elizabeth's face between his fingers, he forced her to look upon the dance of death.

Tarleton's body suddenly went limp; his head lolled forward. Leaping to the rope, the executioner cut him down. Then he passed the body to a waiting carter, who dropped it into an open pine box in the back of his wagon. Sliding the lid over the coffin, the carter jumped into his seat, then drove off toward the forbidding bulk of the Tower. It was all over in two minutes.

Elizabeth gratefully sank down again.

"The knot must have broken his neck," mused Sir Robert. He looked and sounded extremely disappointed. "Such an easy death! I had hoped he would swing longer. I fear your player cheated his last audience out of a good show."

Merely glaring at him, Elizabeth silently drew the lap rug over her gown. The driver made their slow way back through the city and over London Bridge to the south bank, then on to Greenwich Palace. Throughout the long ride, Elizabeth spoke not a word, nor did she look at her sadistic escort. All her thoughts were fastened to the lone gallows tree on Tower Hill.

"I trust you will be in a better mood anon," remarked Sir Robert when they alighted at Greenwich. "You have not much time to dress for our wedding. Then, mistress mine, you had best sing a different tune!" Abandoning Elizabeth on the steps, he stomped angrily away.

When Elizabeth reached the safety of her apartments, Charlotte and Lady Anne greeted her with sobs and embraces. Elizabeth's stoic response surprised and deeply concerned them.

"Oh, *ma petite,* you must be freezing. Poor dear! Let me get you out of this gown...."

"Non!" said Elizabeth hoarsely. "I shall remain as I am. Do me the kind office of taking these ribbons and bells off. And, please, may I have some wine?"

Lady Anne poured a small goblet of warmed, spiced wine while Charlotte took out her scissors from her sewing basket. Elizabeth drank deeply.

"No, Charlotte, do not cut them." She stopped her maid. *"Pull* the ribbons off!"

"Ma petite, it will tear the dress!"

"Aye," said Elizabeth coldly. "Tear it to tatters. That is how I will be married—in shreds and rags. That's all that's left of me now."

Charlotte and Lady Anne exchanged apprehensive glances, then they stared at the stony-eyed, pale girl. Taking a deep drink, Elizabeth began ripping at the colored bits of satin.

"Let the whole court see exactly what I feel!"

Sir Robert La Faye was relieved that the simple wedding ceremony took place in the Queen's private chapel with only a few people present. Originally he had hoped for a more public solemnization followed by a large wedding feast so that all the court would acknowledge his closer ties to the Queen. However, considering that the silent Lady Elizabeth chose to be married in a shocking state of disrepair, Sir Robert decided it was just as well to keep the ceremony low-key. As it was, he had already heard several courtiers whispering darkly about Elizabeth's sanity. As long as he was married to her, Sir Robert did not care what her state of mind was. After a few solemn words in front of a cleric, Sir Robert emerged a very rich, powerful man.

The wedding supper followed immediately afterward in the Queen's apartments. Despite the fine imported French wine and the presence of a gifted lute player, the gathering was anything but festive. Elizabeth spoke only a few words, most of which were directed to the Queen. Sir Robert's bride barely glanced at her new husband. For her part, the Queen was surprisingly solicitous, sitting close to her goddaughter, even feeding her dainties from the royal plate.

Elizabeth deeply appreciated the Queen's sudden kindness. She smiled wanly at her godmother as she ate the sweetmeats that were offered, though she barely tasted what she put into her mouth. Her mind was fixed upon the coming hours. *I must let him touch me,* she steeled herself. *My baby must be safely legitimate.* She was tempted to drink a great deal of wine to blot out what was to come, but she recalled Philip's admonitions against it, and she resisted the impulse. *I wish this night were over.*

After supper, Elizabeth was led away by Lady Anne and Lady Mary for the ceremonial bedding.

"You look too pale, my love," reflected Lady Mary, brushing Elizabeth's hair.

"Wouldn't you?" retorted Lady Anne as she tied a ribbon on the sleeve of Elizabeth's simple shift. "Look at the pig who is her husband!"

Lady Mary sighed and nodded. "Be strong, dear heart," she whispered to the unblinking Elizabeth. Placing her cheek against the younger woman's, she noticed Elizabeth's skin was as cold as her emerald eyes.

"Thank you," said Elizabeth finally, as the ladies helped her into the large bed, strewn with rose petals. "You have both been more than kind to me, and I shall not forget it."

Just then the door opened and Sir Robert La Faye, dressed only in his nightshirt, was pushed inside, followed by the Queen and her guests. Not that the bridegroom needed much encouragement. The bloated toad clambered eagerly into the bed, a silver goblet clutched in his hand.

"Pour me more wine, Seaton," he giggled unpleasantly to his body servant. "I have some thirsty work ahead of me!"

A few people in the room tittered nervously. Sir Robert's eyes narrowed as he glanced at his stiff bride beside him. Then he smiled with forced gaiety at the Queen, her maids and Walsingham, who stood at the foot of the bed.

"As you can see, we are well and truly bedded!" He waved his cup, spilling some wine on the sheets.

"Yes, Sir Robert," echoed the Queen lightly, "before all these witnesses, you are truly wedded and bedded. May you both enjoy a happy marriage until death do you part!"

The Queen kissed her goddaughter warmly on the forehead, tactfully wiping away a small tear that hung in the corner of Elizabeth's eye.

"May you have many happy blessings," Elizabeth of England whispered to Elizabeth La Faye.

"Thank you, Your Grace," Elizabeth answered woodenly.

"And now, good night to you both!" cried the Queen as she swept out the door on the arm of her chief minister, her hushed ladies following.

Sir Robert's manservant was the last to leave. Giving his master a leering wink, Seaton closed the chamber door with a doleful thud.

"Now, my sullen bitch, we are alone." Sir Robert rolled his great bulk on his side. His eyes burned into her with hot lust.

Elizabeth tensed herself, not daring to meet his gaze. Reaching out a paw, he stroked her face, allowing his hand to wander down to her breasts. Elizabeth didn't move. The smell of sour wine mixed with onions on his breath turned her stomach. She wished she could fall into a trance until after he was finished with her. She prayed that he was drunk enough not to notice her belly was no longer flat. Underneath her pillow, she gripped a small vial of pig's blood that she would use after her husband fell asleep. In the morning the stained sheets would be her testimony of virtue, and so insure her child's rights.

"Look at me," Sir Robert snarled. Grabbing her face in a viselike grip, he yanked her toward him. "I said look at me when I speak to you! I have half a mind to tie you to the bedpost and give you the thrashing you so richly deserve, but that would not satisfy my immediate desires. First, I mean to take my full husbandly rights. If you manage to please me, perhaps I will not beat you afterward."

Elizabeth swallowed back her revulsion as she stared into his eyes, now slit with cruelty. Sir Robert's fingers dug into her cheeks. He started pulling at the neck of her shift. The blue band ribbons caught in his fingers. Cursing, he wrenched at them.

A strangled scream escaped Elizabeth's throat as she heard the material rip.

Without warning, the chamber door burst open and six armed members of the Queen's household guard marched in. Elizabeth was shocked into silence.

"Sir Robert La Faye! I arrest you by order of Her Majesty, the Queen!" Sir Walter Raleigh's stern commanding voice stopped the bridegroom cold. The tall knight strode to the foot of the bed. He was dressed in his formal uniform with a wicked-looking rapier hanging at his belt.

La Faye's face turned a blotched shade of purple; a vein stood out alarmingly on his forehead.

Shivering with terror, Elizabeth pulled the sheets up to her chin.

"In the devil's name, what is the meaning of this jest?" demanded Sir Robert, as he hoisted himself upright. "How dare you disturb my wedding night! If the Queen knew . . ."

Raleigh smiled unpleasantly. "The Queen is perfectly aware of this intrusion, Sir Robert. As a matter of fact, she ordered it. Here is her signature upon the warrant." The knight held out an official document, from which dangled a large red seal.

"And what is the so-called charge?" Sir Robert asked, eyeing the soldiers in fury.

"For the murder of Sir Thomas Hayward—" Elizabeth gasped as Sir Walter continued "—for the attempted murder of the Lady Elizabeth Hayward, and for conspiring with the Babington supporters of the Scottish queen against the crown! 'Tis all stated in the warrant."

La Faye's jaw dropped, then he began to tremble. Falling out of the bed, he groveled on the rush-strewn floor. "Mercy, Raleigh! Some enemy has poisoned the Queen's ear against me!"

Raleigh curled his lip with contempt at the quaking mass at his feet. "Be that as it may, I have orders to convey you forth with all possible speed to the Star Chamber. There, you will hear the matter in full, and listen to the witnesses against you."

"Witnesses . . . ?" Sir Robert's face drained.

Raleigh bared his teeth. "Aye, witnesses who have sworn their testimony to myself and to Sir Francis Walsingham. You have but a moment to don your breeches, my lord—unless you care to go as you are."

"Surely there is some mistake?" The accused blubbered.

"I highly doubt it," remarked Raleigh. "Sir Francis is very meticulous when it comes to investigating capital crimes. You have been in his eye for some time. Come!" The imposing knight turned to the guard. "I fear you may have to carry Sir Robert. He appears to have been taken ill."

The soldiers sneered at the gibbering bulk in the night-shirt. Without another word, four of them grabbed La Faye under his arms, and half dragged, half carried him from the room.

Raleigh bowed to Elizabeth. "My apologies for this disturbance, my lady," he said kindly.

She bit her lip to keep her terror from leaping out. "What will happen now, Sir Walter?"

"As the wife of an attainted criminal, you are to be sent from court." But he smiled as he spoke.

"Sent from court?" Elizabeth repeated, her mind jumping from one possibility to the next.

"And all your husband's property is forfeit to the crown. Tomorrow morning, you will be conducted by coach to the Priory of St. Aloysius at Godstow. There you will stay, at the Queen's pleasure." Raleigh's eyes twinkled; his voice softened a fraction. "'Twill be a very comfortable coach, my lady, and the mother abbess is looking forward to seeing you again."

"And Her Majesty? Have I displeased her?" Elizabeth quivered.

"On the contrary, my lady. Her Majesty wishes you sweet dreams this night, and a pleasant journey on the morrow. Have no fear, my lady. You will be in good hands."

For the first time that long terrible day, Elizabeth allowed herself to relax as she comprehended her last-minute reprieve.

"And Sir Robert?" she asked. "What will happen to him?"

Raleigh shrugged his broad shoulders. "The evidence against him is weighty—even more weighty than he is. I believe you will be a widow in very short order. My condolences, Lady Elizabeth." The knight did not look especially sorry as he related these tidings. "Good night, my lady. I shall see you off in the morning." His voice dropped lower. "I have taken the liberty of sending your maid for a warm posset. 'Twill help you sleep." Then he bowed deeply again, turned smartly on his heel and was gone.

Still clutching the sheet, Elizabeth lay back against the pillows and tried to sort out this newest turn in her fortunes. She found it a great comfort to know she was going to Godstow, with Philip nearby in Oxford ready to help when the baby came. Hidden deep in the countryside, there would be few questions asked when Sir Robert's "heir" made a premature arrival. At Godstow, Elizabeth could mend both her body and her spirit.

When Charlotte brought the posset, Elizabeth greedily drank it down. She fell into a deep, dreamless sleep, while her little maid lapsed into a long French tirade over the ruined shift.

"The weather will hold and the roads are frozen hard, my lady. Your journey should be comfortable enough." Sir Walter settled Elizabeth into one of the Queen's closed coaches. A hot brick, wrapped in wool, was tucked under her feet and she was swathed in furs against the bite of the November air. "I shall personally see to it that your maid is on her way to you as soon as she can get the rest of your odds and ends packed. She should be with you in a few days' time."

"How can I ever thank you enough for your kindness?" Elizabeth asked, smiling softly at the gallant courtier.

Raleigh chuckled. "Just put in a good word for me with Mother Catherine." He saw the question in Elizabeth's eyes. "That wonderful lady has a number of us 'black sheep.' I owe her a great deal."

"Black sheep—that's what Tarleton calls . . . called . . ." Elizabeth faltered and bit her lip. She tried not to think about Tarleton yet. She promised herself a long grieving period once she was safely at Godstow.

Raleigh patted her arm understandingly.

"Sir Walter, where is my Dickon buried?"

He looked at his boots as he murmured, "Mother Catherine has him now. He will be well taken care of at Godstow."

Elizabeth nodded. *Then we shall all be together,* she thought. When the baby was born, she would take it to

Tarleton's grave. Perhaps, Tarleton's soul would know his child was there.

"By the way, Lord La Faye was found guilty as charged," Raleigh suddenly announced. "The Queen has ordered him to be dispatched without delay. You will be free of him before sundown."

Elizabeth gasped at the swiftness of the Queen's justice. "I will say a prayer for him," she said quietly. Though she had no wish ever to see Sir Robert again, she certainly had not desired his death.

"Then yours will be the only prayers he shall have," remarked the gallant knight in a grim voice. "Fare thee well, Lady Elizabeth. 'Tis time you were off so that you can reach Godstow by nightfall. I hope we shall meet again—under happier circumstances." Kissing her hand, he stepped down from the coach and closed the door. "Drive on!" he called.

Lying back against the leather seat, Elizabeth stared out the window as the coach made its way through the bustling city. A great weariness of spirit enveloped her. The events of the day before seemed like a nightmare in which she had been but a supporting player. In the space of a few hours, she had lost forever the two men who had so influenced her life: Sir Robert, whom she had despised, and Tarleton, whom she would love forever. Her fingers touched the pilgrim's badge pinned over her heart—Tarleton's last gift to her. *Amor vincit omnia*—love conquers all.

Chapter Twenty-One

The carriage rolled into the priory an hour after sunset. Stiff with fatigue, Elizabeth was chilled to the bone, despite the heavy fur robes. Rousing herself from the numbness that weighed her down, she smiled wanely at the irrepressible Sister Agnes, who greeted Elizabeth effusively.

"There you are, my dearest dear! I have been waiting at this gate for over an hour. Your coachman took his sweet time, I'll warrant!" Sister Agnes smiled at the exhausted driver and outriders, who were too tired from the long journey to protest her remark. "My, how you have changed, my little Robin! La, I should have guessed! And what *would* I have said to that naughty Tarleton!"

Hearing his name, Elizabeth's eyes filled with the tears she had spent the day holding back. Seeing her distress, Sister Agnes took Elizabeth into her ample embrace, patting her comfortingly.

"Please forgive me, my lamb! I don't know where my tongue runs off to sometimes! Come. Mother Catherine has been waiting anxiously for you. I shall see to your things directly. And you men there!" she called over Elizabeth's shoulder. "Don't stand around scratching your ears! After you've taken care of those poor horses, you'll find hot soup, bread and cheese in the buttery. A beer or two for your pains, as well. Step lively! The stables are that way!" Sister Agnes waved the driver and his escort across the courtyard.

Nodding his weary thanks to her, the coachman touched his cap, then ambled in the direction she pointed. The outriders followed suit, leading their steaming mounts. Sister Agnes, her arm still around Elizabeth, took her directly to Mother Catherine.

"You look tired, my child," observed the abbess, indicating a high-backed chair by the fireplace. "Was the journey difficult?"

Sinking gratefully onto the soft cushions, Elizabeth unhooked her woolen travel cloak. "I feel as if I have been to the gates of hell and back, Mother," she answered honestly.

Mother Catherine looked down on her newest charge. "'Twas horrible yesterday?"

Elizabeth shuddered. "I shall never forget any of it. Oh, Mother, if you could have only seen Dickon!" Her tears began to spill down her face. "He acted as if he were giving the greatest performance of his life."

"He was," said Mother Catherine simply.

Elizabeth reflected on this for a few moments, then she asked, "Where have you buried him? I would like to say my prayers there."

"In good time, child. Time is what we have in abundance here." A small bell chimed in the distance. "Now I must go to prayer. You remain here and rest. I'll send someone to fetch you when it is time for supper." The little woman kissed Elizabeth on her forehead. "Always remember, just when things are darkest, there will come a light. You shall see anon."

Elizabeth nodded dully. She did not have the same optimism that Mother Catherine so obviously did.

The abbess softly slipped out the door. Elizabeth stared into the fire, watching the dancing flames weave a special magic of their own. She wept, though she was not aware of her tears flowing silently down her cheeks. Heedless of the safe, warm surroundings, her memories of Tarleton crashed down upon her; his image was pure and clear. Her mind relived the velvet warmth of his kisses. A cold shiver spread over her as she remembered Tower Hill, and the laughing, jesting, dying Tarleton.

A hand rested lightly on Elizabeth's shoulder, stirring her from her torturing thoughts. " 'Tis time for supper?" She hastily wiped her eyes.

A deep voice chuckled warmly behind her. "That's my sweet Robin! Always hungry!"

Elizabeth stiffened, realizing a sliver of panic. The fire in the hearth cast the room full of dancing shadows. She huddled deeper in the chair, too terrified to face his ghost. The warm hand caressed her shoulder tenderly.

"Nay, sweetling," he murmured softly in her ear. "I have not come back to haunt you. I haven't left yet." He brushed her cheek with his finger, feeling the wetness of her tears. Cupping her chin, he gently turned her face to look at him.

Tarleton's liquid brown eyes glowed with love and tenderness. A thrill of frightened anticipation touched Elizabeth's spine. She felt as if her breath were cut off. Bending over her, he brushed her lips with a kiss as tender and light as a summer breeze. It was a kiss for her tired soul to melt into. Raising his mouth from hers for a moment, he smiled again into her eyes. Then his lips recaptured hers, more urgent and demanding this time. His kiss sang through her veins. In one forward motion, she was in his arms; Tarleton held her tightly against him in a crushing embrace. Elizabeth's arms grasped him around his neck. She returned his kisses fiercely, savoring his touch, his taste, his scent. Her body pressed against his, yearning for more. They kissed until there was no breath left to kiss.

"Dickon?" she whispered. " 'Tis really you?"

"Aye," he answered thickly. "I hope so."

Elizabeth began to shake uncontrollably. The reaction from the past twenty-four hours caught her fast in its grip.

Cradling her in his arms, Tarleton sat in the chair before the fire, rocking her as if she were a child.

"Please tell me 'tis not a dream," she shivered. "For if it is, I never want to wake."

Tarleton's lips brushed against her brow. "'Tis no dream, chuck. You are safe with me, and I never intend to let you go again!"

Full of wonderment, Elizabeth traced the outline of his face with her finger, kissing each dearly remembered crease. He was warm, and close, and so very much alive.

"How?" she was finally able to ask.

The imp's grin danced across his face. "I was waiting for that! What a jest!" He chuckled at the thought. "'Tis the best trick I have ever played. Though I must confess, there were a few uncomfortable moments."

Elizabeth gave him a sidelong glance of utter disbelief. "Jest? You call hanging a jest? Dickon, if you only knew what it did to me!"

Tarleton stroked her cheek, sending delightful ripples of sensation coursing through her. "For all your anguish, I am sorry. I pray that you will allow me the rest of my life to make amends for the fright it must have been." Between each word, he planted kisses on her eyes, her nose, her brows, her lips. "I did not know your presence at my execution was part of the plan."

Elizabeth's eyebrows slanted in a frown. "I don't understand. What plan? Whose?"

"Who else? That master of intrigue—Sir Francis Walsingham—and a bit of my own, I must confess!"

Elizabeth's mind spun with bewilderment. How long had this game been played?

"Are you ready to hear a tale of murder, surprise, death—and enduring love?" he asked, kissing her fingers one by one.

Elizabeth nodded slowly, reveling in his warmth, his scent of pine needles, mint and smoke. His caressing lips tingled her skin.

"Then lay your sweet head on my shoulder and listen. Once upon a time a poor wandering fool fell in love with a beautiful lady...."

"Who loved him back," Elizabeth added, tenderly touching a small scar on his chin.

A smile flitted across Tarleton's mouth. "Is this my tale or yours? As I said, he fell in love, and they traveled over the highways of England, escaping from the clutches of the evil La Faye, who would force this poor lady into a hateful marriage."

"Sir Robert! God rest his soul!" Elizabeth shivered. "Dickon, you couldn't know what it was like! After we were married and put to bed, he—"

Tarleton's eyes glittered. "Did he...hurt you, sweetling?"

"Nay, but...I was terrified! He tore at my shift! If Sir Walter hadn't burst into the room just then..."

Tarleton chuckled again, his breath softly fanning her face. "Raleigh's timing has always been impeccable—last-minute, but impeccable. Let me continue." He kissed her nose. "As planned, the poor fool was arrested for daring to love his lady, and he trembled dramatically when the Queen's guards led him away. But, instead of being taken to the Tower, he was conducted by the back stairs to the Queen's apartments, where he met with Walsingham, Raleigh—and the Queen! Quite a lofty company for a fool!"

Elizabeth's eyes widened. "I thought you were brought before the Star Chamber!"

"That is what everyone was supposed to think. Instead, the fool enjoyed a hearty midnight supper in right royal company."

"While the lady lay in her cold bed, and cried until there were no tears left to fall," whispered Elizabeth reproachfully.

Tarleton kissed her eyes, first one, then the other. "Aye, I feared as much. For each one of those tears, I promise you a day of laughter. Now may I go on?"

"Please!" Elizabeth put her head back against his shoulder, in love with the sound of his rich honeyed voice.

"Lord La Faye had been under investigation for some time. Walsingham suspected he played a part in the Babington conspiracy to put Mary of Scotland on the throne, but had no real proof. When I told Sir Francis of your father's death, the pieces to the puzzle began to fall into place. He sent an agent to question members of your household. They related the same tale as you told me, adding their own embellishments. Fortunately, your cook, Jane, has a sharp eye and a good memory. She tried to caution La Faye that the mushrooms he had gathered were poisonous. Sir Robert took them away, saying he would dispose of them. The next thing Jane knew, your father was taken ill. She was too frightened of Sir Robert to voice her suspicions, even to your chamberlain. After all, she fully expected Lord La Faye to become the new master of Esmond Manor. When Sir Francis's agent assured her of royal protection, she was more than happy to speak her mind."

A sudden anger lit Elizabeth's eyes. "Why wasn't I told this before?"

"Ah, but Walsingham did not have all the pieces yet. Also, the Queen found out about your love for me. You said a good many things in your fevered dreams."

"Oh!" Elizabeth buried her head against Tarleton's worn leather jacket.

"At first, Her Grace thought to discourage this love of ours, but when she saw that I returned your love, she decided to use us as part of the ploy against La Faye. That was the hardest part for me, chuck," he whispered into her hair. "To be denied your sweet company. Hanging was easy compared to that. We were kept deliberately apart until All Hallows' Eve. Once we were together, it was expected that you would jump immediately into my arms." He shook his head. "It almost didn't work out that way. I thought my knees would buckle under me when I saw you standing in the firelight. I had to wait until I was sure Sir Robert and the

Queen had come through the door behind the arras and could catch us in a so-called shameful embrace. Meanwhile, you were venting your righteous anger at me."

Elizabeth wrinkled her nose thoughtfully. "So I was a player in this counterfeit?"

"Aye, my sweet. Walsingham called you the 'golden pawn.' I tried to convince him you could act your part, but he is old-fashioned. He didn't think a woman would have the wit to carry it off, nor the ability to keep a secret."

"What?" Elizabeth bristled at the accusation. "Why, he should have seen me in Oxford, or Banbury, or—"

Tarleton stopped her further protestations with a soft kiss. "Do you want me to go on, sweetling?"

"With your kiss or your tale?" she murmured coyly.

"First my story and then much kissing, I vow! Sir Francis is a very thorough man. He had his agent go to Oxford, where he sought out Sir Robert's lodging. There the agent met a discarded mistress named Nan. They say that hell hath no fury as a woman scorned, especially if she has been cruelly beaten and left to pay the bill. Nan told a pretty story of La Faye's political activities for some years past, as well as his lust for your fortune since his creditors were hounding him. After Babington and the others were arrested and executed in September, Sir Robert became frantic with fear. He needed protection. As the husband of the Queen's goddaughter he probably felt he would be safe from implication."

"Why wasn't he arrested before? Why did I have to live through yesterday?" Elizabeth shuddered at the jagged, painful memory of her wedding night.

"The plot thickens! La Faye proved his desperation when he insisted, before witnesses, upon marrying you, despite the fact you were so obviously ruined by me." Tarleton paused and gave her a lusty kiss before continuing. "Upon reflection, Sir Francis came to the conclusion that you and I should disappear, permanently, leaving your estates well protected."

"Property and heirs—that's what the Queen told me marriage was all about," Elizabeth remembered aloud bitterly. "Hang my lands!"

"I wish we could. Instead, they hanged me!" Tarleton laughed.

"But why did you have to...?" Elizabeth could not bring herself to say the hateful word.

"Die? That is one way of permanently disappearing. Also, it would lull La Faye into a false sense of security. The man wanted my blood. And as witness to my downfall, you would have no choice but to go through with the marriage. I confess, I feared for the babe. Is he all right?"

"Aye, now that his father holds me." She studied his profile. "But I saw you hang, my love."

"Did I?" Tarleton paused, as he kissed her deeply, his tongue stirring her senses. Elizabeth moaned softly under his caress. "Is this a ghost who holds you in his arms?" he murmured, his kisses coursing down her neck. "Is this a ghost who kisses your fair throat? Am I so pale and cold, sweetling?"

"Nay!" She giggled as she felt his warm breath tickle her skin. "Oh, Dickon! Don't stop now!"

"Kissing you?" he asked in all innocence.

"In telling me how you died!"

"Oh, that! I was arrested. By midnight, everyone in Greenwich knew of it. By dawn, all of London did. Very early in the morning, I was taken across the river to the Tower, where I spent a pleasant hour or two gaming at dice with the captain of the guards there. By the way, the man is a very poor player, and owes me seven shillings sixpence. Anyway, I slept some, ate a good breakfast, then had a most enlightening conversation with a fellow by the name of Wilt Crossways."

"Who is he?"

"The executioner."

Elizabeth shivered as she recalled the muscle-bound man garbed in black who had put the rope around her beloved Tarleton's neck.

Tarleton smiled down at her. "In faith, he is a reasonably nice sort—if you don't have to meet him professionally. Wilt explained to me the types of hanging, the uses of special knots, and a great many other uncomfortable things. The long and the short of it is this—I was to hang, using a slipknot, then go limp immediately, pretending my neck had been broken. Wilt assured me that a man can swing for some time before dying. Not exactly a comforting thought, but I was in his hands, so to speak. Then the captain proceeded to get me mildly drunk on some very vile malmsey wine until it was time for my final performance."

Elizabeth gazed up at him, her eyes deep green pools. "Weren't you afraid that something might go wrong?" She remembered how magnificent he had been, laughing in the face of death.

Tarleton shook with merriment. "Afraid? My darling Elizabeth, I was terrified! Then I saw you, standing so proudly with your gown covered in love knots, and it gave me heart."

"I only wanted to let you know I loved you," she said softly.

"Aye, you did! You let all of London know! Though I didn't expect you to be there, you gave me the extra courage I needed to take that final step. I think Walsingham knew that. I tell you truly, my love, 'tis a very sobering experience to be hung. Even though I had prepared myself for the moment, when the trapdoor opened underneath me, and I felt myself swinging, I forgot everything in a moment of blind panic. I started fighting for breath. The executioner jiggled the rope to remind me to relax. As soon as I did, they cut me down and threw me into a box. Forsooth, they were not much gentle. I was taken back to the Tower and given another stiff drink. Last night, I rode out of London, arriving here before dawn. I knew you would be coming soon once the final scene was played."

Elizabeth stopped his story with another kiss. Pulling back his collar, she stared at his neck. The angry red burn of the rope was plainly evident on his skin. She traced it lightly with her finger, then kissed the hollow of his throat. She felt him tremble at the touch of her lips.

"If you continue to do that, my sweet lady, I will never finish my story," he warned her in a husky voice.

"Nay, please go on. Why did I have to be married to that whoreson?"

"My Lady Elizabeth! Your language is shocking! What company have you been keeping?" Tarleton mimicked a shrill nag's voice.

Elizabeth laughed. It felt so good to laugh again.

Tarleton resumed his story. "You were legally wedded, and officially bedded to Sir Robert, all duly witnessed. He now had control, ever so briefly, of your properties. Before he had any control over your person, he was to be arrested. Raleigh assured me that he would stop any... activity."

"'Twas a near thing," Elizabeth said tightly.

"Sir Robert was charged with several capital crimes. You, as the wife of an attainted traitor, lost all claim to his estates—formerly your estates. You were publicly sent away from court to the priory—disappearing from the prying eyes of the world. La Faye went to the block. And those blasted estates of yours reverted to the crown. Happily ever after."

"Happily? How can you say that? What's to become of us? I now have no family, no home, no reputation—"

Tarleton kissed her objections into silence. "Everyone got what they wanted. Sir Robert has gone to his just reward—whatever that may be. You have your freedom—forever. And, while the crown holds your estates for your claim in the future, the Queen has some extra revenue for her privy purse. Best of all, I have you. Or do I?" he asked, growing suddenly serious. "Will you be willing to trade your silks and satins for a poor fool who has nothing to give you but his complete love?'' There was an irresistible invitation in the smoldering depths of his eyes.

Elizabeth's fingers again traced the cruel mark of the hangman's rope on his neck. How many men could say they would die for love—then actually do it?

"Of course I will, my dearest, with all my heart,'' she answered.

Exploding out of the chair with a whoop of joy, Tarleton whirled her about the room. "Then let us be off!'' he cried.

"To supper?'' she asked hopefully.

"Damn supper! Mother Catherine has had some poor cleric waiting all this time in that blasted cold chapel for us. There, he will join us in a true marriage, if you can stand being a bride again so soon. Do you think, for a moment, that the good mother abbess would permit you to share the gatehouse with me without the benefit of holy wedlock? After that, I promise, you will get your supper. Please, my dearest love, eat well, for you are now eating for two. Later, you will be soundly and properly bedded by your most loving husband. What do you say to *this* plot and intrigue, prentice?''

Elizabeth snapped her fingers at him. "I say, let's about it, master! We burn candlelight. The chaplain will catch his death of cold, and supper will be ruined if we tarry!'' She hugged him fiercely. "Oh, Dickon, I so love you!''

"And I love you, my sweet Elizabeth—till true death do us part!''

Epilogue

*At the Earl of Leicester's Hunting Lodge near Kenilworth
September 1587*

Smiling with deep affection, Queen Elizabeth signaled the young couple bowing before her to rise. "Truly, it gladdens our heart to see you both looking so well, my dears. You must find country living agreeable."

Even though Tarleton now sported a trim fashionable mustache, his famous imp's smile was plainly recognizable. "I am the happiest of men, Your Grace, especially now that I am in your bright company again."

Tarleton and Elizabeth had not seen the Queen since that last horrible day of October the year before. The young marrieds were very excited when word came to them at their quiet retreat that the Queen was hunting nearby and desired to see them.

"No complaints? You do not miss your former life?" The Queen arched her eyebrow playfully.

"Nay, Your Grace, save that my lady wife has pushed me into this fool's garb of satin and velvet." Tarleton shrugged his shoulders inside the tight-fitting jacket. "In truth, I feel like a stuffed and gilded peacock, ready to be served up in the great hall. Were it not in your honor, I would have asserted my husbandly prerogative and told her exactly where

to put this deuced doublet and hose!'' Tarleton's eyes twinkled merrily as his glance fell upon the golden head of his
lady wife.

"In truth, Your Grace, does not my Dickon cut a handsome figure?'' remarked Elizabeth, gazing proudly at her
well-dressed husband.

The Queen nodded with a laugh. "You would put all the
young bloods at court to shame, Tarleton!''

"That is why I am happy to keep him by my side in the
country,'' Elizabeth hastily added, in case the Queen might
decide to have her beloved jester back in his new guise.

"And you, my dear Elizabeth! You are well?'' the Queen
asked with motherly concern, though the answer fairly
glowed in front of her.

"Exceedingly so, thanks to Your Grace, and to God.''

"Oh?'' The Queen cocked her head. "In that particular
order?''

Elizabeth blushed as she stole a glance at her grinning
husband. "I thank God for answering my prayers to send
me a loving husband, but I am deeply grateful to you, Your
Grace, for making this happiness possible.''

"Just so,'' remarked the Queen, more than pleased with
Elizabeth's reply. "And the child? Is she well?''

"Aye, and thriving, Your Grace! We would have brought
her along with us to show you, but sweet Robin is much
fretful with a new tooth, and when she is displeased you can
hear her all the way to Coventry.'' Tarleton beamed with
pride of his daughter's vocal accomplishments. "With those
lungs she will make a fine singer—as soon as all her teeth
come in.''

"Robin is such a pretty name. 'Tis one of my favorites,''
remarked the Queen, casting an openly fond look at Robert, the Earl of Leicester, her closest friend from childhood. The Queen's "sweet Robin'' bowed at the
compliment.

"Indeed, Your Grace. Robin is also a favorite of mine." Tarleton bowed to his own Elizabeth who dimpled prettily in return.

"Fatherhood agrees with you, I see," the Queen observed. Her brows lifted in surprise to see Tarleton flush a little.

"Aye, Your Grace. In sooth, my lady wife has told me we shall be adding another to our number next year." Tarleton sighed dramatically. "At this rate, I shall be woefully outnumbered in short order."

The Queen smiled with secret satisfaction. "Then I see I have come in good time."

"How so, Your Grace?" Elizabeth prayed the Queen was not going to disrupt her blissful home life.

"With such a growing family, it is time you move to a larger establishment," the Queen observed.

Elizabeth drew in her breath. They had been so happy, living the simple life as a yeoman and his wife on one of Esmond Manor's remote tenant farms. She feared the Queen would to command them to return to the court. But how could that be? After all, the jester was supposed to be dead and the disgraced Lady Elizabeth locked away in an abbey. "Your Grace?" she asked weakly.

Tarleton, understanding his wife's feelings, took her hand in his and squeezed it. To his Queen he said smoothly, "Our lodge is as large as necessary, Your Grace. That way I am able to keep an eye on both my ladies."

The Queen smiled with even more satisfaction. How she loved surprises! Aloud, she remarked. "I have recently been informed of the death of the Earl of Fawkland."

Tarleton's lips tightened as he heard his father's name. He nodded curtly. "Aye, so I have been told."

"He has left no heir," the Queen continued pleasantly.

"Not for lack of trying, Your Grace," Tarleton muttered.

"It would be a shame to let such a pretty place as Breden Hall fall into rack and ruin all for the want of a strong hand and a wise head."

"And for a titled lord, Your Grace," Tarleton reminded her. He tried to keep the bitter taste out of his mouth.

"Ah! Thou hast hit the nut and core of it! Kneel, my fool!" The Queen, still smiling broadly, took the sword which her host, the old Earl of Leicester, proffered to her.

Elizabeth's eyes shone when she realized what was about to happen. As for Tarleton, he looked as if he had been poleaxed as he obediently dropped to one knee on the bare wood floor of the hunting lodge.

"Richard Tarleton, for your many years of loyal service to the crown, for the gratitude your Queen bears you, and for the love, loyalty and protection you have given our most beloved goddaughter, I hereby knight thee." She tapped the blade on one of Tarleton's padded shoulders, then the other. "Arise, Sir Richard, Earl of Fawkland. Arise, and serve your Queen!"

Elizabeth clapped her hands with joy, then looked with surprise at her husband, who still knelt. His face had turned a bright red.

"La, Your Grace! I do believe you have made my good lord blush—a most rare sight." She giggled.

Tarleton shook his head. "Not so, Your Grace, but I beg one further boon of you." His puckish expression played across his countenance. "Since you are wielding that sword with so skilled a hand, could you please cut off this deuced ruff from my neck? I find 'tis choking me worse than a hangman's noose—and I *do* speak from experience."

Laughing, Elizabeth of England granted her newest knight's request. "Now, my Lord of Fawkland, here is your first command from your sovereign. I spy a new countess in our midst. Greet her with a kiss."

Grinning, Tarleton executed a sweeping formal bow. "I am, as ever, your humble servant, Your Grace." Then turning to Elizabeth, he bowed again with mock solemnity. "Countess of Fawkland, will you do me the honor?'

Her heart singing with joy, Elizabeth stepped into his arms. "I have never kissed an earl before," she said demurely, though her green eyes sparkled with mischief.

"Then, prentice, let me show you how 'tis done," murmured the new Earl of Fawkland, as his mouth closed over hers.

* * * * *

Author Note

Fool's Paradise portrays several historical events and figures; Elizabeth I, the Babington Plot, Sir Walter Raleigh, Sir Francis Walsingham, Lady Mary Sidney, Dr. John Dee, the Earl of Leicester, and a most uncommon commoner—Richard Tarleton, the Queen's favorite fool.

Tarleton was as famous for his wit in his day as Robin Williams and Bill Cosby are in ours. Pubs were named for him, and he is reputed to have written several plays, now lost, as well as a number of jestbooks. He was the leading actor of The Queen's Men, a theatrical company founded under royal patronage in 1583. His physical description is none too romantic: curly haired, squint-eyed and flat nosed—the latter being the result of an injury sustained when Tarleton quelled a maddened bear at the bear-baiting pits in London. Tarleton, son of a pig farmer, was born in or near Condover, Shropshire, though the year of his birth is not known. As a teenager, he was discovered "feeding his Father's swine...when a servant of Robert Earl of Leicester passed by. He was so highly pleased by Tarleton's happy unhappy answers, that he brought him to court where he became the most famous jester to Queen Elizabeth." Tarleton was the master of extemporaneous ballads and improvisations, and he is credited with popularizing the jig. Above all, Tarleton is remembered as the creator of the comic rustic yokel, a character who appears in many of

Shakespeare's comedies. He was also the fight choreographer for The Queen's Men. Tarleton eventually fell out of favor with the Queen when his jokes about Sir Walter Raleigh and the Earl of Leicester overstepped the bounds. He is said to have died on September 3, 1588 in Shoreditch near his beloved Theatre and Curtain Playhouses where he had once trod a merry measure upon the stage.